TREASON IF YOU LOSE

SIXTH BOOK IN THE BRIGANDSHAW CHRONICLES

PETER RIMMER

ABOUT PETER RIMMER

Peter Rimmer was born in London, England, and grew up in the south of the city where he went to school. After the Second World War, and aged eighteen, he joined the Royal Air Force, reaching the rank of Pilot Officer before he was nineteen. At the end of his National Service, he sailed for Africa to grow tobacco in what was then Rhodesia, now Zimbabwe.

The years went by and Peter found himself in Johannesburg where he established an insurance brokering company. Over 2% of the companies listed on the Johannesburg Stock Exchange were clients of Rimmer Associates. He opened branches in the United States of America, Australia and Hong Kong and travelled extensively between them.

Having lived a reclusive life on his beloved smallholding in Knysna, South Africa, for over 25 years, Peter passed away in July 2018. He has left an enormous legacy of unpublished work for his family to release over the coming years, and not only them but also his readers from around the world will sorely miss him. Peter Rimmer was 81 years old.

ALSO BY PETER RIMMER

The Brigandshaw Chronicles

The Rise and Fall of the Anglo Saxon Empire

Book 1 - Echoes from the Past

Book 2 - Elephant Walk

Book 3 - Mad Dogs and Englishmen

Book 4 - To the Manor Born

Book 5 - On the Brink of Tears

Book 6 - Treason If You Lose

Book 7 - Horns of Dilemma

Book 8 - Lady Come Home

Book 9 - The Best of Times

Book 10 - Full Circle

Book 11 - Leopards Never Change Their Spots

Book 12 - Look Before You Leap

Book 13 - The Game of Life

Book 14 - Scattered to the Wind

Book 15 - When Friends Become Lovers

~

Standalone Novels

All Our Yesterdays

Cry of the Fish Eagle

Just the Memory of Love

Vultures in the Wind

In the Beginning of the Night

~

The Asian Sagas

Bend with the Wind (Book 1)

Each to His Own (Book 2)

~

The Pioneers

Morgandale (Book 1)

Carregan's Catch (Book 2)

~

Novella

Second Beach

First published in Great Britain in September 2019 by

KAMBA PUBLISHING, United Kingdom

10 9 8 7 6 5 4 3 2 1

Peter Rimmer asserts the moral right to be identified as the author of this work.

PART ONE

RAPE AND PILLAGE – SEPTEMBER 1938

1

The flying boat performed perfectly on the test flight from the Isle of Wight. Dropping the fluted hull of the big, four-engined aircraft onto the placid surface of Lake Constance in Switzerland, Harry Brigandshaw sensed the light kiss of his craft on the water, felt the aircraft settle, and ran her in towards the shore, away from Germany which they could see clearly on the other side of the lake.

"Smooth as a baby's bottom, Uncle Harry," said Tinus Oosthuizen in the co-pilot's seat.

"This is a beautiful aircraft, Phillip," Harry said over his shoulder to the chief engineer of Short Brothers. "If you give your passengers caviar and oysters they'll imagine themselves on the *Queen Mary*."

"Three days from England to Cape Town, Harry. Two weeks from Southampton to Cape Town by boat, but you should know."

"We did it once in ten days with the SS *Corfe Castle* just to prove a point, but the voyage was rough. The engines vibrated the length and breadth of the boat. Passengers complained."

"Lands on the Nile near Cairo. Then the African Great Lakes. The Zambezi above the Victoria Falls. We can land in Cape Town harbour if there isn't a southeaster blowing, then we will divert to one of the freshwater dams."

"Imperial Airways will make a killing. People will pay a fortune to say they've flown to South Africa in three days. Can you see anything on the other side of the lake we don't like, Tinus?"

"Some sailing boats. Three big ones with single high masts, making for the shore," said Tinus.

"There's an official-looking motorboat patrolling what's probably the Swiss–German divide of the lake," said Anthony Brigandshaw from where he was sitting next to Phillip Crookshank behind his father and cousin Tinus. "Do you want to look through the binoculars, Tinus? There's a flag flying on the back of the boat I've never seen before. The men in the boat are all in uniform. If I'm not mistaken, one of them has a pair of glasses trained on us. Some kind of a cross on a red background."

"Swastika," said Phillip.

"There's a small fishing village on the map over there where we'll ask about Gabby and Melina," said Harry looking at his map. "Can't believe too many schoolgirls from Germany holiday with friends on the lake without the locals knowing. By the way Bergit spoke on the phone, I'd think the girls had been here before. They're at school in Switzerland, Geneva. Only Erwin is at school in Berlin."

"Romanshorn looks more than a fishing village, Harry," said Phillip Crookshank, having read the name over Harry's shoulder.

"Good. Then it won't take long to trace the girls and find out what's happened to Klaus. There's a railway line that runs along the shore of the lake."

"The patrol boat is coming our way."

"Where is the divide? They won't come into Swiss water."

"If you taxi at a maximum speed, Uncle Harry, the wash will prevent them getting closer. The slipstream from the propellers will blow their hats off. Now this is fun. I thought all the fun would stop last week when I came down from Oxford. How old are the girls, Uncle Harry?"

"I was trying to work it out. Erwin turned seventeen last month. Why he was at home arguing with his parents about the Hitler Youth. The next youngest is Melina, probably fifteen. Gabby will be thirteen or thereabouts."

"The patrol boat has turned away," said Tinus. "If it rocks any more in our wash it will turn turtle. What happens if we sink a German patrol boat, Uncle Harry?"

"Just keep an eye on them. In all my travels I have never been to Switzerland before. Now we'll have to come in real slow. Phil, this flying boat is going to make Imperial proud."

"Can the girls speak English?" asked Anthony.

"I have no idea."

"Are they going to come back with us to England? They can always stay at Hastings Court."

"I didn't think you liked girls, Anthony? You'll be back at boarding school next week anyway."

"I'm going to get into the Colts this season. The first fifteen Colts. Did you ever play rugby at Bishops, Tinus?"

"Of course, everyone plays rugby in South Africa."

"Drop anchor, gentlemen. The first flight of a Short Sunderland flying boat has arrived in Switzerland."

HARRY COULD SEE the snow-capped peaks of the Alps behind the village. A small forest of masts showed in front of the church steeple. Harry thought the village must have been on the shore of the lake for centuries by the look of the old buildings. With the engines silent, the lapping of water came up to him from below. If no one came out to meet them, there was a small inflatable dinghy they would pump up in the water to its full size. Four retractable wooden paddles went with the dinghy.

Rocking gently in their own swell, they waited. Nothing happened. On a day in late September, Romanshorn was asleep. Looking back out into the lake, Harry could see the German patrol boat dead in the water. It was not moving. Taking the binoculars from Tinus he trained them on the small craft, immediately bringing into focus a man with a pair of binoculars looking at him.

Harry waved, still holding the glasses to his eyes with his left hand. There was no reply; the man, whoever he was, not wishing to be friendly. On the back of the motorboat, to one side of the small engine, Harry could now see a mounted machine gun. The man looking at him dropped his long pair of binoculars onto his chest and made a sign to the man sitting with the tiller in his hand at the back of the boat next to the engine. Even at a distance, Harry heard the motor come to life and saw the puff of white smoke from the exhaust from just above the waterline. Then the boat made off towards the far shore in German Bavaria, the man still standing up looking towards the flying boat, its propellers now motionless.

Harry put down his glasses and looked back at the village. A small open boat with two men was slowly being rowed out to them. The man not rowing waved. Harry put his hand out of the cockpit window Phillip Crookshank had just opened and waved back at the man. The Swiss were friendly. The Germans were not. To make sure, Tinus pushed a small Union Jack on a wooden pole out of the small window and waved it around. Harry wondered if the German standing up in the motorboat had seen the flag. Not that it made any difference. Officially the flying boat was on its first test flight out of England. Making contact with the von Lieberman girls to find out what had happened to their father was a private matter between Harry and the von Lieberman family. Old friends keeping in contact. Even Timothy Kent was still not sure what had happened to Klaus von Lieberman after he had been taken away by three men from his family estate in Bavaria the previous month.

"How do you know for certain he was taken away, Tim?" Harry had asked on the phone from the Isle of Wight to his office at the Air Ministry in London that morning.

"One of the von Lieberman tenants is a friend of ours without knowing it. His wife is from Dorset. They visit the grandparents in Langton Matravers which was how we heard, the local police have been asked to keep an eye open. The whole estate was talking about it for a day according to the wife and her friend in the village. The wife thinks one of the servants at the big house works for the German Secret Police. The girls should know if you find them. The estate is only twenty miles from the Swiss border. If the mother wants to get out of Germany there's a train to the shore of the lake. It's not a crime yet in Germany to hire a boat and go out."

"When did you last speak to the police in Langton Matravers?"

"He's back in Germany with his wife and kids. Not a word since then. The police only report anything unusual they hear out of Germany that might be of interest to us. It was the Secret Police bit that sparked our phone call."

Feeling a bump against the hull of the flying boat Harry brought his mind back to the present. Even police in rural England were reporting anything strange they picked up about Germany.

"I hope they speak English," he said to Tinus who was watching the three tall-masted sailing boats tacking into shore.

"Hello," came a voice. "Does anyone want a lift to shore? What a beautiful aeroplane. It's so big."

"The Swiss speak English, Harry," said Phillip. "Tourism. People always try and speak your language when they are making money out of you. There's more money in tourism than fishing. Are there any fish in the lake? Someone told me mountain lakes don't have fish."

"There's so little wind out there it will be next week before they land," said Tinus. "I think they are trying to come into Romanshorn. There are youngsters on board. Lots of them."

"Any teenage girls, Tinus?"

"They're all wearing the same yellow sou'westers. Beautiful craft. What I wouldn't do to be out on one of those yachts. There's barely a breath of wind."

"Never been on board anything like this before," said a man being helped up by Anthony who had opened the door to the outside. "Who is the captain? You'll want a stamp in your passports. You all British? Jolly good, I think you say. I'm the chief customs officer at Romanshorn. Welcome to Switzerland, gentlemen. Fact is, I'm the only customs officer at Romanshorn. We didn't think a seaplane could ever be this big. The whole town's come out to look. You've made today quite an occasion."

"First test flight out of England. We left the Isle of Wight this morning. Harry Brigandshaw. My co-pilot Tinus Oosthuizen. Flight Engineer Phillip Crookshank. My son Anthony. I'm originally from Rhodesia. We're less formal than the British even though we are British. They call us colonials." Harry had discovered the British upper class called anyone by their surnames, a habit he found faintly rude.

"So you have a British passport?"

"Of course. Can you recommend a hotel?"

"My pleasure, Mr Brigandshaw."

"We'll anchor out here and come into shore with you if we may, Mr...?"

"Tannenbaum. German Swiss. At your service. A test flight? Everything went all right?"

"You'll see flights from England to your lake more often, Mr Tannenbaum," said Phillip Crookshank. "I am the chief designer for Short Brothers who make the plane. Mr Brigandshaw once flew the first seaplane down to Africa."

"How long will you be staying in Romanshorn? There is so much to do, you know."

"Can I go sailing?" asked Anthony.

"There is always sailing, young man. Sailing in the summer and skiing in the winter. We live a peaceful life, God willing."

"Where is the divide?"

"In the middle of the lake. Whatever happens, Switzerland will stay neutral. The police chief in the boat with me wished to be sure your aircraft was not military, you understand. Herr Krock does not speak English. French, German and Italian like every good Swiss, but not English."

"Where did you learn your English?"

"In America. I was a ski instructor in Colorado before I joined the customs service after my old bones began breaking too easily. Snow skiing is a young man's sport. Two of you will come ashore and the next will follow, I'm afraid."

"We have an inflatable dinghy," said Phillip, who had put the dinghy on board to show Harry Brigandshaw and the Air Ministry how easy it would be for a downed pilot to be pulled out of the drink by Coastal Command using the flying boats. "You go on shore with Anthony, Harry. Tinus and I will paddle ashore to show you how it's done."

"Ah, now I see why you brought the dinghy. Never miss a chance, Phil, to make money."

"The hotel belongs to my cousin," said Tannenbaum, beaming at everyone.

Harry smiled as if he hadn't known and followed the customs officer down into the rowing boat, taking his seat in the bow with his back to Romanshorn and facing the flying boat still gently rocking on the swell of the dissipating wake they had created coming in to land. The big wing floats were in perfect proportion to the big hull with the cockpit high above where Tinus was waving at him with the Union Jack on the end of its pole. The German motorboat was invisible to his naked eye. The three sailing boats were closer to shore despite the light wind; whoever was on the boats knew how to sail.

Looking out over his shoulder at Romanshorn and the distant mountains, Harry drew in the pure air and marvelled at how clean everything looked and felt. There were no factories around the shore that Harry could see.

"Champagne air," he said to Anthony as the silent police chief began rowing the small boat towards the small harbour and the forest of masts below the church spire. Harry could see the remnants of a wall that had once circled the town. Switzerland had been at peace in the centre of Europe for centuries. It was protected by the Alps, he remembered, thinking of Rhodesia and his farm outside Salisbury, hoping the centuries would also leave them alone, the African bush, not the mountains, giving them protection.

"You have the most beautiful scenery, Mr Tannenbaum," he said, trying to take it all in.

"We think so. Maybe you stay a week and go up into the high mountains."

"And go for a sail," said Anthony hopefully.

They came ashore at a small pier that guarded the yachts inside the basin, the police chief rowing them silently round the jetty to land them at the bottom of a small flight of steps that led them one by one out of the open boat to stand ten feet above the water. Harry could smell baking, the delicious smell wafting down from a wooden building on the jetty that looked to be more a restaurant than a bakery. So far, no one had asked to see their passports, their word enough for Mr Tannenbaum; Harry doubted the man even had a stamp to imprint their arrival. Anyone coming across the lake from Germany would likely be friends, if not relatives, most tourists arriving in Switzerland from the other direction by rail.

"Is that a restaurant?" Harry asked Herr Tannenbaum. The police chief, after a quick word with the man from customs, had tied the rowing boat up to a metal ring attached to a thick wooden post that rose out of the water and gone off about his business.

"My wife's brother. Wonderful food."

A horse with colourful tassels around its halter was looking at Harry with doleful eyes, the driver in the trap behind seemingly fast asleep. Busily, Herr Tannenbaum put the four cases into the trap.

"Why don't you go in?" he said. "Ferdinand will take the luggage to the hotel and put it in your rooms. Four rooms for a week. My cousin will only charge you for the nights you stay."

Looking at the horse and the waking driver, Harry was not sure which one of them was Ferdinand. With the ringing sound of clip-clopping on the wooden planks of the jetty, Ferdinand went off with their sparse luggage. No one had spoken a word to the driver.

"Does he know where to go?"

"There's only one hotel."

"Please join us in your wife's brother's restaurant. In thanks for bringing us ashore. We can watch from inside for our friends through those windows."

"My pleasure. Every window looks out over the lake. Very popular.

My wife's brother's cakes and chocolates are delicious. He always bakes at this time of day. You are very lucky. Swiss chocolate cake is the best in the world. My wife's brother's chocolate cake is the best in Switzerland. Now, young man, about you going for a sail. Do you see that nice boat over there? It is indeed my brother's. My brother is a very good sailor and will take you out on the lake."

Anthony, looking from the small boat to the sleek yachts with the tall masts still far away, white sails leaning with the wind as they tacked towards the shore, gave Mr Tannenbaum a brief smile and said nothing. Out on the lake it seemed to Anthony the wind was picking up, the three yachts slanting beautifully to the water.

"Will the Swiss chocolate cake be ready now?" he said, changing the subject and the direction of Mr Tannenbaum's family avarice.

"Of course, young man. Just the aroma of them baking makes my mouth water."

"You think our cases are safe?" asked Harry. The small bell attached to the door tinkled as they went inside, the horse and trap having gone from the jetty towards the town.

"Not so many customers at this time of day. No one steals anything in Romanshorn. Where are they going to go? Up in the mountains with small suitcases?" Mr Tannenbaum, finding his own joke to his liking, laughed so much his fat belly above the thick leather belt began to roll in front of Anthony's eyes, causing Mr Tannenbaum to slap Anthony on the back. "You like that one? Now, let us go and sit down. It is so good speaking English. I like speaking English. Very good language, English. That one over there is my wife's brother."

Trying not to laugh at the other side of Tannenbaum's humour, that he doubted the man understood, Harry pulled out a small chair and sat down at the table. Apart from themselves, the wife's brother was the only person in the long room.

"Some friends of mine from Bavaria told me about your beautiful town, Mr Tannenbaum. Please order for yourself whatever you would like. Do you know them perhaps, Frau and Herr von Lieberman? Their children, like my son of the same age, are fond of sailing."

"Maybe several slices of chocolate cake to start with?" With Harry's confirmation the brother disappeared into the kitchen.

"Here they come," said Anthony. It was clear, even to Anthony, they were all in good hands. "Here comes Tinus and Mr Crookshank. That was quick work in a rubber dinghy with paddles."

"It would be. Phil's trying to show off. Coastal Command, Anthony."

To Anthony's surprise the man Tannenbaum looked up sharply. Then the cakes arrived at the table and took everyone's attention.

"Better order some coffee as well," said Harry to cover up his gaffe. "So you don't know my friends Klaus and Bergit? Or their children?"

"Why do you ask?"

"We heard the girls are holidaying on this side of the lake."

"Who told you?"

"Their mother, as a matter of fact."

"Excuse me, got to see my wife's brother in the kitchen."

"What about your cake?"

Without a word, the man stalked off from the table by the window above where Tinus and Phillip were clambering out of the rubber boat below the steps.

Like so many previous times in Harry's life, he told himself, nothing was ever a coincidence. From the outward appearance of a garrulous fool, the man's eyes had changed along with the tone of his conversation. There was no doubt in Harry's mind, the man from customs knew the von Liebermans. Maybe living on a border was not so peaceful after all. Nothing ever was what it looked to be at first sight. The jolly old man underneath the rolls of fat now seemed to have more to worry about than digging up business for his relatives, the reason for the suitcases going off on their own more apparent. Luckily, Harry had not locked the cases so the locks would not have to be broken if the police chief wished to look inside.

"Come and join us, Phil," said Harry through the window that was open to the afternoon sun. "Our friend has gone off for coffee. It's all very pretty but there's a distinct chill in the air. Be careful none of us catch a chill before we fly back to England. You can never be too careful in a foreign country however good the welcome. I hope you both like chocolate cake? These, I understand on good authority, are the best in the world. Really. Believe me. Our cases have gone on to the hotel. How was the dinghy ride?"

"Swift and accurate. I love chocolate cake. Just the smell had my mouth watering from down on the water. We came ashore quickly, don't you think? I put sea anchors out on four sides so the wind coming up won't be a problem. There's nowhere to tie up the flying boat even if we wanted. This little harbour is far too small. What's the matter, Harry?"

"I don't know. After nearly three years as an unwilling guest of the

Tutsis in the Congo, my antennae are always on the alert away from home. She looks beautiful from here, resting in the water. An aircraft should always be beautiful as well as functional."

"We're coming up. Where are the reception committee?"

"That's my point. We've been left here with the slices of chocolate cake."

"I'll come and help you," said Tinus, tying the painter to the pole next to the rowing boat that had brought Harry and Anthony from the flying boat.

By the time the other two joined them at the table there was still no sign of anyone. They were completely alone. Harry passed the slices of cake around to them all. No one spoke while they ate, all of them smiling.

Herr Tannenbaum returned long after the last crumb of chocolate cake had been eaten, Harry not sure what to do in the meantime. He had looked at his watch three times. When the fat man came back he was beaming again, the large bald part of his pate shiny and red, as if he had put his head in a hot oven. It seemed that the coffee had been forgotten. At the same time, his wife's brother appeared with a plate of small cakes and a large savoury dish.

"He says to try his savoury cooking. Baking cakes is a sideline, I think you say. This dish is a fondue. We Swiss are famous for our cheeses. I am proud to say this is my wife's brother's special recipe for savoury melted cheese. We eat it with freshly baked bread by dipping the pieces of bread into the cheese. You will find it is delicious.

"Frau von Lieberman sends her regards, Colonel Brigandshaw. I had no idea you were the Englishman who saved Herr von Lieberman's life. We Swiss are neutral. Herr Krock made the phone call. We are determined not to be involved in the rest of Europe's problems. We are too small. We Swiss pride ourselves on being discreet with privileged information. Herr Krock asks you to enjoy your night at my cousin's hotel and leave first thing in the morning. Now, my friends, let us eat fondue. You see, British flags waved from aircraft can make our friends across the water ask Herr Krock questions. He has explained who you are. A family friend of the von Liebermans. The chances of an official test flight to this backwater of Switzerland was too much for Herr Krock. He has a mind that looks for the not so obvious to keep our little town as quiet as your proverbial mouse. You do understand, Colonel Brigandshaw?"

"Did Bergit von Lieberman ask that we leave?"

"How would I know, Colonel Brigandshaw? Herr Krock made the phone call. Isn't the fondue delicious? Be careful not to burn your tongue. Something easily done when eating a piping-hot fondue. Your cases are in your rooms. Your very good rooms. Now, if you give me your passports I will stamp them with your entry permits. Tomorrow I will stamp them again with your exit permits. We Swiss are, to use one of your words I like so much, sticklers for detail. It is how we have kept our noses clean over so many years. When those yachts tacking towards us out on the lake reach our small harbour, I will tell Melina and Gabby von Lieberman you are here. Their mother said they would wish to be courteous and make your acquaintance, Colonel Brigandshaw. After all, without your chivalry they would not be alive, if you see my point; their parents would not have had the opportunity to marry and have a family."

"Not having met their girls before, it would be good to meet them."

"They are polite, lovely young ladies."

"Are they pretty?" asked Anthony.

"That is for you to see, young man. How did you know, Colonel Brigandshaw, the girls sail from our little harbour?"

"I didn't. You are right. This fondue is delicious."

Smiling at Swiss diplomacy, Harry looked at the three yachts. By late afternoon they would enter the small harbour.

2

*M*elina von Lieberman had been the first to hear the sound of an aircraft engine, both her older brother Erwin and her father Klaus being flyers. To her young ears accustomed to single-engined aircraft from when the family visited the small aerodrome near the family's estate, the sound was different, deeper, and somehow to Melina, menacing. Once she had flown with her father and ever since asked him to teach her to fly an aeroplane the way he had started Erwin on his path to becoming a qualified pilot. Anything Erwin did in his life was perfect, ever since she could remember as a small girl growing up on a big estate that had been in her family for centuries. She had hero-worshipped her brother for being so good at everything he put his mind to, from riding a horse like the wind to flying an aeroplane to emulate their father, an ace in the German Air Force that Herr Hitler was now calling the Luftwaffe. What Melina wanted most in her life was to find a young man just like her brother and marry him.

Melina had listened a full minute before she was certain, the only other sound in the air the occasional flapping of the big sail as it tried to catch enough wind to let the boat tack its way in towards the distant harbour of Romanshorn. With the light wind blowing, they tacked three hundred yards to make ten in the right direction. When she was convinced the engine sound was coming their way, the vibrations more in the air than her ears as the wind came and went, she called across to

Monsieur Montpellier at the tiller. Monsieur Montpellier was the owner of the boat and father of her schoolfriend Françoise. Françoise was sitting on the edge of the boat between Melina and Melina's sister Gabby, ready to lean back with the crew if the wind picked up and pushed the yacht over at an angle to the water.

"There's an aircraft flying this way," she said in perfect French.

"I hear nothing. Where would they land? No aeroplanes fly this way, my dear."

"I can hear it," said Gabby.

"So can I," said Françoise.

For the next few minutes the crew listened more to the throbbing of the distant engines than the sound of the wind in the sails. Some were curious, most were excited at the prospect of seeing an aeroplane.

"Well, Melina, you were right. The engine sound is coming this way," said Monsieur Montpellier, keeping his careful eyes on the sails. "Going about," he called into the still, mountain air before bringing his boat about to continue his tack with the other two yachts towards the distant church spire of Romanshorn, the target of his approach.

"There it is! Just above the water. At the end of the lake," called Melina. "It's a German aircraft, I'll bet. My father and brother are pilots."

They all watched, convinced by Melina's knowledge of aeroplanes that the aircraft was German, the Germans on board smiling, the Swiss not so sure.

"There must be something wrong," said Monsieur Montpellier, standing up for a better look while still holding on to the tiller. "It's going to come down in the lake. Oh, my God. There's going to be a terrible accident."

"I don't think so," said Melina, triumphantly. "German aircraft don't crash. It's a seaplane. Going to land on the lake near Romanshorn. I'm sure they'll know my father. Just look at it. It's touched the water. A big, big bird sending spray high behind into the air. Beautiful. Just beautiful. I feel so proud to be German. Just look how big it is."

In her excitement, Melina was standing. Miles away beyond the lake, the white caps of the Alps made a perfect backdrop for the spectacle. Melina was hugging herself with excitement.

"It's turned towards Romanshorn. I was right," she said, surprised she was the only one who was excited.

"Sit down, Melina, or you'll fall out of the boat and the water's cold," said Gabby, once again in the shadow of her sister, something she hated.

"What a magnificent seaplane."

"Must be a passenger plane," said Monsieur Montpellier, training his Zeiss glasses on the seaplane as it taxied in on what seemed through the glasses to be two of its four engines towards the shore. "Goodness. Four engines. Lands on its hull, the wing floats just to keep it stable. Civilian, not military. I didn't know anything that big could fly. There are no markings on the fuselage or the wings. We are going to have interesting company at the hotel tonight. Everyone be ready. We're going to come around again if the wind will hold. There's more wind over in Germany by the look of the flag on the stationary German patrol boat. The wind over there is moving the German flag."

"Slipstream from the propellers," said Melina smugly. "The motorboat is almost awash. Why did they get so close?"

"To have a good look, Melina. Oh yes, to have a good look. There's a flag being pushed out from the cockpit window by the look of it. A Union Jack it seems. Melina, that seaplane is not German. It's British."

"Then what is it doing here?" said Melina, somewhat deflated as she sat back down again, her young mind beginning to race; even at three months short of her sixteenth birthday the coincidence was far too great.

Ever since Melina experienced her first family fight she had always sided with her brother Erwin, even when she knew he was wrong. Apparently wrong, Erwin always had a good reason. The letter from Erwin to Monsieur Montpellier's house in Geneva arrived for her before they left for the lake and their three-week sailing holiday where they were to stay at the Romanshorn hotel. Monsieur Montpellier owned houses in Geneva and Marseille. Owning the boat at Romanshorn was enough. Madam Montpellier, not being a good sailor, preferred to stay in Geneva when her family went sailing, making a hotel to stay in more convenient than a house for her husband. Françoise had said, when they had first met at school in Geneva, her father was a banker.

The banker was a lot older than his young wife, giving Melina and Gabby a fit of the giggles when they left for the lake, both girls sure their schoolfriend's mother preferred being left on her own to pursue more pleasant arrangements than sailing an old boat up and down a lake. It was Gabby who loved the sailing, Melina on her fourth trip not so sure. Apart from Françoise and Gabby, every person on board was old, a constant change of business friends who came for the day to enjoy being entertained by Monsieur Montpellier. Switzerland, unlike Germany,

Melina had commented sourly to Gabby, was a morning's train ride from anywhere.

With the British seaplane rocking the German patrol boat and the family estate just over the border, Melina wondered if the letter from her brother was the connection. Thinking hard, she let her brother's letter play again through her mind. The letter was postmarked Berlin.

'They've probably taken Father away by now so don't take any notice of Mother. She's hysterical. Mother and I had one terrible row after Father wanted me to leave Berlin. The Hitler Youth have agreed to keep me at school for my last year, father saying we've run out of money. Then I join the Luftwaffe to serve our Fatherland. Germany will rise again, Melina. Never forget that. Whatever they say, Germany must rise again or we are nothing. Father will learn like the others. People are either for the Fatherland or against the Fatherland. Those against, are our enemies. Father, like Uncle Werner, will again be a loyal member of the Nazi Party or he will no longer be our father. Mother must learn to understand. Very soon there is going to be a war that Germany will win. I am so proud to be a German, you have no idea, my darling sister. You too must be proud. The family must all be proud or I can have nothing more to do with them, you understand.'

Two hours later, when the three yachts came into the small yacht basin passing the British seaplane on the way, Melina was sure something was seriously wrong with her family. That her father had done something terribly wrong. On the jetty in front of the restaurant stood Herr Krock with Herr Tannenbaum alongside four men.

"I wonder who they are?" said Gabby.

Melina went cold, her premonition of disaster stronger than ever.

"I don't know... I hope this has nothing to do with what Erwin wrote," she murmured to her sister, once again thinking back to her letter from Erwin.

"What do you mean? Daddy says Erwin's coming home. He'll be home when we get back... Françoise, can we get some chocolate cake? I've got a little money. While your father is tying up the boat we can go to the cake shop on the pier... Look at that, Melina. That man is waving at us as if he has come to meet the boat. Oh good. Maybe he'll buy the cake? Are you coming, you two? Is there something wrong, Melina? You can be so funny sometimes. Now that was a lovely sail."

One by one, the three yachts found their anchor buoys and tied up for the night, having first dropped most of the crew and the passengers on the jetty. Gabby was smiling at Harry Brigandshaw and the young boy standing next to him, having just been introduced by Mr Tannenbaum. She found it funny standing on shore after so many hours on the boat, the jetty still seeming to move despite the swell of the boat no longer being under her feet. Something was wrong with Melina but something was often wrong with her. Gabby had found it better to humour her older sister rather than ask questions. As the youngest of the trio it was her job to tag along behind.

With her mind set on chocolate cake, Gabby was smiling at everyone. Next to the boy was a young man and next to Mr Brigandshaw, another man the same age as him.

Then, quietly she said to Melina, "I remember now, that man saved Daddy's life. That must be his seaplane. He and Daddy were both pilots. Maybe we can go up in the aeroplane? I do hope he buys the cake. Why are you looking so sour, Melina?"

"They are the enemy."

"Don't talk rubbish. The war's been over twenty years. Anyway, Daddy said Mr Brigandshaw saved him from his burning aircraft."

"Erwin says it has just started. Anyway, it was this man who shot down our father before he landed and pulled him out of the wreckage. They were trying to kill each other. They were enemies."

Gabby remembered her mother telling her about their visit to Hastings Court in England and wondered about the younger boy who was of a similar age to her. The boy she noticed was grinning at her. Gabby smiled back at him, making Melina give her one of those sour looks of disapproval she liked so much. Whether it was because he was a boy or English, Gabby was not sure. The other young man was looking warmly at Melina, as if he saw something he liked. Then they all trooped into the cake shop without Gabby having to ask.

For half an hour, while she happily ate her favourite chocolate cake, Mr Tannenbaum, who Gabby knew had lived many years in America teaching Americans to ski, translated the conversation from German to English and back again. Only when Monsieur Montpellier came back from mooring his boat did they speak French, only some of which Gabby understood.

The boy was still grinning at her. Mr Brigandshaw was also smiling at her when he was not talking to someone else. He was, as her mother and father had always told Gabby, a very nice man, despite he and her father being made to fight each other during the war, something Gabby could still not understand. If they were friends now why had they tried to kill each other up in the sky flying their aeroplanes? Of all the silly things that grown-ups did, killing each other to Gabby was the silliest of them all.

Instead of the four men coming back to the hotel, Ferdinand came along the jetty with his horse and trap, stopping outside the restaurant where they had eaten the cake. Ferdinand took four small suitcases from the buggy and put them down on the wooden pier. Then he turned round the horse that for a moment looked at Gabby through the open window with doleful eyes. The horse and buggy clip-clopped away down the wooden planks of the pier. Gabby had no idea what was going on until the young man left.

From inside what Gabby thought of as the cake shop, she watched another man pick up the cases one by one and climb down with them out of sight. Gabby presumed the man was putting the cases into a boat. Then Mr Brigandshaw was leaving. Meeting him on the pier was a coincidence, like many other things Gabby often did not understand. When all the cases had gone from the pier, everyone began shaking hands. Briefly, Mr Brigandshaw again shook hers. Monsieur Montpellier did not seem to know what had been going on from the time he came back for the girls after tying up the boat.

From the window Gabby watched a rubber dinghy push out from under the pier with the four men on board where she could also see the suitcases. Mr Montpellier had now sat down at their table to watch and eat cake with Herr Tannenbaum, whom Gabby knew was the man from customs. The dinghy moved much faster than a normal rowing boat out to the aeroplane. Further out in the lake, the German patrol boat had come back again. The boy waved to Gabby from the dinghy and Gabby waved back. It was a pity, she thought, the boy could not speak German.

Not long after, they all watched the engines of the big seaplane start up, the German patrol boat this time keeping a better distance. Then the plane taxied round and faced out into the lake and into the wind. The four engines made the big propellers go round so fast they became invisible. Gabby watched the seaplane take off. Then they all left the restaurant to walk back to their hotel. When Gabby turned round, the plane was well on its way to fly over the peaks of the mountains. Smiling sadly, Gabby wondered if the boy was waving. Just in case, she waved herself before following her sister, who had lost all interest in the aeroplane when she found out it was not German.

"What was that all about?" she asked her sister back at the Romanshorn hotel.

"I have no idea. Good riddance to bad rubbish."

"Why do you say that, Melina?"

"They're English. You're too young to understand. They are the enemy."

"Why?"

"Erwin says we're going to war with them. Soon. Germany is going to be great again."

"Why will going to war make any difference?"

"Last time we lost. This time we will win. We will defeat the English and the French. Erwin says we must all be proud to be German. Anyway, why was that boy grinning at you?"

"I really don't know, but I liked the look of him."

3

*H*arry Brigandshaw said to Timothy Kent a week later, when Harry was back at the Air Ministry, that it was like eating soup with a fork.

"Every time I thought I'd got something it fell off. The Swiss are inscrutable. Playing both sides without favours. Soon after the girls got off their yacht the German patrol boat was back. It can take hours to make a person to person call from Hastings Court. I think the Germans and the Swiss have a direct line to their police stations. Never once did Herr Krock say a word. Everything came from the bumbling Herr Tannenbaum, who I don't think was quite so bumbling after all. Sometimes it is impossible to do friends a favour, so we left when the suitcases suddenly appeared with the patrol boat in the Swiss water far too close to the flying boat for my liking... Coastal Command will love her. Easy to fly. Easy to land. Quick to launch a rubber boat from the big hatch low down on the hull three feet above the waterline. Even in rolling seas they'll be able to get out and back with stranded pilots. Positioned along the south coast and connected by phone from our radar stations, we'll be able to hit Jerry bombers over the Channel with Fighter Command and pick up any of our chaps shot down in the sea with the flying boats. Coastal Command can be on the way to shadow the dogfights and pick up downed pilots. They'll be in the right place at the right time. Better than patrol boats looking for pilots in the drink from sea-level, especially when there's a swell. Any German aircrew picked up in the sea will be incarcerated and out of the war for its duration, an even more valuable prize than shooting down their aircraft."

"I'll pass it on."

"They've got Klaus, I'm sure. The older girl knew something, the way she looked at me. Same brainwashing as the brother. They were close those two. Bergit said Melina hero-worshipped her older brother. I think she knew what was going on from young Erwin. Get them young enough and you can make them do anything. We were politely told by the Swiss to bugger off after Tannenbaum spoke to Bergit on the phone in Germany to find out who we were. Poor girl. Poor Germany. Poor Europe. Anyone who doesn't agree with Hitler and his Party get their arse kicked. This isn't just about the Jews. It's about anyone who challenges the power of the Nazi Party. You only need a few evil men to turn a nation rotten. If you ask me, everyone is scared shitless including Bergit, worrying about what they will do to her family if she gets in the way. When Tannenbaum said he'd spoken to Bergit on the phone I thought I was getting somewhere, especially when the man said the girls were on one of the yachts on the lake and Bergit wanted me to see them. Then it all fell apart when Melina and Gabby came ashore. One minute we were told we could stay one night only, the next our suitcases appear on the jetty. So that's it, Tim. I've done my best. All we can do for Klaus and Germany is hope. Why is it always the right royal sods in life are the ones who win?"

"They don't have a conscience. Only a purpose. Megalomaniacs don't think like you and me. Just because a man has similar outward features doesn't mean his brain is wired the same way as yours. Even what they say doesn't correspond to what's in their head. They have no scruples killing people so long as it is not themselves, they'll sacrifice an army to save their own skin. Make a bloody army fight for them, telling them so persuasively it's in everyone's best interest who's doing the fighting, the fault only found out when the tyrant takes power and keeps the spoils for himself and his cronies. We've had them all the way down history under different guises, people wanting power. Some use national pride. Some use religion. Many plain fear. Some, the promise of plenty. Most somewhere appeal to man's inherent greed. Rape and pillage are part of all of us, Harry. The chances of any of us coming down through history without being the product of rape is nil. We're all a direct product of the rapist and the raped. Who we are running through our veins, those of us who survived. Meek and mild people don't last very long whatever the Christians will have us think. Nice idea. Just goes against human nature. You did your best, Harry. Nothing to look back on and regret, whatever horror comes out of it. Just makes me even more determined to defend England against tyranny."

"We're going to have to fight them aren't we?"

"Yes, we are. Why don't you send a full report to Coastal Command? Glad to have you back, sir. Sorry about the diatribe. All this wasted effort of mankind gets me wound up and that's a mistake. Never take it personal. Better still, get right out of the way which, looking at the future, is not going to be possible."

By the time Harry Brigandshaw took the train from Waterloo to Leatherhead and home, Timothy Kent's diatribe had sunk in. On a pleasant summer's evening the car at the station started first time. Other city slickers, as Anthony liked to call them, were walking home, distinct in bowler hats and carrying rolled umbrellas. Some peeled off at the Horse and Hound to prepare themselves better for family life. If it did not rain so often in England, Harry would have enjoyed the morning and nightly exercise walking all the way to Mickleham and the house that had been in the maternal side of his family for centuries.

If there was one thing about money that he had learnt in his life, Harry told himself as he drove past the hedgerows and fields, it was keeping hold of wealth was more difficult than making it the hard way in the first place. If a man or country had something of value there was a line of not so lucky trying to get their hands on it by fair means or foul, something his paternal grandfather, whom some called the Pirate, knew all about. Whether the man was a pirate in name or practice, Grandfather Brigandshaw had founded a shipping line, coming up from the ranks in the Merchant Navy, that was the foundation of Harry's English money and the reason his family lived at Hastings Court. Harry's maternal grandfather, Sir Henry Manderville, had done a deal with the devil and sold his only daughter and Hastings Court to the Pirate to relieve himself of the family debt.

"You're right, Tim. We're all a mix of the good and the bad. I wonder what the old Pirate was really like, God bless his soul in heaven or hell."

After badly singing himself a couple of songs to which he neither knew properly the tune or the words, Harry turned the car into the long driveway that led up to his ancestral home. Anthony was back at boarding school. Beth was away on her first term at a small private school in Bournemouth where Tina hoped they would teach her to behave like a young lady, something Harry rather doubted and secretly hoped would not spoil the rebel in his child. Tinus, footloose and fancy-free, was Harry's problem along with what to do with his money to keep it out of reach of the current predators thrashing around in Europe.

Leaving the car in the driveway in front of the old house, Harry found everything surprisingly quiet. Neither dogs nor the younger children had rushed out of the house to greet him on his return from London as usual.

"They've all gone off with Aunt Tina and the chauffeur," said Tinus, appearing on the long terrace that faced out from the front of the house. Above, the false turrets and battlements looked down silently on the summer evening.

"*Including the dogs?*"

"They all piled in. I watched them. How was your day, Uncle Harry?"

"Interesting but not for the right reasons, Tinus. Do you fancy a trip?"

"To the Running Horses?"

"I was thinking of somewhere further."

"You're coming back to Africa?" Tinus, taken out of his lethargy, walked quickly to the balustrade and looked down at his uncle.

"First, we are going to America, ostensibly to see Robert and Freya St Clair. I'm worried having so much of my money in British bonds. I've never been to America... I think Coastal Command will go for the Short Sunderland. I'm to put in a memo. How was your day?"

"Boring, I'm afraid. I need something to do other than loafing around."

"Your new degree will be put to use in New York. I want to diversify my investments. I thought we'd first visit Sir Jacob Rosenzweig at the Rosenzweig Bank. You can assure him his daughter and grandchildren are doing fine on Elephant Walk. He'll want a full report having never seen his grandchildren. Why does religion so often get in the way, instead of helping people's lives?"

"She and Ralph are very happy. So are the kids."

"That's all that matters. The old man must be awfully lonely all on his own in New York. Robert's in New York with his publisher for a month, the children in Denver with Freya."

"When do we leave, Uncle Harry?"

"I thought on Monday. Being a volunteer civil servant gives me some leeway I suppose. I don't have any job description. They seem to ask my opinion when it suits them. Tim does the real work. If they don't pay you they can't very well order you around. I thought we'd fly to America."

"Ourselves?"

"No, Tinus. A scheduled airline this time. You want to go to the Running Horses?"

"Not a bad idea with no one around."

"Come on then. You don't need a coat. It's the new barmaid, I suppose."

"Something like that."

"Do you know this one's name?

"Not yet, Uncle Harry."

To his surprise, the face that came to mind was not that of the barmaid at the Running Horses. Instantly, and not for the first time since leaving Lake Constance, Tinus saw the young face of Melina von Lieberman looking at him in a way that said she would like to do something to him, the stare was so intense. Someone had once told him the line between love and hatred was thin, the strong emotion easily going one way or the other. Looks from girls, however young, said more to him than any words, even if thinking of a girl not turned sixteen would be construed by many as cradle-snatching.

Whether the girl's thrusting look when Tinus glanced up from the dinghy when they came out from the shadow of the pier was meant to show him interest or hatred he was not sure. What Tinus did know was their eyes locked for a considerable time until the dinghy was far enough out in the lake to break the eye contact by distance, neither of them finding it possible to look away.

Not for the first time, Tinus had found girls to be strange creatures he doubted he would ever understand, other than that thrust from deep behind the eyes that spoke to him of primal lust and made his hormones react strongly when he saw deep inside what he wanted from a girl.

Half listening to his Uncle Harry as the car made its way through the evening sun along the English lanes, all he could think of was Melina von Lieberman and what her look at him in the boat had really meant.

Being a Friday night the carpark of the Running Horses was nearly full. A typical English country pub, the Running Horses was part of many locals' lives. Everyone seemed to know each other enough to nod and wave. After that the groups kept to themselves with, to Tinus, that strange habit he was told was British reserve.

When they reached the bar, the new barmaid was being patronised by three young men. His uncle bought the pints and they went outside.

"So, what are you going to do, young Tinus?"

"At this moment I don't have a clue."

"Do you want to farm in Rhodesia? I never used my geology degree, remember. Schooling is to teach us how to think. An educated man does not have to follow his degree. In a productive life we should study many subjects in a wide spectrum."

"I'm not sure."

"A nice young wife and family on a farm is a good way of life. Similar, year after year, but a good life. You could play some cricket in Salisbury. Go into the bush. Take up wildlife photography instead of shooting the poor animals. Why is it some men like to kill big game just for sport? My father began hunting ivory for a living and an elephant killed him in the end."

"Part of me would do that. Build the dam. Put in the rest of the infrastructure to make the irrigated crops viable. Yes, water at home is the key to farming success. But I'm not sure whether in the end I would find myself bored with not enough of interest to feed my mind. It seems so silly not to know now what to do with my life."

"America first. Then Rhodesia. It is time I went home before it becomes impossible."

"When is it going to happen? You really think it's going to be war?"

"Months. Maybe a year. The Americans will sit on the fence and make a fortune. A war in Europe would finally put the end to their depression. Why I want to go and see first-hand where to put some of my money. With your degree in economics you'll know what questions to ask. In wartime, people make fortunes. We can fly to Africa after the trip to New York and take a look at Elephant Walk in the light of a pending war... So you don't want to join Anglo-American and become a corporate man? They'd fall over themselves to employ a young Rhodes Scholar who played cricket for Oxford." Harry sat on a bench and lifted his pint glass. "Cheers, Tinus. Good having you at Hastings Court. I miss a good conversation when you are not here. Anything slightly cerebral makes my wife change the subject. She likes to talk about our children, not the tale of the world. Can't blame her. Probably better with her head buried in the sand. Mostly, there's nothing the individual can do about it anyway. Tina says what's the point of worrying... She's not as nice as the last one."

"Who?" said Tinus, startled, thinking he was referring to his uncle's murdered first wife, who was born Lucinda St Clair.

"The barmaid." For a moment they smiled at each other and drank from their beers.

"Why didn't you pursue geology?" asked Tinus.

"I never found the diamonds. Your father and I went together and searched the Skeleton Coast. Then we went our separate ways. Prospecting is much more fun when you find what you are looking for."

"Didn't you find anything?"

"One large diamond, which is still uncut."

"What did you do with it?"

"It's safe. Safe for a rainy day. Do you know, I haven't thought of that diamond for years. I was in my thirties. When I went home after the war."

Somewhere a pigeon was calling from among the trees behind the Running Horses. The evening was still and quiet, both of them silently enjoying each other's company.

"Do you want another one?" said Tinus having finished his beer.

"Why not?"

At least, Harry thought, he hoped his diamond was safe as he watched his nephew take the empty glasses into the bar. Many years ago, he remembered building the large uncut diamond into the stonework of the new mantelpiece over the fireplace in the lounge of the main house of Elephant Walk. To Harry, it had looked like a piece of worthless quartz it was so big, which was the whole idea. Who in his right mind would stud a diamond into the mantelpiece over the fire, Harry had asked himself? Last time he looked it was still there. Hopefully it still was and would stay there until it was needed, a time Harry hoped would never come.

The best place to hide anything he had found out, was right under people's noses. Even his family did not know what was staring at their backs when they stood in the winter evenings in front of the big log fire 'airing their knowledge'. The smoke from the fire over the years had turned the surface of the uncut diamond black to add to the illusion. Back then, like Tinus, he was footloose and fancy-free, not knowing what to do with the rest of his life.

"Her name is Alison," said Tinus, coming back with two brimming mugs.

"The same as your grandmother who left Hastings Court with my mother when they ran away to Africa. Alison was my nurse and married my father's partner, his mentor and muse. The man whose name you bear, Martinus Oosthuizen. If two men loved each other it was your grandfather and my father. To have such a friendship is one of the greatest joys that can come out of a life. Cheers again, young Tinus. May your life be an interesting one."

"Didn't you find diamonds on the Skeleton Coast?"

"It was after we had parted. Near where the diamonds he had found on the beach in the sand south of Alexander Bay. Those that were washed up by the sea or swept down the Orange River. I was looking for a diamond pipe, the actual diamond deposit forced up from the bowels of the earth where the volcanic heat made them. I needed time on my own to wander, to forget the war and at best remember my dead friends when they were alive and having fun. Living off the gun. Oysters and mussels off the rocks at low tide. Driftwood fires far from the presence of man. Not seeing a soul month after month. Looking up at the layers of the stars. Three distinct layers as clear as crystal with the naked eye. Feeling insignificant but alive. At peace with myself in the end when I decided to go back to Elephant Walk, my mother worried again out of her mind. Mothers always worry, Tinus. You should think of that. My sister worries about you so far away. We only have one family that is our own and it's very precious. My mother still worries about me, she says."

"I miss my father."

"We all do. Barend was on his way home to you all when he was killed. Never forget that."

"Would he have stayed with us?"

"I hoped he would. Your mother hoped so. He had found religion buried at the bottom of the mine thinking he was going to die. He was going to farm the other side of Elephant Walk again. You would have seen. Underneath his wanderlust and hatred of us British for killing his father, he was a good man. My friend. A good, true friend. Don't think back with bitterness, Tinus. Your life is in the future to enjoy. Don't do what your father did and look back in bitterness until it consumed him."

"Maybe Hitler has other ideas about my future."

"There is always someone around with bad ideas. Often the ones who tell you they are good and righteous are just as evil. You can only rely on yourself and take what comes. Some have a long life, some short. But does anything matter except the present moment?"

"I'd like to visit the Skeleton Coast of South West Africa one day and follow your footsteps."

"Maybe you will. The Namib Desert is one of the most beautiful places on God's earth... When we've finished these we'd better go home. Tina and the children will be back by now. Aren't you hungry?"

"Starving. I was going to buy a packet of crisps but didn't want to ruin my appetite for Mrs Craddock's cooking. Why is it some people can cook so well?"

"Another of life's best kept secrets. Better to be born poor to a mother who can cook than born rich and eat lousy food because it isn't cooked properly. Did you know our trip to Switzerland was in all the newspapers?

"Who was it this time?"

"William Smythe, who else?"

4

William Smythe had written about the test flight of the Short Sunderland knowing Harry Brigandshaw was news in England and America. Harry Brigandshaw's disappearance in the Congolese jungle and subsequent resurrection had made him front-page news around the English-speaking world. It had also made William a lot of money as a freelance foreign correspondent. Just the syndication out of Denver, Colorado, channelled by Harry Brigandshaw's wartime friend Glen Hamilton, had made William more money than he earned as a cub reporter on the *London Daily Mail* and reporter on the *Manchester Guardian* put together. From there he had taken his stories to the BBC Empire Service and made himself a household name. Working for himself had proved the way to get on in the world.

Phillip Crookshank had given him the story, not knowing, as it turned out to William, the real purpose of Harry's trip, Crookshank's interest in publicity only to do with sales. While Harry and Tinus were driving back to Hastings Court to sample Mrs Craddock's cooking, William was having dinner with Horatio and Janet Wakefield at a small restaurant off Shaftesbury Avenue that specialised in Bengali cooking.

After years of climbing the ladder of journalism, his old friend Horatio was now the foreign correspondent of the *Daily Mail*, his wife Janet a speech therapist specialising in cures for people suffering from stutters with a thriving practice on the ground floor of their three-storey house in Chelsea. Young Harry and Bergit had been asleep in the top floor nursery when they left to go out to the Bengali restaurant, Janet saying the only food she could never get right was Indian curry. The nurse, Blanche, was in charge of the children allowing the parents to leave the house without a worry.

The house had been paid for from the proceeds of Horatio's half share freelancing in Berlin, before he was taken away by the German police, to be freed by Harry Brigandshaw asking his friend Klaus von Lieberman to intervene and get Horatio back to England. In gratitude, the first-born had been named Harry, the second Bergit, the Wakefields personally thanking the von Liebermans when Klaus and Bergit visited England in July of the previous year.

"I liked the story, Will, but you missed the point," said Horatio. "Okay, this time the test flight of a flying boat was successful and it didn't crash in the jungle. But have you looked on the map?"

"If this is going somewhere go on," said William.

"Lake Constance, and Romanshorn in particular, are as close as you can get without going into Germany to the von Lieberman estate. I tried to speak to Mrs Lieberman on the phone the day your story hit the press but no one would speak to me in English. I asked for both of them with a question mark in my voice and had the phone put down at the other end. How did you learn about the test flight?"

"A chap at Short Brothers tipped me off."

"Harry knows his friend has a problem. Why he used the flying boat to get as near as possible. I'd like to help if I can."

"Why don't you ask Herr Henning von Lieberman, Janet?" said William. "He was your patient for six weeks when the von Liebermans' cousin visited London. Did you do any good for his stammer? Or better put, did he have a stammer in the first place?"

"He was a very nice man and his stammer has improved, he tells me. Considerably improved. You read too much into everything, Will."

"Horatio's up to that trick by the sound of it. Give Harry a ring, Horatio."

"I did. Told me to mind my own business. First time he's ever been rude."

"Now you have got my attention," said William.

"He just chopped off the conversation telling me to leave it alone. He's worried, William. I've never heard him so on edge. All the communication lines to Germany are coming apart. When countries stop talking to each other they get their wires crossed and end up in trouble with their relationships. My guess is something happened to the von Liebermans and Harry went over with a cover story to have a look, found out what he feared, and came back in a hurry thinking he was doing more harm than good. Did the Americans pick up on the flying boat story?"

"Not this time. The public has a short attention span. Glen said Harry's old news but three of the British papers picked it up as you found out."

"There's a man three tables away who's been staring at you, William. Your fame has spread. Someone must have told him who you are. The famous foreign correspondent and radio journalist. How does it feel to be famous and stared at?"

"Why would anyone consider me famous?"

"Don't be modest. It doesn't suit you. Anyway, he's coming over, having worked out I'm talking about him. Chap looks foreign by the cut of his clothes. And young. If he were a woman I would not have been surprised. On first glance with that long hair he looks like a girl."

"Mr William Smythe, I'm sure. My apologies for staring. I was going to call you when I arrived in Britain two weeks ago but thought you would not remember me. Count Janusz Kowalski. Our mutual friend Fritz Wendal sent you to Warsaw the summer of 1936 to report on our air show. As a young pilot speaking English, Fritz pointed you out to me. How is he, Mr Smythe?"

"They murdered and burned him. Of course, I remember you, Janusz. Have you brought any modern aircraft into the Polish Air Force since the air show? Did you receive my message after I returned to England?"

"To join the RAF if Germany invades Poland and defeats the Polish forces? Of course, that won't happen now. The British treaty will make Hitler think twice before invading us. We all feel much safer. Some of my friends fear the Russian Communists on our eastern border more than the Germans in the west, my father in particular."

"Does your cavalry still ride horses?" William was smiling, enjoying his little joke. "Please sit down."

"I'm afraid they do. Very well, of course. The last cavalry in Europe. We believe more in tradition than practicalities of war, Mr Smythe. My young friend is looking lonely at the table all on her own, don't you think? It was rude of me to leave her."

"Bring her over. Mr and Mrs Wakefield. Horatio was incarcerated by what we now call the Gestapo in our press. He too was a friend of Fritz Wendal."

"I did not know. Poor Mr Wendal. It is not good to be a Jew in Germany. In Poland we live our lives in the hope of being left alone. A foolish habit of us Poles for many centuries. I will bring Ingrid over. She is the reason I am in London. She studies interior design. We are going to be married. I am now practising law in Warsaw." The English words came out in detached sentences, as if Janusz was reading from a script translated from Polish.

"Do you still fly?"

"Of course. Mrs Wakefield, Mr Wakefield, excuse me a moment."

"I'll have the waiter join our tables."

"There's an empty one next to you," said Janusz.

"Better still. This is a pleasant coincidence. A student and a junior lawyer cannot afford the fancy restaurants."

"Neither can a working journalist," said Horatio. "Unless he's freelance. How long are you staying in London?"

"A week."

"Have you met anyone in the RAF?" said William.

"Not yet."

WITH CONVERSATION SUSPENDED by the interruption, they waited for the couple to join them at the tables Horatio helped the waiter to push together. For some reason Horatio never understood, every Indian restaurant had square tables so the two fitted nicely together when they finished. He watched William's smile broaden when the girl, introduced as Ingrid with a surname none of them would be able to ever pronounce, sat down at the two joined tables, her eyes fixed on William. After ten minutes, while the five of them split a bottle of Spanish red wine and told each other their brief personal histories, as was the custom on new acquaintance, it seemed to Horatio the girl was less interested in marriage than her friend Janusz, the way she was flirting with William. She also looked older than the boy, who looked to Horatio as if he had only just started shaving.

Listening to, rather than joining in the conversation, he wondered how people so often believed what they wanted to hear without question. According to Ingrid's broken English, it seemed the Royal

Navy, the Royal Air Force and the French Maginot line were more than enough to make Adolf Hitler behave himself and keep his hands off Poland. Having looked more carefully at British rearmament, Horatio knew it would take two more years to bring Fighter Command up to full strength. In journalistic circles the Royal Navy, stretched from Singapore through the Suez Canal to the Mediterranean and out into the North Atlantic, was considered even less prepared; no longer did the Royal Navy rule the waves, able to protect British shipping around the world. By the sound of it at the dinner table, the Poles were relying on something that did not exist, rather like Janusz with the commitment of Ingrid to their marriage.

"How long are you staying with us in England?" Horatio asked in a lull in the two-sided conversation between Ingrid and the clearly infatuated William, something his wife was finding embarrassing by her faint look of disapproval.

"As long as you'll have me, yes?"

It was not clear to Horatio how Ingrid paid for her studies and kept herself in London. On the other hand, a girl with her looks was never likely to be without the support of one or two wealthy friends.

"Where did you meet Janusz?"

Horatio smiled to himself; his wife, always the romantic, was trying to protect the up and coming marriage that Janusz had pointed out when he first stood at their table.

"Warsaw."

"When are you two getting married?"

"We haven't set a date," interrupted Janusz.

Then Ingrid ignored the question and put her had on William's knee under the table, something Horatio only found out the next day. By the time they all went home to their respective abodes, William had given Janusz Harry Brigandshaw's telephone number at Hastings Court and Ingrid had slipped him her phone number, again under the table, the indiscretion hidden by the long white tablecloth that hung halfway to the floor, again only reported by William the next morning. Horatio could see by the end of their interrupted evening that any thought of what was happening in Germany across the Swiss border had gone right out of his old friend William's mind.

"He really should get married," said Janet when they let themselves into their house.

"Something that is not on Ingrid's mind, who it seems would very much like to stay in England and not go home."

"You think that was what it was all about?"

"Polish counts with country estates sandwiched between Russian communism and German fascism do not compete with famous English newspapermen as eligible husbands. And she's got the looks to do what she likes."

"Why do pretty girls always get to choose?"

"Nature, darling."

"Did you choose me for my looks?"

"Of course I did, darling. Now run upstairs and tell Blanche we are home if she hasn't heard. I thought a small nightcap before we retire to bed. More and more I'm convinced your old stammerer Henning von Lieberman was in London spying the land, taking photographs of prime targets such as the London docks and that sort of thing, his therapy sessions with you every morning an alibi for being in London. His father, who is Klaus's uncle by the way, is definitely a Nazi. General Werner von Lieberman doesn't even try to hide who he is. Why should his son be any less of a Nazi?"

"You and Harry Brigandshaw have Nazis on the brain. Pour me a very small whisky and I'll be right down. My first patient is at eight in the morning. Do you really think Hitler will invade Poland and plunge Europe into war?"

"As sure as I am that Ingrid is not going home to marry young Janusz if she has anything to say about it."

"She was just being polite to William."

"Yes, my dear."

When Horatio's wife came down from the nursery not two minutes later she was smiling.

"Why do they look so angelic asleep and in the morning turn back into little monsters?"

THE NEXT DAY in his office at the *Daily Mail*, having been given the lowdown on the previous evening by William over the phone, Horatio studied the blown-up map of Europe that took up the entire wall opposite his desk. It showed each adjacent country in a different colour, sovereign states with wandering tentacles of land that sneaked into their neighbours. Sometimes it was a river that bent the borders which had changed since the first tribes roamed the plains and hills that through thousands of years now showed as individual countries on a map that changed every few years, war or no war, friendship or enmity.

"It's a bloody mess," he said to the map, thinking, like all Englishmen cut off by twenty miles of sea, of the Continent, that part of Europe on the far side of the Channel as not part of Britain. "No wonder they've never got their hands off each other's throats."

"They all want what's theirs as well as yours if possible," said Mr Glass the editor coming into the office. "Never forget the easiest way to get anything is to steal it. We English have been doing it for years close to home. First Ireland, then we forced the Scots into a United Kingdom, and a Prince of Wales onto the Welsh. Anglo-Saxon sphere of influence and there isn't much left worth having. Won't last much longer, of course. Empires have to come and go or we'd have nothing to fight about. The French and the Germans want their own empire. So do the Americans, despite touting their anti-colonialism. Man is avaricious, the reason why we survived top dog in the animal world, but not why I came to see you, Wakefield. I want you to go to Moscow and tell us what's going on. Are they on our side or Hitler's?... And do we want them on our side? They too want their empire and there's only so much to go round. How big is the Red Army? How good is their morale?"

"Will they give me free rein?"

"Of course not. That's why you are so highly paid, to get at the facts without anyone at first being aware. I was going to send you to Berlin but one of our friends said the German government won't let you in, a fact we told the Russians to get you your invitation to Moscow. Even in the polite world of journalism you have to play one off against the other. In politics they call that diplomacy or some other highfalutin word."

"Alone?"

"Take Gordon Stark. Those buildings that look like onions make a wonderful photograph. If you take your passports to the Russian Embassy I'm assured they'll give you visas."

"Do we fly?"

"Don't be silly. You go by train. That way you can see what's going on in the rest of Europe before the whole place blows up. The French are being arrogant as usual, the Swiss are playing it close to the chest and the Poles think the sun shines out of our arse for some daft reason."

"I met a Pole last night."

"Do you know, Wakefield, that sounds quite funny. Go and tell Stark.

Then bugger off to see the Russians. If you leave as soon as possible the Russian countryside won't have frozen over. No wonder we British have never had our eye on Russia. Enjoy yourselves. By all reports, apart from the vodka, it stinks now everyone is meant to live the same. They all call each other comrade, a man according to his needs. That should be fun. All equal together my foot. Man really does have ways of pulling the wool over the common man's eyes so when he opens them properly again he's been screwed."

"Thank you, sir."

"What for?"

"The opportunity. Never been to Russia."

"Just make sure you come back this time. The Russian Secret Police are said to be as bad as the Germans, and this time I doubt Mr Brigandshaw has any of his usual influence in Russia. You can try and persuade your friend Smythe to go as well and give each other that nice feeling of false security. But only if he writes for the American press this time, of course. We don't want him stealing our thunder in England."

"What a shame. Last night he found a new girlfriend. Poor chap never stood a chance. Janet thinks after being snubbed by Genevieve he'll never find a wife."

"Ah, the famous Genevieve. My son watched her last film and said she's the sexiest woman alive. I wouldn't know. Far too old for that. If I suggested sex to Hazel she'd laugh in my face. Get it while you can, Wakefield, store up the memories. You'll need them. Do you know, a friend of mine said in the pub last night that if you find your ultimate woman and put a penny in a bottle for every time you have sex with the love of your life and afterwards, for the rest of your natural life, take a penny out of the bottle for each time you get it the bottle will never be empty. He was drunk of course. My wife thinks sex is somehow dirty. Beneath a woman with high moral standards. They do say you only get the truth from babes and drunks. What do you think, Wakefield?"

"Janet and I are fine. We would have filled up the second bottle by now."

"Must have married the wrong woman. She was so enticing before we married."

"Never judge a book by its cover."

"Shut up, Wakefield."

"Jealousy, sir, is a bad state of being."

"I think I'll find myself a mistress."

"Much better idea. There's always someone for everyone whatever the age. I'll take a taxi with Gordon to the Russian Embassy right now."

"Where do I meet a woman?"

"They're all over the place, Mr Glass. William last night did not know what hit him. When we all went out to dinner he was miserable, dour, finding fault at every turn. When he phoned me just now he was chirping like a bird in spring."

"I need a woman."

"Don't we all? Just don't get caught by Mrs Glass. She frightens the holy crap out of me if you don't my saying so, sir, and she's only to me my boss's wife."

"Discretion. Be discreet in Moscow."

"How long does it take to get to Moscow by train?"

"I have no idea... A mistress. I'll have to think about that."

"They say in times of war, everyone is a lot more free and easy with their affection. Trying to spread and receive seed before it is too late. To compensate for all the dead soldiers. I don't think Darwin explained it that way but it's all part of evolution. The survival of the species."

"They'll be more dead civilians this time than soldiers from your report of Bomber Command. Drop enough incendiary bombs and a whole city goes up in flames... So you think if war breaks out all the young women will be handing it out as a patriotic duty? There's always some good in the bad, Wakefield."

Mr Glass, smiling and humming some kind of tune, left the door open when he left Horatio's office. Horatio thought Mr Glass looked ten years younger. Even the idea was enough to make him straighten up his back.

"There's always a trick or two in an old dog," he sighed, picking up the phone and putting it down again, deciding it was probably easier to go to look for Gordon Stark himself. "Moscow," he said savouring the flavour of the word.

5

The only available seats to New York, refuelling at the Azores, was for the following week. When Janusz Kowalski telephoned Harry Brigandshaw giving William Smythe's name as his introduction, he was invited to Hastings Court for the weekend.

"My friend I came to see in London is studying interior design."

"Bring him along. At the weekend, my wife says the more, the merrier, Count Kowalski. And I do remember sending you a message through William. Any pilot trained by the Polish Air Force would be welcomed by the RAF were the Germans to overrun Poland. We have a way of accommodating our colonies. In the event of war, we will even have a Rhodesian squadron in the RAF, the country where I grew up."

"I do not know this place."

"Nobody does. South of the Congo. North of South Africa."

"I'll look for it on the map."

"Catch the train from Waterloo to Leatherhead and phone this number. My chauffeur will come and pick you up. Likely with a bunch of children. They get bored. A Polish count will send them into rhapsodies, particularly Beth."

"My friend is a woman."

"Beth is nearly fourteen."

"We are only engaged though. Truthfully, I am more engaged than Ingrid."

"You will each have a room to yourselves."

"You are most kind. Ingrid is from Poland and no good at English."

"Can she ride a horse?"

"Like the wind."

Only when Harry put down the phone did he remember Beth was now away at boarding school which was just as well. The young madam had the same eye for making men do her bidding as her mother. The same looks. The same power to break young men's hearts when she grew a few more years, Harry thought, not sure which was worse: a plain daughter or a girl that turned every boy's head.

Late in the afternoon, using the excuse of telling Tina they had a fully-fledged Polish count staying the weekend, Harry asked Tina to go for a walk with the dogs. None of the children were anywhere to be seen.

"It's a lovely evening for a stroll in the woods. Soon, winter will make walking less pleasant. I have a surprise visitor this weekend. Put on your walking shoes and I'll call the dogs."

"What are you up to, Harry?"

"Wait and see. His name is Count Kowalski. Polish Air Force Reserves."

"It's always business."

"That's exactly what I have to tell you about. I have to go to America. Then Rhodesia through Cape Town where I will look at our new house you don't want to visit. If war does break out I won't have the money to maintain Hastings Court at full staff. Many will be called up. Mary Ross in the village has said she'll work at the Goblin factory and won't be available for the manor. They make vacuum cleaners at present but that will change."

"How do I run the house without servants? Every single thing in this house is out of the ark. We don't even have central heating. Coal scuttles to every room. Cleaning out the fires in the morning. Vacuum cleaners! We don't even have one, let alone an American washing machine. The house will grind to a halt. Why are you suddenly going to America?"

"To get out some of my money. You can't just transfer money at will, except to the colonies. There will be ways Sir Jacob Rosenzweig will know about. I don't want my English money all in one place. You have to think ahead the whole time to hold onto money, Tina. You can't just stand still or you'll end up with a rude shock."

"That's your job, Harry. Everyone I talk to says a war will never happen. That we learnt our lesson from the last one. I am not taking the children to live in Africa so don't get any ideas. I'd prefer to take my chances at home than go and live in the jungle."

"You will if the Germans start bombing London. Anyway, Rhodesia is not in the jungle. It's the bush. There aren't so many trees among the waving long grasses that there were in the Congo."

"We don't live in London."

"They'll be flying right over our heads, there and back. Bombers that haven't dropped their bomb load on the target will do so on the way back to lighten the aircraft to get home. Do you prefer the idea of living in an air-raid shelter with your children? Why don't you come with us to South Africa and Elephant Walk?"

"Who's us, Harry?"

"Tinus. We want to finalise the dam."

"Isn't he in London looking for a job?"

"Interviews. He's not sure what he wants."

"If war does come he'll go into the Air Force to join his schoolfriend from Cape Town, André Cloete."

"Why I want him in Rhodesia for a few months if he doesn't take a job right away."

"Even this place is quiet in the week. Imagine that farm in Rhodesia."

"I do, Tina. Every day of my life."

"What about the Air Ministry?"

"You and the children will be safe."

"So you'll stay. You don't even have a proper job."

"I just don't accept a salary. Anyway, more than half would go in income tax. At the top, we pay sixteen shillings in the pound. On Elephant Walk we don't need money. The farm feeds itself. And you won't run out of servants. Even if a world war collapses every economy and makes paper money worthless."

"Why should our money stop here?"

"It won't most probably without a total meltdown across the world. There just won't be anything to buy. Hastings Court will have to go into full production as a farm, which isn't your style. The food will be distributed by the government. However many eggs we produce we will only be allowed to eat our ration."

"Let me go and get my shoes..." Returning with her walking shoes, she asked, "How big is the air-raid shelter you talk about?"

"The size of two cars."

"Don't be ridiculous."

"I'll show you the plans in my study when we come back from our walk. We'll have to make the blocks of concrete on site."

"Now you frighten me, Harry. What's this to do with this Polish count?"

"When Hitler overruns Poland we want their pilots to get out before they're captured and come over here to join the RAF. We're short of pilots. In war, an air force is always short of pilots."

"There are the dogs with Frank. Why do they always bark at Frank?"

"They don't like him. He kicks them when I'm not looking."

"You just don't like Frank."

"I try not to show it, Tina. To treat him the same as my four. I'm going to see Robert St Clair in New York. Have you seen Barnaby recently?"

"No, why should I?"

"You can't shop all the time when you go up to London."

"Oh yes I can. Anyway, Barnaby lives in his own world surrounded by young girls. He's said by his total disinterest he will never take any interest in Frank. That Frank must never know Barnaby is his father. Don't let's go through all that again, Harry. It's boring."

"People change their minds, Tina. I think you will about South Africa and the house in Bishopscourt when war breaks out. Do you ever hear from Albert in Johannesburg?"

"Haven't heard from Brother Bert in years. Never comes home. When Dad said he didn't want his money, Bert took umbrage."

"Your father prefers working for his money."

"What does that mean?"

"I'll get the dogs."

Mentioning Frank and his wife's infidelity was never a good idea if he wanted peace in his home. Harry was never sure which was worse for Tina: Barnaby's rejection of Frank or Barnaby's rejection of Tina. The aristocratic Barnaby had dismissed the idea of marrying the daughter of the stationmaster at Corfe Castle railway station, preferring to keep Tina as his mistress, as she had been when Harry first took interest in her, getting her pregnant with Anthony.

"You want to walk with us, Frank?" said Harry, trying to make amends.

"No thanks, Dad. The Alsatians always bare their teeth at me. The old Spaniels never do that."

"Don't kick Maxwell and he won't try and bite you."

Harry ruffled the boy's hair and watched Frank go off to look at his rabbits. If war did break out, rabbit stew would become a delicacy. Like so many parts of life, it wasn't the boy's fault who had fathered him. So long as he was alive and healthy he was the same as the rest of them. There were even some nice parts in Barnaby St Clair's nature, Harry tried to remember. In a tight corner he would rather have Barnaby around than some of his so-called friends. Barnaby's trouble was women. Once it had been money. Now at the start of his middle age he had too much of it.

Whistling up the dogs whilst waiting for Tina, Harry wondered how different his life would have been if Barnaby's sister Lucinda had not been killed when pregnant with their child. Anthony, Beth, Dorian and Kim would not be alive, which was a strange thing to think about. The chances of life for all of them were so slim, a mathematician would never produce an equation to show a person's likelihood of ever coming into the world. And all for such a short time, he had always thought when looking up at the night sky in Africa showing him the limitless universe.

She was coming out of the house to cross the lawn towards him, her mere presence what some would say was the result of an accident, their meeting on the SS *Corfe Castle* when both of them were going out to Africa. Whether it was an accident, he had never been quite sure. Anyway, there she was walking across the lawn, the mother of his four children, none of whom he would have swapped for the world. Maybe one day, Frank would go to Barnaby. Life took strange turns on its way to the grave. "Shut up, Harry, you're getting morbid," he castigated himself.

Putting out his hand, Harry took Tina's, something he had not done for some time. The pigeons were calling into the still evening from the trees all around Hastings Court. The air was scented with flowers. Insects went about their business while the flowers were still open to them during the last of the day. Small white clouds stood motionless, the way clouds were in the sky in Rhodesia, making the pang of missing Elephant Walk a sudden and physical feeling. Silly of him, he thought. What could be wrong with what he had? A rare evening of summer in England in the home of his ancestors who had fought their own way through life to give him this wonderful one, any mistake of theirs eliminating him in the chain of life, making him never happen. Trying to imagine the world without himself was impossible. Nothing was there. Nothing had ever been there. Without him being alive the world could never had existed... Better to forget Barnaby, and Mervyn Braithwaite who had shot Lucinda to get back at him for something that had never happened. Better to enjoy what they had and let the future take care of itself.

"Those dogs do so love a walk," she said, her small hand in his. "Why don't they ever go on their own?"

"They think we might not be here when they come back. No, going for a walk with someone you love is far more fun than going alone."

"I love the dogs too. Do you think dogs love humans the way we love each other? You can't just ask them. Are we all right, Harry?"

"I just worry about all of us the whole time. Never stop. If I ever did I'm convinced there would be a catastrophe. I always have to be there. To be one jump ahead of events. Outthinking the problems for you and the five children."

"I was talking about you and me."

"So was I, in a roundabout way. Men have to look at life further than the home. You look after our home and I'll look after the family outside of the home. We're luckier than most. Always count your blessings rather than want what can't be had without tearing others apart. That's why Barnaby keeps away. You can't have us both, Tina, and neither can he. You'll take your memories of growing up close to Barnaby as a child to your grave. And your growing up together to become adults and lovers. He didn't want to get married. Probably never will, now. Some men are like that. They don't need other people. Happy with their own company. The thought of growing old alone a pleasure, not a threat. Too often we only look the same from the outside. You can never tell what's in the back of another person's mind. Often, the less complicated a mind, the happier the person. Barnaby is selfish, Tina. Always was from the time I met him as a teenager while I was up at Oxford with Robert."

"Where did Frank go?" Tina said with a faraway look.

"To look at his rabbits."

"Does he feel there's something different from the others?"

"Probably. Just don't ask him. It'll make it worse. He tells me Maxwell wants to bite him and he can't see why. What a beautiful summer's evening. The reason you love England. England only gives us a few days like this a year for our memories to treasure and look forward to again. There must always be something to look forward to."

"When are you going to America?"

"After next weekend. We have seats on the plane on Wednesday."

"I'll miss you, Harry."

"I'll miss you too, Tina. We should both try and remember that more often."

"What's going to become of us?"

"Only God knows."

"Is there a God?"

"Only God knows, Tina. Only God knows, not us. People prefer to believe. Stretching the mind too far can make it break."

"There is so much more of you here, yet you still hanker for Africa?"

"Africa has its own strange pull that can be stronger than blood. I think it's the animals. There are so many more of them. Walk the bush and look down into the Zambezi Valley and everywhere you look you see herds grazing the long grass, browsing the leaves on the trees. The bush is so full of life and not just humans trying to get their own way. Herds of animals grazing look so peaceful. As if that was what life was about, not building a mansion or building an aeroplane to get away. Nature at its best. Life at its best. In Africa I feel so much part of it, so much more alive. In London I'm just another rabbit in the warren, deep underground so to speak, not knowing what is really going on. Here I'm submerged. There I'm floating above it, a spectator to peace and happiness, light of heart."

"Don't the animals kill each other?"

"Only to eat. The lion only kills what the pride can eat. Then they sit in the sun and digest their food, animals grazing around them no longer in fear of their lives knowing the lion has fed. Only man accumulates more than he can spend. Surrounds himself at great expense with useless manifestations of his apparent success. Man by his nature has to show off. Has to be appreciated. Envied. Better than the rest. The lion just wants a good meal when he's hungry and then he's content. Africa is free. Here we are prisoners of ourselves. Of all the rules and regulations that keep us away from each other's throats. From doing what Europe is about to do as the same rules don't bind nations to behave themselves the way laws frighten us with the threat of jail. Oh, no. Africa is real freedom. The African bush. One among the animals. Ask Tinus. He knows what I'm saying. Why I think he won't take one of those careers offered him in London. He's an African who just happens to have a white skin that the bush doesn't see. Only humans see that kind of colour to make themselves seem bigger and better than the rest of them."

"How long will you be in Africa?"

"That trip will take longer than America. Why I want you and the children to come too."

"They're in school."

"Sometimes schools teach them the wrong way to live. So they miss a term, take the books with them and work harder when they get back to catch up."

"When you talk like this I don't understand you one bit. What's wrong with Hastings Court?"

"It's not Africa. What I've been trying to tell you."

"So the threat of war is an excuse."

"Part of it, I suppose."

"Let's just wait and see. Maxwell's seen something. Just look at him run."

6

---

*I*n the end they caught the boat, Horatio Wakefield not prepared to take his chances and travel through Germany to Moscow on the train. They sailed from the Pool of London on what William called a rust bucket up the North Sea, round the Baltic Sea and into the Gulf of Finland reaching Leningrad in the USSR the same day Janusz and Ingrid arrived at Hastings Court for their weekend. The boat trip had amused Horatio after Gordon Stark asked the captain if he could photograph the cargo.

"Lucky to get on board. What's in them crates is the owner's business. We bring back timber from Finland and I mind my own business."

"The markings on the crates suggest military equipment."

"I'm not going to look inside and neither are you."

The rest of the trip had been pleasant, Horatio remarking to Gordon Stark, who had raised the ire of the captain, "My enemy's enemy is my friend. Whatever we think of communism, pragmatism comes first."

Then they landed at the Port of Leningrad and life had never appeared so different. Everyone looked exactly the same. Dressed precisely the same, one big mass of humanity milling around at the railway station waiting patiently, mostly without a word. Horatio had never before seen people drilled into submission, only the start of the process in Berlin after Adolf Hitler proclaimed himself Führer of Germany. It was difficult for the three of them to see if the people were happy, as the faces were inscrutable under the cloth caps that made everyone equal, every one of the caps the same dull grey.

Without any Russian and no one speaking English, they used the one word 'Moscow' pronounced like a cow at the end and hoped the packed train they climbed into was the one they wanted. The rail passes had been given to them by the Russian Embassy in London, the words and alphabet unintelligible to any of them. Trying to find a seat proved impossible. They were going to stand in the corridor packed with the rest of them, not even with a battered tin box of sandwiches, Russian trains only travelling one class in a classless society that had crushed all privilege.

"They are all so grey," said Gordon Stark, hugging the bag that contained his camera. "There is no colour. Even the landscape has less colour than England. Do you think they have to pay for their train tickets?"

"If the state considers they have a reason to travel, like us they are given a free pass," said William Smythe. "Everything is given according to their needs. An apartment. Heating. Schooling. Mostly everything that we have to earn in a competitive society and pay for out of our own pockets. Everything here is owned by the state. Everyone has a job to do. Everyone is told what to do by someone else and God help you if you think for yourself or step out of line."

"Everything you need free sounds good," said Stark looking around at the faces to see if anyone was listening, whether anyone understood the three obvious foreigners in their midst. "Do you notice no one takes the blindest bit of notice? How did we end up on a ship running guns?"

"What else would they want in Russia?" asked Horatio, nervously looking around, his memories of Berlin five years earlier alive in his mind and making butterflies in his stomach.

"Does it remind you two of Germany?" asked Gordon.

"Not really," said William. "So far they don't look frightened. More like a herd of cows content to chew the cud and let someone else worry about the state of the world."

"I wish we'd brought some food. Why didn't the captain warn us?"

"He didn't like us, Gordon. After you wanted to take pictures of his machine gun crates."

"How did you know it was machine guns?"

"The name Vickers on the crates. Vickers make machine guns."

"They make a lot of other things."

"Not long and slim. The Red Army must be getting ready for Hitler like the rest of us. So this is the utopian state where the lust for materialism doesn't officially exist."

"At least in Russia you don't have to worry about where your next meal comes from."

"If you behave yourself."

"In a British factory, if you misbehave yourself you get fired."

"The unions would have something to say."

"There are more ways than one of kicking an unwanted element out on the street."

"So this is better?"

"It would be, if my few kopecks could buy me lunch. How long does it take to get to Moscow?"

"I'm not even sure we're even on the right train. Can either of you read the station signs?"

"The man nodded and smiled when we got on the train at Leningrad. I think he was the conductor, anyway he wore a uniform and was behaving importantly."

"Smiling at sending three Englishmen to hell, maybe. Do the Russians even like us?"

"We were all on the same side against Germany in the last war until the Russian Revolution in '17. Then they had more of their own problems to sort out and stopped the war against Germany. I never found out what really happened to the Eastern Front. I think they just shot their officers and buggered off. Maybe we should all have done the same."

"Was that why the Americans came in on our side in '17?"

"Why are photographers so ignorant?"

"I was only asking, William. I'm not the famous foreign correspondent who gives talks on the BBC."

"Where did you get the kopecks?"

"Lloyds Bank. Some Russian émigré emptied a suitcase of paper money on the manager's desk. The manager gave him ten quid."

"How much did you pay?"

"Two quid for a walletful."

"How much are they worth?"

"No idea until I try and spend them."

"Lucky he didn't get shot," said William.

"Or had his head cut off. The French cut off their heads."

"So much for capitalism. Two quid for toilet paper. Let me have a look, Stark? You'd better burn these. Do you know who that man is on the note?"

"The bank manager didn't know. I asked him. It was only a couple of quid."

"Bugger's a thief. That's Tsar Nicholas, poor sod. They shot him and his entire family."

"The New Republic, or whatever Robespierre called his thugs, cut off the heads of the entire French aristocracy. Mind you, they were a bunch of fops. When you go to the piss house, flush those notes down the toilet, Gordon. You don't want to end up like Horatio in Germany. Never get you out of a Russian gulag."

"What's a gulag?"

"A camp in the frozen north they send the people they don't like."

"Careful, William. One of those chaps looked up at the word gulag. There was a brief flash of fear in his eyes. I'll go look for the toilet."

Eleven hours later, when the train crawled into Moscow station with William declaring he could eat a horse, the same man that had looked at Gordon Stark with fear, looked at him again and smiled.

"Have a pleasant stay in Moscow, gentlemen," he said in perfect, barely accented English before getting off the train and disappearing into the teeming crowd.

While the three of them were contemplating how easy it was to put their lives in jeopardy and hoping nothing came of their indiscretion, Tinus Oosthuizen was walking the heath at Mickleham alone with the dogs trying to make up his mind. There were more problems in his life than trying to keep his eyes off the fiancée of Janusz Kowalski. Unknown to him until he spoke to William Smythe later, like William, Ingrid had been giving him the full treatment back at the house right in front of poor Janusz. Even Uncle Harry had raised his eyebrows, somewhat embarrassed for his young guest from Poland. Later that day they were all due to drive to Redhill Aerodrome and fly aeroplanes with John Woodall.

The first of five interviews had been the most interesting and had brought him the offer of a job. Tinus would have liked to ask Aaron Rosenzweig, the eldest boy of Sir Jacob Rosenzweig and brother of Rebecca who was married to Ralph Madgwick, manager of Elephant Walk, and ostracised by her family for marrying out of the Jewish faith, whether the job offer had more to do with Uncle Harry, who had arranged the appointment, rather than his own credentials and degree.

Strangely, the name of Rebecca had never come up. Or was it so strange, Tinus thought, as he watched Maxwell race away with the old, fat Spaniels trying their best to waddle on behind, one of them barking in overweight frustration.

A job at the London office of Rosenzweigs, a prestigious merchant bank, would have likely put Tinus on the path to riches. The other four interviews over two days, spending two nights at the Williams Hotel in Hackney to preserve what was left of his funds, had been for Tinus a waste of time, job opportunities picked up from the London newspapers. To work for the one company he had always had at the back of his mind, Anglo-American, required a trip to Johannesburg.

It all came down to spending his life making money on paper, matching borrowers and lenders, later floating public companies on the London stock exchange, if he was lucky, always working for someone else and daily commuting to London on the train if he couldn't afford to live in London itself.

Trying hard to concentrate and keep the picture of Ingrid out of his mind, Tinus walked and walked, wondering why making up his mind was suddenly so difficult. A good job was a good job. There were lots of girls in London. Genevieve visited London. André Cloete, his old friend, was stationed close to London. Everything looked simple were it not for the pictures of Africa staring at him in his mind, beckoning, telling him toiling in a city was not the way to spend the rest of his life.

"No bloody way," he said turning round on the spot, his pace quickening as he strode back to Hastings Court.

Halfway down the hill he remembered the dogs. Looking back up the long slope of the heath he saw the Spaniels coming down, trying to catch up. Maxwell stopped, asking by his stance why they were being so slow.

"You dogs eat too much," he said to the Spaniels.

Putting two fingers in his mouth, Tinus let out the whistle that he had learnt to call the pack of Rhodesian Ridgebacks on Elephant Walk. Like a runner out of the starting blocks, Maxwell took off down the hill, both Tinus and the dog now sure they were going in the right direction.

"You're homesick, you fool. Go home. You've done your degree. Go home to Elephant Walk."

Only when he found Ingrid waiting to give him the eye back at the big house did Tinus remember there were no young girls near Elephant Walk. Probably only a couple of dozen in the whole of Rhodesia, and all with their noses stuck in the air. Proof that any shortage in demand could always command its own price, a price far higher than it was really worth.

"The first law of economics, Tinus," he heard Mr Bowden his tutor say in his head. "Probably the first law of life. Always have what the other fellow wants and sell out dearly. The bigger the competition, the bigger the profit."

The way Count Janusz Kowalski treated the wandering eye of his girl told Tinus one thing clearly: in Poland, there was a surplus of pretty young girls, explaining to some extent why Ingrid was trying so hard, throwing her net as wide as possible, not wishing to end up, as Tinus's mother so often put it, 'on the shelf'. Something highly unlikely to happen to Paula and Doris on Elephant Walk, even now Paula was nearly twenty-three years old and in their mother's words, 'about to miss the boat'. Young men looking for an adventure in a new country outnumbered young girls eight to one, even if most of the men were hidden away in the bush.

Maxwell, now far ahead of the pack of Spaniels and sniffing at the large picnic basket filled by Mrs Craddock for their lunch and waiting to be packed into the car to take the men to Redhill Aerodrome, had been the first to arrive.

"We're going when you're ready, Tinus."

"Do I have to change?"

"What for? I've put what flying gear we need in the Austin. Just the three of us. John Woodall knows we're coming. There's a young lad from Australia he wants you to meet."

When they got into the car, Uncle Harry explaining to them two of the big cars would fit into the concrete air-raid shelter he was planning to build for Hastings Court, Ingrid stood on the steps looking miffed. Janusz waved at her, saying something in Polish. The girl looked bewildered.

"Will she be all right on her own?" asked his Uncle Harry.

"Told her to take the dogs for a walk and not get lost. That big dog wants another walk, Tinus."

"Must be difficult in company where you don't speak the language. When are you two getting married?"

"She wants to stay in England and learn English. I try and help now I'm here. The trouble is, not many people speak Polish in England so no one can translate. I've found a Russian émigré who speaks Polish, French and English. The Russian aristocracy were good at their languages.

Something to do, I suppose, when you don't have a job. Ingrid will find it much easier to learn when we get back to London. Anyway, I have to go home. We Kowalskis like to earn our living in spite of the family estate. When I gave the Russian a pound note he kissed me. Where he was born in Russia there were seventy servants on the family estate tending the house and the gardens."

"Don't you worry about Poland?" asked Tinus.

"All the time. Don't you worry about your farm in Rhodesia? That's the trouble with a big estate. People can see what you have. You can't hide it. Wouldn't that be part of your job as a merchant banker? Hiding jewellery so they can take it with them when they run?"

"Where do they run to?"

"America, if they have enough jewellery. Are we going to fly one of your brand new fighters, Colonel Brigandshaw?"

"Not really. More like the plane you were flying when you first met William Smythe in Warsaw. A biplane. Great for aerobatics."

"But not much good against Germans."

"A Tiger Moth. A recreational aircraft. Lovely to fly on a summer's day like today. Two open cockpits. John Woodall is an old friend of mine who runs the flying school. We flew together in France during the war. 33 Squadron. Three flights with six Sopwith Camels in each flight at full strength. We were usually under strength. Pilots, Janusz. Chap crashes a plane we could quickly replace the plane, but not the pilot. Planes are easier to come by than trained pilots."

"What were they like, sir?"

"The pilots?"

"No, the Sopwith Camels."

"Best fighters in France, flown properly. You can help me by passing one of Mrs Craddock's ham sandwiches sitting next to you in that wicker picnic basket. Why I put the picnic basket on the back seat and not in the boot. We cure our own ham the way we cure it in Rhodesia. The taste makes both myself and Tinus homesick, which is why I like them. She'll be all right with the dogs. We'll be back in two hours. You and Tinus will have a chance to fly while John and I have a good chinwag."

"What's a chinwag, sir?"

"Digging up old times. Please don't call me sir. In Rhodesia we are not as formal as you Europeans."

"But you are Europeans."

"We're African. Tinus's family on his father's side have been in Africa nearly three hundred years. Anyway, we Europeans came out of Africa in the first place according to the anthropologists I read. From Kenya. Not that long ago if you think how long life has been on the planet. Of course, when the dinosaurs ruled the world millions of years ago we hadn't begun to evolve. No, we're Africans, Tinus and I. Despite my being born at Hastings Court, something I don't remember. My first memories are the smells and sounds of Africa when I was two years old. So far as I recall, apart from bringing the body of Grandfather to Hastings Court to be buried next to his ancestors, my mother has not been back to England in fifty years... Good, aren't they? Just the right amount of mustard. Homemade bread. Home cured bacon. What more can a man want? Now that's what I call bringing home the bacon... There she is through the trees. One of the first airfields in England. There's someone taking off right now. I never get sick of watching aeroplanes fly. It really is a beautiful day. Please feel free to have another ham sandwich. I asked Mrs Craddock to make lots of them. The chaps at the airfield always ask for Mrs Craddock's ham sandwiches. Can you imagine living in something twice this size night after night? The whole family and the servants. You can't just go to the air-raid shelter when the siren goes off and leave the servants in the old house without protection from the bombs. My wife is finding it difficult to sink in. The last war was in France with the occasional Zeppelin hand-dropping a bomb out of the basket so to speak. This one is going to have hundreds of bombers with levers to open the underbelly and drop a full load right on top of civilians. How do you see it, Janusz?"

"Warsaw in ruins. You only have to look at Spain. What the German bombers did for Franco. Without the German air force on his side, under whatever guise, Franco and his fascists would not be winning the civil war."

"Hitler's testing his armaments. They made a right royal mess of Guernica. Now they've bombed Barcelona. Why you need command of the air in any war of the future. Will you have command of the air, Janusz?"

"No, we won't."

"Neither will we without enough Hurricanes, Spitfires and pilots. Whoever is flying that aeroplane knows what he's doing. A complete loop followed by a dead stick and pull out just above the airfield. Pass me one more sandwich before the hordes get into the picnic basket. While you're flying, I'll have a cup of tea from the flask with John. Maybe I'll take her up for a spin when you two are finished. You remember the old Handley Page, Tinus?"

"Still flies. Tembo really was frightened. Princess won't let him go up again."

"Who's Tembo?" asked Janusz.

"The bossboy on Elephant Walk," said Tinus. "He runs the place. Even Ralph Madgwick defers to him on most occasions."

7

They all stood outside the hangar watching the unknown pilot do his aerobatics while munching Mrs Craddock's ham sandwiches. John Woodall, Tinus could see, had a sweet smile in his eyes as he picked up the second one from the open picnic basket; good, half-sized bread sandwiches with the crusts on, the farm butter yellow at the edges matching the yellow squeeze of the mustard against the thick red of the ham, the edges of the ham covered in a brown sugar coating topped with nutmeg.

"I'd marry a woman just to get a sandwich like this, Harry," said John Woodall.

"How long's he been up?"

"Twenty minutes. He's coming in now. We don't fill the tanks for that kind of flying close to the field."

"Had an Australian in the RFC. Before your time at 33 Squadron, John. There are plenty more in the basket. William Smythe says young Janusz here is as good as they come."

"They can go up together and later swap cockpits if Tinus wants to fly, which is a silly question. Good to see you both. How's the project?"

"Spitfire is on schedule. Tooling up for mass production is the problem. Half the government doesn't take us seriously. Or Hitler, for that matter. They believed what they wanted to hear when Chamberlain came back from Munich. How did you end up with an

Australian at Redhill? Bit far from home. What's he doing in England?"

"Better ask him, Harry. Came over yesterday with a sports job I suppose you'd call it and rented a plane for today. Gave him a student rate. Said he was short of money. Showed me a licence and a letter from his flying club outside Melbourne, wherever that is. Some university. You ever been to Australia, Harry?"

"What kind of a sports job?"

"Looked the same sort of thing as yours, Tinus, only different. Where is the Morgan?"

"Hastings Court. Came in the Austin with Uncle Harry. Had to have somewhere to put the sandwich basket. Go on, Mr Woodall. Have another one."

"I don't mind if I do."

"Come on, Janusz. It's our turn. He's taxiing to the fuel pump."

Watching the two run to the biplane, John Woodall sighed and put his hand in the picnic basket without looking.

"Don't know where you put them, John."

"In my stomach. What I would do to be that young again. All the excitement and none of the pain. They look so bloody innocent."

"They are. Their world is still perfect. Cricket fields. All the history of Oxford. Everything to learn and everyone to help. Not a cloud in the sky. Even their girls are perfect, whatever the girls do to them. I think Janusz likes his girl to flirt. Likes to see her appreciated. They can't even imagine infidelity in someone they love. To them at that age it's real love too, not one bump in the road ahead. Do you think it's instinctively why they like the idea of going to fight the good war at that age? Or all the books they read that makes everyone a bloody hero? Maybe their instinct tells them getting killed young stops them finding out the truth. To die pure and innocent with only love and bravery in their hearts and on their minds. Seems to me every generation does it so there must be something in my theory."

"Blimey, Harry. Have another sandwich. What's got into you? The idea of being wired to die young in war is morbid."

"The start of old age. Nostalgia. Not wanting the children to find out the ugly side of life. Don't you know what I mean?"

"If I did I wouldn't admit it to myself. I still enjoy my life. In particular right now, these ham sandwiches."

"You want some tea?"

"Pour away."

"Doesn't your wife feed you?"

"Not like this. Pilot's name is Trevor Hemmings and here comes youth, as they say, in all its glory."

"Mr Hemmings? My name is Harry Brigandshaw. You're the second Australian I've met."

"Lucky bastard. Mr Woodall said you come from Rhodesia, Mr Brigandshaw. First time out of Australia for me."

"What are you doing over here?"

"Buggering around after finishing at Melbourne University. Like Tinus. Can the Pole fly?"

"We're about to see."

"Like a ham sandwich?"

"Rather. I never eat before flying or I throw up."

"Like a friend of my nephew's."

"Do you fly, Mr Brigandshaw?"

"Just a little."

"Colonel Brigandshaw shot down twenty-three Germans in France," said John Woodall.

"That must make you an ace... They're good. You make them yourself?"

"I helped cure the pork."

"Bloody marvellous. There they go. I learnt to fly with the University Air Squadron. Like Tinus at Oxford."

"You two swapped a life history in ten seconds."

"Only the important bits. Later we're going to race against each other. Tells me he's got a green one like mine. Then I'd better hop it back to my digs in the village."

"Get your bags and stay at Hastings Court."

"Tinus hoped you'd say that. Us colonials have to stick together in Pommy land. My bag's in the hangar. Always travel light, I say."

"I rather thought that would be the case, Mr Hemmings. Always let opportunity knock."

"You know what it's like. Everyone's been young according to my dad. Mum says she doesn't remember. Like pulling each other's legs."

"I expect you'll then tell us what you're doing in England."

Watching the young man eat his way through the ham sandwiches, Harry found out that, since he was only twenty-two, there wasn't much to tell.

"My dad runs a chemist in Collins Street. Not far from Flinders Street Station. Gets the train from South Yarra every morning. The Yarra. Yarra River. Only river in the world that flows upside down. Too thick to swim in, too thin to plough. But you've heard that one. Mum looks after us kids. My prize for getting through pharmacology at Melbourne was a six-month trip home. Dad can't afford it of course, with all the kids. But he promised. Only way he'd get me into the bloody shop. Does all the dispensing and takes all the money himself. Don't trust no one outside family. When I get back I join him. Not a bad do really. Dad's made a living and brought up us kids okay if you ignore Justin. He's wild. Fifteen and wild. Doesn't bloody concentrate at school. Plays footer instead of doing his homework. I tell him you can't make money playing sport. That's why they call it playing. Like talking to a brick wall, Mr Brigandshaw. My dad would go for these. Mind if I have another? There they go. The Pole's flying. We got Polacks in Aussie. Fair go. Right, he can fly. Kind of makes friends quickly, having something in common."

"You'd probably like a cup of tea?"

"Never say no to a cuppa."

"When did you get to England?"

"Couple of weeks ago. Came over round the Cape, going back through Suez."

"Why do you call this home, Trevor?"

"All Aussies call England home, Mr Brigandshaw. A different kind of home. Like where we come from. Most of us don't have too many roots. Don't ask too many questions either. Anyway, this is home even if the Poms sent Great Granddad in a convict ship for stealing a sheep. Funny hey? Then they sent the bloody sheep."

"Did you know your Merinos come from the Cape of Good Hope? Did you stop in Cape Town?"

"Every stop I got off the boat. Probably never travel again. Once you get a wife and kids that's it. Then it's work. Aussie's too far from anywhere and big enough to keep a man occupied looking over his own estate. Never been out of Victoria before this trip."

"So you learnt to fly at university. Like my nephew. You are right, Count Kowalski can fly."

"He's a bloody count? Wait till I tell my sisters."

"How many sisters do you have, Trevor?"

"Four at last count. We're Catholics. Two boys and four girls. Mum says we eat her out of house and home."

"Have you worked at the chemist shop?"

"Every hols. Where the fare came from. Dad paid me in credits."

"Wise man. A few shillings here and there buy nothing of lasting value. You'll remember this trip for the rest of your life. Enjoy it to the full. So you'll join us at Hastings Court? You can drive behind the Austin."

"Too bloody right. You'll like Matilda. Beat the shit out of your nephew's sports car."

"What is Matilda?"

"An old motor cycle he picked up for ten bob and fixed," said John Woodall. "He's going to pay for his flight by helping me fix my car's ignition."

"Does Matilda go, John? For ten shillings. I wouldn't have thought..."

"Like the wind. And like that Morgan of Tinus's it's green for some reason. Only trouble is, it doesn't have an exhaust. You can hear it a mile away. Come and have a look. It's parked in my hangar."

"Shouldn't I bring the picnic basket, Mr Brigandshaw?" asked Trevor Hemmings hopefully.

"Why not?"

On either side of him, as they walked across to the aircraft hangar, both of them were smiling.

"Are all souped-up motorbikes in Australia called Matilda?"

"Most of them. You want to give it a go?"

"That's how you pay for your stay at Hastings Court. Motorbikes are one of my obsessions."

"Good on you. You got a nice house, Mr Brigandshaw? We're pretty open to travellers in Australia. Don't mind sleeping on the floor. Got my sleeping bag."

"I don't think that will be necessary," said Harry smiling, knowing exactly how the young man's mind was working. The best bed on holiday was always a freeload.

With the goggles on his face, the wind in his hair, the haversack with all his worldly possessions strapped onto his back, Trevor Hemmings followed the big Austin, the throttle half open, the power of his motorcycle vibrating up through his loins, and the whole world at his feet. Prepared for anything, Trevor followed the three men he had just met. If supper was as good as the sandwiches at the airfield he was going to eat like a king, something that had not happened very much once the boat reached England and 'home'.

When the car in front turned through the portal of an English country mansion as if it owned the place, Trevor began to chuckle.

"Good on you, mate," he said to the big trees gliding by his side that looked as if they had been in the same spot for centuries. The size and magnificence of the supper grew in his mind as the driveway went on and on, coming eventually to a gravel yard that looked to Trevor behind his goggles the size of Flinders Street Station. The façade was topped with battlements. "Shit. How long's this been here?"

A large Alsatian dog met the car while a pack of Spaniels watched from the terrace that ran half the length of a football field down in front of the house. Between the Spaniels stood a girl with long dark hair and a body made in heaven. His day was just getting better and better. Then some kids joined the girl as Trevor turned off his engine, still astride the bike not knowing what to do, his mouth wide open.

"When you said Hastings Court it was like my mum saying 'come back to Buckingham Palace'. This I've never seen."

"Family," said Harry Brigandshaw. For once the man seemed lost for words. "You can race the bike with the car tomorrow. Tinus will show you up to a room. Don't worry, we don't dress for dinner. Dump your haversack and come for a beer."

"I'm in heaven."

"Only if you let me ride your bike. Enjoy yourselves. My eldest son is away at boarding school. The rest will ask you a million questions. The lady belongs to Janusz and doesn't speak English. Behind her with my children is Tina, my wife, the one waving. I hope you'll be hungry after all the sandwiches. You youngsters must have much to talk about so I'll let you be. John Woodall wants you back at Redhill tomorrow noon to fix his car. There's always a price for everything."

"What's the price here, Mr Brigandshaw?"

"I work at the Air Ministry. We are always looking for good pilots. If you don't want to put on a white coat and serve at the chemist shop, the RAF might give you a job flying their latest aeroplanes. Supper's at eight. Tinus will give you the lay of the land. We'll be eating on the lawn behind the house on a night like this. I've learnt to make the best of good English weather. Welcome to Hastings Court, Trevor Hemmings."

"How long's your family had this place?"

"Six hundred years, round about. Not the exact same house. This one is Elizabethan at its core. We came over with William the Conqueror."

"Saw a good film back home, *Holy Knight*. About the St Clairs in

Dorset back there. Meant to be true according to the write-up. Began with the Battle of Hastings. Genevieve and Gregory L'Amour. Now she's really something."

"My first wife was a St Clair. My friend Robert St Clair wrote the book. Ask Tinus all about Genevieve. Did you know Gregory wants to be a pilot? Said if war breaks out with Germany he'll come over from America and join the RAF. You're all about the same age. Don't mind that dog, he just wants to go for a walk."

"Well I never! How are you and Tinus Rhodesian, if you don't mind me asking?"

"That is a long story. You see that second-storey room to the left with the window open? My father put a ladder up to that window and eloped with me and my mother and the nurse. The nurse is Tinus's grandmother. We all ran off to Rhodesia to get away from my grandfather. When he died I inherited this place. Nothing's really complicated when you work it out. I want to go back to Rhodesia. My wife wants to stay in England. So here we are."

As Harry went inside to book a call to Sir Jacob Rosenzweig in America for the following day, he was thinking how far Robert's book had gone. First tickling Maxwell behind the ear, Harry picked up the receiver and waited for the operator. Then he booked his person to person call across the Atlantic and noted the time on the small note pad attached by a cord to the telephone.

PART TWO

NEVER MISS AN OPPORTUNITY – OCTOBER 1938

1

Sir Jacob Rosenzweig was seventy-one years old and had just found his second wind in life when the call came through from Hastings Court. Unlike Harry, who he knew by reputation and from speaking to on the phone, both aware of their unspoken family connection, he did not live with his wife or any of his four children.

The three children in England visited when it suited them; when they visited, the subject was always money. Apart from Rebecca, far away on Elephant Walk, he had never been certain the children were his own. When they married, he and Hannah, it was family business, two good Jewish families to be tied by marriage to each other. Then, as always, the banking world in Europe was small, cementing relationships by mingling blood more important than any short-lived love.

Once, when Hannah was having more trouble than usual with her lover, she had briefly seduced her husband, later giving birth to Rebecca, the only person on earth Sir Jacob had truly loved, a love taken away by the obsession of his business clients to keep the blood of the Jews to themselves.

Ralph Madgwick, the man his daughter ran away with, was a gentile and that had been the end of it if he were to prevent all the years in business history from unravelling. He was not the first Jew to make such a sacrifice to preserve his race. He was sure he would not be the last.

Survival came first, happiness much later in the five thousand year quest of his people.

"It is strange to know a man so well and not have met him, Colonel Brigandshaw. I hope there is no bad news." Sir Jacob was on edge. Ever since he had been told by the telephone exchange a call was coming to him from Colonel Brigandshaw in England he had worried about Rebecca and her children in Rhodesia.

"None whatsoever. So far as we know, everything is well. Aaron has offered my nephew a job which he is mulling, for which I thank you for your introduction."

"Then what can I do for you from so far away in America?"

"Not so far in four days' time when I arrive in New York for my first visit. No, I wish to reciprocate your kindness. Business, Sir Jacob. I wish to diversify my portfolio to include America. You are the only man I would come to for such advice. Robert St Clair will meet us at the airport. He was my brother-in-law before my first wife was killed. Robert and I are old friends from our days at Oxford. I believe you financed the film Gerry Hollingsworth, the one-time Louis Casimir, made of Robert's book, *Keeper of the Legend*. I understand the introduction came from Max Pearl, an old customer of Rosenzweigs and Robert's publisher."

"You are well informed. Please make time to call at my office when you arrive in New York. Keep your second night free for a dinner party at my apartment in Abercrombie Place."

"That will be the night of the fourth."

"The fourth it shall be. Seven for seven-thirty. We are overlooking Central Park. Miss Cohen will give you an appointment in my office. We, you said?"

"My nephew and I."

"I will ask Max and Robert. A pleasant way to finally meet, Colonel Brigandshaw. Should you wish to bring..."

"My wife will stay in England."

"My wife too stays in England. Has never lived in America. One visit in thirteen years to be exact. And no, I am never lonely. Quite the contrary." Why he had referred to his previous loneliness he had no idea.

When Jacob returned the handset to its cradle, he was smiling. He would tell Vida at dinner. A dinner party. The first they would throw together. Then he sat back in his chair to think of the new woman in his life.

Vida was from Germany, her family dead, her money gone, the

maturing glory of her beauty still startlingly apparent to an old man. From adversity, they had found happiness. It would be most interesting on the night of the fourth to find which one of them brought up the subject of his daughter first. To be polite, he would give Harry Brigandshaw five minutes. Then he would want to know. From what Harry had said about his nephew, the boy had recently been on the farm in Rhodesia. If not pictures from a camera, Sir Jacob would hear pictures of his grandchildren from the boy's mind. It would finally bring them alive. Make them real. Whoever said old age was boring had never lived his life.

"The world indeed is small, Miss Cohen. Put Colonel Brigandshaw in my diary for seven o'clock on Tuesday night. We are going to throw a dinner party."

"Good news, Sir Jacob?" asked his secretary.

"The best. One of my young guests for Tuesday recently visited Rebecca."

At half past one on the Monday afternoon, Robert St Clair was wondering what had happened to his friend. The plane was two hours late and no one at the Imperial Airways desk knew what was going on.

"Well, he can't have lost himself in the jungle this time."

"Pardon me, sir?"

"Last time he crashed and spent two years living with a tribe of Tutsis."

"I don't understand, sir."

"Neither do I. The first time I flew someone told me how many parts there were on an aircraft that had to work perfectly to keep us up in the air. Then we took off. To calm my nerves I lit a cigarette. When I stubbed out my cigarette the ashtray fell on the floor. Been a nervous passenger ever since. Do we know what time the aircraft took off from the Azores?"

"They don't tell ground hostesses information like that, sir."

"Then they should. All things come to those who wait."

The girl was smiling at him in a 'now what are you going to do' kind of way. She was having a bad day like the rest of them waiting in the concourse.

"So we're both in the same boat."

"They'll Tannoy the aircraft's arrival. Go and have a cup of coffee. There's a very nice cafeteria you can see down there through the glass doors. Have a nice day."

Slumping on a bucket seat Robert began to think back. The girl was right. There was nothing either of them could do. Using his fingers, mental arithmetic not being his prize subject, Robert tried to calculate how long he had known Harry Brigandshaw since the days they had met at Oxford when he could still stand on his own two feet.

Like so many friendships it had started casually in a crowd, no one making a formal introduction, two undergraduates the same age finding the spires and quadrangles overpowering while making a show of feeling quite at home. Harry taking a degree in geology came to Robert's mind. His own Bachelor of Arts in history had been about as much use in his life to come. Neither of them had ever used their degrees.

"Must be thirty years ago."

The man sitting next to him looked up from his book and went on reading. The girl on the other side had ignored him after a first quick look, saying, without words, that old men were not of interest. Bored, her legs crossed, she had gone on bouncing her knee.

"What are you reading, old chap?"

The man showed him the cover.

"Not one of mine."

"I don't steal books."

"You waiting for the London flight?"

"We all are. They don't exactly land every ten minutes."

"Just trying to pass the time."

Freya and the kids had stayed in Denver. Genevieve, his niece, was in town, along with Gerry Hollingsworth who was raising money for *Holy Knight*. Robert was bored stiff like the girl in the bucket seat next door.

"My name's Robert St Clair," he said to the man with his nose in the book, hoping the name would ring a bell and start a conversation. For all Robert knew, they would be waiting around all afternoon with nothing to do.

"You've got to be kidding!"

"So you've read my books?" said Robert smugly, looking at the girl out of the corner of his eye to see if there was the same reaction in that direction.

"What books? Never read except at airports. If I haven't finished it when I go I throw it away. Same when I fly. I'm George Manderville from Virginia. If I lived in England they'd call me Sir George Manderville Bart."

"You're Cousin George! Are you waiting for Harry?"

"And Cousin Tinus. Somehow I remember from Harry you and I are related, Bob."

"Harry's first wife was my sister, Lucinda."

"I'm sorry. That story don't run right. Harry told me how Lucinda died. I'll be blowed. Sitting here all this time and not saying a word. Came all the way up from Virginia to meet his plane. Thought I would surprise him. Harry's first time in America. Now, tell me, what sort of books do you write? Instruction books? Everyone writes instruction books. All this new machinery. I can't even write a letter myself."

"*Keeper of the Legend.*" Miffed by the girl still ignoring him, Robert was going all out to impress.

"Now that's not true. That one was a film."

"Based on my book."

"You got to be kidding. Never knew they made films about books."

"What do you do in Virginia, George?" The girl was still bouncing her leg.

"Grow tobacco. Like Harry in Rhodesia. Did you know my father sent him his first seed? Us family have to stick together. Only trouble is, I inherited the damn title and Harry got Hastings Court. And I can't even use the damn title in America. You get born right and it still don't help none. Did you hear that, lady?" said George leaning across Robert. "This man here wrote the book that made the film that made Gregory L'Amour famous. Now you got to know the name Gregory L'Amour, lady. Every pretty young girl in America knows Gregory L'Amour. My name's George. I'm from Virginia. Don't tell me you're waiting for Harry Brigandshaw?"

Without saying a word, the girl got up from her seat and walked away down the airport concourse.

"She thinks we're spinning a line."

"Why don't we get ourselves a cup of coffee?"

"Much better idea, Robert. We'll go get ourselves a drink in the bar. This is a celebration. This is a family reunion. If we get drunk it don't matter how long Harry takes a-coming. Take all day, for all I care. Just came up to meet Harry. You got anything better to do?"

"Not at the moment, George," Robert smiled, getting to his feet.

"What they done to you, Bob?"

"The Germans blew off my right foot in the war. I stump a bit but I still get around. Amazing what doctors do with prosthetics these days. If you listen carefully you can hear the new foot clicking when I walk."

On the plane, still half an hour out of New York, an oil seal in the right engine having been replaced was doing nothing for Harry Brigandshaw's nerves, Harry was tapping his fingers on his right knee, watched out of the corner of his eye by Tinus Oosthuizen.

"You don't like flying, Uncle Harry. I never knew."

"I like flying when I am in control. How can they replace an oil seal halfway through a flight? Pilot should have sensed the seal about to blow. They're just taxi drivers, not pilots. Well-paid taxi drivers relying on the ground staff instead of themselves. In France I worked in partnership with my mechanic to stop a problem before it happened. Always look for trouble. Remember that, Tinus. You can't land in the sea and repair an oil leak."

"Why don't you ask the pilot if you can sit in the cockpit?" asked Tinus.

"They don't want an old man telling them what to do. Anyway, he's the captain. It's his job to get us to New York. I hate being late. I hate being flown. I hate what's going on in the world. And why are you smirking?"

"We'll be landing soon, Uncle Harry. Genevieve will be at the airport too. Our rooms are booked in her hotel. I'm excited."

"That smirk said something else."

"Relax, Uncle Harry. You're even making me a little nervous. I never think what could happen when I'm flying."

"Robert said he'd meet the plane. Have you made up your mind?"

"When we get home. I want to walk the bush alone for a couple of days. Then I'll know what to do with my life."

"Do you think I should put money into *Holy Knight*?"

"Films are a gamble that usually lose. Like putting on a play. As your financial advisor, with a brand new degree in philosophy, politics and economics, you'd be safe in government bonds, guaranteed by the Bank of England. But what the hell. The first film made Hollingsworth and Rosenzweig a fortune. Have a piece of it, Uncle Harry, if Genevieve and Gregory do the film. I'd guess it's just as much the actors who bring the crowds as the film. Why do some people photograph and film better than others? I've known Genevieve for too long not to see what's going on. But if anything, I'd put my money on Gregory and Genevieve, not the film. They both make people want to be like them. Everyone wants them as lovers. The boys and girls who never date can have a perfect fantasy. It makes them feel better about themselves after they've seen one of their films. As if they were part of it. Hero and heroine for a day. Better than reading a book as they don't need the same imagination as when they have to picture Robert's words. On the screen, there it is. Gregory is the knight and Genevieve the perfect lady. Exactly as they are. You don't have to think, just sit back in your cinema seat and enjoy. If I had any money I'd put it on Genevieve and Gregory."

"Tinus, you are biased. I think we are starting our descent. He's been wiggling the flaps a couple of times. Well, here we come, America. The country will never be the same. Do you know, I really do feel different. Europe is suddenly so far away. All its problems left behind."

"Maybe I'd better have a look at America," said Tinus. "Do they recognise an Oxford degree?"

"When Cecil Rhodes made his will and laid the foundation for his scholarship he put America in the Trust as a beneficiary. All members of the Commonwealth and America are allocated Rhodes Scholarships. Rhodes still thought of America as part of the empire. The renegade child that went on its own. Oh yes, they'll recognise a Rhodes Scholar. And your degree from Oxford. Why ever not?"

"I might just have a word with Gerry Hollingsworth."

"Does this have more to do with Genevieve?"

"I'm young, Uncle Harry. Risk is in my blood."

"And not in mine anymore."

"It would be if you put money into the film."

"And you stayed near to Genevieve in America to look after my investment! Better think about that when you are all alone walking the bush. Elephant Walk needs looking after. Ralph Madgwick is going to want his own farm one day to leave to his children. I wonder if Jacob knows Rebeccas's pregnant again? How strange it is we know more about his family than Jacob. I'd hate that. Family to me is the most important part of my life, nephew."

"You can still have a family in America if you start your own."

"I was right. We're going down slowly. My ears are popping."

"So are mine. Sometimes it gives me a violent headache that only goes when I land. Welcome to America, Uncle Harry."

Tinus, smiling, noticed his uncle had stopped tapping his right knee with his fingers. Then the butterflies ran wild in his stomach at the thought of seeing Genevieve again so soon.

It was not as easy as before for Genevieve to be out in public alone. Dressed in a headscarf and a large pair of dark glasses that caused odd looks but no recognition, she had seen and overheard her Uncle Robert long before he went off to the bar with the older man he picked up sitting in the next seat. She had seen the young girl put her nose in the air as she walked down the concourse, and hoped she'd trip. Genevieve knew talking to Uncle Robert would blow her disguise, his strong British accent announcing to the world her presence for everyone at the airport to hear.

Like Tinus, though unknown to her at present, she was nervous, wondering how they would both feel seeing each other again, even after a month. What they had between them was something neither of them spoke of. The fear that made her tremble with cold in the afternoon heat was going to be told in a few minutes. Tinus was finished with England and going home to Elephant Walk, their paths never again to cross.

"This time I'm going to seduce him and to hell with it," she whispered to herself, pulling the headscarf further forward to cover her ears. "That'll make it or break it." Standing next to a pillar, trying to look like the rest of them, she listened to the loudspeaker announcing the flight had landed, her last chance to get what she wanted almost at hand.

Moments later Uncle Robert stumped his way out of the bar with his new friend as everyone moved to the gate where the passengers from the new flight would come out into the concourse after collecting their baggage.

"How are you, Uncle Robert?" she said, putting her index finger to his lips.

"How long have you been here?"

"As long as you."

"This is Cousin George from Virginia. Harry's Cousin George. Thinks Hastings Court belongs to him. He's the new baronet after Harry's grandfather died in Rhodesia leaving no sons. A bit like your father, I suppose. Have you ever thought, Genevieve, that were you a boy you'd inherit the St Clair family title?"

"Only if my parents had been married, Uncle Robert. But yes, I have. Now your Richard will inherit after my father dies."

"Only if I'm dead first. How is he? How's Mother?"

"He's fallen in love with the pigs and cows. Smithers is miserable in the London flat on his own. I worry about both of them, the valet and the master I suppose you'd call them in a book. How long will it take for them to come through?"

"Heaven knows. Nobody here tells me anything."

"Gran misses Grandfather and doesn't much care anymore. I don't want to get old."

Cousin George, struck dumb, stood looking at Genevieve, now no longer wearing her dark glasses, without saying a word. The girl who had ignored Robert came up to her all excited with a small notebook and pen in her hand.

"May I have your autograph?" she asked obsequiously.

"No, you can't," said Genevieve, delighted at the chance of getting her own back. "You were rude to Cousin George and my uncle."

"What a bitch."

Genevieve smiled at how quickly people changed when they couldn't get what they wanted.

"Not as big a bitch as you, darling," Genevieve said in the cockney accent she had only known as a child.

"Well, I never."

"No, you never will."

With a big grin Genevieve once again watched the girl walk away, this time with everyone watching.

"What was that all about?" asked her uncle.

"Women talk. Now, what were we saying?"

"Half an hour. Takes them half an hour to get their luggage. All that speed of flying gets down to a five minute slow walk from the plane to the airport building, to stand around looking at each other waiting for their luggage. They take them off the plane one by one."

"Buy me a drink. I need one. We can watch for Uncle Harry and Tinus through the glass partition from the bar."

"It would be my pleasure, Miss Genevieve," said Cousin George crooking his arm.

2

The next day in the kitchen of Abercrombie Place, Vida could see no difference between herself and a household servant. She was not one thing nor the other, neither paid housekeeper nor wife. The scullery maid was cutting the vegetables while Vida did the cooking, the only difference being she would get to eat the food sitting with the guests at the dining room table, all of them not knowing where she fitted in the picture or whether there was a picture to fit in. It was her last throw of the dice.

For years she had watched the Jews being pushed out of Germany. Their possessions stolen, their lives only spared if they had money to buy their way to another life. Palestine, being a British Protectorate, had shut its doors, turning back the ships laden with refugees fleeing Germany for their lives. Only America was still the promised land. America was where people wrote back, urging their Jewish relations and friends to sell what they had and cut their losses.

America was where Vida had set her sights, and in 1936, eighteen months before she met Jacob Rosenzweig with a forged introduction, she had begun to make up a story that would carry her through the rest of her life and, hopefully, make her rich or at least not live from hand to mouth, frightened of her future. Young and poor was one thing, she told herself as she had planned her future. Old and poor without any family quite out of the question. Someone, somewhere, had even said to Vida: 'The Lord helps those who help themselves'.

First, she had laid out her assets in her mind. She was thirty-two years old. Prettier than most. And, by the luck of spending two years in England, looking after the children of a Jewish family in Kent, she spoke English fluently, even if she spoke with a strong German accent.

To get herself into America Vida knew she had to be Jewish with a hard luck story that fitted the American image of the oppressed Jews in Europe. The first part was to concoct a story that would make the Americans feel sorry for her, to make them pour out their sympathy to a young woman left all alone. The Jewish underground in Berlin whispered of rich men in America who used their wealth to bring the best of the Jews out of Germany, young people with education or old people with money.

With little time for anyone to check credentials, Vida used her friend who worked as a printer to make up her degree and give her the appearance on paper of having more than a poor secondary education. Payment for that was cheap; all she had to do was sleep with him which for Vida with Kurt was a pleasure.

Telling her family, none of whom were Jewish, the family having emigrated from Lebanon in the previous century, that she was going back to England as a child nurse to younger friends of her family in Kent, she had booked her passage to America. Even her Wagner surname was false, the name she said she had taken to hide her Jewish ancestry from the Nazis.

By the time Vida landed third class in New York, having used herself and her mother's jewellery as payment, she was the epitome of a Nazi victim of hate, her family dead, most likely because of her father's political beliefs, no one knowing what had happened to them. Only by luck had Vida avoided being sent away. It was the luck of speaking English that made her story plausible. She could explain herself. Make the Americans understand. Make people cry at her story, and, most important, as she had always understood, make people feel sorry for such a terrible story and want to give her help.

Finding Sir Jacob Rosenzweig had been the easy part of her journey. Inveigling her way into his life only a little more difficult. He was lonely, past the age he thought possible to indulge in female comfort. Even Miss Cohen had missed what was coming when Vida walked into the Manhattan office of the Rosenzweig bank of New York and given the secretary her letter of introduction from a well-known Jewish family in Berlin who, soon after giving her the letter, had unfortunately been imprisoned in a Nazi concentration camp, their business and factory confiscated, something Vida was well aware of when Kurt concocted the letter on the Jew's forged company letterhead.

Dressed in black, Vida was shown into the chairman's office. Smiling, she had begun the process that had led her to the kitchen preparing for the first of what Vida hoped would be many more dinner parties, and a trust fund, if not a ring on her finger if the old goat could be persuaded to divorce his wife. She could still hear his happy words of astonishment the night she seduced him.

"You look so much younger than forty, my dear."

Forty, she thought, sounded just right, the lie supported by the white streak in her black hair, a pigmentation flaw since birth. If he had known she was thirty-two he might have questioned her authenticity and smelled a rat.

"I'm going to change for dinner, Amy."

So far so good, she told herself as she left the kitchen to dress for dinner, the food certain to be perfect, her father a chef in one of Berlin's top restaurants.

"It's all in the preparation, Amy. Buying the right food. Being organised in the kitchen. You can't make good food out of bad ingredients."

They were going to serve themselves from the buffet when Amy brought the trays of food to the long dining room. Soon after moving into the apartment at Abercrombie Place Vida had fired Jacob Rosenzweig's cook.

"Why waste money? I can cook as well as Mabel. Never waste money, I say. My mother, bless her soul, was a stickler for avoiding waste."

All day alone in the flat, the old bag might have found out the truth. By then, the old goat, as she thought of the tall, wiry Jacob Rosenzweig, was besotted. Mabel was asked to pack her bags and given six months' pay.

"It's always better to be generous," she had smiled into his face, sitting on his bony old knees while Jacob sat on the couch.

"Now we are alone," he had said with a boyish smile.

To Vida's surprise for such an old man, the old goat was permanently horny, a word she used in her mind, picked up in England from the father of the children she looked after during the day, and the man who had told her money was more important than happiness, that without money everyone found life hard and sad. That money was not the root of all evil but the power to do what she wanted. It had worked for the father of the children in her care, now it was going to work for her. With real money she could tell the whole damn lot of them to go to hell.

Not only was it the first dinner party, it was the first time the dining room was being used. With his new lease on life Jacob had bought the apartment next door, broken down the common wall and joined the two together. A woman half his age was not going to be prepared to sit in the lounge looking at an old man wearing slippers. She needed to be entertained in the best way possible, by entertaining others. What was the point of having so much money, he told himself, if it sat in his own bank? With Vida by his side, the Rosenzweig apartment at Abercrombie Place was going to be known the length and breadth of Manhattan Island as a mecca of entertainment, where the best in film, literature and business came together to express their views.

With Harry Brigandshaw in the offing and the renovation complete, their first introduction to the world of entertaining was made in heaven, even if that young star of film, Gregory L'Amour, was out of town; there was always a second opportunity to fill in that gap, Jacob told himself happily. When Jacob told Vida Genevieve was coming to dinner the light of his life's jaw had dropped making Jacob feel so good he burst out with a peal of happy laughter, something the walls of the apartment had not heard in abandon since Rebecca ran away back to England and on to Rhodesia to marry Ralph Madgwick.

Adding to a film star, a Hollywood producer, a New York publisher and a famous fighter pilot, he knew buying the next-door apartment had been worth every cent. The recently purchased dining room table that had originated in a French salon during the eighteenth century seated twelve people in considerable comfort, a long, beautiful piece of mahogany that stretched the length of the two original rooms, the connecting wall having been removed by Jacob's builder.

At one end he would hold court. At the other end would sit Vida in all her beauty with her beautiful foreign accent to charm the guests. Like a good game of tennis, they would play the brilliant conversation between themselves up and down the ornately decorated table spread with the new silverware from Christie's, bought for him in London without one word reaching Aaron his eldest son to be reported to Aaron's mother and Jacob's wife. Everything was going so smoothly Jacob felt like hugging himself.

At four o'clock, Jacob did something he had not done once before in his life; smiling to everyone, he walked out of his office on a Tuesday afternoon before the office closed.

"You have Colonel Brigandshaw's appointment in my diary, Miss Cohen?"

"Three o'clock in this office tomorrow afternoon."

"Splendid."

"You don't have an appointment, Mr Rosenzweig."

"I'm going home. Have all my guests confirmed?"

"Mr Hollingsworth is bringing a friend as you asked. His wife is home in California. Mr Pearl too but won't be bringing a young friend. Colonel Brigandshaw will partner his niece, I think he called her, his nephew a friend of Genevieve's."

"Colonel Brigandshaw was married to Genevieve's aunt, God bless her soul. The Goldbergs?"

"Unfortunately, the chairman of the board said he and his wife would not be able to attend. They have a prior engagement."

"A shame Mr L'Amour is out of town. What about the flowers?"

"They are to arrive an hour before the guests together with the flower arranger. Why not a caterer, Mr Rosenzweig?"

"Vida is the best cook in the whole wide world. She just loves doing everything for me, Miss Cohen."

Miss Cohen waited for the lift doors to shut before shaking her head and gave the closed door a bitter smile.

"She'll have me out if I'm not careful. Poor Mabel. Everything! I'll bet she does everything."

Only when she sat back at her desk, the space outside the glass door empty in front of the lift, did she recognise the true origin of her emotion. Miss Cohen at thirty-eight, two years younger than the new girl from Germany who had bowled over her boss, realised she was jealous. Wondering why she hadn't tried seduction herself, she wound the letterhead into the top of her typewriter and began hitting the keys as hard as possible, reading off her shorthand of Jacob's words as she furiously typed.

"Who would ever have thought he had it in him?" she mumbled to herself between clenched teeth. "I've wasted ten years of my life here.

Instead of running around New York all the time it was staring me right in the face."

Jacob was still smiling as he walked into Tiffany's ten minutes later. Even though he was not the dashing young man from fifty years ago, working in his father's London office on the pittance of a salary 'commensurate', as his father had put it, 'with his knowledge of merchant banking', he now had the money to buy his lady diamonds to place round her beautiful neck. He would make Vida happy the way she was making his whole life worthwhile once again, invigorated by the transfer of her youth to his old body. He had done so much for so many and put up with Hannah's affairs, now it was time before he died to spoil himself, to enjoy himself, even make a fool of himself if that was the way it turned out.

"Can I help you, sir?"

"Diamonds. Diamond necklaces, to be precise. I would like to see your diamond necklaces."

"How much do you wish to spend?"

"As much as necessary. Tonight we throw our first dinner party. Tomorrow, who knows. Do you think being selfish is wrong, young lady?"

"Buying diamonds for a lady is not selfish."

"Oh yes, it is."

"How old is your wife?"

"She is forty, so she says. And no, you don't have to look that shocked. The lady is not my wife."

"Let me see what I can find."

An hour later spent in pleasure, Jacob pointed out the necklace he wanted.

"Please send the bill to my bank."

"It doesn't work that way, sir. We have to know the bank will honour your cheque."

"But the bank is mine."

"We all have our own bank."

"I own the bank, kind lady. Sir Jacob Rosenzweig, late of Rosenzweigs London. Now plain Mr Rosenzweig of Rosenzweigs New York. You have heard of the Rosenzweigs, Merchant Bankers?"

"Yes, yes I have. Can you confirm your identity?"

"Please phone Miss Cohen at my office."

"Right away, sir... So you wish me to send your office the bill?"

"Indeed, I do."

Taking out a wallet from the inside pocket of his jacket, Jacob handed the girl his business card.

Gerry Hollingsworth described it later to one of his cronies in California as the whore giving him money for her services; banks entertaining their borrowers was new to him. In his experience, finding money to make a movie was all 'sell, sell, sell'. Only one in four ever made money. But the bank taking equity in the film, owning part of the cinema rights, meant Gerry as producer of the film was not required to give old Jacob Rosenzweig his personal guarantee for the bank loan to finance the making of *Holy Knight*. If the film failed to make a profit they each lost their own investment, both of them writing off the film to other more profitable projects.

Unlike Max Pearl, the publisher, sitting opposite across the dinner table, the money for the film came before anyone knew what it even looked like. At least Max had had the chance to read the complete book before he published *Holy Knight*. Had the chance of making a judged assessment of its worth before committing a cent to the publication. The poor sod who had to 'sell, sell, sell' was the author Robert St Clair, sitting next to him, and without a bestseller to his name what chance would he have had in the rat race of commerce, Gerry asked himself? When everyone wanted to 'have it made' before they committed a cent of their own money. How many times had he said 'it's a something' to some wavering investor like Harry Brigandshaw on the other side of the table looking bored.

Giving a sidelong look at the lady at the top of the table, Gerry would have put money on the necklace round her neck being brand new by the way it sparkled. All the diamonds he had given away dulled down without regular cleaning. Twice Gerry had seen her fingers go up to her throat and touch the diamond necklace, as if to make sure it was still there. And diamonds they were, of that Gerry was certain. The real thing had a very specific look to it, like the rare face of an honest man.

Of course he knew the prize of the evening was Genevieve sitting next to the young man with the same odd way of speaking as Harry Brigandshaw, an accent to Gerry that sounded like speaking with a clothes peg stuck to the nose, and the one with the nasty questions when it came to putting Harry's money into the film. To some extent, the well-known author in Robert St Clair was a prize. Even Max Pearl as a well-established publisher would be asked to literary circles.

So that had to be the answer to the evening; Jacob was showing off his wares and his power to the girl at the end of the table, the not unattractive girl who was wearing the diamonds and wisely keeping out of the general conversation other than to smile and to listen. Lucky old bastard. Young enough to be his granddaughter, if Gerry knew anything about young girls on the make.

Making a mental note to find out who she was, Gerry idly studied the rest of the décor in what looked like a spanking new dining room. Max Pearl was holding court on the subject of Jewish poets, a subject Gerry, a Jew converted to the Church of England in a second step out of trouble, the first being changing his surname, knew nothing about. Gerry did not even look Semitic, something prominent in the face of the girl listening with bated breath to every word gushing out of his well-oiled mouth as Max warmed to his subject, helped by the odd pull from his glass of expensive wine.

The cut crystal chandelier, over the centre of the long, antique table covered in George the Third silver, was the central point for the interior decorator, whoever he was; what Gerry would describe in a film as the central point, the commanding presence that dominated everything down below. An exquisite vase, solitary on a pedestal and brimming with fresh cut flowers, stood behind the lady sitting at the head of the table. Between the Georgian silverware were lines of flowers in shallow holders, each of which were joined back to back down the centre of the table. Instead of keeping the different types of flowers apart, just the heads floating in the slim troughs of shallow water were mixed, giving a flow of colour from one end of the table to the other, a touch that had caught Gerry's professional eye when Jacob first ushered them into his sumptuous dining room, the sideboards groaning with trays of food in ovenproof pots and covered dishes brought in by a bemused girl through the door that Gerry guessed led to the kitchen.

Whoever had decorated the room or arranged the flowers knew what they were doing, as did the cook, Gerry found out, when he helped himself to his supper, lifting the lids from the covered dishes one by one, the large whisky he had drunk in the lounge on arrival sharpening his appetite. Next to him he watched the girl he had brought from the agency helping herself to food, the girl still struck dumb by the presence of Genevieve. The agency girl wasn't the best he had seen in New York but good enough for one night just the same, the thin waist and large bottom just to Gerry's taste when it came to his women. Something that once, long, long ago, had attracted him to his wife.

Sipping his wine, his stomach pleasantly full, Gerry watched them all around him, wondering what each of them were really thinking in their heads. Staring more at Genevieve, something he had done since finding her and giving her a part in one of his films, he was confronted by the mismatched eyes that first made men look at her, one blue, the other almost the colour of coal. But then they flashed at him with a daggered look of annoyance, and Genevieve held her spread fingers over her face to keep his look away from her, a gesture he knew all too well, his level of frustration peaking instantly at the rejection. Only when she looked at the young man, who had asked too many good questions at the meeting in his hotel earlier in the afternoon, did her expression change to a soft and dreamlike wanting, the yearning written plainly all over her face. Forcing himself to remember how much money Genevieve had made for him, Gerry turned his attention to the whore in the seat next to him, trying to rack his brain for her name.

"Sonja," she said quietly so no one else could hear, a professional who knew her job without having to be asked a question.

Liking the girl just a little, Gerry took a sip of his wine, first raising his glass to Harry Brigandshaw in the hope of cementing the deal he hoped they would make before Harry left for Africa.

Then he turned back to the girl he had hired for the evening, putting his hand on her knee just under the table, the girl moving his hand far down and back up again, over the silky smoothness of her flesh, making Gerry forget everything else in the room. Then he smiled; if there was one thing Gerry hated in life it was amateurs and this girl was not an amateur. 'If a job's to be done, do it properly,' he told himself, the girl stopping his hand just before he reached her panties. 'The rest, as it should do, would come later,' he told himself removing his hand.

Idly he wondered how old she was, a question, like all the other times, he never asked. She did her job. He did his by paying her. It was the law of life. The way it should be. The way he liked. Emotions, when it came to women, always got in his way.

Then his eyes strayed back to Genevieve, one of the few women who had come into his life and got away. Maybe it was the challenge of one still to be had that kept him going. Kept him making his films. And, like old Jacob at the end of the table, kept him making the money that kept the world going round. The money, without which everything in the modern world, a world they were all forced to live in, would stop. Trade, he told himself, it was all about trading. Keeping the flow of money going from one to the other.

"Is she all right, Harry?" he heard Jacob say as he brought his mind back to the guests at the table. Making the world go round.

"They are all all right, Sir Jacob," said Tinus, bringing Gerry out of his private thoughts.

Then Gerry watched the three of them look at each other across the table, Gerry wondering who they were talking about, his mind racing, looking for an angle in his ongoing battle with Rosenzweig. What could young Tinus Oosthuizen know about that could interest Jacob Rosenzweig so intensely? Like remembering the young man's name, a name that had been confirmed after the meeting with Brigandshaw, there was something else to be found out about Jacob Rosenzweig; information in Gerry's world was often as important to trade with as money. At least the young girl who had come with Genevieve was flirting with him. Probably wanted a part in a film. Again, he would find out her name. Unlike some people, Gerry was no good at remembering names until he needed them. He was in New York another few days. Gerry only liked young girls. Then the girl smiled at him, making up his mind; she was worth a small fling. Who knows, he said to himself, she might even be worth a part in a film.

As evenings went in New York, it was a pleasant one. Generally, people were getting what they wanted including the woman at the end of the long table who, once again, had touched the diamond necklace decorating her throat. 'Bugger must have spent a fortune,' Gerry told himself, wondering why.

For Harry Brigandshaw there was an element of *déjà vu*. The weekends at Hastings Court, surrounded by strangers with everyone in the same boat trying to have a good time, reminded Harry of the dinner party. What people wanted to say to each other was left unsaid in favour of trivial, polite conversation or a dissertation on poets that Harry suspected bored Max Pearl as much as everyone else.

Jacob wanted to talk about Rebecca to Tinus, the last in the room to see his daughter and grandchildren. Gerry Hollingsworth wanted his money for the film. Robert wanted Freya who was back in California looking after their children. Genevieve would have preferred to be alone with Tinus by the look of her watching his nephew. And the young girl, hanging on every word spoken by Gerry Hollingsworth, would have more likely preferred to talk about getting herself a part in a movie.

For Harry, the only way to talk to friends was around a campfire. With the lions roaring in the background. His back to a log. The Zambezi River at his feet. The crimson red of an African sunset reflected in the slowly moving surface of the river. The sparks from the big fire rising to the lower boughs of the riverine trees as the birds of Africa called out to each other, telling each other where they were roosting for the night for when the quickly fading light was too dim to see. To have around him men sparring with their words. So when they spoke what they said was worth the listening. Something of value to add to the mutual pleasure of watching the fire burn. The day's travels in the bush tired all their bones. Each with an eye on their own spot on the ground where they would sleep round the same fire, taking turns to feed it to keep the predators from coming too close. Each doing in his turn what was necessary from individual habits formed from years of living in the bush. Tomorrow's breakfast baking deep underneath the dead ashes of last night's fire wrapped in river mud clay, the birds cooking just right for the dawn.

He was a much simpler man than those sitting around him at the dining table other than Tinus. All the great display of wealth would never for Harry compare to the Zambezi River, the morning calls of Egyptian geese echoing stridently in the dawn. Only in Africa was he free to roam without the questions, the rules, the obligations. What had made men live cheek by jowl with each other in great cities was beyond Harry's comprehension. Rebecca was the lucky one, living on Elephant Walk.

"Jacob, do you ever take a holiday?" he asked during a lull in the conversation.

"Where would you like us to go, Harry?"

"Elephant Walk. My nephew and I are going out to the farm when we leave America. I have the mind to build a great dam across the Mazoe River to irrigate thousands of acres of oranges. Tinus has made a preliminary study. Why don't you come with us? Fly to England and take the boat to Cape Town. Fly to Salisbury. Ralph will meet us at the station."

"Are you looking for money to build the dam?"

"No, Jacob. As I said on the phone, I wish to give you some of my money to invest in America."

Only when Harry had finished talking did he realise everyone else had stopped too.

"Bring Vida, Jacob. Give her a holiday. Maybe Africa will be to your liking."

"Oh, I'll like it all right. But what would Rebecca say? Never go where you're not wanted, Harry."

"It was her idea to Tinus," Harry lied.

"Who is Rebecca?" asked Vida into the silence.

"My estranged daughter," said Jacob. "Ralph is my son-in-law."

"I can look after Abercrombie Place while you travel," she smiled.

"Anyway, the invitation stands," said Harry trying to recoil from what was becoming an awkward situation. "If war breaks out the journey may be impossible. Why I am going so soon. Like here in New York, I want to have my affairs in order in Africa before the world goes mad again."

"Vida, shall we all take coffee in the lounge?" said Jacob Rosenzweig getting to his feet, his crumpled napkin left next to his half-finished bowl of apple crumble.

When Jacob reached the lounge ahead of the rest of them he dabbed his eyes and recovered his self-control, the invitation, coming out of the blue, having caught him unawares. What was so far away was suddenly very close. The girl called Amy brought in the coffee but the evening was over. Like a sand castle on the beach at Brighton Jacob had watched as a child when the sea came in, all his hard work was collapsing in front of his eyes. The others were making their excuses to go their respective ways. No one liked being made to feel uncomfortable.

Harry Brigandshaw was the first to leave, the one with nothing to lose, avoiding Gerry Hollingsworth on his way out with his nephew, Genevieve and her friend close behind. Robert St Clair was the next to go. Max Pearl, drunk, closely followed. Hollingsworth was all for sitting around for a nightcap by the look of him, the girl he had brought not caring one way or the other. There was only one way to get rid of Hollingsworth in a hurry.

"Gerry, you've got your money for *Holy Knight*," said Jacob, tired of all the innuendo.

"Wonderful, Jacob. We'd better be off. Lovely evening. Everyone thoroughly enjoyed themselves. I'll come across with the papers tomorrow."

"You do that."

"Here's my card," he said to the girl leaving behind Genevieve. "Give me a call."

"Thank you, Mr Hollingsworth."

"Call me Gerry."

Genevieve, half out the door, came back and took her friend by the hand.

"Goodnight, Mr Hollingsworth," said Genevieve pointedly.

Then they were alone, Jacob and Vida, the diamond necklace no longer quite as important.

"We're not going to Africa, are we?"

"No, Vida."

"She'll always be your daughter. That can never change. Like your love for each other. Thank you for the diamonds. It's late. Let us go to bed so I can rub your shoulders."

"I can't change anything."

"None of us can, Jacob."

"The food was perfect. She and the children are safe in Africa. You are lucky to be out of Germany. The situation there is only getting worse... Tell me, what else can a man do?" he said after a long pause.

IN THE TAXI on the way back to the hotel where they were staying on the same floor as Genevieve they were quiet. Harry had paid for another taxi to take the young girl home, Harry not wishing to face another unfortunate moment. The girl had still been clutching the business card given to her by Gerry Hollingsworth.

"Do you think he means it, Genevieve?" the young girl had asked as her taxi arrived.

"Oh, he means it. It's just what he means is different to what you think is going to happen."

"Does it matter if I get a part in a film?"

"Probably not."

The girl had been smiling as she climbed into the back of her taxi while Harry was busy giving the driver money and the girl's address.

"Why did you bring her tonight, Genevieve? You know I don't play around."

"To help balance the table places a little, Uncle Harry. To give the girl a chance."

"Will she get one?"

"Depends on Mr Hollingsworth. There are hundreds looking for fame and fortune. Do you think it matters?"

"Probably not. If it doesn't bother her afterwards. None of us are saints even though we like to think so."

They were almost back at the Independence Hotel before Harry spoke.

"Like trying to help Bergit von Lieberman, I just think I've done more harm than good."

"She didn't ask me to invite her father to the farm," said Tinus.

"I know, I lied. He won't come. Some family rifts are so deep they can never be crossed. I was a fool. Should have kept my mouth shut. Well, Tinus, are we going to invest some of my money in making a film of *Holy Knight*?"

"I don't think so."

"Neither do I. My bet is tomorrow, when I see Jacob, he won't mention Rebecca... Do you think that girl is just after his money?"

No one in the car answered the question.

For some reason, Genevieve was brought to mind of William Smythe when the taxi stopped outside her hotel. Then she remembered: the Independence was the same hotel she and William had had their one-night stand. Thinking she was no better than the rest of them, she said goodnight downstairs and went up alone in the lift to go to her room. There she felt empty. As if her world had nothing in it worthwhile. That being a star of film was hollow with nothing inside. Tinus had not even tried to take their friendship where she wanted it to go.

"By the time I'm thirty I'll be as hard as nails like that girl with her claws in old Jacob."

It was a long time into the night before Genevieve began to fall asleep. After all, Cousin George had missed nothing however much he had wanted to go to the dinner party.

"He's going back to Rhodesia and that damn farm," she had said to the empty room before dropping off. "So will Uncle Harry, if he gets the chance. Life just goes on round and round, no one seeming to get anywhere."

She had heard Sir Jacob Rosenzweig confirm the money to Gerry Hollingsworth for *Holy Knight*. Her last thought before falling asleep was about Gerry Hollingsworth. At least someone had got what he wanted. Racking her brain, she could not now remember the name of the girl she had brought to the party. Maybe the girl too had got what she wanted. Genevieve hoped so.

She woke once briefly before the dawn, thinking of Tinus in panic. In her nightmare his aircraft had been going down in flames into the sea. When she went back to sleep she was straight back into her nightmare, tossing and turning, soaking the sheets with her sweat.

In the morning she found the bed in a mess and her head was aching. She had missed breakfast, looking at her watch. Uncle Harry and Tinus would have gone about their business in New York. Turning over, Genevieve went back to sleep and slept until lunchtime. The phone ringing brought her awake.

"We've got the money."

"I know. Heard him last night."

"But today he signed. Come and have lunch, Genevieve."

"Why not? I've got nothing else to do."

"I'll be right over. Don't go away."

Thinking that life could be a lot worse, Genevieve resigned herself to her fate.

3

The meeting at the Rosenzweig Bank with Jacob was not what Harry expected. Rebecca was not mentioned, as if the subject had never come up, as if his daughter living on Harry's farm in Rhodesia was none of their business. Behind an office desk, Sir Jacob Rosenzweig was a lot more formal. Two other men were in the meeting. They owned a factory on the outskirts of Chicago that made and filled tin cans, the same cans that had been used to send food to the troops fighting the Germans in the trenches during the last war. The machinery in the factory required replacement to treble the output of the factory.

After the war, Harry and Tinus were quickly told, the factory had been allowed to run down as the demand for canned food dropped when the armies of Europe went home to lick their wounds and eat fresh food forever after, disdaining anything that came out of a tin. The two men wanted a large amount of money. Harry was asked if he would help.

"What security?" asked Tinus, taking hold of the discussion.

"When that war of yours starts all over again, buddy, Tender Meat will be awash with money. You can charge an army what you like, the same way we did last time."

"Can you now?" said Harry, the sarcasm lost on the two men from Chicago.

"You can bet your bottom dollar."

"So how does my uncle fit in?"

"You give us the money and get a big fat interest for doing nothing. Two per cent over the bank rate. How does that sound, junior?"

"And if war doesn't break out?"

"Buddy, that just isn't going to happen the way you lot in Europe are sparring with each other."

"So we take the risk and you take the profit?"

"Buddy, we do the work. That's just how it works. This is America. You English want to make money, you got to listen to Uncle Sam."

"What has the American government got to do with this 'deal', as you put it in America? And I am not English. A colonial, like yourself."

"We kicked out the British back when. No offence, Jacob. We're Americans."

"I would require five years' accounts. Full balance sheets. Full profit and loss accounts. Audited, of course."

"What the hell for? You're just lending us money. Isn't that right, Jacob?"

"If you require my uncle's money to restart your moribund factory we would require forty per cent of your equity and two seats on your board."

"What the hell for?"

"To make sure we get back our money. To share with you the reward, sixty per cent of something is better for you than one hundred per cent of nothing if these figures presented by the bank are correct. If you wish my uncle to join your gamble on the outbreak of war in Europe, we wish to share the profit. Interest at two per cent over the bank rate and our purchase of forty per cent of the net worth of Tender Meat which on these figures is worth nothing. Your machinery is out of date. You don't own the building of the factory or the land. You barely at present make a profit. Our gamble is whether you know how to restart what was once a successful factory using your past experience. Without our money, gentlemen, it is my opinion you will go bankrupt within the next two years."

"You've got to be joking, junior."

"I never joke with other people's money."

"We don't have five years' audited figures."

"Then you don't have a deal. My uncle has another appointment downtown in twenty minutes. We have to hurry, Uncle Harry. I'm sure Sir Jacob will fill our friends in with the rest of the requirements if they wish to borrow our money. Good day, sir. Good day, gentlemen. I did so enjoy the dinner party, Sir Jacob."

"Very much so," said Harry lamely as Tinus got up to leave the office, the only man standing.

"We'll be in touch," Tinus added.

Outside down in the street looking for a taxi Tinus was grinning.

"We don't have another appointment, Tinus," said Harry. "That was the only one scheduled today."

"War profiteers. Making money out of dead soldiers. We can throw the whole bloody thing out on the balance sheets. Those two I wouldn't trust further than I could throw them. Tender Meat indeed. By the time you get anything into a tin can it has to be tender."

"Did they teach you all that at Oxford?"

"Word for word. Never underestimate the English. Mr Bowden's words, not mine. Especially the ones with the pukka accents. William Smythe was right. The Americans want us out of the colonies. They even want us to go to war. I'm surprised that factory survived the depression, which still isn't over, by the way, looking at those figures. America needs a war in Europe to get its economy going. We spend the money, they supply the goods. Perfect for America."

"You were rude to them, Tinus."

"I'm a colonial. They expect colonials to be rude. Everyone does."

"They'll never come back."

"Oh yes they will. When they talk all sweet and nice I want fifty-one per cent or no deal. You have to control the cheque book, Uncle Harry. Control the company or you have nothing. To quote Mr Bowden, 'owning a minority of a private company isn't owning anything at all'."

"I'm glad I gave you the Morgan."

"So am I. Driving that sports car during three years at Oxford was a perfect pleasure." Tinus was grinning, his adrenaline pumping.

"And they taught you more than good manners and how to play cricket by the look of that meeting."

"I learnt to play cricket at Bishops. Our Alma Mater. What time are we meeting Cousin George for dinner?"

"He's coming round to the hotel at six o'clock."

"Then let's go and look at the river. Who knows when we'll be back in New York."

"Making money out of the plight of soldiers doesn't appeal to me."

"Doesn't appeal to me either."

"I like the idea of a walk."

"Let's go see New York."

4

The owner of the Italian restaurant lived over the shop, something Harry found out later. The receptionist at the Independence had given Tinus the tip. By the time Cousin George arrived there was still no sign of Genevieve. Her note had said she was celebrating with Mr Hollingsworth and Gregory L'Amour, who was back in town, along with the rest of the crew who had been on call to help the producer get the money they all needed to make *Holy Knight*. Tinus, a little miffed it seemed to Harry, had made no comment. The cab driver said he knew the way and dropped them off outside the restaurant. None of them had any idea which part of town they were in.

"Just go straight in," the cab driver said ominously.

"Don't look at me," said Cousin George. "I'm of Canadian descent who farms tobacco in Virginia."

"That much we have in common, George. A couple of hicks," said Harry.

Opening the restaurant door for his cousin George, Harry smelt food that instantly made his mouth water.

"It seems Jean knows her restaurants," said Tinus complacently, quickly closing the door to follow the cab driver's instructions, while trying not to look over his shoulder for the New York mafia.

"So you know her name," said Harry.

"In America they wear their names on their sleeves, or in Jean's case on her lapel. I think displaying her name is obligatory in American hotels. Genevieve would have liked this place. Cosy. Informal. Not a dozen tables and all tucked into nooks and crannies."

"Just the place to do business in private," said Harry, looking around.

"Jean sent us," said Tinus to the man who had greeted them at the door.

"Come this way."

"What wine would you suggest, Mr Russo?"

"How do you know my name?"

"Over the door into your restaurant. We are from Africa, my nephew and I. Please bring us food and wine that you would eat and drink with your wife."

The man went off giving them a suspicious look after pointing to a table next to a pillar.

"They're going to murder us," said Cousin George. "I don't think he's ever heard of Jean. How did your meeting go with the bank?"

As they sat down a large, round bottle of wine covered with raffia was plonked on the table. The table was already set with cutlery and glasses.

"Enjoy. I come help you drink it later. Very expensive. My wife make you her ravioli. Everything from Italy. All the ingredients from Italy."

"You don't know Jean?"

"Never heard of her."

"Independence Hotel."

"Expensive hotel. I bring second bottle shortly. Enjoy."

"He's drunk," said Tinus happily.

"So long as his wife's sober... They want us to invest in cans of meat, George. War profiteers before the war starts. Can you use some capital on the farm, George? Your father sent Grandfather the tobacco seed for us to get started on Elephant Walk. Keep it in the family, so to speak. I'm never good doing business with strangers."

"Why don't you come to Virginia and see? Every farmer can use more money to increase his gross turnover. The overheads on a farm stay the same. Got to grow more."

"I'd like that. Tinus didn't like the firm Jacob brought along today. Didn't like the directors. They called him junior. What do you need money for in Virginia?"

"To buy the farm next door. The equipment I already have can farm his land."

"Now you're talking my language. Putting money into an idea I can't see for something that hasn't happened is not my idea for a good investment. I want to see what I have bought. Want to be sure my money can't be stolen. Farmland, now that's an investment. Something you can safely leave to your children. Not something that is here today and gone tomorrow. My ideas have been building ships, designing new aircraft. Not some get-rich-quick scheme that when it works gives nothing but money. No satisfaction. Not something you can look at and be proud of when you get old. I never understood the point of making money for the sake of making money and using it to show off. I want to be able to enjoy what I have. I enjoyed expanding Colonial Shipping. I'm doing the same on the farm. Look at it. Be part of it... Can we fly, George? Time is short. How far are we from your place in Virginia?"

"This is America. The home of the Wright Brothers. I think Russo is coming to join us. Tinus, start pouring the wine. That Genevieve is sure some girl. Where'd she go tonight? Oh well, farmers with titles they can't use are no good to a girl like Genevieve."

"They got the money from Jacob Rosenzweig to make the *Holy Knight*," said Tinus. "There's more to making films than appearing on screen. Even her Uncle Robert got roped in. It's business for her tonight. I'm sure she'd prefer to be here."

"Do you two have something going?"

"I wish we had, Cousin George. I'm just a kid without a job. How can I compete? Better to stay good friends than make a mess of it."

The restaurant began to fill up. Groups of big men with fat stomachs. One table, the only big one, was entertaining women as far as Tinus could see round the pillar. Thinking of Genevieve finding somewhere more important to be, made him flat after the high from showing Jacob Rosenzweig what he could do, the job in London still on the table if he wished to pick it up. They were just friends from before Genevieve became famous, taking her out of his range. There were always so many people around. People wanting something for nothing. Better to be alone on the farm in Rhodesia than get his hopes up. Better to know his limitations. Her world would always be more exciting than his.

What he hated most was the way Gerry Hollingsworth looked at her, the thought of them together now giving Tinus a feeling of revulsion. Gregory L'Amour was a young man who envied Tinus being a pilot. If anything had happened between them it was their affair. That was natural. An affair with an old lecher who thought his stars his property made Tinus recoil in disgust. Just the thought of his hands on Genevieve.

Maybe his Uncle Harry was wrong, he thought. That making so much money could buy a temporary possession knowing more money was coming in to pay for the next passing fad. That everything in life was temporary, to be bought and used and thrown away, while the search went on for something else on which to spend the money. That possessing a girl like Genevieve was no different to possessing a new car, something to be had and shown off like all the other possessions. Which brought Tinus back to why people like that needed all that money: because without their money they were nothing, which made Tinus feel better about Gerry Hollingsworth and how he thought of him.

In between the ravioli and the homemade ice cream, Tinus watched Russo join them and help drink the wine. The man was a happy drunk, amusing everyone. With a smile on his face from the wine and Genevieve in better perspective, Tinus sat back and listened to the ebullient owner of the small restaurant.

"This is my whole life, from upstairs where I live to downstairs where I work. We don't go further than here. Why should we? Good food and good wine. My friend playing the most beautiful musical instrument in the world over there, also my cousin. My wife in the kitchen. New friends every night. This, my friends, is how to live. I am a most happy man."

"I'll drink to that," said Cousin George.

"So will I," said Tinus. "To happiness. To hell with the wealth."

"Elephant Walk," said Harry, raising his glass.

"Virginia," said Cousin George.

"To life," said Russo.

Smiling, Tinus continued to watch them quietly, having said enough for one day. Russo was drunk, no doubt about it, with the three of them not so far behind.

"To peace," said Tinus so quietly nobody heard above the talk and the man playing something that vaguely resembled a violin. Once at Oxford Tinus had seen a picture of a man standing up in a gondola playing such an instrument but never found out its name; like Russo's cousin, they both used a bow to make the strings give forth the sound.

Later, when the two bottles of wine were finished, they ordered a third. Cousin George was by then sentimentally talking about his children. Russo cried just a little, at how beautiful his daughters looked. Even Uncle Harry went through a sentimental moment talking about his own though strangely, for Tinus, leaving out any mention of Frank.

When Russo's wife joined them, a woman as round as she was tall, still with a beautiful face, she didn't seem to mind her husband being drunk. She was still wearing her apron from the kitchen. The beautiful daughters were nowhere to be seen. The party at the big table with the girls was making a lot of noise. Russo waved at them, smacking his lips to his hand. The big, fat men at the other small tables did not look so menacing to Tinus. With all the wine he had drunk, Tinus was glad he didn't have to work the next morning. He hoped Genevieve was having just as good a time. Very quickly the wife became drunk too, making Tinus think she had been drinking in the kitchen; that all Italians drank and enjoyed themselves.

By the time the fourth bottle of wine appeared on the table the people from the big table had joined them, bringing their chairs. Two of the men sang a sad song while Russo's cousin played in the background looking sad. One of the girls began to cry. Looking at her, Tinus could see she was very drunk. One of the men who was not singing sadly wiped the tears from her cheek. The girl cried some more. Even Tinus felt the song was sad, not understanding any of the words. Everyone in the room was having a wonderful time.

Tinus began worrying how Russo was going to collect the money. At the end a very pretty girl came down the stairs from the apartment above and gave every table a bill. She was smiling. Uncle Harry left the girl a big tip on the plate. Mrs Russo gave Uncle Harry a kiss making everyone bang on the tables. Tinus thought Uncle Harry would have preferred the daughter to give him the kiss.

Tinus remembered falling into the taxi on top of Cousin George when they finally got outside. They were all laughing, everyone declaring undying friendship with Russo. Everyone from the restaurant had come out on the street to see them off. When Tinus looked through the back window of the departing cab everyone was going back inside. Uncle Harry shook his head, looking at Tinus.

"Now I know why that first taxi driver had a note of warning in his voice when he dropped us at the restaurant," Uncle Harry was saying. "I don't think Russo charged us for all the wine. I'm going to sleep like a log."

When they reached the Independence Tinus was the only one still awake. His Uncle Harry was snoring. So was Cousin George. Jean was not on the desk. The old man who must have been the night porter gave them their keys. They were all being quiet.

"Now that was a night," said Cousin George.

Passing the door of Genevieve's silent room, Tinus found his door, fumbled the key, waved at Uncle Harry having the same trouble at the next door to him and went inside. Without thinking of pyjamas Tinus went to bed, falling asleep the moment his head hit the pillow. For a moment he had thought the room was going round.

5

_____

When Tinus woke his head was pounding like someone on his door.

"Go away."

"It's Uncle Harry. Let me in, Tinus. The men from Chicago are downstairs wanting breakfast."

"What time is it?"

"Eight o'clock."

"I thought war had broken out with all that pounding."

Tinus got up in his underpants and let his uncle into the room.

"You look awful, Tinus. Jean phoned up to my room. Said two men were in the lobby. I asked 'where's the lobby'. She said on the first floor. You have to be careful in America. Everything is different. The ground floor is the first floor, the lobby the reception. The two men are probably still standing at the desk. They want to buy us breakfast."

"How can you sound so cheerful?"

"They told me they want to sell us forty per cent. Get your clothes on. In America they start their business over breakfast."

"God forbid."

"Hurry up, nephew. The nice men are waiting."

"This time, Uncle Harry, you can do all the talking. And remember, fifty-one per cent. And I want those figures."

"Strong coffee, waffles with maple syrup. Scrambled eggs with a side dish of jam. You'll feel much better. What they offered me on the breakfast menu yesterday. Can you imagine scrambled eggs with jam?"

"I'm going to be sick."

"Then hurry up. I will be downstairs in the restaurant with our guests. I've never seen anyone work so quick in my life."

"You'd work that fast if you were going bust. Running out of money tightens the sphincter."

"Have you seen Genevieve?"

"Not yet... Now, move, please."

"Yes, sir!"

"Quieter, Uncle Harry."

"We flew every morning at dawn when the weather permitted."

"But not with heads like mine. Did I imagine it but was there a pretty girl at the end of the evening?"

"Russo's daughter. She collects the money. Now that's what I call a family. And yes, she was very pretty. Like her mother, I guess, when her mother was the same age. Cousin George is booking our flight to Virginia just up the street."

"You two were snoring in the taxi!"

"A couple of old dogs who know the tricks. We both forced three pints of water down our throats before we went to bed. Flushes out the hangover. Trick I learnt in the RFC. Can't afford to have a hangover in a dogfight. You'd be wise to remember that, Tinus. Germany has issued a ruling to confiscate Jewish property, and German troops are starting to subjugate the Sudetenland. It's getting worse and looking very ominous. It was all in the paper I found under my door. Do you know, I rather like America."

"Give me five minutes and I'll be right down. I feel bloody terrible."

The shower helped. Gathering his thoughts and trying to remember what he had said the previous day to the Americans from Chicago, the words of his tutor Mr Bowden came back to him. Mr Bowden had been prone to giving impromptu lectures, the personal words to Tinus often more important than formal lectures in the classroom.

"You can't work on a hangover, Tinus. The brain is scrambled. Better to leave it alone. You'll have to redo the work anyway. Anyone who thinks he can do good work drunk or with a hangover is a fool. In business, you have to drink, one of the hazards of doing business. The best men of the business can recall drunken conversations word for word and use alcohol to find out what the opposition is thinking. Drunks blurt out the truth and don't remember what they said, giving you an advantage. Try and keep behind with the drinks. One of my previous students drinks a glass of water between rounds. You'll find your own method. There is no difference between a drunk and a fool. A fool and his money are easily parted is an old cliché but like so many old sayings it is very true. Never be dishonest in business or the dishonesty will come back to haunt you. Always. Letting another man spill information is not dishonest. It's his problem and not foul play. Never forget that, Tinus. The only reason we have successfully run an empire, like the Romans, is our honesty. And you never, ever do business with a dishonest man. You couldn't bribe a Roman official. You can't bribe the British. When everyone is made to be honest the world runs smoothly. When the British Empire goes as many wish, there will be much jubilation among those who would like to be dishonest. For a short while. People who wish for something like that should be careful of what they wish for. The moment the rules are broken, the system will collapse. Always be honest and you will succeed in life. You will be able to live with yourself. Letting a man get himself drunk is a good way to find out if he is honest. From the mouths of babes and drunks comes the truth. Just remember what I said. Never, ever, do a deal drunk or on a hangover or you will live to regret it. You won't find that in the economics of business. There's more to life than book learning. Most of it is common sense. Just think, Tinus. Always think."

Downstairs in the almost empty restaurant Tinus said not a word, remembering the advice of his tutor. Trying to think clearly was impossible. Even the smell of a cooked breakfast made him want to be sick. How his Uncle Harry seemed so bright was beyond his comprehension, despite Uncle Harry drinking all the water before he went to sleep. There was no sign of Genevieve or Cousin George in the hotel restaurant. The two men engaged in the conversation with Uncle Harry looked at him every now and again, expecting, Tinus thought through the throbbing in his head, another attack. Maybe, after all, the hangover was working to their advantage. Within a brief interplay between the two men and Uncle Harry their percentage of ownership rose to fifty-one per cent. Uncle Harry was offered the non-executive chairmanship of the board of directors. The rate of interest on the Brigandshaw loan rose a full percentage point. It seemed to Tinus, drinking his black coffee, his Uncle Harry was enjoying being back in the game of business. When the two men got up to go, shaking his hand and the hand of Uncle Harry, Tinus silently gave up his thanks to Mr Bowden for making him keep quiet.

"So we have a deal, Harry?"

"Oh, I'll have to think about it, gentlemen. My nephew hasn't said a word. I'm just a farmer from the bush. He's the one who makes the decisions. He has a top economics degree from Oxford University."

"Didn't you own Colonial Shipping before your aircraft went down in the jungle? Mr Rosenzweig told us after you two left his office."

"I inherited everything. When I had apparently died the United Kingdom Department of Revenue made the executors of my will sell my shares in Colonial Shipping to pay my death duties. Between the time of my apparent death, when they assessed my estate, and when they forced the sale, the shares in my family company had dropped along with the Wall Street Crash making the executors sell all my shares to cover the debt. When I came back from the dead they gave me back my money. Lucky me. By then, what they gave back was a lot more than the poor chap who bought the shares could get for them. I kept the cash. He kept the company. My money is now worth more than double his. No, I'm a farmer. We are going down to Virginia this afternoon to look at buying a tobacco farm. Now that's something I know about."

"Mr Rosenzweig will get you five years' audited figures as soon as possible. It'll be a pleasure doing business with you. The news from Germany is not good."

"Have a nice day, gentlemen, I think you say in America. Sometimes I wonder if we speak the same language."

"Money always talks."

"I'll remember that, Clint. It is Clint and not Clinton?"

"Clinton's just fine, Harry. Did anyone ever call you Harold?"

"Not that I remember. We all know how to keep in touch."

"I'm sure we'll understand each other."

"I hope so. Here comes Cousin George. I inherited the family estate. George inherited the family title, which isn't any good to him in America."

"Isn't that Genevieve?" said Clint in wonder.

"Yes, it is. She is the niece of my first wife Lucinda."

"Too complicated. Sorry about the divorce."

"Not when we get to know each other. My first wife was killed."

When all four of them, Tinus, Harry, Genevieve and Cousin George, sat back at the breakfast table, Clint and his partner on their way back home to Chicago, Harry turned to Tinus.

"Brilliant. You never said one word."

"Are you going to buy the company?"

"That depends on you, Tinus. When you've studied the figures. How's your head?"

"Terrible," said Cousin George and Tinus simultaneously.

"Who were those guys?" asked George.

"Tender Meat Company," said Uncle Harry. "When do we fly?"

"Five-thirty tonight. I met the lovely Genevieve coming down to breakfast."

"I'm starving," said Genevieve.

"So am I all of a sudden," said Tinus.

"I always make people hungry," said Genevieve, sadly. "Where are you going now?"

"Virginia. To buy a farm. How was your evening?"

"Boring. Hollingsworth when he wins is a pompous ass. How was yours?"

"Tell her about Russo's daughter, Tinus," said Harry looking from one to the other. "He's got a hangover. I want to see Jacob when we come back to ask his opinion. He wouldn't have introduced us if they were crooks."

"We go back to California tomorrow," said Genevieve. "Tonight would have been our last night together. This is our last meal together until we meet again."

Trying not to look at Genevieve in case she saw the look of panic and loss, Tinus picked up the menu and ordered what he assumed was a typical American breakfast; steak, eggs sunny side up, sausage, corncake and French fries.

"What is corncake?"

"Canned corn in batter and fried," said Genevieve.

"French fries?"

"Potato chips," said Cousin George.

"Bring the lot," said Tinus, still not making eye contact with Genevieve.

Working on the principle it was better to feed a hangover than starve the problem, Tinus waited for his food in the hope it would make him feel better. The coffee had begun to take effect, making his heart beat faster.

"How's André?" she asked.

"He's fine. Trying his best to get a transfer to Fighter Command."

"Give him my love."

"Of course... So quick isn't it?"

"The food hasn't come yet. Oh, the trip. Everything's fast over here."

"I thought we'd have..."

"There's a park round the corner. Why don't we go for a walk together?"

"Here it comes. I say, that is a lot of breakfast. Yes, why not. Just so silly, really. Here today and gone tomorrow." Tinus was trying to be flippant to hide his feelings.

"Eat your breakfast. How much did you drink last night?"

"Too much. After the first three glasses of wine it doesn't seem to matter so much. I always drink too much when I'm enjoying myself."

"Was she that nice?"

"Only appeared at the end. To give us a bill and collect our money. Italian families are real families. I liked them."

6

Outside the hotel Genevieve looked up at the sky, a thin line between the tall buildings. There were a few clouds but no sign of rain. Taking Tinus by the hand she led him away into the morning sun, walking on the side of the road that caught it. They just held hands. There was no pressure. Tears pricked at the back of her eyes. The change from make-believe to reality had been too swift. From all the razzmatazz to a boy and a girl holding hands walking along to the park. It took them less than five minutes.

In the small park the leaves were falling from the trees, the wooden benches deep in autumn colours. There were other lovers in the park. Real lovers, not the ones she played on film. None of the couples noticed them, too immersed in each other to look. The wind had ruffled her hair that had grown to the length of her shoulders. This week her hair was the colour of a light strawberry. Not even the colour of her hair was real. Tinus was more real than any of the men at Hollingsworth's celebration. Everyone had gushed. All over her. So pleased. Laughing. They made out it was all so important, including themselves. Gregory had had to buck her up, told her to smile for the man with the camera. Now, with Tinus, the previous night seemed so unimportant yet they were going to part.

"Why are we always saying hello and goodbye to each other, Tinus?"

"Did you ever think that without Uncle Harry we would never have met?"

"Can't we do something, Tinus?"

"What? Your world has been made. Mine still has to come."

"What are you going to do?"

"Probably nothing of my own volition. The world's catching up. We won't have a choice anymore. None of us. It's all running downhill so fast. Uncle Harry knows a lot more than he's letting on. You only have to read the newspapers. Even the papers over here are saying it's a matter of time. Then I'll join the air force and the rest won't matter. Elephant Walk. Rosenzweigs. Tender Meat Company. Love. Money. Family. It won't matter. We'll all be fighting to survive."

"You could hide in Africa."

"Anyone can hide. It's staying hidden that's the problem. How long would the few of us in Rhodesia last if Britain goes down the drain? We're all part of the same empire. Without the body the limbs will fall off. A fascist or communist world run by thugs would be an unhappy world. Mr Bowden says it isn't communism or nationalism where the problem lies but in the thugs who manipulate the new ideas that are supposed to give everyone everything they want. One day it's follow Christ and be saved. The next day Karl Marx will give you the rich man's money. Hitler will make you proud to be German. No, we'll have to fight for our way of life to survive. There won't be an option. It's gone too far. The thugs want power, not communism or fascism or any other damn ism. They want the power and your money. All I ever want is to be left alone but people never let that happen. I'm too young to understand. Maybe I will one day in the distant future if I survive."

"Then what's the point?"

"Man's been asking that question all his existence, which is a very long time according to Mr Bowden. Trying to find a point. Trying to find a god. Trying to make sense of what we are doing."

"Then why are we here, Tinus?"

"I have no idea."

"Maybe it's to love each other."

"Nothing is that simple."

"Why don't we try?"

"Try what?"

"Loving each other."

"If only life was that easy, Genevieve. How long have we got?"

"About another hour. Then I have to pack. I'm always damn well packing. Always going. Never getting anywhere."

"Maybe we will one day."

"What?"

"Love each other. Maybe one day they'll all go away and leave us alone."

While Genevieve and Tinus were making each other miserable at the thought of packing, Harry Brigandshaw was thinking how far the family had spread since his ancestors stormed ashore from the Norman fleet to fight the Saxons at the Battle of Hastings in 1066. Cousin George, now the direct male descendent, had gone off to do his shopping. They had talked on alone at the breakfast table, getting to know each other as friends rather than relations.

"Your grandfather's uncle was my great-grandfather is how it worked. I suppose I should be English but back then a fourth son without money wasn't any use to anyone, Harry. So he went to seek his fortune in Canada."

"Did he make any money?"

"Not a penny. By all accounts the chap was a charming bum. Beautifully spoken. Perfect manners. Everyone loved him."

"Your grandfather?"

"Another bum. Roamed the frozen north of Canada. Some say he collected animal pelts. Went off one day and never came back. For years Grandmother brought up my father on charity. There were only the two of them. She was a tough old bird. Always telling me and father stories of the illustrious Mandervilles. That back in the old country we had an ancient title and a country estate. Must have been why she married Grandfather, believing all that bullshit. He never believed a word till the day he heard back from your grandfather, Sir Henry Manderville, God bless his soul, saying Father was the heir to the baronetcy. That all the other male heirs had died out. He did say he had a daughter and a grandson but that you could never inherit the title and it had to go to the next male in line, was what he said. A lot of women would argue about that these days now they have the vote. Do you know, Harry, it did something to my father. Made him want to make something of himself now he had some esteem. That Grandmother's stories he thought were bullshit were in fact true. That in our veins ran the blood of ancient knights. Father was bumming around like the rest of them round about then. Lumber jacking. Cutting great fir trees for someone else. Father was about the same age as Tinus when the first letter came to him from my old grandmother, enclosing your grandfather's letter. He was the last of the Mandervilles. It was up to him to carry on the line. He had to find a good wife and have seed as it says in the Bible. Father finally came to his senses. Instead of cutting trees for someone else, living in a lumber camp, bunking in one of the row of beds with the rest of the crew, he got himself a concession in Virginia. By then he knew how to fell trees. Being single with no real home back anywhere he hadn't spent his money for five years."

"What did he call your farm?"

"Lily Water. You'll see why tomorrow. Tonight when we get home it will be dark. Tomorrow I'll show you everything... You know, Harry, up close that Genevieve is real pretty."

"I'll tell Merlin you said so next time I see him."

"Who's Merlin?"

"The Eighteenth Baron St Clair of Purbeck, Genevieve's father."

"So she's got a title like me?"

"She's a bastard. Like me. Now that's another long story. My father eloped with me and my mother from Hastings Court when mother was married to the eldest Brigandshaw brother."

"But aren't you his son?"

"Mother was pregnant when she married him, by the youngest brother. We all ran away to Rhodesia where Father was a white hunter along with the farm he called Elephant Walk. We all have our family tales, Cousin George. Nothing in life comes to us simple. Just life itself maybe. I'm looking forward to seeing your Lily Water... I'm going up to my room for a sleep. Now the initial discussions are all over with Chicago I need some sleep."

"We'll take a cab to the airport?"

"Looking forward to meeting your family. This is proving quite a trip."

"There's one point I don't understand, Harry, before you go up. How did you as the son of the youngest sibling inherit?"

"My Uncle James Brigandshaw left me his shipping company and Hastings Court, that he had inherited himself from his father, some called the Pirate. I had no idea what was coming. I'd have stayed in Rhodesia for the rest of my life. It's a lot easier running a self-contained African farm than a shipping company with the largest freight business in and out of Africa. The largest fleet to the Cape. Sometimes, if not always, inheriting great wealth is more of a burden than a pleasure. Believe me, George, you're far better off on Lily Water than sitting in an office in the City of London. However plush. However much respect people show you, meant or otherwise. My father roamed the African bush free as the rest of the animals. That's the way to go through life. Not cooped up in an office."

"Refresh my memory again on why you inherited Hastings Court?"

"It was through Uncle James, not Grandfather Manderville. What with property tax and no income, most of the land having been sold off, Grandfather Manderville made a pact with the devil. In exchange for my mother marrying the Pirate's eldest son and heir, he gave my mother's father enough money to live off. Hastings Court came as part of the deal. So the Brigandshaws, not much to speak of, became part of an old, blue-blooded family with a mansion to match. Bit like the bullshit told you by your grandmother. Grandfather Manderville went off to live in Italy. Only later did he join his daughter in Rhodesia after she ran off with father. Where we all lived happily ever after."

"And your father?"

"He was killed by the Great Elephant. The biggest elephant in Africa. A legend from the Congo to the Cape. I think father would have liked it that way. At first, he had killed elephant for their ivory. The tables were turned. Only when we are young do we want to shoot wild animals. Some of us. In those days Africa was a lot more wild. Millions and millions of animals roaming the vastness of the bush. Only a handful of people. For me, I can only shoot for the pot. Man is carnivorous. We all like steak and eggs like I ate just now. Only when you come face to face with the live animal, before you eat it, does what you eat become real. A living beast much like ourselves. We've eaten flesh from the start. Will go on. Man does what he likes and afterwards makes what he does look acceptable. Like my Grandfather Brigandshaw, who bought a baronetcy for himself by giving money to the Tory Party, I think it was. And died alone in the Great Hall at Hastings Court, a man, in his mind, of consequence. And how could I complain? Without his being alive I would not exist. Now, if you don't mind, that nap calls. You know where to find me, George."

"Isn't life just strange?"

"You never know. Maybe one of your children will marry one of mine and bring it all together again."

"But you didn't inherit the Brigandshaw baronetcy?"

"Of course not. Uncle Nat's son is the current Brigandshaw baronet. Down the male line Uncle Nat, the bishop, just got what you received, a worthless title, and passed it down to his son. Never see the cousin. Thinks I stole his money. His inheritance. What can you do? We are who we are. That's all that matters. Lily Water. What a lovely name. He thinks, like you, he'd be better off with the money."

"Not me, Harry. I'm happy. I'm the last in a great direct line and proud of it. You keep Hastings Court and your grandfather's money."

"But, George, we're going to use it to buy a farm."

"Then we'll be partners, Cousin Harry. Partners. And that's different."

While Uncle Harry was sleeping back in his bed, Cousin George off on a walk to think through what they had said, Tinus saw the charabanc full of tourists pull up in the street next to the park. A pair of lovers had caught his eye, looking annoyed, the pair nearest to them on the grass. Following their look to the disturbance, Tinus understood why. All the tourists were talking at once, every one of them carrying a camera. Their peace, like the lovers', was over.

"Better get up and go, Tinus. That bus is trouble."

"One of them has seen you, Genevieve. The price of fame. She's yelling your name at the whole damn busload at the top of her ugly voice."

The couple on the grass, not ten yards away, were now looking at Genevieve with their mouths open. Like a stampede of heifers, as Tinus described it afterwards, the busload of tourists began to converge. Genevieve, resigned to her fate, got up to meet them. Within a minute she was surrounded. Tinus, who had also got up, was ignored. Genevieve broke out her best smile to his surprise and posed happily for their cameras. Anything that could be written upon was thrust in front of her. Fumbling in her handbag, Genevieve found a fountain pen, took off the top and pushed it back on the bottom in a resigned, familiar fashion before getting down to work. The crowd was shrieking and giggling, men and women, old and young. Tinus watched them from where he had stepped back to a safe distance.

"Who are you?" asked the girl who had first seen the bus coming.

"Tinus Oosthuizen. From Rhodesia."

"Is she your girl?"

"We've never had the time to find out."

"You've known Genevieve a long time? Since before?"

"Before what?"

"Before she became everyone's property, by the look of that mob. Why do people only behave like that in a crowd?"

"It's like a swarm of locusts except they don't eat the grass."

"We're going now. Have a nice day."

"Did they ruin your day?"

"Only a little. We have the rest of our lives together. You'd better go rescue your girl before they eat her alive. Good luck."

Looking from the togetherness of the couple's departing backs to Genevieve surrounded by pushy people made Tinus envious. The girl didn't have to finish what Tinus knew was left in her mind; 'you'll need it'. The girl and boy were arm in arm. Patiently, Tinus waited, forgotten, just a young man on the fringe of a crowd in whom no one was interested.

"Get me out of here, Tinus," Genevieve mouthed.

Genevieve broke away from the crowd and stood next to Tinus.

"Why do you do it?"

"My job. They pay a few hard-earned cents at the box office to see me. That's the only way I meet my audience. *Private Lives* was different every night. I felt the audience. You connect in a live theatre."

"They think they own you!"

"They do, Tinus. Something I must never forget. Take my arm. Firmly. Now walk the long walk back to the hotel if we can't find a cab. It's over. I might as well pack. That's how it really is. I'd hoped to forget for an hour."

"This is madness."

"This is my life. Mother said they'd tear me apart. The way booze is tearing her apart. I can't even help my mother, let alone myself. I'm sorry, Tinus. For a moment it was lovely."

"I can't ever compete with this."

"I know. Everyone has their price. Before all this I was a discarded girl with unmarried parents, with a mother who preferred to get drunk. Ostracised by everyone for none of my own fault. The butt of my parents' mistake. This was my way out. I can't go back now. If I told any of them I was a bastard they couldn't give a damn. Silly, isn't it?"

With a broad smile on her face, waving at the crowd, they made their slow way out of the small park. A taxi was waiting. The girl, still arm in arm with her companion, gave Tinus a wave.

"She called us a cab."

"Aren't we lucky? And cheer up, Tinus. Smile. You'll get used to it."

After he bundled Genevieve into the back of the cab, Tinus stood up to his full height to look around. To see if there was any more trouble. The girl from the grass was still watching him. Tinus waved his thanks. The girl gave him a sympathetic smile. Tinus ducked down and got into the cab. The crowd, if anything, was getting bigger. They sat at opposite ends on the back seat, saying nothing, looking at the back of the cab driver's head. A dark cloud had taken away the sun.

When they reached the Independence they separated to go to their own rooms.

"This is goodbye, Tinus."

"I know."

"At least you've come face to face with the problem."

"So they'll never leave us alone."

"Probably not. Say goodbye to Uncle Harry. I'm going to pack and go."

"You can always call me. Like you do, sometimes."

"I'll try."

"Why are you crying, Genevieve?"

"Don't be such a bloody fool."

Opening the door to his own room, Tinus went inside. He was smiling. Always the most difficult in life to attain was the most worth having.

Then he climbed into bed and fell asleep.

When he woke in good time to go to the airport, his hangover gone, Genevieve had also left. Jean was back at the desk when Tinus went downstairs with his one small suitcase.

"Any messages, Jean?" The door to Genevieve's room had been open, a girl inside cleaning the room.

"Not this time, Tinus."

"Russo's was a real gas."

"Have a good trip. Your cousin and uncle are outside with the cab. Thank you for staying at the Independence. You've still got your key in your hand."

Tinus put the key on the desk, his last physical connection with Genevieve. By then Jean was busy talking to someone else. Like in the park, he was no longer important.

*W*hen Tinus woke the next morning the sun was shining into his room. Feeling normal after yesterday's hangover he got up and stood at the window. Lily Water, spread out in front of the house, was as pretty as its name. In the small garden were children playing, their treble voices music in the morning air. The same huge woman he had met briefly the previous night was sitting in a solid-looking rocking chair watching her children. A man came out of a long, long cabin with four windows down the side and looked up at the sky, much the same way Tinus looked up at the sky first thing in the morning on Elephant Walk; everything on a farm was regulated by the weather. The man said something that Tinus could not hear. Two more men came out. They all walked off together. There was no sign of Cousin George or Uncle Harry as far as he could see.

They had arrived at Lily Water after midnight, all of them tired. The old pickup truck had been left at the airport by Cousin George when he flew from Richmond to New York to meet his cousin Harry. The three of them had sat in the cab with Cousin George driving, the gear lever firmly stuck in Tinus's crotch. By the time they reached Lily Water after a long drive he was stiff in both buttocks. His right foot had gone to sleep. All the way, Tinus had found it strange driving on the wrong side of the road. The first set of headlights coming at them on the wrong side had sent Tinus into a panic. By the time they reached Lily Water he was used to it. The huge lady had given them supper round the fire. The fire made the small room look cheerful. There was no ceiling, only rafters and a wooden roof. The woman was twice the size of Cousin George with hands the size of hams.

Looking out the bedroom window, Tinus thought he remembered her name was Thelma though he could not be certain. Cousin George, in the middle of his introduction, had disappeared into her arms along with his words. She had briefly held him out at arm's length to get a look at him before enfolding him again. Cousin George had made strange sounds of affection before being put back on his feet. Without doubt she was the largest woman Tinus had ever seen. She wasn't so much fat as big. If everything about her had shrunk in half she might have looked more normal. Looking at them together the first time the previous night had made Tinus want to giggle. When he had looked at his Uncle Harry, his uncle would not make eye contact in case he too burst out laughing. Then she shook their hands and Tinus felt her strength. A practical woman, she had fed them and let them go straight to bed. Cousin George must have phoned her from New York as everything was ready.

Outside all the colours were browns and reds as far as he could see down a valley. Only the fir trees still had all their pine needles looking green. Right in the front of the garden lawn, not twenty yards from the woman, was a large natural pond full of lilies. They were different to the lilies in Africa by the look of them. Further down the valley was a series of ponds fed by rain water down the slopes of the hills. If he had not seen the msasa trees on Elephant Walk in the spring, the same reds and browns of new growth, not the falling leaves, he would have said he was looking at the most beautiful place in the world. Best of all there was not one ugly sound of man, not even a dog barking. Just the treble sound of the children's voices until the woman clapped her big hands and they all ran to go inside. Surprisingly easily for such a big woman, Tinus watched her get up from the rocking chair in one smooth movement to follow her brood. Only then could Tinus see her face, a face of total content and happiness making Tinus envy his cousin George.

Then he put on his clothes and went to look for everyone, hoping to find himself a cup of tea, or failing tea, a breakfast cup of American coffee.

By then Tinus knew he was going to enjoy his stay with Cousin George. The old grandma had to be somewhere to complete the family picture.

"Hello, I'm Cousin Tinus."

One by one the children came and gave him a hug. Grandma smiled a toothless smile. It seemed to Tinus, drinking coffee in the morning did not require Grandma's false teeth.

"What's your name?" asked Tinus surrounded by the children. He had sat down at the breakfast table next to Grandma. Without asking, a mug of coffee was put on the table in front of him by the big woman.

"My name is Henry," said the boy Tinus thought to be between six and seven. With such a big mother it was difficult to tell by the boy's size. "I'm named after Sir Henry Manderville, our illustrious ancestor."

"Who told you that?"

"Grandma."

Smiling, Tinus ruffled the boy's hair.

"I'm George the Fourth," said the boy next to Henry, which did surprise Tinus, his mind thinking of the kings of England, George IV long dead. Then he realised the boy was more likely to have been named after his father, his grandfather and great-grandfather.

"So you got your father's name. And what's your name?" Tinus said to the third boy standing next to the girl.

"Bart. Henry got the first part of our illustrious ancestor's name. I got the last part. Sir Henry Manderville Bart."

Looking at the satisfied look on grandma's face Tinus understood where the names came from. Grandma had still not said a word.

"And you, little lady?"

"I'm Mary-Anne. I'm going to marry a duke."

The children all stared at him before going off outside to play with an old dog that wagged its tail. The facial hair around the muzzle of the dog was white with age. The backdoor to the kitchen was open to the morning despite the chill wind blowing up the valley. The stove fire that had boiled the water for the coffee was giving out heat with the fire door open. Following his look out the door to the children surrounding the dog, Grandma gave him a toothless grin, put down her empty coffee cup and left the kitchen, pulling herself up by her hands with the help of the kitchen table. When Tinus looked round he was alone, the woman whose name he thought was Thelma having walked out the door and followed the children. Not sure what to do, Tinus stayed sitting at the kitchen table drinking his coffee.

Not long after, Tinus heard Uncle Harry and Cousin George come back from an early morning ride. He could hear the jangle of bits and the neigh of the horses. Then he heard his uncle talking.

"So from what I understand, the first tobacco seed came to us from Virginia before the war, in 1913. You were a child then. My grandfather planted that first seed on instructions from Cousin George, your father. Back a few years ago we got some more, better seed, that doubled our yield of tobacco in the lands. That was you, I am assuming? My memory is a little hazy. Grandfather Manderville was running the tobacco on Elephant Walk."

"Let Grandma tell you, Harry. That's if she's had her first cup of coffee and put in her teeth. She doesn't talk till then."

"Morning, everyone," said Tinus standing at the outside door to the kitchen. "This is such a beautiful place, Cousin George." The children by then had gone off somewhere with the dog and were nowhere to be seen.

"How many hands you got, George?" asked his Uncle Harry.

"Six at the moment. Live in the bunk house. They come and go. Lot of people out of work in the cities after the crash. They come here for food and a place to stay. Do the planting and hoeing. In America we don't grade the tobacco on the farm. Dry it in the barns. Flue cured. Bale the leaves and send it off to Reynolds. They weigh it and send us the money to the bank."

"How do you know it's right?"

"We have to trust them, Harry. Is Grandma in the kitchen, Tinus?"

"No, she isn't. Went off somewhere."

"Any coffee? Where's Thelma?"

"Went off with the kids. There's plenty of hot coffee on the hob."

Smiling, Tinus stepped aside to let them in at the door. He was right. The big woman's name was Thelma. "And here comes Grandma."

"Grandma, tell Cousin Harry about the first tobacco seed sent to Africa."

"Your pa of course sent it, George. Having sailed around the world, he returned to me in Canada. I made him find his English cousin, only we found Cousin Henry in Africa and wrote to him. By then his older uncles were dead without producing sons, and your pa was the last of the Mandervilles. Your grandpa had long gone so we headed to Virginia and your father worked as a planter on a tobacco plantation. He told Cousin Henry he owned it. Stole some seed and sent it with all those instructions to Africa. Your pa worked his way up and got his concession.

Sadly he's dead now but now we got our own farm and that's the truth. Pleased to meet you, Cousin Harry."

Tinus, watching, saw Grandma had put in her teeth.

"This is Cousin Tinus."

"We've met. Couldn't speak. Don't put my teeth in till I had my coffee. Cleans out my old mouth, hot coffee."

"George and I are going to buy the farm next door, Grandma. George wants to be the biggest tobacco farmer in Virginia."

"That's my grandson. Always did say he had good blood in him even if the good blood didn't show itself for a few generations. You come and have your coffee and tell me all about it, Cousin Harry. So you knew Sir Henry Manderville Bart?"

"He was my grandfather."

"I want every detail. Don't you miss out nothing. Not many families got knights in their ancestry. Makes me feel right proud. When you going back to England, Cousin Harry?"

"After we come back from our trip to Africa. We leave the day after tomorrow."

"Then start talking. Got no time to waste."

Tinus, not part of the conversation, finished his coffee and went for a walk to get a closer look at the lily ponds he had seen from his bedroom window.

"Now where do I start?" he heard his uncle say from the kitchen.

"From the very beginning."

"I'm a Brigandshaw not a Manderville. All I know is what I heard on the farm in Rhodesia from Grandfather Manderville."

"Just don't leave nothing out."

"Well, like my first wife's family the St Clairs, the Mandervilles came to England with William the Conqueror. They were Normans, or Norse Men, originally from what we now know as Scandinavia. They fought the Saxons at the Battle of Hastings and conquered England for their king. In exchange, the Norman knights were given English land..."

Only half listening, Tinus made his way across to the lily pond and dipped his fingers in the water. Just in front was a frog sat on a lily pad. The frog took one look at Tinus and jumped off the flat, round, green pad of the lily leaf into the water. From further down the valley Tinus could hear the voices of the children. The dog was barking excitedly. Tinus, sitting himself down on a small bank, looked out over the water. The white and yellow flowers of the lilies were open to the morning sun.

Birds were calling to each other from the surrounding trees. Probably, he thought, all this was going to be part of his future if Uncle Harry bought the farm next door for Cousin George; a tobacco farm in Virginia; a meat canner in Chicago. It was a start, he thought, tossing a small pebble into the centre of the pond and watching the ripples spread and spread. Then Tinus stretched out and lay on his back to look at the sky and think of Genevieve. So far as he could see, there wasn't a cloud in the sky.

PART THREE

IT'S EASIER TO KNOCK IT DOWN THAN
PUT IT UP – SEPTEMBER TO DECEMBER 1939

1

Ten months later their whole world went upside down.

The mechanised divisions of the German Army powered their way into Poland. As the French and British ultimatum expired, a state of war between France, Britain and Germany came into effect. Shortly after, the countries in the British Commonwealth, led by Australia, Canada, New Zealand and South Africa, declared war on Germany. America, Sweden, Norway and Belgium declared themselves neutral.

Three days later the Polish Army and air force were defeated. Russia and Germany partitioned Poland between themselves. Shot down twice, Janusz Kowalski, with nothing left to fly, his father arrested by the Germans, began making his way in the ensuing chaos towards the Polish port of Danzig on the Baltic Sea leaving Ingrid behind in Warsaw, all forms of civilian communication destroyed by the German Army.

Riding a bicycle, dressed in peasant clothes, Janusz made his way among the people fleeing the German advance. Alone, frightened, mourning his friends, he arrived in Danzig the same day André Cloete landed his Hurricane in a French field, spearheading the British Expeditionary Force into Continental Europe. In Melbourne, on the other side of the world, Trevor Hemmings boarded a Dutch ship bound for England.

· · ·

A WEEK later at Hastings Court, Harry Brigandshaw was pacing through the house waiting for his call to be put through to Tinus Oosthuizen in Rhodesia.

"Can't you see the bloody lines are busy," the operator had shouted. "Wait in line like the rest of them. There's a war on. Stop wasting my time."

"I'm sorry. It's my nephew."

"I don't care if it's the King of England. Get off the bloody line and wait your turn."

Everyone Harry knew was on edge. Anthony, having turned sixteen in May, had said at breakfast he was going to lie about his age and join the Royal Air Force. His mother's face had turned white. Beth, two years younger, had pulled a face.

"I can fly," Anthony had said.

"A Tiger Moth, Anthony," Harry had replied.

"It'll be all over before I'm eighteen."

"And what about school?" asked Tina.

"I hate boarding school. They won't let me play in the school teams because I stopped growing. They call me the runt."

"I went on growing at Oxford," said Harry.

"You're just saying that, Dad."

"I can prove it. When I went up to Oxford I was eighteen years old and five foot five inches. It says so in my first passport. When I renewed it five years later I was five foot nine. You can have a look, Anthony."

"They made a mistake," said Anthony, sounding unconvinced.

"They don't make mistakes on passports. Believe me, son, you'll grow. Sons are always taller than their fathers."

"Mr Banford said at school a boy is taller than his mother. Mum's only five foot three. I made her measure herself against the wall. I'll always be a runt."

"Who's Mr Banford?" asked Frank, almost the same height as his brother and nearly three years younger.

"My PT teacher. He's also the rugby coach."

Frank looked smug and went on reading Harry's morning newspaper.

"It says here that rationing starts next week. I'm going to make some more rabbit cages and go into business. How much will I get for a pound of rabbit?"

"They'll make you sell the meat to the butcher at a government price. No one's meant to make money out of war."

"Then you'd better sell your shares in the Tender Meat Company, Dad. When can I go to America?"

"Don't be rude to your father, Frank," said Tina.

"I want to go to America and make money. I want to be rich so no one tells me what to do. Ant, you're going to be a short-arse like our mother."

Tina, sitting next to Frank, without thinking, gave him a backhander across the face, hurting the back of her hand.

Exactly at the same moment, the air-raid siren began to wail from the top of Headley Heath.

"What's that?" screamed Tina.

"The air-raid alarm. They're testing the system."

"Germans coming," shouted Frank, banging the breakfast table with the back of his tablespoon, the slap on his face having had no effect on his pleasure at the chance of annoying his brother.

"I'm going outside," said Kim, the youngest. "I don't like quarrels."

"Sit where you are," snapped Tina, the siren alarm stopping abruptly.

"Can I go too?" said Dorian.

"I was right," said Harry. "Now they're sounding the all clear."

"You can all go," said Tina. "Get out of my sight."

"We're going to play in the air-raid shelter," said Dorian. "Why is it so cold inside, Dad?"

"The concrete blocks are still damp."

"There's water on the floor."

"The man in Leatherhead is making duckboards."

"Are we having ducks when we sleep in the air-raid shelter?" asked Kim.

"Duckboards are raised wooden slats. We used them in the trenches so as not to get our feet wet. When we have to go to the shelter we will take paraffin heaters and paraffin lamps. Warm it up and dry it out. You'll see."

"Why don't we go to Rhodesia?" asked Frank.

"Because your mother does not wish to leave England."

"They're testing that bloody siren again, Harry. That is now the alarm call. Why don't you put a call through to Tinus and find out what's happening? Could we get on a boat to Cape Town? I'm scared, Harry. For the children."

"Why are you scared, Mum?" asked Anthony. "With France and

England as allies, Hitler will be defeated by Christmas. Why I want to join the RAF now."

"Why don't you go into the garden, Anthony? I hate that sound. Is there anyone living in the Cape Town house?"

"Only the caretaker," said Harry.

"Can we get the boys into Bishops?"

"When I asked the headmaster last year it was all right. I'll go and book a call to Tinus."

"What will you do, Harry?"

"Stay in England. When it's over I'll join you. I hope they've finished the dam on time. Tinus was supervising the planting of the citrus. We'll need irrigation on the small trees after this year's rains. Are you serious, Tina? You've always been adamant about staying in England."

"That damn siren's got on my nerves. When will Hitler invade France?"

"André's already gone over with his squadron. The BEF are already there in strength. We'll stop them."

"Three days to overrun Poland."

"The Russians did a deal. You can't trust anyone in politics. I'll try to book a call. The lines will be busy. Everyone wants to make a long-distance call."

"Do you think he really will grow some more?"

"Oh, Anthony, I'm certain. It's in his genes. He'll be a big boy by the time he's twenty. There it goes again. The all clear."

"That bloody siren gives me the willies."

"You'll get used to it, Tina. If you stay in England."

"I'm going. With the children."

"That is good news. What about Frank's rabbits?"

"He can gas the lot for all I care. He's not taking them with him. He's always got something to say. He likes hurting people."

"That was a pretty good backhander." Harry was grinning at his wife; it was Frank's first whack. "Not bad. Next time give him one for me. You know the old adage, spare the rod and spoil the boy. He's so damn like him. That's what makes me so mad. Both of them like getting under other people's skin. Rubbing them up the wrong way. One of these days Frank and Anthony are going to end up in a fight."

"All boys fight. It's part of how they are made."

For a bad moment, Harry had thought Tina was going to admit Barnaby St Clair was Frank's father in front of the children. Getting up from the breakfast table, Harry had gone into the hall and booked his person to person call to Rhodesia.

At three o'clock in the afternoon, the same operator put through the call.

"Mr Oosthuizen is not available."

"Just put me through. It doesn't matter who answers."

"Three minutes and no more."

"Thank you... Who's speaking? Mother, it's Harry. Where's Tinus?"

"On the train to Cape Town. Can you hear me? Who's speaking?"

"Harry."

"What's going on, Harry?"

"We're at war."

"Have they dropped any bombs?"

"Not yet."

"Do you want to speak to Madge? When are you coming home? You know they won't let you fly at your age."

"Tina may come with the children. What's Tinus doing in Cape Town?"

"Catching the boat. It seems from his days at Oxford he's on the RAF reserve. They've called him up."

"Three minutes!" called the operator.

"Who's that, Harry?"

"The Leatherhead operator. Got to go."

Before his mother could say goodbye, the line went dead. Beside him Tina was looking up at him enquiringly.

"What's Tinus doing in Cape Town, Harry?"

"They've called him up. He's joining the RAF. There's a troop ship going to Cape Town I heard in the office. There must be people wanting to join up in South Africa."

"They won't call you up will they, Harry? To fly?"

"Not yet. They want me to go down to Uxbridge next week. The CO is an old friend of mine."

"Thank God Anthony is too young. And Frank."

"The last war went on for four years. Better take them to Cape Town or Rhodesia."

"What is there at Uxbridge?"

"The control centre of Fighter Command. Where the radar units down the south coast call in what they see from their screens. The nerve centre of the RAF if the Germans come across the Channel. Underground. Away from German bombs. Near the airfield."

"Are we going to win this war, Harry?"

"Not with Neville Chamberlain as Prime Minister. Rumour has it Churchill will form a coalition government with the Labour Party. Make Clement Attlee his deputy prime minister. Then we'll see what's what. I wonder if Tinus had time to finish the dam? I need a cup of tea."

"I need a drink."

"Then we'll have one. Together. I haven't had a drink at ten past three in the afternoon since I left the Royal Flying Corps in 1918. If we can't celebrate we can drown our sorrows."

"Why do nations always want to fight each other?"

"You'd better ask history."

2

While Harry and Tina were drinking gin and tonic, Barnaby St Clair was looking out of the second-floor window of his four-storey Piccadilly townhouse at the beginning of autumn in Green Park across the road. Everything looked different. What a week ago held the promise of peace in the comfort of grass and trees now had an air of menace.

"Stop hovering, Edward," snapped Barnaby. "Go and find another room to clean."

"Everything looks the same yet everything is different," said Edward, Barnaby's valet.

"Exactly what I was thinking."

"How will they know to sound the alarm siren? No sooner you hear the aircraft they'll be on top of us dropping bombs. Last time all we had was the Zeppelins drifting into England. Plenty of time to take cover from an airship."

"They have chaps on the coast with binoculars. Aircraft spotters. Harry tried to explain the radar. Bounces a signal off metal somehow. They all have telephones. Harry says we'll be given plenty of warning to go down to the air-raid shelters."

"I heard they are giving everyone gas masks. They think Jerry will drop cylinders of mustard gas. Like the waves of yellow gas he sent over our trenches when the wind was blowing right. He'll asphyxiate the lot of us. Friend of mine took in just a whiff before he got his mask on. Been coughing ever since, poor bastard. Doctor says he'll be coughing six times a day for the rest of his life. I've cleaned out the basement. What happens if Jerry drops incendiary bombs?"

"We'll fry, Edward. Try hiding in our own basement. Don't be damn silly. The RAF will have shot them down long before they get to London."

"They'll have fighter escorts. The Polish air force didn't shoot down one of them according to the *Daily Mirror*."

"Of course they did. The *Mirror* always likes sensation. The Poles didn't have our Hurricanes and Spitfires. Harry says the Germans have nothing to compare. Once they've shot the German fighters out of the sky the slow flying bombers will be sitting ducks."

"My friend said Jerry bombers bristle with machine guns. How else did the Poles give in so quickly? Jerry has tanks that go fifty miles an hour."

"Mechanised infantry."

"What's the difference if you don't have an air force and you're riding horses into battle? *Mirror* says the Polish cavalry were still mounted on horses. Anyway, they won't call us up this time!"

"Haven't you heard of the Home Guard?"

"What's that, sir?"

"To protect the island if the Germans invade. Every able-bodied man under the age of sixty. No one is going to avoid this war, men or women."

"The *Mirror* said last week it would be over by Christmas."

"Then they'd better make up their minds. I met one of their reporters at RAF Benson. Having an open day for celebrities and the press to recruit pilots. Came from somewhere in the Baltic, or his dad did. Bruno. That was his name. Bruno Kannberg. I'll have a word with him if we ever meet again. No point in frightening people or making them complacent. I'm going for a walk in the park, Edward, while I still can. And you're right. Everything feels different."

"They'll have to make different sized gas masks for the children."

"I suppose they will. At least we didn't have that problem last time."

"They called it the war to end all wars, sir."

"I do remember, Edward. It was just twenty years ago. Every damn part of it is still vivid in my mind. Yours too, I expect Edward. We'll just have to keep our chins up a second time."

In Green Park Barnaby found strangers were looking at him, trying to make eye contact. For a moment he thought there was something wrong with his appearance or there was something left over from lunch on the side of his face making him put up a hand to find out what was wrong. Then he saw the same person looking at a man sitting alone on a bench. The two smiled at each other. Strangers acknowledging each other's existence, a very un-English practice Barnaby had only seen during the last war.

'They're looking for reassurance,' thought Barnaby.

The leaves on the trees were dark green, the last colour of green before turning brown and falling off to the ground. In a month it would be autumn in the park followed by winter; cold, short days when walking outside needed a thick overcoat, gloves and a scarf wound round his neck. At the fourth person he passed, Barnaby smiled, receiving the same smile of reassurance in return; London and England were going to survive, they seemed to say to each other.

England had not been conquered since 1066. Many had tried and failed, the Spanish, the French, the Dutch; only the Romans and the Normans had ever succeeded. The park felt different, no longer a place of menace. Looking back through the trees across the grass and over the traffic down Piccadilly, Barnaby could see the second-floor window of his house, the same window he had been standing at before his brief talk with Edward. At forty-two, they were both too old to be fighting men again. He was too old to ride a camel through the Arabian Desert fighting the Turks, or anyone else for that matter. His body was no longer the taut athletic one that had taken him through the war with honour until the moment when he failed.

'Fifty quid,' he thought. 'I've got more than that in my wallet right now, all because I borrowed the money to pay my debts.'

Always, in the same discussion with himself, Barnaby was sure he would have given back the money had he not been caught and told to go back to England from Cairo at the end of the war and resign his commission before he was cashiered in disgrace. A cold sweat broke out as the memory came back, jolting him, making him remember the fear of ostracism from the people that made up his class.

A disaster, in the end, prevented by Colonel Parson, his CO, after Barnaby had gone on the boat out of Egypt with his tail between his legs and fear in his belly, a far greater fear than anything brought on by the Turks. So little money now, so much money then, the cold reality of recollection still forming a knot in his stomach.

Even Colonel Parson would not want him back in the army. Once a thief always a thief. Not even a desk job to let him feel he was doing his bit to repay what life and England had always given him, the life of privilege and success despite the errors on the way that still came back to haunt him on a walk in the park. For whatever reason he was no good to England anymore, except to smile reassurance at passers-by that bombs were not going to drop from the sky at any moment.

Now he had all that money and nothing to do. The girls, all the girls, were beginning to merge into one in his mind, the same woman in the same passing face, exciting for a moment and soon forgotten, the face, the body, soon forgotten, just another girl passing briefly through his life to momentarily take away his boredom. Some of them had used the word love which made him laugh at how easily everyone mistook lust for love and hoped it would last long after satisfaction.

A pretty girl caught his eye making Barnaby give her a smile, a different smile to the smile he usually gave to girls. She smiled back and passed on down the path, leaving Barnaby with a feeling of friendship in adversity rather than his usual predatory expectation.

'Well,' he told himself sitting down alone on a park bench away from the path, 'it's over, Barnaby. Fighting wars. Chasing women. Even the excitement of making money.' Only then did he begin to laugh at the irony of life; he'd had it all, most of it not mattering a damn in the end. Did Tina sometimes think of him, he doubted? With five children she had enough on her plate not to dwell in the past.

The same pretty girl was passing back the other way along the path in front of him ten yards across the lawn. This time she avoided his look. Barnaby looked around. It was too early in the day to go for a drink. Closing his eyes in the September sun that dappled him through the leaves of the tree above, Barnaby quickly fell asleep, an ability to nap on demand learnt in Palestine during the months and years with his mounted regiment hunting the Turks.

When Barnaby woke, feeling refreshed, no longer in the trance of a knot in his stomach, it was six o'clock by his watch.

A little stiff in the joints from the wooden park bench, he got up and went to look for a drink, avoiding eye contact with anyone as he walked down Piccadilly to Piccadilly Circus and his favourite pub on the corner where he ordered himself a pint of bitter.

3

*W*hile Barnaby was enjoying his first pint of beer, across the pond in America, Bruno Kannberg was walking down the street in New York on his way to an early lunch appointment with Max Pearl, his publisher. As the American correspondent for the *London Daily Mirror* he was trained to be on time for an appointment, especially one that was important. Looking at the passers-by, they seemed to Bruno to be their usual confident selves, the news from the old world having changed nothing in their lives. Looking at them, Bruno doubted the war in Europe even crossed their minds.

When it came to their meetings Max Pearl was always late and Bruno always early.

"Five minutes early for an appointment, Kannberg," his London editor had said when Bruno started his first job at the *Mirror* in 1931, "and five minutes late to a party to give your host that last few minutes to get ready."

Smiling to himself as he walked, the words of Arthur Bumley had once again controlled the subconscious of his mind as they did so often in his life. He was five minutes early for his appointment.

Boy Rising to the Stars had sold more copies in America than *Genevieve*, pleasing his wife Gillian who enjoyed living in New York after their two-roomed flat in London. Bruno's real reason for the lunch was to ask Max for more money, his wife having spent what was already in the bank, the new idea for a book the excuse to get Max to give him lunch.

There was a small bar near the entrance to the restaurant he could see through a window. At twenty past twelve the place was half empty. By Bruno's watch as he opened the door, he was exactly five minutes early, having cut the pace of his walk two blocks back on the four-block walk from his office. To Bruno's surprise Max was already seated on a high stool at the bar.

"How much do you need, Bruno?" were his publisher's first words.

"A thousand dollars. She spends money like water."

"Tell me. I'm on my fourth wife. What you got for me, Bruno? Better be good. There's no such thing as a free lunch. So the Brits, the Frogs and the Krauts are going to blow each other to pieces again. Don't people ever learn? What are you going to have?"

"Gin and tonic."

"You English are so predictable."

"Don't you worry about the war?"

"None of our business. Why we have the pond between us. No one can get at us. If you look as if you're winning we'll come and help you out so we can share in the spoils. Otherwise it's business as usual. As we did the last time, American industry will make money, kill off the depression. Roosevelt is playing his cards well and America is right behind him. No sane man starts a war, let alone interferes in one that's started."

"Don't you worry about your fellow Jews in Germany, Max?"

"Anyone with brains got out. You can't spend your life worrying about other people, Bruno. Now that's a good barman. Overheard what you want. Down the hatch, Bruno. I picked that one up from you. Did anyone worry about your father, the White Russian, when he made a run out of Latvia? Of course not. Poor bugger was on the wrong side. But look at you. You did all right. Life often turns out for the best just when it's looking the worst. All those Jews fleeing Germany for America will do us all a power of good. Hitler's doing the Jews and America a favour. It's all just politics, which is money. Do you know our factories are gearing up for full production? That friend of yours and mine, Bruno, he's going to make a fortune out of the Tender Meat Company. Now that Harry is one smart cookie. Your good health, my friend. What you got for me? I like you Bruno. You always make me money. One of my tricks as a publisher is to choose good authors with expensive wives who keep their old man's face to the grindstone."

"Gregory L'Amour is going to join the RAF," said Bruno, clutching at straws. "Wants to be a real-life hero. I want to write a sequel in instalments. You sell first to the magazines for a big, high number and afterwards bring it out in a book. Keeps them on the hook, so to speak. Brave American coming to the old country's help. There's nothing more satisfying than sending another man to do your work for you."

"She can have five thousand, Bruno. Five whole thousand. That's one hell of a good idea. When's he going to England?"

"I'm not sure."

"Maybe she gets the five grand when you are sure, Bruno. Drink up. I'm hungry. This one's on you, Kannberg. All you got to do is make sure."

By the time the main course arrived at Max Pearl's usual corner table, the Thespian was full, the noise having risen to leave their small bubble of conversation unheard by the diners around them. The Thespian was close enough to Broadway to use a theatrical name and be patronised by what some liked to think of as people of letters. Especially, Bruno knew, when they were thinking of themselves. Max liked the restaurant because it was next to his office. The food was good and diabolically expensive, giving Bruno the problem of writing a cheque without any money and being charged with fraud or explaining his real predicament to Max Pearl.

Bruno's monthly cheque as American correspondent for the *Mirror* barely covered the rent, let alone his wife's entertaining now she was married to the man who wrote the biographies of the stars, something she took great pleasure in telling anyone who crossed their path. Now a lady of leisure instead of a London shorthand typist, his wife Gillian lived in a world of her dreams while Bruno picked up the bills.

As he had said to Arthur Bumley on the transatlantic phone while trying to borrow money from his editor, "it doesn't matter what I make, she spends it."

"Are you getting enough, Kannberg?"

"Barely."

"You married her. Have fun. Even when you don't want it anymore you'll still be paying. You're welcome to America's divorce laws."

"I don't want to divorce her!"

"Watch this space. Write another book. You're on a treadmill, Bruno. Have a nice day, as they say in America."

"They're not coming into the war."

"Oh, they will, when we can't pay their bills after we ask for credit. When we owe them enough for out-of-date destroyers, they'll come in on our side to protect their own financial interest. Their greed will give us the credit. We just need to run up the bills and make them big enough to fight for."

"We're all Anglo-Saxons."

"You're not, for one. Give my love to Gillian. Tell her from me to keep up the good work."

"Thank you, Mr Bumley, for the loan," Bruno had said sarcastically.

"My pleasure."

Bringing his mind back to the present, the price of his fillet steak still sticking in his throat, Bruno tried to concentrate on his publisher's words.

"Those two girls over there are in the wrong place. Happens once in a while. They mix up thespian with lesbian or I'm a Dutchman. Just look at them holding hands across the table. Should be a law against it."

"There is."

"Only for men. Women can do to each other whatever they want. That's Gerry Hollingsworth over there, Genevieve's producer. My word, the place is full. He'll know when L'Amour is going to England. Go and ask him."

"It was just an idea. I need money, Max. Gillian again. If I pay for this lunch with a dud cheque they'll lock me up."

"And a damn good one. You don't have to get out of your seat. He's coming over. Maybe he'd like to join us for lunch with his girlfriend."

"I can't afford it, Max."

"Then you shouldn't invite me to lunch. I'm a popular lad. Plenty of people would like to buy Max Pearl lunch."

"You invited me."

"After you asked to be invited. Under false pretences. Gerry, old buddy! Come and join us. Bruno here is paying for lunch. Who's the new girl? Have you finished making *Holy Knight*?"

"Why I came over, Max. We have a problem. Your client, Gregory L'Amour, wants to go to England."

"When?" said Bruno jumping up from his seat.

"Right away, Bruno. How nice to see you. Gregory doesn't give a damn about the film all of a sudden. He's gone all heroic. Wants to go down in flames. Genevieve won't marry him. Can't you help?"

"I'm sure he can, Gerry. If you buy him lunch. Bring the girl right over."

"Didn't you recently get married, Max? Second or third time?"

"The day an old man stops looking at a pretty girl he might as well be dead. It was the fourth, and more expensive the bigger the age gap."

"Why are you laughing, Max?"

"Better ask Bruno. He knew Greg was going to England before any of us. He's going to write a sequel, *The Real Hero*. Make me a fortune. If you're a good boy I'll sell you the film rights."

"How long do you need him to finish the film?" asked Bruno.

"A month, if we concentrate on just filming his scenes."

"I'll have a word with Genevieve. Wouldn't it be best if we cross to your table, Mr Hollingsworth?"

"The world's gone arse about face."

"I thought it was arse over tit," said Max, picking up his glass and the bottle of wine.

"That comes later when the real war starts. I'm calling this part the *Phoney War* in my column."

"Nothing phoney in Poland."

"We weren't in that one," said Bruno. "We only think of what affects ourselves."

"You can leave the plates," said Max. "The waiter will bring them. Why won't she marry him?"

"Says she doesn't love him. Do you know, I've spent half my life trying to get into her pants?"

"So has half of America, Mr Hollingsworth. In their minds. What's her name?"

"That's what she calls me. She won't call me Gerry and I'm her producer."

"I know, Gerry. Isn't Genevieve a bit young for an old fart like you? And what about your wife?"

"Her name is Petronella," said Gerry Hollingsworth, ignoring the question about his wife.

"I thought it was Hannah."

"The girl at my table, Max. I'll fly you to California, Bruno. When can you go?"

"Tomorrow. I'll want that five grand, Max."

"My pleasure. What a story. I'll leak it to the press to get it started. So he can't go back on his tantrum with Genevieve. We'll say our hero is first going to finish making his film. Then he's going to a real war. The true American hero. Do us both a power of good, Mr Hollingsworth. Your films. My books. Nothing like a glut of good and free publicity to make money in the entertainment business."

"Please stop calling me that."

"Where's she from? Petronella?"

"New York."

"This lunch is getting better and better. To girls like that, one old fart's as good as another. You did tell her I'm a famous publisher, Gerry, before you so rudely left her at your table all on her own? Waiter. Throw away what's on those plates and bring it all over again. I'm hungry."

"Do you think they'll charge us twice for the steaks, Max?" asked Bruno.

"Who cares? We're rich."

"Don't you worry about Gregory getting himself killed?" Bruno found trying to force a man to go to war was beginning to prick his conscience.

"He's the one who's going to get all the glory, young Bruno. Not me. By the time they've finished squabbling in Europe and made up again there'll be millions dead. They're going to bomb the shit out of each other."

"Maybe Genevieve will marry him," said Gerry Hollingsworth hopefully. "It costs money to build a star."

"Splendid! Famous actress sees off famous actor to war. Bloody sensation in the papers. Have the whole bloody country crying."

"I meant marry him to stop him going to war, Max."

"Oh, he's going to war. Said so in England. They won't let him back out now. The newspapers will hound him. Ask Bruno. I'm going to phone Glen Hamilton in Denver the moment I get back to my office. He'll tell that freelancer in London. Writer under the syndicated byline of William Smythe."

"And if he gets killed?"

"He'll be an even bigger hero," said Max on a roll as they reached the other table.

"This is Petronella," said Gerry Hollingsworth as he began the introductions. "The old guy with the bottle of wine is Max Pearl. The young man is Bruno. Bruno Kannberg. Wrote the books on Genevieve and Gregory L'Amour. He's coming with me tomorrow to California to save our bacon. Petronella wants a part in the next film. Pity you only publish books, Max."

"Maybe Petronella wishes to write a book?"

"I doubt it," said Gerry Hollingsworth nastily.

"Could you help me write one, Max?" asked Petronella sweetly.

"Of course I could, darling. Would you like some of my wine?"

"Just a little," she giggled.

Standing a pace back from the others as waiters moved in the new chairs, Bruno doubted the girl was out of her teens. Just as he was pondering the girl's age and what to say to Genevieve when he found her in California, Petronella gave him a wink. Even young, they come tough in America, thought Bruno changing his opinion of the girl.

"And what do you do, Bruno, apart from writing books?"

"Make money for my wife."

"Do you love her?"

"Yes, I do. Ever since I saw her I've never looked at anyone else."

"Lucky you. Come and sit down. Tell me all about Genevieve. How she started. You see, Gerry told me it was you who wrote her book before he went across to your table leaving me all alone. All I want is to become an actress. Maybe you know some of the tricks?"

Glancing at Gerry Hollingsworth, Bruno kept his mouth shut as he took his place at the table. Five grand, he thought, hoping it would be enough.

"What's her name?" asked Petronella ignoring Gerry Hollingsworth's look of annoyance.

"Gillian."

"She's a very lucky girl. Do you have any children?"

"Not yet. My wife says we don't have enough money for children. It's always about money. However much you make."

"That's why I want to be a successful actress. Isn't it, Gerry?"

Without having to be told, Bruno knew the girl was sliding her hand along the inside of Hollingsworth's leg, making Hollingsworth's eyes glass over for one brief, intense moment. Then the girl smiled at a job well done and bought her hand up from under the table and went on eating her lunch, letting the men talk, her control of Gerry Hollingsworth firmly in place for the moment, making Bruno smile; everyone in America had an angle, everyone trying to get what they wanted.

For the rest of lunch, the war in Europe was never mentioned. At the table it seemed to Bruno everyone had got what they wanted. The noise in the restaurant had now reached a crescendo as each table made its point, people interested only in themselves, their personal bubbles, safe and secure. Bruno doubted there was one person in the room not beating their own drum, each oblivious to the other's intentions.

4

While Bruno was enjoying his second platter of steak, now without fear of it sticking in his throat, far away on the South Atlantic coast in Cape Town Tinus Oosthuizen was eating his supper in the Mount Nelson Hotel. This had once been the British headquarters of Lord Milner during the Anglo-Boer war which had ended for his family when the British hanged his grandfather for treason, his grandfather's only crime 'going out' for his fellow Boers when as a Cape Boer he was a subject of the Queen. Sitting alone at his table in the majestic colonial dining room, the irony was not lost on Tinus, nor the irony of General Jan Christian Smuts, now Prime Minister of the Union of South Africa, taking South Africa into the war to fight alongside his old enemy, England.

What had been the Boer Republics of the Transvaal and the Orange Free State were now part of the Union, alongside the Cape and Natal, the whole British-Boer conflict turned upside down with the losers ruling the country. There was even talk in the *Cape Times* Tinus had read that morning before he took the short drive to Uncle Harry's new house at Bishopscourt, that if Churchill became Prime Minister of Britain, Smuts would be invited to join the British War Cabinet.

Tinus found the Bishopscourt house grander by far than Uncle Harry's description, Mr and Mrs Coetzee, the caretakers, living in splendour in the nine-bedroomed colonial house with six servants, three in the house and three in the ten acres of gardens, as different to Elephant Walk for his Aunt Tina as chalk was to cheese.

The Coetzees, delighted at his fluency in Afrikaans, had shown him around as if they owned the place, more of a reality to Tinus than fiction. Declining their offer to put him up until his boat sailed for England, Tinus had driven his hired car back to the Mount Nelson Hotel and the distractions of Cape Town. After months on Elephant Walk supervising the infrastructure of pipes and pump houses, with not a young woman in sight, Tinus had better ideas on his mind than saving money. The *Capetown Castle*, which Tinus hoped would be full of young women, was due to sail in only a week.

When the cable from André Cloete had arrived on the farm telling Tinus to 'put his arse in gear and get over to England', he had lied to his mother and grandmother by saying the RAF had called him up, that his Oxford University Air Squadron had put him on the Royal Air Force reserve of officers, officers who were now being called up for the war.

A week after arriving in Cape Town, somewhat satiated by the nightclubs of Cape Town, buoyed by the bravado of youth, Tinus boarded the *Capetown Castle* on his way to England and the war that, apart from the British and French declaration, had not yet started.

BY THE TIME the *Capetown Castle* was sailing out of Table Bay, the newspapers in America were in a feeding frenzy at the heroics of Gregory L'Amour. Glen Hamilton, editor of the *Denver Telegraph*, had made clippings of the headlines from around the country, not sure what he had started after receiving the phone call from Max Pearl in New York.

'*Now Hitler will think again*'
'*America to the rescue*'
'*American knight to the rescue of Europe*'
'*All over by Christmas now they have Gregory*'
'*Flyboy goes to war*'
'*Our hero Gregory*'

"HE's NEVER FLOWN a plane or ridden a bloody horse," said Glen in disgust.

"Sells papers," said Robert St Clair sitting comfortably in the chair on the other side of Glen Hamilton's desk. "Assuages the public's guilt at staying neutral whichever side they would want to be on. Don't forget your press finds it necessary to pander to the wealthy Jews in America. And they want America to fight Hitler. Now. Build up Gregory L'Amour and the job's half done for the newspaper barons. All hot air and only Gregory gets hurt. They keep the Jews quiet and don't upset their buying public, one man off to war, now that's leverage. Freya feels sorry for Gregory being dragooned off to fight but thanks to God America is minding its own business. Every time she thinks of the war and looks at the children she shudders. Won't let me think of going back to England. I've written to Mother suggesting she visit America, more to salve my conscience than believe my mother will set one foot outside Purbeck Manor. Merlin will take it as a nice gesture. Anyway, with my one foot they won't want me getting in the way. Merlin's far too old this time. Barnaby may try and lie about his age. He's got nothing to do. Chap's bored. Some fools think war's exciting. Hopefully Barnaby had enough excitement in Palestine to see sense. Probably forgotten he nicked fifty quid, so you never know."

"What are you talking about?" said Glen, putting the clippings aside and changing the subject.

"Oh, that bit is a long story, but all Barnaby had to do was ask Merlin for the money. By the end of the war my brother Merlin had made a fortune out of Vickers shares. The war made Merlin rich, Barnaby a thief, and blew my foot off. Not that Merlin didn't pay his dues in the trenches. He was in charge of the Vickers machine guns on a long stretch of the front by '18. If Gregory gets killed the newspapers will send him to heaven by making him a saint. Hollingsworth will make a film. Pearl puts out a bestseller. The papers will make another fortune. Sorry, Glen. Not having a go at you. Life is life. I hate war."

"I was there with Merlin in France, remember?"

"As a reporter. You lot only came in in 1917."

"You think America will do that again?"

"They've done it. Declared themselves conveniently neutral. Why not? Every country does what's best for its people. Why, you making such a song and dance about Gregory sells papers. Everyone knows this is a world war that affects everyone. Now with Gregory on his way in a few days people in America, where I now conveniently live with my wife and children, will think America is doing its bit."

"Sometimes I forget you are English."

"Well, don't. We're a mild lot until we get pissed off. You'll let us stop the Germans as we did last time and then come and help. If I was Roosevelt I'd do the same damn thing. Any day now the German air force is going to be bombing London. They'll outflank the Maginot Line. Go round the French army. This time we won't have time to dig a trench across Europe. Those mechanised divisions are too fast. They'll stop at the Channel. You watch. And all the French heavy guns in their impregnable redoubts will be pointing the wrong way while the German Army marches into Paris."

"And the French, what do they do then?"

"They'll do a deal. Most Englishmen would rather go to war with France than Germany. Remember the Prussians arriving just in time at the Battle of Waterloo saved Wellington's bacon."

"Weren't your ancestors Norman?"

"Stop trying to have a go at me, Glen, to make you feel better. Actually the Normans were Norsemen from Scandinavia. Not French, even though they spoke French. Mostly we English fight alongside our Anglo-Saxon cousins, the Angles and Saxons as they were when they conquered England."

"And the British Expeditionary Force being sent to France?"

"They'll have to get out. The Royal Navy will bring them back. Thank God we still have a navy the Germans are too weak to fight. You watch. It won't be over by Christmas despite sending Britain Gregory L'Amour. Chances are the British Commonwealth will be all on its own with America across the Atlantic watching from a safe distance with a smirk on its collective face remembering their war of independence with England. And if Freya has her way I'll be watching safely with the rest of you."

"So Genevieve won't marry him?"

"Not even to stop him going to war. She's in love with Harry's nephew. Has been for years. Luckily he's safe on the Brigandshaw farm in Rhodesia. Harry's going to send his wife and children to Cape Town where he bought a house a couple of years ago. Tina hates the African bush. Won't live on the farm in Rhodesia, but she'll live in Cape Town. Lovely climate. You see, everyone wants to be safe from war, Glen. And why not? Only fools rush in where angels fear to tread."

"Is Gregory L'Amour a fool?"

"He's young."

"That doesn't answer the question."

"Oh yes it does. We're all foolish when we are young. Don't you remember? Why didn't you stay in Denver in 1917? Even as a reporter you could have had your head blown off. At that age it's glamorous. You're looking at a converted fool in me. War is terrible, you only find out when it happens. That's the trouble with the world. With writers like me glamorising war. With Hollingsworth putting the same glamour on film. All the kids want to rush off to war and make themselves heroes instead of living their ordinary little lives. You can't smell it in a book or a film. It's the smell and the noise. Putrid flesh in no man's land that no one wants to go out and bury. And it's happening all over again. Time and time again."

The bit that pleased William Smythe when the story broke through Glen Hamilton in London, was the real reason for Gregory L'Amour's heroics: she wouldn't marry him; Genevieve wouldn't marry him. That part was never written in the newspapers or the value of the story would have lost its point. Still treasuring what had turned out to be a one-night stand in the Independence Hotel, however William looked at it, Genevieve was still a free woman. Any chance was better than none. Women grow old and lose their power of attraction. Film stars went out of fashion. If Genevieve did not marry he would still be there to soften her fall. Pick up the pieces. Put them back together. Give her a family and make them both happy for the rest of their lives.

They would live in a small cottage in Cornwall, William with his money from freelance journalism writing a book instead of a column, the house and car paid for from his savings. Money invested for the children's private education. Everything planned to be happy away from the turmoil of modern life, the backbiting, the politics, the bitterness and rivalry. Making money, as William put it to himself, out of some poor sod about to get himself killed. Even their rivalry over Genevieve did not prevent William seeing the truth. All the British headlines: '*They're on our side*', '*He's coming over*', '*Look out Adolf here comes Gregory*', were to make money for the newspapers by making their readers feel better while their world collapsed around them in the reality of modern warfare that William, briefly in Warsaw before he ran for his life, had seen with his own eyes. The power of modern guns that could blast their way through anything.

"They could send ten thousand Gregory L'Amours and it wouldn't make any difference," William said to Betty Townsend, putting down the newspaper. "It's all bullshit. The bugger can't even fly. You remember all that twaddle at RAF Benson when Harry Brigandshaw got them to open the Bomber Station and invite the press? Well, they got what they wanted."

"Maybe he did too. Making play play is not the real thing. Why do kids run around with tomahawks yelling like Red Indians on the warpath? They want to be part of a fight. Are you going to take me out to dinner? It's eight o'clock and I'm hungry. Why don't you be nice to me? Men should be nice to their secretaries. Especially when there are only two in the office. What are you going to do, Will?"

"Get drunk, I suppose. You need a man much younger, Betty."

"They're all running off into the army now the regular army is going to France. That chap André Cloete we met at Uxbridge is already there."

"How do you know?"

"He writes to me. Not all men are like you, Will."

"Betty, please. You're my secretary. You know the rules. I can't afford the time to train a new secretary. There's a war on. And there goes that bloody siren again."

"They're coming, Will. It'll soon be too late. Can't I at least get drunk with you in the great tradition of the Fourth Estate?"

"I'll buy you a drink in the pub."

"That's better."

"So's that. It's the all clear siren. Must be testing again."

"When Gregory does arrive London won't take any notice of the bloody siren. You can buy me a sandwich in the pub."

"They've got pickled eggs in jars. Shit, I'm tired."

"Do you still love her?"

"Of course I do. Doesn't everyone love Genevieve?"

It surprised William how quickly the feeling of comparative normalcy came back to him. The Green Man looked the same. Horatio Wakefield was at the end of the bar and waved. So many faces were familiar, men from the world of newspapers chewing the day's cud in case they missed something. Often the reason, William supposed, that the London papers had an uncanny habit of telling the same stories.

Two of the men gave him a glare. He had given Horatio the exclusive when Glen Hamilton phoned from Denver saying Gregory L'Amour was trying to break his film contract to join the RAF. If the boy had seen what William had seen in Warsaw he would have been more careful to avoid a fight.

Just a few days ago the dreadful feeling of extreme panic, gut-wrenching fear, and here he was walking into the pub with a pretty girl on his arm and only the occasional practice siren telling him a war was going on. That England, again, was at war with Germany.

It had almost become inevitable the moment the French went into the Ruhr to attack the coalfields when the Germans had defaulted on war reparations stipulated in the Versailles Agreement. Now, barely two decades on, the monster had grown another head and invaded Poland, Hitler and the Germans having bided their time to build up their strength.

From dive-bombers and strafed trains, the threat of German Panzers just down the road and the full power of *Blitzkrieg*, to the familiar smells and smiles of the Green Man, a pub that William knew could have been anywhere in England at that moment.

"Glad you got out in time," said Horatio putting out his hand. "And thanks again for the story. Mr Glass was delighted to pay you handsomely for the story and put one over Arthur Bumley at the *Mirror*. They all picked up the story quickly but that's journalism. Our sales went up twenty per cent the first morning I broke the story, made the public feel closer to the people who are going to fight this war. Is he really coming over?"

"I don't know."

"What made him make such a public display? Hello, Betty. Now this is nice, bringing your secretary, William. What's going on?"

"Nothing," said Betty. "Though it's not for the lack of trying. I'll have a small shandy, Horatio. How's Janet?"

"You said you wanted to get drunk with me. Genevieve won't marry him but don't put that in the paper. I still have some hope."

"You see what I mean?" said Betty.

"Looking around you'd never think there's a war on," said William. "They're all pissed off with me for giving you the L'Amour story and not them."

"What are friends for?"

"Give her a gin and tonic. I hate getting drunk with a sober drinking companion who remembers what I said the next day. I was on the train, Warsaw to Bromberg the day the Germans crossed the border. Arrived at Danzig when the German air force was dive-bombing the docks. Boat to Copenhagen and a flight to Croydon."

"You were lucky."

"Luckier than you, Horatio, getting out of Berlin in '34. I'm still shaking despite everything staying the same in London. Give me that drink. I need it... To Gregory L'Amour, gentlemen," William said raising his voice. "The Yanks are coming. God bless the Yanks." Then he smiled at Horatio. "Nothing like rubbing it in. Next time I have in my possession such juicy information I will start a bidding war. Life's all about money, they say. There they are, Betty, in that big glass jar on the counter. Help yourself to a pickled egg. The girl's hungry, Horatio. Still growing?"

"Why don't you just resign, Betty, and seduce the bastard? Janet's fine. She had a letter yesterday from Germany. Her patient Henning von Lieberman. Posted in Berlin before the war broke out. Took longer than usual to reach London."

"How is Herr von Lieberman?" asked William sarcastically.

"Wanted to tell my wife how much easier he speaks. I thought it was rather nice."

"Man's a Nazi. Spouting his mouth off with Janet's help."

"They probably all are now," said Horatio, ignoring the jibe at his wife. Janet was convinced Herr von Lieberman was a 'perfectly nice man'. "Arthur Bumley says that if the French had kept their hands off the Ruhr we wouldn't be in this mess now. The French still haven't forgotten the Franco-Prussian War."

"We English have a long history of blaming the French for our ills."

"What was wrong with his speech?" asked Betty without much interest, her mind concentrating on the idea of seducing William.

"He had a stutter. My wife's a speech therapist. Makes more money than I do."

5

While Betty Townsend was listening to the conversation of William and Horatio, getting bored at being ignored, across town in Holland Park, Rodney Hirst-Brown, one-time Chief Clerk of Rosenzweigs Bank in London, was walking into the Crown, smiling all over his face. Rodney, having spent most of the day pleasantly wandering around the London docks taking photographs with his Leica camera, was feeling pleased with himself.

"Double whisky, Henry," he said to the publican, one of the few people Rodney hoped was his friend.

"Your new business must be going well, Rodney."

"Never better, Henry. A man has to work for himself to make money. All these years at the bank were a waste of my time. Photography. That's my business. Make it a Chivas Regal."

"We are chipper. Doesn't the war dampen your spirits?"

"War is always good for business."

"Never asked, but what kind of photographs do you take?"

"That's my big secret, Henry. Never divulge the secret of making money or one of those chaps down the bar will copy the idea and put you out of business."

"Must be nude girls with that smile on your face. Cat got the cream."

"How did you guess? After all the years coming in here, you know me, Henry."

"Not calling you up this time, I suppose? Didn't you say you were a lieutenant in the last war fighting the Turks in Palestine?"

"In the desert. Past it now. Can't use me this time. Did you ever hear of the Honourable Barnaby St Clair? Self-made millionaire. Sponsors West End shows and female singers. All young girls. Brother's Lord St Clair. Same officers' mess in Cairo. Chap was nearly cashiered. Should have been, according to my information. The CO paid in for him. Stole fifty pounds. Just shows how the thieves of this world stick together. Now just look at him. All the money he wants and all the young girls."

"Never heard of him."

"Quite the man about town."

"How's Mrs Leadman?"

"Much more civil since I rented a second room next to mine."

"What for, Rodney?"

"A dark room."

"You develop your own photographs! I am impressed."

"All top rate photographers develop their own photographs," said Rodney, giving the landlord of the Crown what he hoped looked like a lewd wink.

"Suppose so. If the chemist did the developing they'd have you arrested. You've turned into a real card. Same again? That one went down quick enough. Must be thirsty business photographing all those women. Well, I never."

Only when he had sold the second double whisky from his most expensive brand did Henry move down the bar. It always paid him to talk to the customers. Make them feel important. Make them feel at home in a public house. Most of them were lonely, the ones that came in on their own.

'Wonder what he's stealing this time?' he asked himself. Everyone in the bar knew Rodney had been fired by the bank for stealing, though no one ever said so to his face. 'Everyone has something to hide.'

"What's he into, Henry?" whispered the next man down leaning over the bar.

"Nude photographs."

"Bugger me."

They were all smiling, including Rodney Hirst-Brown. The letter from Berlin with the money had been stuffed under his door the previous day. There was no postage or postage mark. Clean, one pound notes. A list of instructions. Each time there was a drop, the man waited for Mrs Leadman to leave the house before letting himself in through the front door with Rodney's duplicate key and putting the letters under the door to Rodney's small room at the top of the stairs.

All Rodney had to do was take the photographs, develop them in his dark room and give them to the man who brought him the money. Rodney never met the man. There was an address in Putney where Rodney pushed his envelope through the letter box in the front door, not even ringing the bell. The same way he had given the man the key to Mrs Leadman's front door.

"Like taking candy from a kid," he said to himself, raising his glass. "What harm could ever come from taking photographs of ships?"

Meeting Herr Henning von Lieberman when the German was in London having therapy for his stutter had been nothing else but a pleasure. In many ways getting his own back on Aaron Rosenzweig and the Jews for Rodney being fired for stealing one pound and twelve shillings from the bank was even more motivation for Rodney than the money.

After nearly two decades' loyal service at the bank, reaching the height of chief clerk for his hard work, they had never tried to listen to his story of why he was forced to borrow the money to pay back his bookmaker before the man carried out his threat to break both his legs. So little money when a man had it in his pocket. So much when there was no way to turn. Something wrong with a system that paid the chief clerk five pounds a week while the directors lived in mansions with access to millions. Every time he thought about his last conversation with Aaron Rosenzweig his blood boiled.

"It's not the amount, Hirst-Brown. It's the dishonesty. You're just lucky we don't wish to go to the police."

"What do I do now, Mr Rosenzweig?"

"You should have thought of that before you took the bank's money. We can't have thieves working in the bank now can we?"

"He was going to break my legs."

"Really? This is England. People don't go around breaking other people's legs. What the board would like to know is what else you stole?"

"Are you going to give me a reference?" Rodney had said in frustration.

"Don't be ridiculous. You'll be blacklisted, Hirst-Brown. Better than going to jail."

Looking back on his last interview with Aaron Rosenzweig, Rodney began to boil all over again. Whatever the Germans did with his photographs they were welcome. The man had ruined his life for the princely sum of thirty-two shillings.

Ever since getting the sack, Rodney had channelled his frustration and hatred at the Jews, telling anyone he met what he thought of them. 'Bloodsuckers' was the word he liked to use, never once allowing his thoughts to suggest to himself his predicament was his own damn fault.

As usual, no one came across to talk to him. Rodney waited patiently for the landlord of the Crown to give him a few brief words in exchange for another round. When he finally left the bar, Rodney was drunk, feeling better about himself for the first time all day.

6

---

*S*ix weeks later, Gregory L'Amour ducked his head to walk
through the open door of the aircraft and, from the platform at
the top of the steps, looked down on the hordes of people who had been
waiting hours for his arrival in England. Gregory, looking out over the
sea of expectant faces staring up at him, silent, waiting for him to say
something, as if the fear of war had locked their jaws, wondered what the
hell he was doing here.

"Well, it's too late to backtrack now," he said quietly.

"I doubt Croydon Airport has ever seen so many people meeting a
flight," said Bruno Kannberg right behind, still just inside the door of the
aircraft, not wishing to spoil the picture for the press of Gregory standing
there all alone in all his glory.

"Look as if they've come to witness a hanging by the deathly silence."

"Wave, Gregory. To them you are Robin Hood. They want you to
smile."

Gregory, taking his cue from Bruno, instead of taking direction from
whoever was directing his latest film, moved forward to just above the
first step that would take him down to the tarmac and raised his right
hand open-palmed, then he waved. Instantly the crowd responded with
a cheer.

"Just be yourself, Gregory."

"If I became myself I'd piss in my pants at what my big mouth has got me into."

"Then play the part."

"This is real, Bruno. Down there they expect me to go and fight a real war, where the characters get killed once and for all. How the hell do I get out of it?"

"You'll be fine. The RAF will be fun."

"Are you going to join up?"

"I would, Gregory, but as you know, Gillian wants us to live in America. We'll start the first chapter right here getting off the aircraft. *The All American Man*, remember. Max says every magazine on both sides of the Atlantic is vying for the rights. We'll tell the readers how proud you are right now. How much you want to fight the tyranny of Hitler. How much you sympathise with the Jews. That last bit's important. The Jews in Europe are going through a hard time right now."

"I'm scared shitless, Bruno. Why don't you tell them that in your magazine?"

"Robin Hood and Sir Richard Saint Claire were never frightened when they went into battle to fight the good fight. Wave again, Gregory. Wave again. Down there are your people. They adore you. Just look at their smiling faces. They were silently sad. Now they are cheering."

"And will weep no doubt at my funeral. Except they'll be alive and I'll be dead. I'm too young to die. What am I doing here? How did those first words of bravado at Uxbridge get me here? How did you all let it get out of hand?"

"You let it get out of hand when Genevieve turned you down. Don't blame us."

"I'm turning round."

"Not now. *Holy Knight* is finished even if it was in a hurry. When she sees how brave you really are, she'll change her mind."

"Do you think so?"

"Women like real heroes. You're going to be a real hero, Greg."

"I'm going to be a dead hero, Bruno."

"Go on down to them. They're waiting for you. Just look at them chanting your name. This is going to make the first instalment blow Max Pearl's mind."

"Isn't that Tinus Oosthuizen I met with Genevieve at Oxford?"

"Probably. She said he had joined up. You mean the chap in uniform?

Yes, that looks like him. That's Harry Brigandshaw's nephew. Harry's the famous fighter pilot. You're in good hands."

"How's he in uniform so quickly? He was in Rhodesia when Genevieve said no."

"University Air Squadron. He's been a pilot for years. Now off you go, Gregory, before you make a fool of yourself standing around. The 'All American Man' strides forth. He doesn't dither around."

"Give me a push."

"Are you serious?"

"My feet are like lead. They won't move. Please, Bruno. Before they all see my knees shaking."

As Gregory L'Amour stepped down on the first step, gripping the rail, Bruno right behind him with a strong hand in the small of his back, the brass band at the back of the crowd began to play the *Star-Spangled Banner*, strengthening Gregory's resolve. The music spurred him on. Drowned out his cowardice. Changed his fear to a resigned resolve. Once again he was in the kind of dreamlike trance he felt when making a film.

At the bottom of the steps, Tinus Oosthuizen was the first to shake his hand. Gregory felt he was standing tall. The smile on his face was real.

"How did you get here, Tinus?"

"By ship. I wanted a sea voyage to think."

"Any girls on board?"

"Plenty."

"Where do I go from here? Bruno Kannberg said I'm booked in at the Savoy."

"Squadron Leader Kent is waiting with a staff car. You remember RAF Uxbridge outside London, where we first took you after our meeting on the river? That's where we are going for you to apply to join up. Then to Redhill for flying lessons. This will be the last time the press will get a look at you. Make the best of it. Hello, Bruno. How's Genevieve?"

"She said if I saw you to give you her love."

"Here I am. Still getting used to the uniform. Doesn't take long. You'll be staying at Hastings Court during the flying lessons. You're American, Gregory. So far America is neutral. We're all working on it."

"And if I'm no good at flying?"

"Don't think of it. You'll be fine. Like riding a bicycle when you know how. Oh, and please, no interviews. Don't answer any questions. This time it's for real... That bit they're playing now, that's the RAF's anthem, so to speak. Martial music. Stirring stuff don't you think? We thought *God Save the King* a bit much for an American. Up the revolution, I say. We Boers sympathise with you Americans. South Africa is all right now. Sometime everyone has to fight for independence."

"Hey, where are you going?" said Bruno.

"Say goodbye to Bruno, Gregory."

"What about the press?"

"The stunt's over, Bruno."

Nobody took any more notice of him as the passengers, now getting off the plane behind Bruno, passed either side of him. Gregory, with the tall, thin Tinus in the grey-blue uniform with the snow-white wings on his breast, passed on into the crowd.

Moments later Bruno could see the car as they got inside, the magazine story disappearing in front of his eyes. Max Pearl had said to stay in England for as long as the story ran. Bruno gave the spectacle in front of him a wry smile that went unnoticed. It had happened before to every journalist. What to do next was his problem.

Looking back at the aircraft that had bought them from America, there was no one else coming down the movable steps. Two men in overalls were pulling the contraption away from the open door of the aircraft. Luggage was being handed down from the luggage bay at the back of the plane and put on a trolley. The Royal Air Force must have sent someone to wait for Gregory's suitcase using the ticket to match the number on the case.

When he looked back, the staff car had drawn away leaving the crowd to mill around, the press like wolves who had lost their quarry. Someone would have to cancel the rooms at the Savoy. Without Gregory L'Amour or a story there was no way Bruno could see Max Pearl footing the bill for a suite at the Savoy. Bruno had imagined a few days of luxury controlling the few interviews he was going to allow the other members of the press.

"I'll be buggered," he said as the crowd dispersed. "Now you see it. Now you don't."

Following the rest of the passengers Bruno went to look for his luggage. Then he went to the ticket office of Imperial Airways, presented his open half of the return ticket and booked his flight on the same aircraft back to New York. Now there was nothing in it for him it was best not to call on his full-time employer at the *Daily Mirror*. It was out of his hands. Everything was suddenly out of his hands, the money from the new book drying up in front of him.

Imagining Gillian's look of disapproval when she learnt they were back to a newspaperman's salary, Bruno wondered when he was again going to get any sex. Sitting on a bench, looking at his luggage, he racked his brain for another celebrity to write about until his mind went blank. At least Max Pearl had paid for the return flight. As usual, Bruno was broke.

A month later, with his biographer back in New York as the American correspondent for the London *Daily Mirror*, Gregory L'Amour moved into the same suite at the Savoy Hotel occupied by Henning von Lieberman when Henning was receiving speech therapy from Janet Wakefield in 1937 while recruiting his sleepers. The winds of winter were blowing across the British Isles with gale force velocity.

For the first time Guy Fawkes Day had not been celebrated with bonfires and fireworks across England in case the beacons of fire in the night brought down German bombs on their heads. Nothing, so far, had happened in Europe so far as Gregory could see from the papers. What the fuss about Guy Fawkes Day was all about, Gregory had no idea.

The autumn days at Hastings Court with Tinus and the famous First World War pilot had progressed with the mornings spent at Redhill Aerodrome learning to fly a Tiger Moth, a biplane similar to the aircraft flown by Harry Brigandshaw in the war. Harry had taken him to Redhill to meet John Woodall the first day and followed his progress from Hastings Court after that.

John Woodall, who had flown with Harry in the war, taught him to fly in three weeks. When shown properly, Gregory found flying no more difficult than driving a car, only the consequence of a mistake being different. When a car went off the road it landed in a ditch. An aeroplane falling out the sky was more difficult to climb from after the crash. The day he was to fly solo, Harry had taken him to Redhill without the chauffeur and watched.

"You are going to make a good pilot, Gregory. When I next speak to Genevieve on the transatlantic phone I'll tell her how you're doing. Are you going to marry her? The newspapers think so. But that's none of my business."

"Will they let me join the RAF?"

"I'm not sure. You filled in a form in triplicate at RAF Uxbridge when you arrived but you have to understand you are an American. America is neutral. In the Spanish Civil War Americans were running off to fight for both sides in the conflict and that was stopped. Did you find a birth certificate for your great-grandfather? You told them at Uxbridge he was British."

"The Holts, my real name, L'Amour the one that sounds better for the films, were not your aristocracy. People went to America in those days to get away from something. They say he was from Lancashire but I don't know the parish to look for the entry of his christening. When the immigrants arrive in the States they dump the old baggage to start all over again. I've got a man on it in Liverpool but all he has is the name. Apparently there are lots of Holts in England. His name was common. Eric Holt. That's all I know. Even his middle name has been forgotten. Grandfather said Great-Grandfather hadn't stolen sheep or they would have sent him to Australia as a convict. Didn't do much in America. Neither did Grandfather. People don't really. Just go through life and die of old age if they are lucky. I don't think I can claim British nationality through Great-Grandfather. Maybe I'll have to wait for America to come into the war and fly as an American. At least now I can fly. My guess is they want my film name more than they want me?"

"I'm afraid so. It's all part of the diplomacy to get America on our side. There's only a thin line between politics and war. They cross and recross each other. Churchill has to wait for a war to become our prime minister."

"So everyone is using me?"

"Not me, Gregory. No, maybe that's wrong. I do what the Air Ministry tell me to do."

"So they're using you. Your war record. Your crash in the Congo I read about in America with everyone else. How did you get out in the end?"

"Bribed the Tutsis with guns. For them, no doubt, to use to kill their eternal enemies. The Hutus and the Tutsis have been warring with each other longer than the collective memory of both tribes. Hatred passed down from father to son. It's just the same in Africa only we don't write about it in England. We write about the English killing the Boers, not the Matabele killing the Shona, which they will go on doing in my part of Africa until one of the tribes is obliterated or their women absorbed. Man behaves the same wherever you find him. To win we look for allies. Like America. Like the Shona were happy when Cecil John Rhodes destroyed the power of Lobengula, the last King of the Matabele, freeing the Shona from being preyed on by the Matabele impis that stole their cattle and young women."

"You've lost me."

"Like your great-grandfather. People come and go, never heard of again, only remembered by those who have a reason to remember them. I often wonder with a feeling of guilt how many lives it cost for me to get my freedom from the Tutsis after De Wet Cronjé died of malaria two years after being crippled in the crash. Sorry, other people's stories are boring. Where are you going to now, Gregory?"

"I'm going to move up to London to await my fate. I will remember these days of calm."

"Good idea. There's more to do in London for a young man. The calm won't last much longer. Probably until the spring, when the weather is better for killing people. Then we'll be at each other's throats. Can I suggest something, Gregory?"

"Of course."

"This isn't your fight. Go home. You're American. Only when America is threatened do Americans have to fight."

"You know something!"

"Just a little. You can do more for England back in America than getting yourself killed over here. The vast majority of our pilots in the last war died through accidents, often before they ever went into combat. Believe me, there's no glamour in war. It's horrible. From a nightmare you can wake up to a beautiful day. From war you never wake up. Even if you come out alive. It stays in your head. Like those guns I gave to the Tutsis when they brought me down the lake. The children will miss you. Probably talk about Gregory L'Amour for the rest of their lives."

"Thank you all for your hospitality. And the flying at Redhill."

"It's a pleasure. The chauffeur did most of the work. Maybe tomorrow we can go up on the same train to London."

"When are your family going to Cape Town?"

"Soon. Very soon I hope. I want Tina and the children out of the way when the balloon goes up."

"Will you give this small box to Tinus when you next see him?"

"What's in it?"

"A rabbit's foot. I found it among the yew trees when I was looking at the graves of his ancestors. So many of them stretching back so far into history. I sent it up to London and Bryers hung it on a chain. They'll be proud of him, all those silent ancestors. It'll bring him luck, I hope."

"The fox eat the body and leave the feet. All that's left is the feet. What a nice thought, Gregory. It's always the thought that really counts. He's asked for a posting to the same squadron as André Cloete. They were at school together in the same cricket side. All three of us went to the same school in Cape Town, though I was a bit before their time. Well, there you have it. Another step down the path of life. I often wonder where it all really ends. Rather like this rabbit's foot. Could the rabbit have ever thought his foot would fly in the sky? You see, Tinus will hang it round his neck. Like a talisman. You can be sure of that."

The message had been given to Gregory in the hotel lobby when he came back from his walk along the embankment of the River Thames, a wistful journey to remind him of a happier time with Genevieve while rowing a boat on the same river upstream near Oxford and the university.

"Who left the message?" he had asked, his heart pounding.

"Didn't say, sir. Call came through at six o'clock our time from New York."

"Was it a man or a woman?"

"*Fred*? Was it a man or a woman you spoke to for Mr L'Amour?"

Everyone in the lobby stopped what they were doing to look at him, the girl at the desk giving him a sweet smile, savouring her moment in the limelight.

"A girl, Dolly."

"Did you hear the accent, Fred?" asked Gregory.

"They all sound the same from America."

Ordering a meal in the suite instead of eating alone in the restaurant to be stared at, Gregory had waited for his call from Genevieve, excited to tell her he was now a pilot, that he had flown the Tiger Moth solo, only bouncing twice when he came in to land that first time on his own. For Gregory, it was the first real achievement in his life.

Twice he asked the lobby when the call was coming through, watching the phone for the rest of the time as he ate his supper, not noticing what he was eating. When the phone rang in the silence it made him jump.

"Mr L'Amour, you're through."

"Genevieve!"

"She's somewhere in California, Greg. How are you, buddy?"

"Who's that?"

"Gerry Hollingsworth, you idiot. Who do you think it is? By now you should know your producer's voice. We want you back in New York for some reshoots. The editor doesn't like three of the rushes."

"How did you know where I was?"

"People who cost me your kind of money I keep an eye on. How's the RAF, Greg?" His tone of voice that told Gregory that Hollingsworth already knew.

"They won't let me join unless I have my great-grandfather's birth certificate. He was English," he added lamely.

"Too bad."

"I've learnt to fly."

"That's my boy. We'll put it in the papers."

"Where's Genevieve exactly?"

"I'm not going to tell you. But when you get back to New York after your gallant effort to help the British, she'll be at the airport, guaranteed."

"Along with the newspapers, I suppose."

"You suppose right, lover boy. Get your pretty arse Stateside before she changes her mind. We want the premiere of *Holy Knight* in New York. You'll be a sensation with all the attention in the papers. Sometimes it's the thought that counts, Greg. The British will always love you. A real live hero. The all American man."

With realisation dawning, 'the thought that counts' echoed in Gregory's mind.

"Did you do a magazine deal with Max Pearl?" he asked sarcastically.

"Of course. Not all of us have been taking flying lessons. Some of us do real work like making money. Bruno wants you to donate half your royalties to the British Red Cross as a gesture."

"Oh, does he? I suppose all is good between him and his wife."

"Never happier, Greg. Have a nice day. Your ticket home is in the lobby. Time and place on the ticket. I'll give Genevieve your love."

With the rest of his food going cold, Gregory stared at the silent telephone back on its hook.

"They've got me by the balls," he said.

Then the feeling of relief set in, making Gregory sit down while his body and mind went limp. Money, he thought. Money always won in the end. The stunt was still on. Gerry Hollingsworth had somehow manipulated the whole damn lot of them. Then he went back to his cold dinner and finished his food. It was turbot in a white cream sauce. Suddenly the food was quite delicious.

"Hope the rabbit foot works, Tinus," he said to the empty plate. "Poor bastard."

As usual in his life, everything was once again out of his control. All the nonsense about Great-Grandfather Holt's birth certificate had come from Gerry Hollingsworth and Max Pearl. They had all cooperated for the publicity. Including the British.

"Must have lobbied someone in the American Embassy. Who knows?"

Then he began to think of home and America, putting the Royal Air Force out of his mind, the face of Genevieve with the mismatched eyes swamping everything else in the room as he rejoined his world of unreality leaving it all in a state of trance.

7

*T*wo weeks into November, with Gregory L'Amour safely back in America, again parted from Genevieve, Aircraftman Second Class Hemmings was receiving his first plate of egg and chips at RAF Cardington where he had been inducted that morning into the Royal Air Force, his blue battledress uniform making his midriff itch. Everyone eyed each other, no one saying much in the queue as everything was so new and unfamiliar to all of them, the present and the future.

"Where you from, mate?" Trevor asked the man next to him as they both accepted their plates from the cook serving with a long spoon from behind the counter.

The man spoken to looked at him, his eyes getting bigger.

"Blimey. A bloody Australian."

They each took their plates, knives and forks to a long bench table, sat down and began to eat their food in silence.

"Chips with everything," said the man still looking at his plate.

"What, mate?" said Trevor Hemmings.

"Chips with everything. What they serve up in the RAF. Bloke from home what joined up day war broke out said we got chips with everything. Forty-eight-hour pass for finishing his square-bashing. Now he's gone to learn his trade in radar. Why do they think we got to learn to march and hump a rifle? You going to Hednesford, Aussie?"

"Same as you, mate."

"What's your trade?"

"Flying aeroplanes."

"Don't they make you blokes officers?"

"No bloody idea. Just joined up today. Ran out of money, chips are bloody lovely. Trevor Hemmings. From Melbourne. Down under, you blokes like to say. You going to finish your chips? Mum says I got worms. Always hungry. Why I had to join up."

"Why'd you come to England?"

"To join the RAF."

"You don't make bloody sense. Have the whole plate."

"Thanks, mate. You're a beaut. So here we are about to spend eight weeks at Hednesford, wherever that is, bashing the square, learning to be a soldier."

"Why didn't you tell 'em you fly? Sent you to flying school I'd think. Straight away. Papers always talking about us being short of pilots."

"I was hungry. No, you got to start at the bottom. They'll ask all of us at Hednesford if we want to apply for an Officer Cadet Training Unit. They all work the same, mate. The rules. Everything in triplicate. You'll see. What's your trade?"

"I'm going to be a cook. Better than these soggy chips."

"Not even tomato sauce. In Oz we spread everything with tomato sauce. Eggs included. Good luck to you."

"Been to England before?"

"Oh yes. On a holiday. Ran out of money then too. Bloody money. Went back to Dad's shop."

"What's he sell?"

"He's a chemist. White coat behind a counter, bit like you as a cook judging by the bugger with the long spoon. I hate working in a chemist. Can you pass the salt?"

Not for the first time in his life, as he looked around the canteen, Trevor wondered what he was doing. The war and getting on the boat had been more of an excuse than any show of patriotism. A way out of the rut and the boredom looming over the rest of his life. Getting his degree in pharmacology had been fun outside of the subject itself. Playing sport. Trying unsuccessfully to get into the pants of all the girls. Drinking beer. Going to the beach. Surfing the waves. Being young without a care in the world while Dad picked up the bills. Life as a student had seemed endless, the days flowing pleasantly along from one to the other. But it ended. Like all good things in life, he had told himself.

The six months' holiday which had taken him to England the previous year once he had his degree had been a pleasant life until he went back to Melbourne to work for Dad, the money he earned serving in the shop in Collins Street in the vacs drunk to the last pint of beer.

By the time Australia joined England declaring war on Nazi Germany the long year serving in the shop had been enough to last him a lifetime. Dispensing drugs to old men and women was not his cup of tea. Only once in a while did a young, good-looking girl tinkle the small bell in the shop giving Trevor a brief ray of hope in his life.

To pay back Dad for putting him through Melbourne University he had agreed to work for three years, the same length of time it had taken to get his degree, at a small salary, living with Mum and the girls at home and watching his younger brother Justin still enjoying his life at school.

Wisely, Trevor thought, young Justin had no pretensions. When he finished school Justin was going off to work on a sheep station in Queensland, make some money and bum around the world letting the future take care of itself. Justin played the guitar and would be welcome in the outback where songs sung even by an amateur were at a premium. Justin was sixteen, the youngest of Mum's brood and seven years younger than Trevor. Very rarely did Justin go into the chemist shop and only when Mum sent him on an errand.

"You won't catch me trapped behind that counter, mate. You can shove that one. Ride a horse and play guitar, that's me. You have the money, Trev. You're welcome. I want to do something with my life. The whole Far East is just above us. Grandad might as well have stayed in England, you two cooped up in a shop in Collins Street. You'll end up like Mum and Dad with six kids working the rest of your life to feed 'em. No ways. A big sheep station, that's me. Everything's paid for. Bunk and grub. What you earn you save. How much did Dad ever save? No bloody ways, mate. Out of school, then I'm off. See the back of my heels Justin. That's going to be me!"

"There aren't any young women in Northern Queensland, Justin."

"Then I'll have to fuck the sheep, won't I?"

"You're a crude little bastard."

"You can say that again."

The Dutch boat had taken Trevor from Melbourne to Perth in

Western Australia before making its way up the coast into the Java Sea, calling at three ports in the Dutch East Indies before landing him in Singapore for three days where the ship loaded cargo for Europe, the hatches open night and day as the stevedores loaded the cargo into the hold. The top two decks of the ship were for passengers, all in one class, the deck area not big enough for a swimming pool.

In the humid heat, the voyage went on to Ceylon and the slow run up through the Suez Canal. There were no young girls on the boat, which made Trevor think more and more of Melbourne and the chemist shop in Collins Street. He could still see the look of sadness on his father's face when he went. Not a word from his mum. They all knew the war in Europe was just an excuse. All the effort of putting him through university just money down the drain, their own lives mirrored in the bored eyes of their eldest son as he had gone to work from the clapboard family house in South Yarra that badly needed painting, the money for paint spent instead on their son's education with nothing much to show.

They had all gone to the docks to wave him off, including all the girls. Trevor had thrown down streamers from the rail of the boat as the tugs pulled the vessel from the pier towards the harbour, Trevor going ever so slowly out of their lives. When the coloured streamers broke, that was it. The parting. What Trevor knew in his heart was the end of his life living with the family he had been in all of his life. His mum was crying, he could see that from the rail.

The girls had just thought it was fun going off overseas to war.

Within a few weeks of landing in England not sure what to do, Trevor had run out of money. The recruiting office was in Woking. No one really asked any questions. With the forms filled in they had given him a rail pass to Cardington, and the canteen where he found himself surrounded by Englishmen, all reticent, none of them talking, keeping whatever they wanted to say to themselves. A few looked furtive. A few looked sad. None of them appeared to be enjoying themselves.

"I'll bet they're doing better than this at Hastings Court," he said under his breath to his empty plate.

The idea of bumming a weekend off Harry Brigandshaw a second time in his life had crossed his mind. By the time it did there wasn't the money to go to Redhill and fly the Tiger Moth. People were happy to be taken advantage of once. Twice was bad manners. Justin would not have minded, Trevor supposed, his new uniform itching under the belt. There was no point in crying over spilt milk. He had made a mistake. Sitting on the bench all alone surrounded by people, Trevor wanted nothing else but his job in the shop dispensing drugs to old men and women, hoping for a pretty girl to ring the bell as she opened the door, Trevor smiling his welcome, straightening his back, waiting to fly a quip.

Then in his mind he walked up and down Darling Street, most of the homes in the long street lived in by friends he had known all his life, the small gardens tended, words tossed over the fence, the place that had always been his home. Day trips to Frankston on the train to walk the dunes down the coast, swim in the sea, throw out a line, the fish mattering little, the friendliness and beauty of the place more important than the catch.

To Ginty's parents in the big house for tea, a real tea so a boy could stuff himself, make the cook feel proud. Sometimes staying over in a home he could only dream of for himself, the parents' wealth never once pushed in his face; regular people whose hard work and luck had made them rich enough to own a summer place down the coast away from the crowd, for family and friends to enjoy with each other, always plenty of kids, always plenty of laughter, never a fight or a nasty word, so far as Trevor could remember over the many years of all those long summers. Even the flies were less aggressive in Frankston, flies that now he would put up with, not even swatting the little bastards as he sat in the sun on the beach. He could smell the salt from the sea. Hear the rolling waves. Feel the soft sand between his toes.

"Wake up, airman!" shouted a man in his ear, bringing Trevor to his feet not sure where he was for a split second, shattering the dreams in his mind.

"This isn't a holiday resort!" The corporal glared at everyone. "The bus leaves for Staffordshire in half an hour. Square-bashing, you lucky people. Stop gawping, airmen. This is the air force. Here, you do what you're told. You don't daydream in front of an empty plate. Didn't someone tell you there's a war on? Jerry's going to bite your arse if you don't look sharp. Quick march!"

Trying to make it look as if he was marching, pushing his arms out, stamping his feet, Trevor followed in the shambles that left the canteen.

"You're a bloody shower," bellowed the corporal behind them, the only person in the room now enjoying himself.

In Trevor's right hand was the kit bag with all his possessions which he'd been told not to let out of his sight when they made him change into his uniform, the arms and legs too short, the part of his skin under the piece of belt still itching. Blanking his mind, Trevor followed orders until he was on the bus on his way to his basic training unit in a place he had never heard of until today. When he managed to find a seat on the bus, his kit bag on his knee, he was wet, cold and miserable.

Three days before Christmas, while Officer Cadet Hemmings was on his way to Flying Command in Scotland, looking out of the window of the train at the snow drifting down on a cold countryside, Tina Brigandshaw was finishing the children's packing at Hastings Court to get it out of the way before her last houseguests arrived for a festive holiday. Once again she had asked her parents to come up from Dorset for Christmas without success, her mother and father preferring to stay in the old railway cottage where they felt comfortable. She had gone down to Corfe Castle by train to say goodbye to avoid the chauffeur-driven car. The children had been left at home at the request of her mother, like the car and the chauffeur.

"Never the twain shall meet, Tina. Like Bert, you made your choice to better your station in life. Anyway, your father doesn't like travelling so far as Johannesburg, or Hastings Court for that matter. We are comfortable where we are. If the Germans want to find us we'd like to be in our own home, not where we don't fit in. The children don't want to tell their friends their grandfather is the stationmaster of the smallest railway station in England, they'd be embarrassed. Bert said he'd fly us to South Africa to get away from the war. What would your father do without his job? He'd have nothing to do. At our age it's important to have something to do. The war doesn't affect us here. The pickles are in the store cupboard alongside the bottled plums. The Victoria plums were good this year. The fox hasn't got any of the chickens and Mr Pringle still shoots the odd rabbit. You entertain your fancy friends and leave us out of it, luv. How are the children? Growing up, I suppose. That's when they notice the class difference and that won't do. We're not ashamed of ourselves. Why let the children feel awkward? Lady St Clair stopped by last week with the dogs. She's lonely without his lordship. Now there's a lady. We had a cuppa together in the kitchen in front of the stove while she warmed up. Cold as charity it's been this winter. You take them to Cape Town, Tina. When you see Bert tell him I think of him. That I'm proud of him. Just we all live different lives. Can't change that. If you come down on your own again you can always have your old bed for a couple of nights and we can have a good natter. Wars never go on forever. Or maybe they never stop."

"They're right, of course," she said to Anthony, who was helping her pack.

"Who, Mother?"

"Your Pringle grandparents. The cottage was a lot more cosy than this old house. I've never found out how to stop the draughts. Stand in front of the fire, the front's hot and your back freezing. I do believe that's the last one. I hate packing. The servants can help bring down the trunks. After Christmas two more of them are leaving. One into the army, the other to work at the Goblin factory. Some new government contract. They've stopped making vacuum cleaners. Where's Frank? He was meant to be helping us."

"Frank doesn't like work."

"Oh, well. He won't have much work in Cape Town. The house is half this size with six servants. When Carter Paterson arrives they can bring the trunks down with the help of the servants straight into the van. We won't have to see the big trunks again until we reach Cape Town. The *Capetown Castle* is going to be fun for all of us. Tinus came back to England on the same boat to join the RAF. Are you looking forward to the trip?"

"No, Mother. Father isn't coming, remember."

Tina looked at her eldest son. "He should. What can he do now he's too old to fly? It's just silly. He always says he's more African than European. I don't understand your father, Anthony."

"Oh, they need him all right. There's a lot more to fighting a war than flying an aeroplane."

"So he says. Didn't he do enough last time?"

"Apparently not. He and the rest of them. My history teacher says they should line up all the politicians in Europe and shoot the lot of them. I don't agree with him. Dad says what would we do without Neville Chamberlain. That without him we wouldn't have radar down the south coast and no good fighter aeroplanes to keep the Germans out of our skies. When I'm eighteen I'm coming home to fly Spitfires."

"The war will be over by then."

"I don't think so, Mother. The fact the Germans haven't invaded France doesn't mean they're not going to. Just look what they did to Poland in a week. Mr Straker says they'll walk all over the French. Mr Straker's my maths teacher. He should know. He was in the last war, his trench was next to the French."

"We won the last war. We and the French will win this one. And you are not coming back, young Anthony, even when you turn eighteen. Your father will see to that. He hates war. You'd better go now to get to the station on time. Tinus is bringing his Polish friend. They both have four-day passes from Tangmere. The rest of the guests start arriving tomorrow."

"Are you sad?"

"It's always sad when something comes to an end."

"You'll come back to England."

"Probably. Probably not. Your father wants to live in Rhodesia when the war's over. By then I won't have the strength to argue with him. Sometimes it's easier to do what everyone wants."

"Elephant Walk. Such a funny name if you think about it. Cheer up, Mum. It's Christmas."

The hauliers, Carter Paterson, arrived soon after the boys went off to pick up Tinus at the station. There would be plenty of time for Harry to find out what was going on at Tangmere. To find out what it was like to have fought the Luftwaffe in Poland flying obsolete aircraft, as much sitting ducks in the air as on the ground.

"At least the lad took my advice and escaped to England," Harry said, looking at his wife. "Wonder what happened to that pretty girl he brought here last time? Are you sad leaving the house?"

They were seated in front of the fire drinking tea and eating crumpets dripping in their own farm butter, the door open to the stairs and the hall.

"Was that, am I sad leaving you, Harry? Come with us, for God's sake.

They don't need you here. You say yourself if the Germans attack London they'll be right over Hastings Court. What's the point? Why put your life on the line when it isn't necessary?"

"There probably isn't one, Tina. There often isn't. I've always had a feeling that I have to be at the heart of a problem or everything will go horribly wrong. Like the dam over the Mazoe River. The pump station and the sapling orange trees are in but the engineers came home the moment Tinus left. What's the use of a half-finished concrete dam? All that effort and the water's still flowing down the river unchecked."

"About as much use as an air-raid shelter in a direct hit."

"It's more psychological. People feel safer in an air-raid shelter. They're going to bump the railings on the stairs with that one. Belonged to my grandfather Brigandshaw. One of his old sea chests. Where on earth did you find it?"

"Mrs Craddock. She knows everything in this house. If you ask me she'll be glad to see the back of us. Before I arrived she ruled the roost with an iron fist."

"She's very fond of you and the children."

"The children, maybe. She'll look after you. Will any more servants leave?"

"I'm closing up all but a suite of rooms. Hastings Court won't be entertaining after this Christmas. Some of the chaps on leave, maybe... You see what I mean! They've clobbered the bottom part of the stairs. Hey, watch that, lads! Been there a long time that piece of wood. Let Jerry knock it down."

"Sorry, sir. This thing's heavy."

"You're probably not the first poor sod to say that. It's a real sea chest. From the days of sailing." Harry got up from his chair and walked to the open door of the morning room.

"Must have been stronger in them days. Where you going?"

"South Africa. My wife and children."

"Lucky buggers, guv. All that sun and no Hitler."

Harry watched four of them struggle with the chest made of teak, the domed lid kept firmly in place with two thick iron straps, the iron pitted with age. Looking up the stairs, Harry could see portraits of his ancestors on the wall looking down in disapproval, the paintings dark with age, only the eyes showing, the rest barely discernible. Harry shivered as if someone had walked over his grave.

"I'm going to put those portraits in the basement," he said to Tina, sitting down again.

"Why not in the air-raid shelter? You'll be all together. Master and servant. And the ancestors."

"I did my best. The concrete blocks are two feet thick."

"Horrible place. Like sitting in your own coffin, waiting. Sorry. Not necessary. I just don't understand why you don't leave the place and come with us on the boat."

"They didn't," said Harry pointing towards the hall and the portraits that climbed the wall of the stairs. "Who else is coming for Christmas?"

"The usual crowd, Harry. To make laughter rise up to the old rafters. Good wine, good food and making merry in the grand old tradition of England," she said with a touch of sarcasm. "Did I tell you Mother had tea with Lady St Clair? Lady St Clair wants to die. Nothing left to do. Must be creepy at Purbeck Manor. Just the old girl and Merlin. Mum says no one goes anywhere near them."

"Not even Barnaby?" said Harry, adding his own sarcasm.

"Not even Barnaby, Harry. London's still full of young girls. More than ever with the army in France and all the young men getting their call up papers. What would he want with the old Manor? Mum thinks she's her only friend. Mum and Mrs Mason. They're all as old as the hills. What's the point of getting to that age?"

"We all get old, Tina. If we're lucky."

Janusz Kowalski looked silently out the window as the train slid into Leatherhead Station. Everything had changed from his last visit to Hastings Court. Then he had a country, a father he knew was alive. Ingrid was with him in the flesh if not in the full spirit of acting like his fiancée. Summer in the countryside of England. They still had an estate in Poland; only God now knew what had happened to the house, the farm and all the people.

A lawyer, if not yet a good one without the knowledge that only came from experience. Ingrid. Where was she? Partying with some German officer? Using her charm? Decorating the flat for a German Frau in a home confiscated from a fellow Pole? Using her sex appeal? Enjoying the excitement of new men whatever the uniform? Or was she dead? A patriot under all the frivolity that had driven him to distraction, the desire for her so intense even thinking of her now made him want to scream. The smell of burning aircraft came back to his nostrils. His own flesh. Twice, not even firing his guns at the German planes as the

Germans flew rings round his squadron, picking off his friends one by one.

The fear and loathing as he escaped to Danzig. The small fishing boat that had got him out to sea with a young fisherman as frightened as himself, everyone fleeing the Germans in any direction, the guns just behind them as they fled, big guns and small. Relentless. Only the small boat taking them away, the small sail catching the wind, the open boat going out and away from the man-made horror engulfing his country.

"If you don't get out now you'll end up at the next station," said Tinus next to him. "They won't be meeting the train at Ashtead. There's Anthony waving like a lunatic."

"I was thinking, Tinus."

"I know you were. Why I didn't want to interrupt. Come on. It's about to stop. Otherwise you'll have to jump."

"I did that twice."

"This time the ground is a lot closer. You'll be all right. They won't shoot down a Hurricane. This time it will be your turn. You can show us the tricks. I haven't seen combat. You can take revenge for your friends. Cheer up, my friend. There is always hope."

"Don't wish for combat, Tinus. You go first. I'm a better jumper."

"That's better. Got to laugh or you cry. My goodness. It's young Kim. The whole tribe of the Brigandshaws. Nice of the CO to give us Christmas leave together."

"Your Uncle Harry put a good word in is my guess."

"Probably. It's bloody cold with the carriage door open. Here we go."

Both with kitbags over their shoulders, both in civilian clothes, they stepped out onto the platform as the train jolted to a halt.

"Must have seen us up front, Janusz. Anthony! Frank! Dorian! Kim! What a welcome. We're going to have a good Christmas. Where's the carriage, boys? Home, James, and don't spare the horses."

"Your carriage awaits you, sir," said Anthony with a mock bow and sweep of his right arm.

"Do we hug or shake hands?"

"Shake hands. You might be Rhodesian, cousin. We're English."

They were all grinning at each other as Tinus went from cousin to cousin formally shaking their hands including the just ten-year-old Kim and eleven-year-old Dorian.

"You remember Janusz from his last visit to the Court?"

"Where's the lovely Ingrid?" asked Anthony, gallantly.

"I don't know."

"Gosh, I'm sorry. Have I put my foot in it? Let me carry that kitbag, Janusz. I'd join up myself but Mother won't let me. We're going to South Africa. Finally going to South Africa. All except Dad. They're still fighting over Dad staying, in a polite sort of way. With everything packed it's more like a wake than Christmas. The food will be all right. Well-hung pheasant. I shot two of them. Suckling pig from the farm. Oh, we'll eat all right. You'll both have to make us laugh, Mother in particular. She doesn't want to go and she doesn't want to stay. By the way, Tinus, the chauffeur's name is Dent."

"Just an expression: home, James, and don't spare the horses."

"Is that all you've got?"

"They don't give us much in the air force."

"What's it like? The Hurricane?"

"Turns better than any German aircraft."

"I can't wait to fly one."

"You'll enjoy Bishops for your last two years at school."

"One year. Then I'm coming back."

"Finish your schooling. Then you'll go to Cape Town University. You can't do much in life without a good education. You've got your whole life to think of, Anthony. Think, you can play rugby and cricket at Bishops."

"I don't want to play sports. Waste of time."

"What do you like doing?"

"Annoying my brothers and sisters."

"Pile in, everyone. There's enough room in the Austin. Thank you, Dent. Back to the Court."

"Hello, Dent," said Tinus. "How's tricks?"

"I go into the Army Service Corps after Christmas."

"Well done... Why's it so cold in England?"

Fleur Brooks, born Jean Brooks before she took her stage name from a novel, plain Jane not suggesting a career in classical or popular music, had already arrived at Hastings Court when Tinus and Janusz drove up in the Austin with the boys. She had brought down the whole band, explaining to the manager of the Mayfair she needed a holiday before the proverbial shit hit the proverbial fan.

"You'll just have to make do, Martin. There are dozens of small bands wanting a Christmas gig. Share the happiness. Hastings Court and Harry Brigandshaw are special to me. And you if you work it out. He was responsible for us playing at Lord St Clair's last party before he died. Where Celia and I crossed over from pure classics to what you hear today. Our public at the Mayfair will appreciate us more when we come back after Christmas. Just don't invite Mr Noël Coward to fill the four days."

"He doesn't sing anymore in nightclubs. Too busy writing plays for the West End stage. I suppose André Cloéte and Tinus Oosthuizen will be there?"

"Only Tinus, I hope. If he can get a Christmas pass. Harry's working on it. André's somewhere in France with his squadron."

"Isn't the whole air force in France?"

"Chamberlain insisted we keep most of the fighter squadrons in England, to defend our island."

"He has his finger in every pie."

"Thank goodness, according to what I hear. But I'm just a woman. What would I know about fighting a war? So there you have it, Martin. Can we go?"

"Are you going to play?"

"Only for fun. They are the nearest I have to friends after you and the band."

Then she pouted sweetly at the manager of the Mayfair and pinched his cheek, licking her finger and rubbing the pinch with her saliva as a follow-up.

"Careful, Fleur. I'm married."

"Can we go?"

"You'd better."

"Oh, goody, goody gum drops."

"Where do you find your expressions?"

"That one came from my first school. Really we do need a break."

"Will Barnaby St Clair be in attendance?"

"I don't think so. There's something with Barnaby and Harry's wife. Barnaby and Tina grew up close to each other in the Isle of Purbeck. Whenever I have tried to find out, people avoid the subject."

With all four members of the band in the car, Fleur had used up all her petrol coupons to drive from the flat she shared with Celia Larson in Paddington to Hastings Court, seventeen miles south of London.

When the big Austin arrived driven by Dent she was looking out of the window in the drawing room across the terrace to the well-kept driveway that fronted the house. One after the other the children spilled out of the car. Immediately Fleur smiled, and not at Tinus who was waving at her where she was standing behind the closed window against the cold. One of the boys was so different to look at than the rest, it was ridiculous. And then she understood. The second in line of the boys was a dead ringer for Barnaby St Clair. Next to her Celia began to giggle.

"He does get around, doesn't he, Fleur?"

"What are you talking about?"

"Barnaby St Clair and that boy in the drive."

Only then did Fleur turn around to see if anyone else had heard. Harry Brigandshaw was looking straight at her, his back to the fire. The man didn't even flinch.

"Is that Tinus arriving?" he asked. Fleur's window was nearest to the fire.

"Down in the drive."

"Good. He's like a son to me. His own father was killed. The only thing I now regret is teaching him to fly. He's a good pilot. That always helps."

"I'm sorry, Harry," Fleur mouthed.

Harry gave her another, smaller smile. Then it was over just as Tina walked into the room where half the guests were still drinking tea and eating sandwiches. All the crusts had been cut off the bread making the triangular sandwiches very small. No one else seemed to have heard Celia's *faux pas* so far as Fleur could see. If any of them had, they were keeping it to themselves. Moments later, Celia was giving Tinus a hug and the discord was lost in the tea party chatter.

Having seen what she saw, Fleur was fascinated. She stood watching the boy, with hooded eyes, as the house party got into its stride. She and Barnaby had a lot in common. Both took sex for what it was, mutual gratification; in their case mutual satisfaction. Neither of them read love into a night in bed or expected anything more from each other than perhaps a repeat performance. All the talk of love never dying was false hope. Wanting to have a man's children, the power of nature wanting to reproduce itself. Wanting to spend their lives together just because they had thrashed around naked in the same bed was to Fleur, as it was to Barnaby, an abject lesson in self-deception. They had parted as lovers as easily as they had come together.

Barnaby had formed a company to record the band's songs. Like so many rich men who did not care whether the project succeeded, like his backing of plays on the West End stage, it was all means for Barnaby to give himself a wider range of girls from which to select what he fancied.

Typically, the record company had turned into gold. Making money had not even been Barnaby's aim. Fleur knew the man had enough money to last him more than one lifetime. Going to bed with Barnaby had been as much for her pleasure as his, any financial reward a by-product. The luck that came with a good idea. For Fleur, who knew she was chronically selfish, the idea of a husband and three demanding children was not on her mind, which was why the boy fascinated her. Making her think about Barnaby, the daddy. Making her stand back from herself and think, something she usually preferred not to do.

Young Frank was so like his father without knowing it, Fleur wanted to laugh. Likely, the boy had no inkling of his heritage, of why he was so different to the rest of the Brigandshaw boys who all showed traits of Harry, a man who was nice to everyone, not a nasty bone in his body. Certain the boy was unaware of his true father, Fleur was equally certain Barnaby knew all about his son and chose to take no interest, let alone wanting to claim him as his own. Barnaby was just as selfish. What would he want bringing up a son, even one so much like himself? Fleur, feeling guilty at not wanting kids, tried to put the boy out of her mind to concentrate on the frivolous.

When the palaver broke out with the dog, Fleur, despite herself, had seen what had happened before the Alsatian bit Frank, sending his mother into a tizz, demanding from Harry the poor dog be put down, shouting that dogs that bit small boys should not be allowed in the house. The bite, as far as Fleur saw, was pretty ordinary, a snap reaction to Frank kicking the dog hard when he thought no one was looking. The kind of kick Fleur could imagine Barnaby executing at the same sort of age just to see what would happen; so much of what Barnaby did in his life was only to see what would happen.

Like young Frank, Barnaby was easily bored. Barnaby was a good chaser but rarely wanted what he chased when it was caught unless he was hungry. West End plays, once he had shown he made money out of them, like the record company, now bored him stiff. Fleur knew she bored him too in or out of bed, something she did not mind. Like Barnaby she had got what she wanted at the time and was happy to move on, something André Cloete had not been able to understand. André wanted women to want him after he was finished. That man had ego problems, from Fleur's point of view.

"We are what we are, the moment we are born," she told Celia. "The little bugger kicked the poor dog to get a reaction. I'll bet when he was younger he pulled the wings from butterflies. It's not even malevolence. The boy's bored. Straight out of Barnaby. He'll either end up stinking rich or go to jail. That poor dog! I'm sure Tina must know. Harry does. For a brief moment I thought Harry was going to give the kid a clout. Isn't life fascinating? We can't stop what we do, even do the right thing if we wanted to. It's all been passed down, the good and the bad. All this nurture business is a lot of rot and there's the proof right over there. Barnaby has had no influence over his life other than giving him life. But there he is, a little Barnaby, Celia."

"You just don't like Barnaby."

"Of course I do. He's very valuable. For what it's worth, a damn good lay. At least be honest on that one, Celia. We're just girls together. Neither of us ever get jealous of each other. Why we are such good friends. But just look at that boy, the spitting image. One day they are going to recognise each other for what they are. The same person. I hope I'm not around. Two Barnabys kicking dogs and pulling wings off butterflies would be too appalling... Oh, just look at that. We're going in to have drinks. Then we are going to be fed. I'm starving. If the dogs came in as they did last time I'll slip that poor Alsatian a bone under the table. You have to have dogs under the table at a medieval feast. Now, girls, you must all do me a favour and stay sober enough to play your instruments. Suckling pigs, someone said, on the spits in the inglenooks at both ends of the Great Hall, head on. To the Great Hall, or whatever they call it now. We'd better enjoy this Christmas. You never know with a war on. None of us may ever get another one. Why I always enjoy my life. You just never know. Men get horny just before they go to war. Four days, girls. Enjoy yourselves. Let the night begin! I'm hungry and not only for suckling pig. This time, at the end of the feast, we'll play our music standing on the table so all the men can see our legs. Make merry! Make merry!"

"It's only seven-fifteen, Fleur. Another fifteen minutes," said Celia. "Then we can start drinking booze."

Phillip Crookshank, the chief engineer on the Short Sunderland flying boat, had never seen anything like it in his life. Neither had his wife, Mavis or the two children off somewhere in the big house with the Brigandshaw children, both Phil and his wife having happily lost all control of the two boys within an hour of arriving at Hastings Court.

They had come all the way from their small cottage in the Isle of Wight, not three hundred yards from the beach, a beach that when they left in the morning to catch the boat and the train, was being pounded by six-foot high waves hurled at the shore by a storm from the English Channel, making the crossing to the mainland interesting. Mavis had been seasick, the kids screaming at the wind all the way across, their words plucked from their mouths as their father held each of them firmly by the hand.

"There's a fire burning in every grate in the house," said Mavis while they were changing into evening dress. "How many servants must she have? Just to lay the fires and bring up the coal scuttles would take two strong women a month. How many rooms are there in the house? How long's it been here? I've read about these kind of old mansions but never been in one. Your friend Tinus can't be changing for dinner. All they had were kit bags when they arrived."

"There's a war on. Maybe Harry will lend them something."

"Are the kids all right?"

"They can't go anywhere."

"I could get myself lost in this house for the rest of my life. What does it mean, seven-thirty for eight?"

"We go to the drawing room, where we had tea, for drinks at seven-thirty and on to the Great Hall at eight to stuff ourselves with food. John Woodall says the food is good. He always comes for Christmas."

"Who's John Woodall?"

"Runs a flying school at Redhill. Flew with Harry in the war. Harry says they are not going to order the Short Sunderland just yet. Concentrating on bringing Fighter Command up to full strength. Going to rely on the navy to fish downed pilots out of the drink. We'll just have to see. They worry the flying boats will be sitting ducks for the Luftwaffe. You look really good in that dress, Mave. Did you see those girls in the band when we arrived? That was their day clothes. Can you imagine what they'll look like tonight?"

"Down, boy! How did Harry manage to get them for Christmas?"

"They are houseguests. Just like us. Anthony said they are going to give us a gig anyway. Friends of Harry's. Harry seems to know everyone worth knowing. Ant said the girls come up from the village to help at times like this. I'll ask him how many bedrooms. Likely nobody's counted. This four days is a bit like the last supper. The family, all except Harry, are going to South Africa. The war effort has ravaged the servants. Most of the house is being closed up for the duration of the war."

"It's twenty past seven. Better start wending our way. I don't even know which way to turn when we go out the door into the corridor. Tina says all the young kids will be kept in the nursery where it doesn't matter if they wreck the place. Looked to me like dozens of kids. She's organised, that woman, I'll say that for her. Wouldn't live in an old pile like this if you paid me. Despite fires in every room and two in the reception rooms the house is still freezing."

"Hardy lot, the Brigandshaws."

"Weren't they Mandervilles who built this place hundreds of years ago? How come Harry said his family have been here for centuries?"

"Harry's maternal grandfather was a Manderville. Sir Henry Manderville Bart. They brought him back from Rhodesia where he died. Buried him with all the others among the yew trees, according to Anthony. Somewhere at the back of the house. Ant says some of the headstones are so old they've sunk into the ground out of sight."

"That boy's a fount of information."

"He flew with us to Switzerland with Tinus in the flying boat. Test flight, or so they said. I wonder what the von Liebermans are doing for Christmas? They also have an old pile in Bavaria. Harry flew the plane."

"I know, sweetheart. I've never eaten suckling pig off a spit."

"It's the crackling you go for."

"Anthony again?"

"Of course. Come on then. Let the evening begin, my darling."

"First give me a kiss."

"Always my pleasure."

In the corridor, all the lights were on with people coming out of their rooms dressed in their best like Phillip and his wife.

"I hope that boat was all right," said Phillip. "That wind was powerful in the Solent."

"I am sure it has weathered worse storms than that... This is fun, Phil. You too look nice. Did I ever tell you how happy I am being married to you?"

"Every day. You see, that's my real job in life. Making you happy. They say later we are going to dance."

"This must be Camelot."

The four young girls were dressed exactly the same when they entered the drawing room a little after half past seven. Silk black sheaths that hugged their bodies to the knees where the material was pleated, the clothes made by Fleur's dressmaker to Fleur's design.

"When we twirl, darling," she had told her dressmaker, "we want to show the men a good bit of leg. Just up to the knee. The rest is their imagination. What we play is important but how we look gets their attention. We're young and sexy. Flaunt it, I say; one day we'll be old and wrinkled. Enough movement at the top of the dress to show them what we have. You'll have to be careful with Margaret or they'll fall out. She really does have a big pair, the lucky girl. Sort of slope the bottoms, or the fannies as they call their arses in America. We're in the entertainment business. I promised Martin to fill the Mayfair. Life's all about making money. Making people come back for more. Funny, Margaret has the biggest boobs and the biggest instrument. A double bass that she strokes with a bow. That girl makes stroking strings so sexy you can hear the men ache. Is that material pure silk, Priscilla?"

"All the way from Greece. Best silk in the world."

"Didn't know Greeks made silk."

"Start of the silk route to China. From antiquity. They're going to be expensive, Fleur."

"You think I care! Barnaby St Clair is paying for them. It was his idea. Wants us photographed in them for the box of our new record. They get ten 78s in the cardboard box and a picture of us girls on top. Barnaby thinks the picture will sell the record. Every record shop in London will have them on display."

"Who's Barnaby St Clair?"

"Long story, Priscilla. Just make us look sexy. Charge what you like. We're friends, remember."

Following in behind, Janusz Kowalski, dressed in his ordinary clothes, thought he at last had arrived in heaven, all his worries forgotten in the wiggle of the girls' behinds, the black silk riding the four little bottoms to perfection.

"Eyes up, Janusz," said Tinus. "Good, it's Pimm's tonight. Harry serves them in those silver cups with fruit and cucumber. The fruit and cucumber come from the heated greenhouses on the estate. Even the war doesn't stop that one unless they run out of coal for the boiler. Large hot water pipes run all round inside the greenhouse. Hot house, some call it."

"They're the size of buckets."

"That's the idea."

"Why didn't you say we dressed for dinner before we left Tangmere?"

"Then we'd have been in our number ones and I didn't want to wear uniform over Christmas. Let's just forget the war and enjoy ourselves. I must say Cousin Anthony looks rather dashing in his first dinner jacket."

"Who's that gorgeous girl with him?"

"I don't believe it! All dressed up! Aunt Tina must have had something to do with that. I wonder if Uncle Harry has seen her. That's my cousin Beth. She turns fifteen next month. My word, they do grow up quickly."

"Every man in the room is trying not to look at her."

"The other boy is Oliver Stokes, Anthony's best friend. They were both at Radley together. Now Anthony has left to go to South Africa. Friendship rather like André Cloete and myself at Bishops. They're going to miss each other. Do you want to meet Beth?"

"She's far too young."

"So was Melina von Lieberman but it didn't stop me looking. Didn't stop Anthony for that matter. Still talks about her. Funny how the first girl that takes your fancy stays in your mind. There was a girl on the boat coming over... But enough about that. We ended up in one of the lifeboats."

"I thought your first love was Genevieve?"

"Maybe. Genevieve is unobtainable. The other girl wasn't, if you see what I mean. Do you still think of Ingrid?"

"All the time. I know she's still alive."

Tinus heard the change of tone in his friend's voice.

"Back to the girls in front, old boy. Try and enjoy yourself, Janusz. There's nothing you can do about Ingrid now. Would you like a Pimm's No. 1 Cup? Very British. Get you pissed as a newt if you drink enough of them. Just look at that! All four of those girls are straight into the Pimm's. Come and meet them. Celia! Fleur! How are you all tonight? You remember my friend Janusz Kowalski? Unfortunately we don't have dress suits tonight."

"That doesn't matter," said Fleur holding out her gloved hand for Janusz to shake. Then she looked straight into his eyes and licked her lips slowly. Without knowing it she took Ingrid clean out of his mind. "I love pilots. Do you like music, Janusz?"

"Good music is my favourite form of entertainment. Count Janusz Kowalski at your service, madam."

"Fleur, please. We play in a band not an orchestra anymore. Do you know Brahms's *Third Symphony*?"

"Of course."

"Good. Later you'll hear what I've done with the main theme. With a cello, a double bass and two fiddles. These drinks are wonderful. Make you tight as a tick, Tinus. Isn't that your African expression? Come and tell me and Celia what you've been up to. No, Janusz, you too. You don't get away from me that easily."

"Flying aeroplanes," said Tinus. "Not much else. All men together."

"You poor darling. Have a Pimm's Cup. Cheers! Happy days."

"They were following me all the way down the stairs," said Mavis Crookshank as they entered the drawing room together, the cocktail chatter all around them. "What's in that enormous silver bowl Harry's dishing out with a ladle? If I had to run the gauntlet of all those ancestors every morning coming down to breakfast, I'd take them down. Gave me the creeps. Just the eyes following me as I passed their portraits. Some were dressed in weird clothes that went back to the ark. So dark from age, only the light bits showing."

"Pimm's No. 1," said Harry.

"How did you hear what I said?"

"I didn't. Everyone asks. The No. 1 is a gin base. Two and three are rum and whisky but you never see them in the shops. The trick is to tip two bottles of Beefeater gin into the punch bowl to strengthen the gin in the Pimm's bottle. The fruit's in the cups already. How are you both? Did you see my daughter? Sent her straight back upstairs to change, or at least I tried. Didn't take any notice. Tina had taken her up to London to pick the dress. Fifteen next month! Little girls one day, women the next. I think she takes after her mother. Going to give all the men a hard time. Some say it's better to have ugly daughters. Give you less trouble and have better lives. They don't expect so much. Happy to find a husband to look after. Oh gosh, there she is over there. Quite the centre of attention. Fifteen next month, for goodness sake! We don't have snacks in here. Ruins the supper. You won't go hungry tonight. That dress suits you, Mavis. Have a good evening. If you drink too much and can't find your bedroom, ask for help. We're all friends here. Two Pimm's Cups at your service, Mr and Mrs Crookshank. Phil, do you remember that restaurant on the pier at Romanshorn? I can still taste the cake. Enjoy yourselves."

Each holding a silver cup they walked away, Harry by then busy with another couple. Harry's brief expression to them of surprise clear: he had no idea who the new couple were.

"Tina likes the house to be full," said Phil.

"You need an army to fill this house. I'm not sure if I can find the bedroom sober. And if that girl's not yet fifteen I'll eat my hat. She looks twenty. How do we know when to go into supper?"

"They strike the gong. The girl who brought the new scuttle full of coal told me. Her name is Mary Ross. From the village. You were in the bathroom. She and her brother Herbert both do casual work at the Court. Herbert's going in the army. Mary's got a job after Christmas at the Goblin factory. Government contract. She said it's very secret so she wouldn't say what they are making."

"Do you always talk so much to young girls?"

"How did you know she was young?"

"And pretty, or you wouldn't have wasted your breath on her."

"She's also working with the kids in the nursery."

"Poor girl. My own screaming kids are fine. Other people's must be hell. I can taste the gin. This is just my kind of party. I'm going to get this one down and have another before they ring the gong. I never imagined real people lived like this. He's such a nice man."

Smiling to himself, Phillip Crookshank looked around the room. All women liked men who paid them a compliment.

"And he meant it, Mave."

"Meant what?"

"The compliment. Harry liked your dress. Let's go and talk to John Woodall. He's all on his own."

"Doesn't he have a wife?"

"I've never asked him."

"Then I'd better not. Did that once, poor man's wife had just left him. Now that's what I call a roaring log fire. Your friend John Woodall's found the best spot in the room."

Looking at Beth surrounded by young men reminded Tina of what she had lost. She was jealous of her daughter, something she would not admit to herself. There was Beth in her first long dress with something in life to look forward to. Soon, very soon, the first of her children would be on his way. Anthony, without question, was now a young man. Confident. Assured. Not even self-conscious, ribbing the girls in the band, their figures on display for everyone to see. And enjoy, by the expression Tina saw on the Polish pilot's face. Amazing, she thought, how quickly men forgot their problems when sexy girls came around.

All she had was Harry, serving the Pimm's himself instead of allowing Herbert Ross to do the job. A son that no longer needed her. A daughter stealing the thunder that had once always been hers at a party. Hers to choose who she smiled at. Hers to choose who she wanted. She was old, on the rubbish dump, and it made Tina wonder what point there was in her life anymore. All she could see, looking ahead, was a life of more and more isolation as the world left her alone, no longer important, with no longer anything to give that anyone wanted.

All the work she had put into the house party was for the benefit of all the other people, none of them interested in her once they had received their invitations. They were all looking around each other to see what they could find. The old men and women were talking war and politics, which bored Tina to distraction. What could any of them do about the war except get out of the way as she was going to do on the third of January. Sail away! Sail away with nowhere to go but round and round like the Flying Dutchman. Nothing to find on land that could really interest her, just another middle-aged woman, lucky enough to have found herself a rich husband and made herself a brood of children, all only interested in themselves and what they wanted day by day from life.

Harry, chatting away to every new guest as they collected their drinks, annoyed her. Not once had he looked up from the damn punch bowl and smiled at her. No one was even looking at her anymore, standing alone at her own party, drink in hand wondering what the hell to do next.

"Mrs Brigandshaw, there's a fight going on in the nursery. It's Frank. The other boy has a bloody nose and Frank still wants to punch him. Can you help?"

"All right, Mary. I'll be up in a moment. They won't ring the gong for another twenty minutes. Don't you think it's going rather well?"

"Down here it is, madam. Upstairs it's hell."

"I'll be right up. Do you have a boyfriend, Mary?"

"Oh yes, madam. He's lovely. Going in the army with my brother Herbert."

"Just don't have any children if you value your sanity."

"I'll try not to, madam. Please hurry. I don't know what to do."

Taking one swift look around her drawing room, Tina gritted her teeth and smiled. No one else took any notice. Going out the room and up the stairs she hated every one of the ancestors now staring at her. Mocking her: 'You got what you wanted but what did you get?'

Just before opening the nursery door where all the noise was coming from, Tina wiped the tears from her eyes with the back of her hand and walked into the mayhem, catching Frank with a backhander that knocked him sideways. To Tina's surprise her son began to cry. In front of everyone.

"Cry baby," said the boy with the bloody nose, the blood dripping down his chin.

Tina glared at him.

"What's your name?"

"Paul Crookshank. He started it. He hit me first."

"All right, Paul. It's all over. Frank! Come here. I want you two to shake hands."

"That hurt, Mum."

"It was meant to. Now shake hands. I don't want another word out of either of you. Mary doesn't have time to run up and down with you two fighting. You should want to be friends not enemies."

By the time Tina left the room to go downstairs she was feeling better. The back of her hand hurt where she had caught Frank on the side of his face while the boy was off balance. Then she heard someone, probably Harry, ringing the gong down in the hall at the bottom of the long flight of wide stairs. They were going in to supper.

For a brief moment on her way down the carpeted stairs she was sure one of Harry's ancestors was smiling at her from the wall, as if to say it had all happened before. Making a mental note to ask Harry which old woman was portrayed in the painting, she reached the banister at the bottom of the stairs, picked up her feet and followed her guests into the Great Hall.

"There you are, Tina," said Harry smiling. "I was looking all over the place for you. Is everything all right?"

"Everything is fine, Harry," she said, taking the crook of his arm.

"What have you done to your hand?"

"I gave Frank a backhander. He'd bloodied the Crookshank boy's nose."

"Must have been a good one. That's going to bruise."

"It was. It felt good. I need to do that to Frank more often."

"All right up there now?"

"I made them shake hands."

"Good for you. That's the way to do it. What a swell evening. What are we going to do with Beth? She didn't take the blindest notice of me when I tried to make her change that dress."

"Nothing, Harry. Nothing. I'm hungry."

"So am I. I'm going to miss you."

"You mean that don't you?"

"Of course I do. You're my wife."

Following behind the couple, unknown to Harry, Mavis, with the gin beginning to swill in her head, entered the Great Hall side by side with Phil, both unaware of their eldest son's bloody nose, both enjoying their brief freedom from the kids.

"That's the biggest Christmas tree I ever saw," said Mavis. "Why's it so warm in here? The roof goes on up into the cold darkness high above the arches. I've never seen arches in a room outside a church."

"Everyone look for their names on the table placings," called Tina from inside the arched door, studded with iron, the archway rising ten feet above Phil's head. "If you can't find yourself come back to me. I've tried to put people with like interests close to each other. Part of the fun is finding where you sit. There are open bottles of wine on the table. Help yourselves. Harry says don't be shy. We didn't give you the traditional daggers to eat with. Far too messy. Find your place and sit tight. Everything will come to you."

"It's medieval," said Mavis.

"It's meant to be. In the old days when they'd eaten and drunk too much they passed out under the long table. Anthony says that table is so old they don't know who built it inside the Great Hall. They must have cut the oak trees into some kind of shape and fitted the pieces in here. Ant says there are holes from the knots that show right through the wood. Parts of that table are three feet thick. Flat on top with just enough room to get your knees under the round bowl of the tree trunk."

"Medieval."

"That's when it was made. Let's start here and work our way round. You're right. This old hall open to the rafters is as warm as toast. Who do you think we are sitting next to?"

"The fairy lights go right up the tree. Look how the tinsel reflects the coloured lights. The coloured glass balls move round for some reason. Must have taken a week to decorate the tree. Where do you think they got it from?"

"Out of the garden, Mave. Round the mausoleum there are cedar trees the height of the church spire that tower above the yew trees."

"How did they cut down the Christmas tree without smashing the lovely branches? Just look at all those open wine bottles down the centre of the table. How awful if one fell through a knot."

"The dogs are inside."

"Good. I'll feed that Alsatian a bone. There must be places for forty people down each side of the table. Big, wooden platters at each place. How do you think they serve the food?"

"On bigger platters. Carve the suckling pigs, the sides of beef by the looks of it from here, in the inglenooks onto big platters or troughs. Then two servants hoist them on their shoulders by the handles. Where the expression came from, 'feeding at the trough'."

"Now you are pulling my leg."

"You just grab the meat from the trough and shove it on your plate."

"What about vegetables?"

"Just mead and wine in Old England. Who wants Brussels sprouts?"

"I think we get up and go to those side tables."

"Also possible, Mave. Here we are, Mrs Mavis Crookshank between Mr Phillip Crookshank and Mr John Woodall. You can ask him about his wife after the second bottle of wine. Look at Ant. Got one of the band girls on either side of him, now that's nepotism."

"Phil, you're tight from the Pimm's."

"You made me drink the second cup to keep you company. I think we just sit down at our names, pour ourselves a glass of wine and wait to see what happens."

"I've never seen anything quite so splendid."

"I can't pull you out a chair. Everyone sits on the same wooden benches. Can you climb over or shall I pick you up and plonk you down?"

"I think a bit of the up and plonk is called for. Just be careful with me, Phil."

"How's that?"

"Perfect. Now I know where the heat's coming from. There's hot air going up my dress from the floor. The floor's hot in places. I didn't think those two fires at either end could cook all the meat and heat this cavern."

"Red or white, Mrs Crookshank?"

"Red please, Mr Crookshank. There are no Christmas hats."

"Didn't have them back when they built this table. Hello, John. We've got Mave in the middle. Plonk yourself down. Red or white?"

"White to start with. I'll try the red with the beef. Have you ever before seen anything like this?"

"Just what I was saying," said Mave. "It's a bit early, but happy Christmas."

"Happy Christmas, everyone," they said in chorus.

PART FOUR

KNIGHTS OF NEW – SEPTEMBER TO NOVEMBER 1940

1

Having secured a trust fund from Jacob Rosenzweig, Vida Wagner spent her days inwardly purring like a cat. She was rich for the rest of her life. Once a week she did her best to have sex with the 'old goat' as she thought of her ticket to riches. Sometimes it worked, sometimes it didn't. The old man was seventy-two but even the trying seemed to make him happy for the rest of the week.

"Just to have someone warm in bed with me is wonderful, Vida. Old men get lonely. You give me life again. Make what I do worthwhile instead of a constant pursuit of money I will never have time to spend. Friday, my lovely German darling, we are having a celebration. You can show everyone again your wonderful cooking. *Holy Knight* has been a spectacular success at the box office. Max Pearl and Gerry Hollingsworth are bringing girls. Robert St Clair, his wife Freya. Denzel Hurst the director is coming with his wife. Denzel also directed *Keeper of the Legend*. Glen Hamilton of the *Denver Telegraph*, he and his wife are visiting with Robert and Freya in New York, so coming too. None of the stars I am afraid. Genevieve and Gregory L'Amour are in California and don't seem to like travelling anymore. It's said Genevieve doesn't socialise now there's a real war going on the other side of the Atlantic. After Gregory's debacle trying to join the RAF, he avoids the press. We are going to have another of your wonderful dinner parties everyone talks about for weeks afterwards, my clever darling. Oh, and you'd better phone Gillian Kannberg. She and her husband have been good to the film with publicity. Bruno's writing another of his books so he says, won't tell us who this one is about. I'll ask Max on Friday."

When Jacob had gone off to work at his bank, Vida had smiled to herself, the purring gently soothing her body, bringing only nice thoughts to her mind. For five minutes of foreplay and not much else beyond throwing a dinner party once a month, her payment was splendidly out of all proportion. Her scheme worked out in Germany to change her life, purporting to be a Jewish victim of Hitler, had been more successful than her wildest dreams. One forged letter of introduction to the head of a New York bank and here she was, richer than anyone she had known before in her life. And the war was going Germany's way with the whole of Europe under the German jackboot other than England, an England close to capitulation according to newspaper reports, making Vida mentally hug herself with excitement.

She had made up her mind. When Germany won the war with American connivance through non-participation, she was going back to Berlin to flaunt her wealth. The besotted 'old goat', so happy to get his life back again, had not put one stipulation in the wording of the trust. She was free as a bird. Kurt, for forging her papers, would have his reward. Germany would dominate the world, Berlin its capital.

From being a penniless thirty-two-year-old of Lebanese extraction, she would go home in triumph, a real German, the Wagner name she had used in her false papers to America, her real name for the rest of her life.

"Amy, we're throwing a dinner party on Friday. Make me a coffee."

"Yes, madam."

The purring went on. That was what she really liked. Respect. Being called madam by a scullery maid. No longer a nanny for Jewish families in England to order around.

Then, while Amy was making her coffee, she went to the phone and called Gillian Kannberg to invite her to dinner. It was called the Battle of Britain by the paper she avidly read while waiting for the exchange to put through her call. The *New York Post* was all doom and gloom in its reports from London.

"And they are losing it," she read with satisfaction.

"What are they losing, madam?" said Amy from the kitchen.

"The war, Amy. Britain is losing the war."

"I read it was touch and go. Another paper said the RAF are shooting down five German planes for every one the Germans are bringing down. That the RAF pilots who bale out in time are back in the air the same day in a new aircraft the British factories are turning out."

"What do you know, Amy?"

"Only what I read in the papers. My boyfriend says we Americans should go and help. That if we don't, we'll be next. He thinks the Japs are going to side with the Germans. That fighting a war on two fronts will leave us Americans in a right royal mess."

"The Japanese would never be so silly as to go to war with America. They have enough on their plate with their war against China. America and Germany have always been friends. Hurry up with my coffee."

"The coffee pot is just coming to the boil. I know you like it hot."

Only when Vida was halfway through the cup of coffee did she reflect on the irony of her situation. Only in New York did it pay to claim to be Jewish. Everywhere else, the Jews were trying to hide. Luckily Jacob went to shul at infrequent intervals, taking her when he went. Whether he believed the full extent of her story was a worrying question. Twice in shul, Vida had got the procedure wrong, explaining afterwards shul in Germany had been different, that ever since Hitler came to power her family had maintained a distance from their Jewish religion.

'Men believe anything when it suits them,' she thought, her lower lip twisting upwards. 'It's how they are made'.

The call to Gillian Kannberg had been brief. In Vida's opinion the woman was a social climber out of her depth. Every time Vida had seen Gillian with Bruno she understood; the girl had her husband under her thumb which, she smiled to herself, was all a woman required to be successful in life. They had the same thing in common, the two of them. They were both on the make. Both with men besotted by them.

Later, Vida went for a walk in Central Park, opposite their apartment in Abercrombie Place. To pass the time she looked at people's faces, many washed by the sun. None looked worried. None looked concerned. The war in Europe was nothing to do with them. Genevieve and Gregory L'Amour in *Holy Knight* were more real to them on the screen than the stories of war from Europe. Most New Yorkers she watched in the park were smiling. With the war effort in England frantically buying American goods, the depression was finally over. Good times were going to roll for everyone, the pursuit of money a pastime once again in vogue.

Vida looked carefully at each of the faces passing her by. There were many with expressions she mostly understood, expressions each of them had cultivated to see them comfortably through their day. Inside each of the heads behind the faces, like inside her own head, was a squirrel's nest of plans and expectations, all of them centred on themselves. Like Vida, all of them, she knew, were scheming something or other, the park and the trees only fleetingly noticed, each head an island unto itself. Only a squirrel not far up a tree, looking her square in the eye, knew what she was thinking.

"Just as well I can't ask you what everyone's thinking," she said to the squirrel as she picked up her stride in the sun, the leaves and trees suddenly real to her.

A row about money began the moment Bruno Kannberg reached home from work. If he had had any money he would have gone to the small bar near the office to talk over the war with his fellow journalists, the war Arthur Bumley in London had said on the phone was reaching a critical point.

"They're hitting the radar stations, directly attacking Fighter Command at the airfields and command centres. They know where to attack. Another month, the RAF will be exhausted, not enough pilots left to fly. In Kent and Surrey the battle's right over their heads. A monumental struggle. Churchill sent a squadron of Blenheims last night to bomb Berlin. To give the Germans a small taste of their own medicine. Bomber Command isn't strong enough to take the war to Germany. They didn't have adequate fighter escort. Tell your American friends to write in their papers we need some help."

"How long can the Luftwaffe take their casualties? Even when their pilots bale out they are out of the battle. Prisoners of war."

"We don't know, Bruno. The fog of war. We don't really know what's happening in our own squadrons. Two chaps fire on the same Jerry and both claim the kill."

"Don't we know our own casualties?"

"That we do. The numbers are terrible."

"Is Tinus all right?"

"How do I know? Tangmere's taking the brunt of the fight with the rest of the stations near the south coast. They won't tell us the truth. Propaganda on both sides."

"Won't bombing Berlin make Hitler bomb London?"

"I think that's Churchill's hope, God help us. Take the fight away from Fighter Command. Give them a chance to regroup. The pilots are on drugs to keep them awake. Some pilots are going up four times a day as the waves of German bombers come over. Thank God for radar. They don't have to patrol, looking for the Germans. They can sit on the ground and wait to be scrambled by telephone from the command centres. They're pulling squadrons down from Scotland, so we just heard. We're out of reserves in the south."

"I'd better come home and join the army."

"Stay where you are. Do your job. You'll do more good making the American public see sense. We're fighting their war as much as ours, single-handed. No, not single-handed. Thank God again for the empire, for the Canadians, Australians, South Africans and New Zealanders. We've even got Rhodesians in the RAF and a squadron of Poles who escaped when Poland collapsed. Your old friend Harry Brigandshaw wants to get back in the air. They won't let him. Say he's too old. My guess is losing Harry would be bad for British morale with all the publicity if he crashed. When's Gregory L'Amour coming over?"

"Poor chap feels terrible. Max Pearl is not publishing a book of my magazine serial. Gregory pulled it. Are you all right, Mr Bumley?"

"Found myself a girlfriend. Billy Glass at the *Mail* suggested it. We're both in a rut... I'm all right."

"Does your wife know?"

"Don't be bloody stupid. She thinks I can't get it up anymore. How's Gillian?"

"The same. Spent every penny I've made."

"Tell me about it. Good sex costs money."

Without the price of a round of drinks in his pocket there was nothing he could do. The worst sin in Bruno's eyes was leaving a drinking session when it was his turn to pay for the round. He had never done it, and despite Arthur Bumley's suggestion to talk to his American colleagues he went straight home to find Gillian grinning all over her face, a sure sign she wanted something.

"Marvellous dinner party at Jacob Rosenzweig's residence. Hollywood. Publishers. Max will be there. And we're invited. You are so clever writing books about the famous. Vida phoned. She's such a dear. Bet she's glad to be out of Germany. They don't like Jews in Germany I'm told. I've just got to have a new dress. At that kind of level you can't be seen in the same dress twice. I'll stun them again. There's a lovely shop on Fifth Avenue. Has just what I want. I'm sure Vida will be showing off a new piece of jewellery. Jacob's so generous. Well, I'll just have to settle for a nice new dress. Jewellery like hers is out of the question for the moment. Maybe you'll write a bestselling novel about the rich and famous. All our new friends."

"We don't have any money."

"Just enough for a dress, Bruno. You know how nice I can look."

"We don't have any money."

"Ask that nice man Max Pearl for an advance on the new L'Amour book."

"Gregory's pulled it."

"What on earth for? Then the one you've been talking about. Who's this one about? You don't have to keep secrets from your wife. I hope the person is very famous. The more famous they are the better it sells. Max is rolling in money."

"I don't have a new book."

"But you told everyone you did."

"I lied."

"Well, you'd better think of something sharp. There are lots of famous people in New York."

"Don't you think of your parents in London?"

"Of course I do but they're there and I'm here. What can I do? Father's a grocer. Everyone has to eat."

"There's food rationing."

"What can I do about it, Bruno? I get us an invitation to a top-notch private dinner party at a rich banker's home and you're more worried about my mother and father than you are about what your wife's going to look like on Friday night!"

"There's a war raging over England. You're English. My father's Latvian and I worry about England every moment of the day. Arthur Bumley says the war's coming to a head. We may lose. Instead of arguing with you about some stupid dinner party I should be right now getting my American friends in the Fourth Estate to write about England, to call for help from America. Convince the American public it's going to be them next if we lose the air battle raging over England. It's your bloody country, Gillian. Arthur's worried out of his mind, thinks Germany's about to bomb the centre of London, not just the docks. That's right, London docks. They bombed the East End last night."

"Art the Bumley's an ass."

"Don't you call him that!"

"How dare you shout at me. Get out. Go and get drunk with your low-class friends. See if I care. All I want is a damn dress. Is that too much to expect from your wife? Sometimes I wonder why I bothered to marry you, Bruno Kannberg. There were dozens of men I could have married."

"Shorthand typists marry clerks, live in semi-detached houses in Wimbledon if they are lucky. Spend their entire lives paying a mortgage and scrubbing the floors."

"Some of them would have got rich."

"None of them. I'm going where I should have been in the first place. Earning my salary by doing what I was told by my editor."

"So I don't get the dress?"

"No, you don't."

"Then get out. You'll regret this, Bruno. You'll pay for this. Mark my words."

When Bruno came home drunk four hours later having borrowed twenty dollars from a friend in the bar, Gillian was in bed, sitting up, polishing her nails. Without looking at his wife, Bruno got in the other side of the bed. For the first time since meeting Gillian West he had no desire to make love to her. Turning his back, Bruno went quickly to sleep, his mouth wide open, ready to snore. In the night he dreamed of London and the bombs coming down.

In room twenty-eight at the Independence Hotel, Robert St Clair woke in a cold sweat. In his dream the bomb had made a direct hit on Barnaby's town house in Piccadilly, blasting out the wall of the bedroom and sending Robert down the stairs atop the grandfather clock as it shot downwards to the ground floor of the house, bouncing off the wooden bannisters. Still alive at the bottom, Robert found the blast had taken off his left foot. Then he woke screaming, Freya trying to hold him down.

"I've lost the other foot, Freya."

Carefully, slowly, cold sweat soaking the sheets, Robert felt down with his right hand looking for his only foot.

"It's still there."

"Of course it's still there. What's the matter?"

"Barnaby has taken a direct hit. I was in the house sleeping. It's all back. The funk. Reading London's being bombed. The same stench of the trenches. Rats, water, and bodies decomposing in no man's land."

"I'll make us some tea. They have a tea maker somewhere in the cupboard. The man who showed us the room said we don't have to call room service. Some of the guests prefer their privacy. You're shivering."

"I was always shivering in the trenches. We all were. From cold and fear. You never got used to it. Merlin said the same. In the desert it was just cold fear before an attack according to Barnaby. You didn't know where they were in the folds of sand."

"You're not going. That settles it."

"You can't boast about your brave ancestors half your life and leave England in the lurch when it matters."

"What can you do for them in England? You should stay with me and the children."

"You're American. The children are too small. You'll be all right with your parents in Denver. I'll give the family moral support. If we don't all do our bit, England will go down. I'd phone Barnaby now if I thought I could get through. The tea machine's in that cupboard, I think. The bellboy was pointing that way when I gave him five dollars for bringing up the bags. Oh no, I must go home. They expect it of me. I'll do some writing for the propaganda department at the War Office. All that morale building. It was so real. The dream was so real."

"I'm coming with you on the boat. You stay or I go. Who's going to make you tea in the middle of the night?"

"The children need you."

"So do you. Mother can cope. Give her something to do. Don't argue, Robert. Either you stay or we both go. We can both stay with Barnaby."

"If my brother still has his townhouse. It was so vivid. I came down the stairs on the grandfather clock that stands on the second-floor landing. What time is it?"

"Three in the morning. A nice cup of tea will get you back to sleep."

"You sound like Mrs Mason at Purbeck Manor."

"I know. Wipe yourself with the towel. You're drenched in sweat."

"You always think of me and the children."

"That's my job. It also gives me pleasure. I like looking after the people I love."

"It was nice of Gerry Hollingsworth to come all the way from California to see me off. With his wife. You know Sir Jacob's married? She lives in London. Jacob's wife never visits America. A marriage of convenience for family financial reasons that didn't work."

"To see us off, Robert. I'm coming with you on Saturday."

"You don't have a ticket."

"Then I'll smuggle myself onto the boat. Chances are it's half empty. They're all coming this way away from the war. I'll phone my mother in the morning. Do you really want tea?"

"Not anymore now I found my one good foot. Turn out the light and give me a cuddle. If I start sweating again, wake me up."

"I don't think he's brought his wife."

"We'll find out at Jacob's dinner party on Friday night. Do you mind my only having one foot?"

"It's not the foot that counts. Come here, lover. They say people make love more often in wartime."

"Now I know why you're coming."

Down the corridor in room thirty-six Glen Hamilton was sitting up in bed talking to his wife. As was their habit, they talked to each other about what was worrying Glen in his job.

"It's three in the morning. You need some sleep, Glen. For tomorrow. You can't function on three hours' sleep."

"He's right. Bruno is right. If Germany wins the Battle of Britain we'll all be living in a fascist world."

"Fascism. Communism. Capitalism. They're all the same, a way to make money for the few and keep the masses under control when built-in religion doesn't work anymore. The Catholics have the answer. Put the fear of God into a child before he is seven and the man will behave himself. Now Darwin has come along and tried to prove we evolved from the slime so the power-hungry are trying something else. Religion was the best. Self-policing. God all around you all of the time. You can hide from the police but not from God. And make them all give ten per cent to the church for its trouble."

"That's really cynical, Samantha."

"I hope so. Wouldn't it be awful if it was the truth? That religion is one big confidence trick which you only get to prove when you're dead and can't argue with the church or get your money back."

"Democracy is better than fascism."

"Plato, I think it was, the philosophers all blend into one in my mind, said the next worse thing to tyranny was democracy. All those stupid people voting to get what they want for themselves. Democracy is just as easy to abuse. All you need is a sleazeball with a big, persuasive mouth. Sound familiar, Glen? That sermon on Sunday was bullshit."

"It's in America's best interest to help England."

"See, what I said. All you have to do is convince a gullible public and we're off to war in our chariot. If the spoils are worth it and the price in blood and treasure minimal, everyone cheers. That's democracy. No sane man volunteers to go to war. Do any of them know what they are fighting about? The governments, I mean. The man in the street never knows. War, an extension of diplomacy someone said. If he won't give you what you want, give him a belt round the ear. We're just fine in America as we are, leave them alone. When they've finished struggling with each other to find out who's the big gorilla we'll see what's in our best interest. Don't let Bruno Kannberg get you writing pieces telling everyone we should go to war."

"And if Hitler invades America?"

"It's a big pond."

"Or the Japs?"

"What have the Japs got to do with it?"

"We're stopping them getting oil in their fight against China. You corner a rat, it turns on you. What else can it do from a corner when its lifeblood is threatened?"

"Your imagination is running riot again, Glen Hamilton. Freya has the right idea. If Robert wants to run back to England and put his head in the noose, let him. She's got the kids."

"Robert's English. Very old English. They have deep patriotism bred into them."

"Still doesn't mean America has to go to war. All we have in common is the language. The rest of America is a melting pot of every tribe on earth. Why it works. We don't have clans. Factions. We all want one thing, the good life. Most of us have it. Everyone has the same opportunity. Let the Europeans scratch each other's eyes out. They wanted the fight, let them have it. A second time. You'd think they'd done enough damage to each other the first time. Russia's keeping out of it. So must we. Now there's a problem for the future. Communism."

"You just said they're all the same."

"Communism threatens the American dream of all having the chance to get rich."

"Now you are yanking my chain."

"Probably. No one ever solved the world's problems for very long, certainly not at three in the morning. There's always a new one. Go to sleep. I love talking to you, Glen, but a girl needs her beauty sleep. You think the kids are all right?"

"Of course they are. Goodnight. Thanks for listening. Sometimes I like to get it off my chest."

"I know. We've been married a long time. We're interested in each other's problems. Not just our own. That's why we work, you and I."

2

Genevieve watched the Pacific roll into shore all morning, only one thought in her mind: Tinus was fighting for his life, the only hope in her future about to be destroyed. The letter from Uncle Harry was wet in the sand at her naked feet, the phone call in her mind, cut off in full flight, Uncle Harry sounding cheerful compared to her own mental misery.

"There's no contact on a daily basis with Tangmere at the moment. Keep your chin up, Genevieve. He's a good pilot."

"Is he all right?"

"Nothing comes out. Security."

"They'd tell you."

"It's a bit hectic at the moment. The RAF has its hands full. I'll give him your love when I see him. They won't let me fly in combat."

"Thank God for that."

"Silly, really. I test flew the Spitfire before it went into squadron service. Now they say I'm too old. Too old when they've ironed out the problems! I'll try again if it gets any worse."

"What do you mean 'any worse', Uncle Harry?"

"We're losing pilots. The Germans more than us."

"I'm going to be sick.

"Just keep your chin up."

There was a click and the line had gone dead, leaving Genevieve the rest of the day to ponder on her own, rereading Uncle Harry's old letter in reply to her own, looking for solace where none could be found. All day the blue sea had rolled in, not once penetrating her thoughts as the fear and misery ebbed and flowed through every portal of her mind.

"There you are, Genevieve. They've been looking for you all morning."

"Leave me alone."

"He'll survive. I'm trying again to go over."

"Then you're as big a fool as Tinus. He was in Rhodesia. All he had to do was stay put."

"Anyway, they won't let me. I've joined an American ancillary squadron. We'll be in the war soon, you'll see."

"Gregory! Do me a favour? Go away."

"You can't mope all day. Come and have some lunch. Get drunk. Do something other than worry. He's a good pilot. The best pilots came through the last war."

"What do you know about it?"

"Only what I heard from Harry Brigandshaw. He should know. Twenty-three kills."

"And all dead. Germans or English what's the difference? Uncle Harry said he's going back into combat if it gets any worse. He's over fifty. How bad has it got when old men have to fight?"

"At least have a drink. When it's all over you'll laugh at yourself for moping on the beach all morning."

"When's it going to be over, Greg? You know the papers are calling it the Battle of Britain. Britain fighting for survival. I want to go home."

"What can you do?"

"Be nearer. Not knowing is horrible. I can make them smile."

"Not with a face like that you won't. Why don't you go to New York to see off your uncle if you want to go to England? Could have caught the same boat. Why's he taking a boat anyway?"

"Doesn't like flying."

"The Atlantic is swarming with U-boats."

"Now you're really helping. Uncle Robert goes all the way through the trenches and drowns at sea. All right then. Let's you and I get drunk at the hotel. If anyone tries to talk to us, punch them in the face. Everybody wants a fight these days. He's going to die, Greg."

"No, he's not. Most soldiers survive wars. If they didn't, they wouldn't fight wars. There are always survivors or where are the heroes? Don't you remember anything about our films? The swelling music when the victor triumphantly returns from the wars to the love of his life?"

"That's comforting. Do you realise what you just said?"

"Sort of. I'm trying to help."

"I know you are. Why don't you find yourself a girlfriend?"

"I don't want one. You know that."

When they arrived for the dinner party at Abercrombie Place, Bruno Kannberg gave his first genuine smile in the presence of his wife since getting into bed next to her drunk. Vida, literally, looked down her nose at Gillian wearing the same old dress, Gillian's stare fixed with envy on the diamond drop earrings, missing the contempt in the other woman's eyes.

"It is so nice of you to come," said the banker's mistress in her German accent that some men found attractive.

"We always try and help. Just a few flowers for you, Vida," said Bruno.

"How is your new book?"

"Coming along just fine. Hello, Robert. Not like yours of course. You remember my wife, Gillian?"

"What a lovely dress," said Freya, unaware she had put her foot in her mouth.

"Ah, Mr Kannberg," said Sir Jacob Rosenzweig. "We wanted to thank you for your articles praising *Holy Knight*. All publicity is good publicity but yours went beyond the call of duty. Yours was more than we might expect. The same magazine as Gregory L'Amour. When's the book version coming out?"

"Hello, Bruno," said Max Pearl. "This is Marsha. He'll come round when he's short of money. They all do. Money always talks. Marsha is a friend of Petronella who is here with Gerry Hollingsworth. Don't you remember Petronella from the Thespian restaurant? You wanted a loan, I seem to remember. Gillian! Ravishing as usual. Do you like Vida's new earrings? So pretty. So expensive."

Bruno listened to the flow of trivia wash all round him, very few words meaning what they said. They drank cocktails handed them by a maid in a short black dress that flared at the knees. The cocktails were in tall glasses with cherries on sticks. Bruno watched his wife drink the first one straight down and take another from the tray when the girl wasn't looking, offering the tray to the wife of the man who had directed *Holy Knight*, the film.

Robert St Clair was on edge with no one mentioning the war in England. Bruno thought it was likely deliberate. The morning papers in New York had talked about U-boats stalking the shipping lanes between America and Europe. In packs. The British were going to give their merchant ships Royal Navy protection and send them to and from America in convoys to stop the U-boat packs attacking them. Bruno presumed Robert St Clair had read the morning papers. His wife had, by the look of her. Poor Freya was smiling with difficulty. Bruno wondered if the poor woman would ever see her famous husband again after the boat sailed in the morning. Wisely, Bruno avoided the subject, trying, like the rest of them, to behave as though nothing untoward was happening in the skies over Britain. The twinge of worry about his parents in London was now constant at the back of his mind, like a toothache, only with a toothache he could go to the dentist and have the pain taken away.

They had not said a word to each other, Gillian going into one of her sulks the moment the dress was unobtainable. All her tricks were back. The flash of thigh and breast that usually made him capitulate to every one of her whims. This time it had left Bruno cold, the spoilt brat in his wife dominating his wife's sexuality, drowning it out, turning him off, making him wonder if the power she held over him from the day they met had gone. Out the window. Each new flash having no sign of an effect.

Then Petronella smiled at him, the smile that every man and woman understood, and the game of sex was on again, making his wife look from one to the other before she understood. For Bruno, it was his day of liberation. In a room of people he preferred another woman to his wife. And all over a stupid dress not worth a tenth of its price, the tag from a Fifth Avenue shop worth far more than the dress itself, the snob value, the show-off value that Bruno had never been able to understand.

There she was. A shorthand typist in a short black dress. Pouting. Petulant. Concerned with herself. A woman he had thought himself in love with. Bruno began to laugh.

"What are you laughing at?" snapped Gillian.

"You, Gillian."

"What do you mean?"

"You blew it," he said, leaning close to her ear. "You blew it, darling."

Even Bruno knew the 'darling' sounded sarcastic. Maybe it was meant to. Moving into the dining room Bruno found his place and sat down. He was his own man again. In control of his life. The jealous lust that had controlled his life was gone.

"Tell me about your next movie," Bruno said across the table to Gerry Hollingsworth, sitting opposite next to Petronella. "Is Genevieve in the film? What's happened to Gregory? Reading the movie magazines you'd think both of them had disappeared off the map. The RAF must have done something to him. Amazing how stars rise so quickly. And fall just as quickly. One minute they are all the news and next you never hear of them."

"They are both at my house in Long Beach. Genevieve only talks about England. Her mother and father. The mother has a flat in Chelsea. She's worried stiff. Our David and Ephraim are in the army. Both joined up after the evacuation at Dunkirk. When are you joining the British Army, Bruno? I'm too old, thank goodness. We'll all have to face up to it in the end, even America, Max. No, they don't want parts in a film. At the moment Genevieve wants to be left on her own. Wouldn't surprise me if she went back to England. It sort of gets you, being so far away when your friends and family are taking the brunt. Instead of running away I should be doing something for the war effort."

"It's with me all day long, Mr Hollingsworth."

"You're not going to England?" said Gillian.

"There's a point where it doesn't have to be thought about. I'll just do it. Apart from your films, I know nothing about going to war. I suppose it's like anything else in life. We soon find out when we have to."

Looking round the dinner table, Bruno saw they had all put down their knives and forks. For the first time in the evening no one was saying a word. Not even Gillian.

"I'm sorry," he said and went back to eating his food, ignoring the 'come on' look from Petronella as she found his foot under the table, rubbing the inside of his ankle with what felt like her stockinged toe.

Finally, the war in Europe had walked into the room in New York. A big, ugly threat understood by every one of them and bigger than all.

3

S ir Jacob Rosenzweig, watching them all from the top of the table, had his own worries. The phone call had come through to his office late in the afternoon, Jacob taking the call without asking his secretary the name of the caller, a practice he found rude; if someone wished to talk to him they had their own reason, not for him to censor the call before he knew what it was going to be about. The voice at the other end was far away, right out of his past, a voice he had never expected to hear again.

"It's Hannah, Jacob. How are you?"

"Hannah?"

"Your wife, Jacob. I've changed my mind. I want to come and live in New York."

"Hannah, it's been years. I have my own life in America."

"So I heard."

"Well, you can't live at Abercrombie Place."

"Why not? London's dangerous. In case you haven't heard over there, there's a war going on right over our heads. Any minute a bomb's coming through the roof. Remember, I gave you your children."

Jacob, silent, contemplated what he considered a lie. Only one was his: Rebecca. The legality was different, all five being born to Hannah while they were legally married.

"Have you heard from Rebecca?"

"I paid them a visit. It's criminal with all your money, Rebecca's husband someone's employee. They should farm their own land if they want to be farmers. All beats me."

"Did you see the grandchildren?"

"Of course I did."

"What are they like?"

"Boys and girls. I'd live with them in Rhodesia if they had their own farm. Mrs Brigandshaw was anything but polite to me. Said the farm manager's job went with one house. We don't like each other. Who does she think she is, telling me what I can and can't do? I think she had spoken to Ralph. Why did you let that man marry our daughter, Jacob?"

"I didn't, if you remember. Rebecca ran off with him."

"You'll just have to kick her out as I can't stay in London. We have blackouts every night. All the windows have to be covered with black curtains, as if the Germans don't know what's below."

"What are you talking about?"

"Vida, I think she calls herself. You're old enough to be her grandfather for heaven's sake. Haven't you any idea of decorum, Jacob? She's only after what she can get out of you. If we weren't at war with Germany I'd have had her properly checked out. Gold-digger. There's no fool like an old fool. I will bring decorum back into your life when I arrive in New York on Wednesday. If she's still there when I arrive all hell will come down on your head, along with the best lawyers in America. Have you forgotten I'm your wife?"

"As a matter of fact, Hannah, I had forgotten."

Looking at Petronella looking at young Bruno Kannberg made Jacob realise the world had indeed been turned on its head. Gerry Hollingsworth did not seem to mind. Gerry Hollingsworth, who had once been a Jew named Louis Casimir until he changed his name by deed poll to escape the tribe of Israel. Watching Gerry the way he seemed not to mind Petronella flirting with Bruno gave Jacob an idea. He would put Vida in another flat and see her just the same. Hannah never said she was going to do something and changed her mind. They had lived in the same house separately for years so nothing would have to change. It might even be cheaper if the Germans bombed his house in Golders Green. They wouldn't have to talk to each other except on social occasions, when other people were around. With luck Jacob could find Mabel and give her back her job as the cook.

Then his mind slipped off thinking about Rebecca. How much he had missed his daughter. How the two of them had first found the apartment in Abercrombie Place together. Somehow tears came into his eyes. Vida was still having her contest with Gillian Kannberg, twice leaning so close to the younger girl the drop diamond almost swung into Gillian's face. Maybe Hannah was right. All Vida wanted was money. It was all about money. It always was about money. It probably always would be.

"Are you all right, Sir Jacob?" asked Robert St Clair.

"Bad news this afternoon, Robert."

"One of your children killed in the war?"

"No, none of the boys are fighting. Aaron runs the bank in London. He's forty-five. Just bad news. Well, you haven't got long to go now. I'm coming to the boat to see you off. With Vida. She insists we are there to wave you off."

"Freya is coming."

"You have a lovely wife," said Jacob feeling sad, knowing he had missed something important in his life, the love of a good woman.

"I know, and it gets better the older we become."

"The children?"

"Staying in Denver."

"Wise. Very wise. Many of the English children are being sent to Canada. Can I pour you another glass of wine?"

It just could not get better, thought Vida the next day on their way to see off Robert St Clair and his wife. The 'old goat' had told her over breakfast, giving Vida what she hoped was her best theatre yet as she played out her part to perfection.

"You can't send me away, Jacob. What will I do? I want to live with you, not in a flat all on my own. New York is so big and strange for a German. If it wasn't for your protection I don't know what I'd do. A woman in the shop yesterday told me to go back to Hitler. I'd just asked for a pound of tomatoes for the salad last night when she demanded to know where I was from. I told her, after she was nasty to me, that I'm Jewish. Only then did she calm down. Heard my German accent and flew at me. As if the war was all my fault. You said you were divorced from your wife. That you hadn't seen her for years. I'll be so miserable on my own I'll want to cut my wrists. Just when my life was so wonderful, Jacob. Oh, what am I going to do?"

"I'll visit you whenever I can."

"You say that now. She won't let you."

"I said we were separated."

"What's the difference? She wasn't in your life when I agreed to live with you. Oh, Jacob, I want to die."

She had looked up from her despair to see if he was swallowing the lies in her words. The 'old goat' was actually crying tears, his eyes soft and so understanding she wanted to laugh in his face.

"I'm going to end up all on my very little own, Jacob. I'll just have to be brave. Chin up, as you British say. Well, if she's coming next Wednesday I'd better move into a hotel. She's legally your wife, now I hear, so what can Vida do? A small hotel. I couldn't live alone in an apartment. Well, we'd better go. They'll be waiting for us at the boat. What a lovely dinner party last night. I love all your friends. Well, that'll all be over. Would you like me to ask Mabel to come back? Most rich wives can't cook. One minute my cup was spilling over, now it's empty. The taxi is waiting downstairs. We'll hold hands all the way. Cheer up, my darling. Life could be worse."

"You don't know Hannah."

"We could be living in England and have a bomb dropped on our heads."

"You'll still have money, Vida. Your trust fund won't change."

"It's not the money that counts. It's you, Jacob."

By the time they arrived at the side of the dock Vida was convinced she had missed her vocation in life. She should have been an actress.

They were all there from last night. The men not going off into danger were joshing with Robert St Clair, telling Vida she was not the only hypocrite in New York. Gerry Hollingsworth said twice he would soon be over, having no intention, the moment the ship sailed, to leave America, whatever his sons were doing in the war. Max Pearl slapped Robert on the back, wishing him luck. The American journalist shook hands silently; apparently, Vida understood, they had met during the last war before Robert lost his foot. For some reason Bruno and Gillian were not talking directly to each other. There was a look of relief on Bruno's face, knowing he was not going on the boat. Gillian glared at her, as if Vida had what she wanted. If only the fool knew life was always better with a young man.

"The ship can outrun the U-boats," Robert was saying, his wife not looking so convinced.

"God speed," said Jacob, shaking Robert's hand.

Vida, bubbling inside at the thought of her freedom, wanted to dance a jig. Then it was over, the guests from the previous night going their separate ways as the ship sailed out of the harbour. None of the men left behind said a word. All, Vida knew, were thinking the same thought: thank heaven it wasn't them on the boat.

Silently wishing the U-boat captains good hunting, Vida went home to Abercrombie Place for the last time, having told Jacob she could not prolong her pain of pending separation any longer. By the time the 'old goat' came looking for her in the hotel behind his wife's back she would be in California, waiting for the Germans to win the war. Then she would go home. Oh yes, she thought, thinking of Kurt. Never again would she be forced to prostitute herself for money. Like any successful man she would be independent. A woman of means. A woman in control of her life. No longer dependent on the whim of a man for her happiness, a man who underneath all the blather was only thinking of himself. Anyway, she thought, what would old Jacob have done with the money otherwise?

4

$\mathcal{W}$hile Vida was rationalising with herself, three hundred and seventy miles south of where the squadron of RAF bombers had dropped their bombs on Berlin, Bergit von Lieberman was contemplating the behaviour of her daughter Melina. Were it not for Erwin being her brother she would have said the girl was in love with the boy, all the fuss that was going on. Gabby, her younger daughter, seemed indifferent to the arrival of the prodigal son.

Klaus von Lieberman, looking out of the window of the old family house, had his back to his wife, his hands clasped together, not moving. For a moment Bergit thought of going up behind her husband, wrapping her arms round his waist and whispering everything would turn out all right, that seeing his only son, named after General Erwin Rommel in deference to a lifelong friend, would be an occasion of joy and happiness after all the pain the boy had deliberately caused his father.

"I don't understand all the long faces," said Melina in German. "Were it not for Erwin, Father would still be in jail."

"Don't be rude, Melina."

"You don't know Erwin like I do. He would only do what was right for the Fatherland. What's the matter, Papa? We're winning the war. Erwin said in his last letter it will all be over before Christmas. We've smashed the RAF. Our men can invade England if England fails to surrender. Then Germany will control the whole of Western Europe and the

Americans won't raise a finger. The Russians have been given half of Poland. The Jews no longer have money or power. The Third Reich will last a thousand years."

"You are a seventeen-year-old girl and don't know what you are talking about," snapped her father without turning round or unclasping the hands behind his back.

"Erwin does."

"Erwin thinks he does. They all think they do at that age."

"What are you so worried about?" wheedled Melina. "Erwin says every victor in a war is right. No one argues with the winner. How can they? Everything will go back to normal. The von Lieberman estate here in Bavaria will last as long as the Third Reich. Uncle Werner says without the Nazi Party you would have lost the family estate."

"What do you know about that?" said Klaus, turning round to look at his daughter.

"That we won't have to pay back the mortgage to the Rosenzweig Bank when we win the war."

"Rubbish. Of course I will pay my debts. When I have the money."

"After the war, the estate will be rich again. The tenants paying their rent in full. If you want to pay it back I'm sure they'll let you."

"Now that is big of them. You can't renege on a debt, however many wars. The fundamental concept of capitalism would collapse. Let alone the law. The world would be in perpetual turmoil."

"Not with Germany in control. And again I quote Erwin, he says we will police the world so well, no one will be allowed to misbehave themselves. That war and riots will be a thing of the past. Everyone will be forced to live in peace and harmony. Troublemakers. Activists. These people will be put in jail and never let out to stir up the common people again. Erwin says there has to be discipline, without discipline the human race will cease to exist. The world needs a master race to look after them. We Germans are the master race. Just look at the British Empire. That little firebrand Gandhi is stirring up revolution. Hitler would hang him from a tree. No one would ever mention his name again. Erwin says that little man will have Muslims and Hindus at each other's throats the moment Gandhi kicks the British out of India, throwing the world into religious wars for centuries. The British have gone soft. We'll take over their colonies next year and toughen them up. The world will prosper with peace and order without those few individuals making trouble for the rest of us."

"How often does Erwin write to you? We never see the letters."

"Every week. He doesn't send them through the post. I have to burn them after they are read. Of course the Party don't mind. It's Erwin. Thinks everyone is a spy. That many Germans are against Hitler. That some people make money out of turmoil."

"Well, Melina. Here he comes. A whole entourage of the faithful. The taxi from the station is full of young officers. Was that why you smartened yourself up? You knew who was coming. Oh well. Better play the gracious host. Hope you are right. If the RAF has been destroyed, how come they just managed to drop bombs on Berlin?"

"Erwin says the Führer is going to bomb London. That will finish them. Once we start bombing central London the British will surrender. How many in the taxi, Father? I don't want to be seen at the window like a schoolgirl, Gabby. Oh, this is so wonderful. Erwin has come home for a visit. Now everything will be all right. Please be nice to him, Daddy."

"There's not much else I can do if I don't want the Party on my back. At the moment they do seem to be winning."

"Don't you want us to win the war?"

"Of course I do. The quicker it's over the better for everyone. Everyone in the world."

"That's more like it, Papa," said Melina, going up to him at the window and giving him a hug. She looked out of the window onto the wide gravel driveway where a taxi was disgorging its passengers. Then she saw Erwin looking up at their window and waved, both of them smiling at each other, their happiness meeting through their eyes.

Klaus watched them, sick to his stomach. They were all bomber pilots and navigators. Boys rather than men. Joking and laughing with each other, the Luftwaffe uniforms little different to the one he had worn as a young pilot in the air war over the trenches. They were just the same. Fighting for the Führer this time instead of the Kaiser, the brainwashing little different to his own. A man not for his country was always labelled a traitor. Good advice when speaking against the policy of the country was never tolerated. Looking at them smiling and laughing, not a care in the world, young men together enjoying their camaraderie, Klaus knew he had been a fool. Instead of arguing with them when they took him away to Berlin in 1938, he should have agreed with everything they said. The rest of the male members of his family were right, including the boy down below who had given both his parents so much worry. The old saying came to his mind, 'if you can't beat them, join them'.

His old adage of staying out of the way, staying out of politics, had not been a success. She was right, of course. His eldest daughter at seventeen was right. If Adolf Hitler won the war and conquered the world for Germany, no one in their right minds would care to question his methods or whether he was morally right to do what he did. All the great heroes in history had started as thugs. The British hated Napoleon; the French still thought him a hero. You just had to win to get people's respect. For a good many years Napoleon had been a winner until the Prussians sided with the British at the Battle of Waterloo, knocking Napoleon off his pedestal, the irony not lost on Klaus as he watched his son, the pilot, with pride.

The German tribes were once again on the warpath, who was he to complain? The French had been greedy at Versailles, rubbing the collective German nose in the manure. Now Germany had marched into Paris, no one was demanding reparations anymore, after they had attacked the coal mines in the Ruhr as if Germany was some common debtor who had reneged on its debts. Maybe the French greed had got them what they deserved. Maybe Hitler had no alternative but to restore the military might of Germany, but building arms behind the backs of the Allies until he was powerful enough to fight. Maybe if the victors had been more magnanimous they would have left Germany with another alternative. Sometimes bitter enemies became friends.

With a weary heart at man's stupidity, Klaus unclasped his hands from behind his back, turned to his family and smiled. Then he crossed the big room that overlooked the terrace above the driveway and walked out to meet his son; whatever the Hitler Youth Movement had done to indoctrinate the boy, Erwin was still his son, would always be his son.

"All we have to do is beat the British," he said as he passed through the open door. In the flash of saying his thoughts out loud he had a picture of Harry Brigandshaw in his mind. The smiling, concerned Harry Brigandshaw who had flown a flying boat to Romanshorn to see if his old friend had need of help.

Downstairs, all the boys saluted him. Formally, one by one, Klaus shook their hands.

Servants, all smiling, were unstrapping the pile of suitcases attached to the back of the taxi, the driver helping instead of sitting in the cab. Everyone was in good humour, the autumn day warm on their backs, pigeons calling as if to welcome the four young men. Bergit was waiting for them on the terrace, the girls standing just behind their mother eager to get a good look at the young officers. Klaus swallowed hard, feeling as old as the hills. One of the men made them all laugh together; his wife, the girls and the boys. The suitcases went into the old house followed by the rest of them.

Erwin had kissed his mother on the cheek, no sign of the rudeness the boy had shown three years before when he stormed out of the house and walked the miles to the station, leaving for the Hitler Youth Movement to finish his education and later place him, a trained pilot taught by his father, in the Führer's Luftwaffe. On the beautiful summer's day in their ancestral home it was as if nothing had ever been the matter. Klaus wondered how many other times in history the youth of his line had come home before going into battle.

When they all came down twenty minutes later Klaus was still standing on the terrace in the sun, wondering what had happened to estrange him from his son. Had the boy anything to do with the three men who had forced him into a car and driven him to Berlin after the seventeen-year-old boy had walked out of the house a year before? Were the Nazis coercing anyone who they thought disagreed with the policy of the Party, who failed to do what they were told without thought or question? Had his uncle, General Werner von Liebermann, played a part? Did it matter now, standing in the sun looking at the boys and girls dressed in riding clothes ready for a romp in the forest, not a care in the world, seeing only what was right in front of them?

The men looked even more like schoolboys than before when they were wearing their uniforms. Melina was slapping her shapely thigh with her riding crop, making the gesture blatantly sexual without knowing what she was about, the instinct built into her mind by nature, Klaus hoped. Gabby, at fifteen, knew the boys, by the look on her face, were thinking of more than her company for a ride on a horse. Everything was in the immediate present, nothing they said in the future or the past. No one had asked if he wanted to go with them. He was the 'old man' they deferred to, who had flown in the last war, a man they showed respect. They had likely not thought he would like to go riding.

Bergit came out of the house to see them walk across to the horses, saddled ready for them, the grooms holding the reins of the horses, all smiling. His wife had the same look of resignation on her face. They were both being left out. Neither was expected to join in the fun. The older generation had had their fun.

"Did he say anything?" Klaus asked when his wife came to stand next to him.

"Not a word."

"They all seem happy. Comrades in arms. I remember it well. At that age they all think they do nothing wrong."

"No wonder Melina was all of a jump. It all happens so quickly. Was it the same with us, Klaus?" She looked up at his face, trying to smile.

"Different but much the same. They looked a nice bunch of boys. Why, suddenly, are they here?"

"That I did get out of our son. To quote our Erwin, 'We're going to bomb the hell out of Britain until they stop fighting the war and agree to our terms this time.' They are going to bomb the cities after Berlin's air raid."

"Rest and recreation before the big battle. They did that to me before I was sent to my squadron in France."

"That's where he's going. To a bomber station somewhere in France close to the English Channel. Poor Harry. Is Anthony old enough to fly?"

"Not yet. Maybe they had the sense to go to Africa."

"It's going to be over soon. That's the good part. Civilians won't be able to stand up to constant bombing."

"They show off every line of their bodies in those damn riding clothes."

"Who?" said Bergit sweetly.

"Melina and Gabby."

"We have pretty daughters. You should be happy."

"I hope you're right. That it's over quickly. That the RAF is out of the fight. Whoever wins the battle for air supremacy will win this war. You can take the whole German Army to the English Channel but if you don't command the air you will never get across. If our dive-bombers can hit the ships of the Royal Navy with impunity, the Luftwaffe will sink the British fleet before it can interfere with the landing of our troops."

"They'll surrender before we have to invade."

"If we command the air. How long are they staying with us?"

"Two days. Make the best of it, Klaus. Let bygones be bygones. Those boys are the future of Germany. It's out of your hands. You did your bit when you had to."

"Not very well. You forget Harry shot me down."

"I thank God every day that he did. That you were captured. That you were unable to fight and get yourself killed, Klaus von Lieberman. Why don't we take the dogs for a walk? It's a lovely day. It's all going to be all right. You'll see. He's a lovely boy. They all see sense in the end."

"It all seems so far away."

"Long may it seem that way. We don't want a war in Bavaria."

Jürgen Mann, the second pilot, caught her eye the moment Melina von Lieberman swung up onto her horse, flooding her with a rush of desire that caught her off balance. For the first time she was not in control of her eye contact with a man. The man's look was that of lust tinged with aching sadness making her usual snooty look in return impossible. Once she was caught looking at him with her own desire she was lost. Very few young men came to the von Lieberman estate, none in the uniform of a German officer or the riding habit of a gentleman. In Switzerland at her school for girls there was only Monsieur Montpellier, Françoise's father, to keep under control and he was too scared of his wife to take it further than a look. There was no doubt now in Melina's mind that she was ready for a man, the combination of Jürgen Mann and the rhythm of the horse setting her on fire.

When the horses were given rein they tore away down the forest path. No one thought of danger, whooping as the trees flashed past, the horses enjoying the ride as much as the rest of them. Gabby, Melina saw out of the corner of her eye, was holding on for dear life, a mix of fear and excitement etched on her face, her hands white on the reins, her knees dug hard into her horse's flanks.

Erwin was a length in front, the first to jump the trunk of the tree fallen across the path. One after the other they took to the air, adrenaline pumping, the boy for a moment out of her head. Then he turned in the saddle, his balance perfect above the crupper, and smiled.

When the horses were blown, the group of horsemen and women collected under an oak tree for them all to catch their wind. None of them had ever been happier in their lives.

"You ride well, Melina. Erwin said you were good on a horse. My word, it's like an aeroplane, feeling the animal's power between my legs. When the war's over I'll take you up in my aeroplane. Christmas. By then we'll be country gentlemen again. Even Erwin. He loves the Party for what it's doing for Germany but he doesn't want to go into politics." Melena watched him dismount, mesmerised.

They were all laughing again. There was thick moss on the ground under the tree. They all dismounted after Jürgen, letting the horses move away to graze the grass in the glade between the trees, where the sun had given life to the grass. The reins fell over the heads of the horses, trailing in the grass. There were birds high in the oak tree none of them could see, only hear. In a moment Melina was sitting next to him on the soft moss, their backs to the tree, side by side.

"This is so beautiful," said Jürgen, the sadness of his first look now mirrored in the tone of his voice. "The trees and the forest."

"Did you grow up on a farm?" she asked softly.

"Oh yes. Many acres. I could never live my life in a city. Erwin likes Berlin, I don't know why. All the noise and dirty smells. Can you hear the owls at night calling to each other? Sometimes at home when the moon is up you can hear the foxes bark. Now that's something. Birds and animals calling in the night. Do you think birds and animals love each other, Melina? When you kill a fox, does the family mourn his death? Feel sorrow? Wonder where he is? Miss him? Do birds fly together because they are happy together? Happy to be in their flock among friends? I've wondered all my life."

"Are the horses all right? Won't they go off on their own?"

"Then we walk home, you and I. May I touch your hand?"

"Yes."

"I don't want to die before I have time to love. Don't tell Erwin I told you that. He'll think I'm soppy. Not fit to fly an aeroplane over England."

"Have you flown over England?"

"Not yet. I've never been to England. I just hope I never have to land there before we win the war. If we all stop talking we'll hear the pure sound of nature, not all the sounds of man."

"How long have you been a pilot, Jürgen?"

"Not very long. None of us have except Erwin. Can I hold your hand, Melina?"

"Yes." His hand was soft like a girl's.

"That's so good. Makes me feel safe. I'll remember the feel of your hand. I know I'm silly. Not tough like the others. None of us are tough like Erwin. I could stay under this tree forever holding your hand."

They were alone. The others had gone to look for Gabby's horse that had trotted away between the trees. A rabbit came out from its hiding place in the bracken and had a look at them. By then, Melina had made up her mind to comfort him. To comfort the brave man before he went off to fight. To love him only for a night, if that was all life had to give them.

"Stay awake tonight, Jürgen. I'll come to you. You're so brave. All of you are so brave. We can hold hands in the moonlight and listen for the bark of a fox."

"Will you, Melina?"

"Don't tell Erwin."

"Everything is so short. Suddenly everything is so short."

"When you hear me imitate the hoot of an owl, call back to me like the owls. Leave your door ajar so I know where you are. Are you close to Erwin's bedroom?"

"Next to him."

"He must never know. No one must ever know."

"I'll lie awake waiting for the hoot of an owl."

"When you hoot and hear me reply, you'll know it is me. They are easy to imitate when you have lived here all your life. I can hear them coming back. Stop holding my hand."

They both tried to find a moment with Erwin alone. To talk to him. To explain. To wipe out the silence of three years. Only Melina had received her letters, most of them kept to herself. Bergit knew Melina was as proud of Chancellor Hitler as she had been of the Kaiser. Asking Melina for information about her son had mostly ended in an argument. For Melina, whatever Erwin had done was always right. Gabby, two years younger than Melina, four years younger than Erwin, had not felt the same influence, the extra age difference keeping them apart. By the time they went into dinner, Bergit understood. He was never going to allow them to talk privately, always making sure not to be left on his own giving his parents a chance to dig up old wounds.

"He doesn't want to talk to us, Klaus."

"What's there to say?"

"He could apologise to his mother."

"I don't think so. The Party never apologises. I'm still a member, whatever they did to me. Uncle Werner made sure of that. They want us all to conform. My guess is someone told him to keep his trap shut. Not to bring up the subject. That I was now a faithful Party member. What he thinks is another matter. I've caught him looking at me a couple of times. A wary look. A look of knowing more than I do. At that age we all think our parents are dinosaurs. That we know what's best. We all want to change the world at that age, thinking we know better. The world just stays the same old mess, generation after generation. We get born, grow old hopefully, sometimes gain a little wisdom and die the same way as our ancestors. The world will always be the same. Nature is far stronger than us. Nature dictates who we are and what we do. Some call God nature. I don't think it matters what we call what has made us so long as the species survives. That's what we leave behind. Our children. Not some great new way of governing ourselves that makes everyone nice to each other. Mother and son included. Leave him alone, Bergit. He'll talk to us when he's ready. There isn't any point in starting an argument right now. Anyway, I'm hungry. What's on the menu for dinner? Don't tell me. Roast lamb with your homemade mint jelly. Roast potatoes that are pre-boiled. Dumplings. Sauerkraut on the side. A big, sherry-filled trifle Harry Brigandshaw's mother showed you how to make on our honeymoon on Elephant Walk. Erwin's favourite supper."

"How on earth did you guess, Klaus! The way to a man's heart is always through his stomach. Especially a boy's."

"He's a man, Bergit. Nearly twenty years old."

"Which makes me feel old. May I take your arm and go into dinner?"

"Of course you may."

"Isn't it wonderful to be happy? Gabby's growing up. Just look at her."

"It's the way the boys look at her I don't like."

"Are fathers jealous of their daughters?"

"Of course they are. If any of those boys tried to touch them I'd likely want to kill him."

"And then they get married."

"That's different. They go through a church; God blesses the union."

"Then we have grandchildren."

"Please, Bergit. I feel old enough around the boys as it is."

"None of them have turned twenty-one."

"How do you know?"

"You can still see the dew behind their ears. Enough talk. I'm hungry. Did you open the red wine, Klaus?"

"A good German always lets the red wine breathe for two hours before drinking. My father told me. His father told him. I'm not sure it makes any difference. Only the ritual makes the difference, which makes the wine taste better."

"Men! They'll all be hungry after their horse riding. Wasn't it a beautiful autumn day?"

. . .

THE NIGHT WAS the worst time for Jürgen Mann. When the pretence was over. On his own in the pitch dark, fear flooded him. He hoped his navigator on the twin-engined Dornier bomber, Hans Bengler, was having a better night's sleep in the room two doors down the corridor. Eating too much roast lamb had given Jürgen indigestion, stopping him from falling asleep as he should have done in the aftermath of so much food.

As he tried to sleep, putting her temptation out of his mind, he knew she would never come to his room in her own home where her parents were sleeping so close. She was seventeen years old, still afraid of her parents in a matter of such appalling consequence. What with the indigestion and the fear of what her father would do to him if Melina was caught in his room in the middle of the night, his mind raced as he lay in bed.

Later, panic took hold as fear reared real and violent from the dark in front of him, making Jürgen jump out of bed and go to the open window. It was pitch dark outside, the moon not yet up, the lacework of the stars in the heavens not enough to light anything on the earth. The stars twinkled. Only the planets stood unblinking in the sky looking down on him. Slowly, the panic subsided. At least, he told himself, holding onto the sill of the window at the same level as his hips, it would be a quick death when the British shot him down, unlike the four years that still tormented his father, making him mostly incoherent. The war in the trenches had not destroyed his father's body, only his mind, forcing the man to live in hell for the rest of his life, leaving Jürgen's mother with no means to help. His mother ran the family estate. Did everything hoping one day he would do the work. Driven by the collapse in the German economy after the war, her fear of losing the estate as well as her husband, his mother like many others with nowhere else to turn had supported the rise of Adolf Hitler, 'our only chance of survival as a family', as she put it as the financial situation on their estate grew worse and worse.

"May the bombs on my plane explode and kill us," he whispered to the night. "Please God don't let me burn to death as my plane falls out of the sky." A devout Catholic, Jürgen crossed himself, hoping it would give him the strength in his mind to feel better.

Far away, beyond where they had ridden their horses, an owl hooted. Jürgen listened, smiling when the bird's call was answered by its mate.

"Thank you, God," he said, the call of the bird soothing his panic, the fear of burning to death over England the following week subsiding too.

A cool breeze came up from the direction of the owls and with it the smell of fresh-cut hay he had seen lying on the fields waiting for the pitchforks to turn it in the morning, the winter food for the cows almost ready to go in the barns. From that moment the looming war for Jürgen was far away.

The moon appeared above the hills, a half-moon giving light to the land, a pale light with long shadows, no colour to be seen. Slowly as the moon rose Jürgen could see the shape of the trees. To the far right a glint of moonlight on the water, a lake or pond, Jürgen did not know. Leaning with his elbows on the windowsill he pushed himself nearer the night outside, trying to better smell the hay. For a long while his mind stayed blank.

The owl call so close startled his mind, bringing back the panic and the fear. It hooted again. It was her! Summoning his strength, Jürgen made a sound that might have been an owl. The sound came back to him with barely a pause.

Closing the window to the night as softly as possible, his heart racing with a new form of panic, he went to the bedroom door and slowly turned the knob. The door came open, letting him smell the dust in the corridor. Like a thief, Jürgen stole back to his bed, pulling the sheets up under his chin. He waited. Now the moonlight was pouring into his room, letting him watch the door open and close, the girl in his room. Melina crossed to the window and carefully pulled the curtains. The springs made noises from under his back. A hand found his hand. Her body found his body. Thanking God for not dying a virgin, Jürgen Mann made love for the first time in his life, the rest of the world excluded from his mind. Then she kissed him softly on the lips and went. Not a word. Not a sound. Soon after Jürgen fell into a dreamless sleep, himself and the world at peace. She had opened the curtains and the sash window to let in the night.

In the morning there was blood on the sheets. Taking his pocket knife from the pocket of his trousers he had hung over the chair before going to bed, Jürgen cut himself over the stains on the sheet, making a trail of blood run up over his pillow to forestall any suspicions the maid might have.

Smiling, Jürgen bound up his arm with his handkerchief and dressed and went down to breakfast. He was a man in the true sense of the word, no longer afraid. If they shot him down in flames he would be remembering making love to the most beautiful woman in the world. At breakfast, only his eyes said thank you to Melina. It was enough. She had understood his fear. Then they went out riding through the fields of hay.

"What happened to your arm?" asked Erwin.

"I accidentally cut myself."

"Sleep all right?"

"Never better. And you, Erwin?"

"The moment my head hit the pillow. Roast lamb's my favourite."

They had taken their lunch and swimming costumes in the saddle bags hung over the rumps of the horses. The water Jürgen had seen glinting in the night was a small lake on the other side of the forest. Only half the von Lieberman estate was under cultivation. The old trees of the forest had been growing for centuries. Far away were the Alps and the safety of neutral Switzerland. Someone had said to Jürgen, Switzerland would be left out of the war, a safe haven for the money of the rich.

There were wild ducks on the water. The water was cold, fed by the Alps from far away, trickling down through the rocks and earth to the plains through the forest. Melina kept close to Erwin. Gabby was next to Hans Bengler. Ferdinand Engel, the second navigator, had a faraway gaze, not looking at the girls when they came back dressed in their bathing costumes. It was strange seeing a body for the first time he had held so close. They were all laughing, making little jokes. The sun was warm though a cool wind was blowing down to the lake from the Alps.

They swam first. Ferdinand, the clown, pretended he was drowning in the middle of the lake, having changed his faraway look. They all raced out to him knowing what was going to happen, leaving the girls behind close to shore. Erwin ducked his navigator for Ferdinand's trouble. They all laughed. Everyone splashed at everyone. The ducks got up off the water and landed further down the lake where the deer were watching them splashing, poised for flight. When the ducks came down on the water, the deer bounded away to the safety of the forest. Jürgen gave them a one-handed wave from the water. Then they all swam back together and ate their lunch wrapped in towels having found a place to sit out of the wind.

Both girls were very beautiful. No one spoke as they ate. The horses had gone off down the lake looking for better grass to eat, the saddles left with the saddle bags where they were eating their lunch out of tins that fitted inside the bags. The tins had had different pictures on their lids.

Jürgen's had a beautiful picture of an eagle in flight. Everything he tried to remember for later on, when they were up in the air waiting for the search lights to light up the cockpit bringing the shells up from the British guns, bringing the British night fighters to shoot him down. End his life so soon. Without her seeing he looked at her as much as possible, the better to remember her face. Once, Erwin caught him looking, making Jürgen turn red in the face. Erwin's look was not friendly, a flash of anger amid the peaceful picnic on the shore of the lake.

From then on, Jürgen did not look at her, or Gabby. Ferdinand was back staring into space. Soon after, once again dressed, they went to look for the horses. They rode back, Ferdinand trying his jokes. Erwin wasn't laughing. Could the man have read Jürgen's mind? The fear came back. Everyone he knew was frightened of Erwin. It was not the father he should have worried about in the middle of the night.

Never once had Jürgen seen Erwin with a woman. But that went for all of them. When they went out from base they all went together. Men out together in town. In the beer gardens. Drinking tall, earthen mugs of beer, their worst sin getting drunk, breaking into song. No one was allowed to look at the girls. They were men together. Comrades in arms. In a book by Cicero, Jürgen had read in the German translation from the Latin, the Roman Legions were the same. Men together. Some of the men of Rome did things to each other but never to girls. It made the bonds of soldiers closer. Made them fight better, according to Cicero.

Forcing himself not to look at Melina, Jürgen stared straight ahead from his horse. They might have been just as brave in battle for all Jürgen knew. He was glad not to be a Roman soldier. He was glad not to be a virgin. Erwin was never going to find out from him.

When they reached the house at the end of a long, slow ride through the lovely country, the tension with Erwin was gone. They were comrades. They were laughing again.

They all ate wild boar for supper in the dining room. There was wine on the table. They drank too much wine on the last night. Not once did he look at her. When Jürgen went to bed the sheets and pillowcase had been changed. The maid had said nothing. Jürgen fell asleep the moment his head touched the pillow.

In the morning, Jürgen gave the maid all the change he had in his pocket. Then he went down to breakfast for the last time. They were all in uniform. Ready to go when the taxi arrived to take them to the station and back to the war. Jürgen never knew whether the owl again called in the night. When he shook hands with Herr von Lieberman, Jürgen felt like Judas Iscariot. The betrayer. His suitcase was on the steps leading down to the driveway with the other baggage. Ready to go.

The taxi arrived. Erwin had preferred to order the taxi. The servants strapped the luggage to the back of the car. They had all shaken hands with the host up on the terrace. They all got in, Jürgen making sure he was the last. One last time he turned round and looked at her standing away up on the terrace. She smiled. A small wave. Jürgen smiled. Saluted her formally and got in the taxi. He could not see her from inside. Neither could Erwin, whose mother Jürgen had seen crying next to Melina when he made his salute. To stop themselves thinking, they were all laughing again as the taxi drove them away.

Melina had stood just back from her mother, to the right of her shoulder so her parents were unable to see the expression on her face. The look followed by the salute sent the same smile to Jürgen Mann in the taxi as the one she had sent to Tinus Oosthuizen in the dinghy at Romanshorn before Harry Brigandshaw flew off in his flying boat no wiser as to what had happened to her father. The look was quizzical, trying to sum up men and decide what to do with them in her life. Was she the sort to swap men like some women she heard of changed their clothes? Was she the family woman who wanted to be a mother? Sex had been a great disappointment, the man now driving away with her brother breaking through her virginity with one almighty thrust and not much else.

Melina smirked to herself at what must have happened to the sheets in Jürgen's room. Back in her room with the lights on there had been blood all down the inside of her right leg. What a mess. For her the excuse was easy. It was her time of the month. The cut arm at breakfast had almost made her burst out laughing. What had he done with the sheets? In her life the practical side dominated whatever she had in her mind.

She had seen Erwin's looks of hatred on the lake, giving her a surge of pleasure almost similar to the one she had had on the horse that made up her mind to seduce Jürgen Mann. Erwin was jealous of Jürgen. Melina knew she would like to see men fight over her, the more blood the better. Did her brother secretly want her body? She hoped so. A weapon that big would protect her life. She would always be able to extract from Erwin whatever she wanted. The idea swirled in her mind as the taxi drove slowly away down the drive, the man she had seduced looking back through the rear window, too far away to see her expression of puzzled indifference. Whatever the excitement was all about she now had no idea.

"What a nice young man," said her mother interrupting the speculation in her mind. "What a nice thing to do. He saluted me. I think that is just so nice."

"He had his cap on," said her father who, despite all his trying had failed to get a word from Erwin on their own.

The whole business was ridiculous. She knew Erwin had nothing to do with her father being taken to Berlin. Erwin had told her so in one of his letters. Why one of the servants, a member of the Party holding rank in the Nazi Party far higher than a servant, delivered his letters. The same man who had shopped her father, sick of his liking for the British. Harry Brigandshaw in particular. They had taken in her father to frighten him. To make him toe the Party line for what was to come. The Party, according to Erwin, were using her father's friendship with the Englishman to further their ends, 'whatever that meant' she had thought when she read the letter. Nothing was ever what it seemed. Like the salute she had just received and not her mother.

Happy her period had come that morning, why she had taken the chance the night before, Melina gave a vague wave to the face in the back of the taxi window. She was bored again. Nothing to do now her days at school were over in Switzerland, the government not wanting its young girls to leave the country now Germany was at war. All life was an experience. Melina just hoped the next experience would be better than the last. That the next man would slake her thirst for men, not leave her hanging in the air.

Thoroughly frustrated, Melina went to look for the dogs, hoping a walk in the forest would calm her down. She was no longer a virgin. That was something.

"Can I come with you?" asked Gabby.

"No, you can't."

Walking away she left her sister standing with her mouth open, making Melina feel guilty at her rudeness.

The hay was being turned to let the underside dry out in the sun making the field mice run for their lives from the talons of the hawks. Melina watched them. The hawks, with the benefit of telescopic eyes, swooped again and again out over the fields. She could not see whether their talons were clasping mice at that distance. A cock pheasant called stridently from the long, uncut grass at the side of the field where the scythes had been unable to reach.

The elderly field workers took no notice of Melina or the dogs, happy to be working in the sun, pitching the hay. The thought of having to put up with Gabby and her parents, day after day, kept niggling her mind. She was bored, no longer the subject of the airmen's attentions, their eyes searching her body hungrily at every opportunity, Melena making them believe she had no idea what they were thinking.

The years of boredom ahead seemed endless, ending in a loveless marriage to some besotted neighbour who for some reason wanted children to go through this same process all over again. There had to be some excitement. Sneaking out of her room in the dead of night had been exciting. The desperation of Jürgen Mann wanting her had been exhilarating. Maybe another time, when he knew better what to do, the act of making love would be more rousing, more fulfilling. She wanted to be satiated by a man, not left hanging. The only lifeline thrown in the two days had come from Erwin.

"You should go to Berlin, Melina. You can't sit at home for the rest of your life hoping some stranger will come along and cart you off to his castle. The Party needs secretaries, girls of good education to work in the office. You speak good enough French and English. Did that school of yours in Geneva teach you how to use a typewriter?"

"Of course not."

"There are secretarial colleges in Berlin. Cousin Henning will know how to get you in. He's great. Uncle Werner's son. Uncle Werner is powerful in the Party. He tells the other army generals what to do. Cousin Henning does something with the Party. Won't say what. You might like him. Quite a dash with the girls. Some girls like older men. Father shouldn't complain having to pay your college fees in Berlin now he doesn't have to pay the Swiss. Write to Cousin Henning. The man has a bit of a stutter but that can't be helped. Went to England in '37 to visit a therapist friend of Harry Brigandshaw's. They say the stutter was less pronounced when he came back. One of the chaps in the Party said it was just an excuse to visit London. Who knows? Everyone has something to say. The man should have been more careful. You don't ever tell anyone what was in my letters?"

"Of course not, Erwin. Mother just thinks Strauss eavesdrops her phone calls. She has no idea he delivers your letters. Why does he do it for you?"

"I got him into the Party. I needed someone to keep an eye on Papa in case he did something stupid. I look after him. If you shout your mouth off too much the Party can have you eliminated. Father is a good man. Just naïve. He thinks everyone is nice until they turn on him. I'll write down Cousin Henning's address."

"I think I remember him."

"You probably do. People look different when we are young. Be careful."

"Are you going to be all right, Erwin? I worry about you."

"Of course I am. I'm invincible. 'Go with the flow' is the latest phrase. When we win the war all this subterfuge won't be necessary. Berlin, Melina. You'll like Berlin. And the Party. You have the right attitude. What do you think of my uniform?"

"Very smart."

"I think so. You see, I do look after you all despite what Papa thinks. He's just so old-fashioned."

The dogs were barking at a hedgehog with its quills up making Melina break out of her thoughts to laugh at their frustration. One of the dogs had pricked his face on a quill and was wiping his nose with his paw. They could smell the food but not get at it through the quills.

"Berlin," she said looking up at the blue sky. "What a lovely name. If Cousin Henning is as easy as Jürgen Mann, I'll have him round my little finger in no time."

Feeling better now she had a good idea, Melina called the dogs to heel. She would walk back home and tell her father she wanted to go back to school, an idea she hoped he would be surprised and happy to hear.

"Men! They are so easy to manipulate," she said smiling as she strode away with the dogs.

Then she waved at the workers in the field.

5

While Melina was confronting her frustration, on the other side of the world, Justin Hemmings was confronting a similar situation. His girlfriend did not want to have sex. He had his hands on her tits and his trousers down but she would not let him go any further, crossing her legs under her skirt making the progress of foreplay impossible. As luck would have it, he had the house in South Yarra to himself and now the opportunity was going to waste.

"All right, Frieda. You can trust me."

"What you said before, Justin. Now look at me."

"You're a proper darling."

"I'm a virgin."

Afraid to admit his own predicament, Justin pulled on his trousers and pulled out his packet of cigarettes. At seventeen he wasn't meant to smoke, but with the parents and all four sisters away from Melbourne the opportunity for him to appear to Frieda a man of the world was not to be passed up.

"Want a fag, darling?"

"You don't smoke."

"Do now. Are you sure you don't want a fuck?"

"You're plain crude, Justin. Just look at me."

"That's why I'm asking. I wouldn't ask Patsy, now would I? She's fat and bloody ugly. They come back tomorrow."

"Thank God for that. You're a bloody animal, Justin Hemmings. When are you going up north? If my mother could see me now. I'd better go before Dad comes looking for me. He knows your dad's away. Skin you alive if he knew what we were doing."

"You think he'd come here?"

"Where else would we be? You don't have money. The pubs won't let us in, we're too young. I'm not at home. Doesn't take a genius to work that one out now does it?"

"Your dad's not a genius, that's a fact."

"Don't be rude or I'll slap your face. Let's have another glass of your mum's gin."

"Now you're talking."

"Just don't get no ideas."

"I said you can trust me."

"How old do you think I am?"

"Sixteen, darling. Sweet sixteen. I'm not going up north after all. I'm thinking of going to England. Trevor's got his wings. Bomber Command. Did you read the RAF bombed Berlin? I want to be a fighter pilot."

"You're too lazy to get on the boat let alone learn to fly. What would the RAF want you for?"

"R double-A F, darling. Royal Australian Air Force. They're looking for pilots."

"Said you were going to England."

"Whatever. I'll get the gin."

"Has Trevor been in combat?"

"We don't know. His letters are censored by the RAF. He sounds okay. Got a new motorbike. Second hand but new to Trevor. He fixes them."

"What's your dad going to do if you go?"

"Serve the cough drops himself."

"You're lucky I came in the shop for mum's cough drops. It's a job. Wish I had a job. Want to leave school. What's the point of school?"

"Don't ask me."

"Did you learn anything?"

"Not much."

"Then they won't let you in the RAAF. Heard you need maths to fly. You didn't get the change right in the shop. Your dad had to help."

"I'll go up north. You count sheep to get to sleep. As long as you sleep who cares if you get it wrong? Are you sure you don't want to have sex?"

"Quite sure, thank you. Quite bloody sure. I'll try a fag."

"That's my girl. Life's one big experiment."

"Put some orange squash in the gin."

His luck was Frieda of the cough drops lived down the bottom of Darling Street, pedalled up the hill on her bicycle. Her old man had a beer belly the size of a cow's udder so their chance of being disturbed was nil. The old man didn't own a bicycle, let alone a car, his transport the tram that went past the gate. Justin could hear the tram coming when it started up the hill, plenty of time to put their clothes on. The mother didn't care much what they did. Frieda's mother worked in the offices in Collins Street, over the chemist shop owned by Justin's father. Mrs Gooderson was the cleaning lady for the Australian head office of the South British Insurance company. How Frieda came to be in his dad's chemist shop buying cough drops for her mum. Keeping home and working all day, Mrs Gooderson was tired. She wouldn't come looking for Frieda.

There was only one good slug of gin left in the bottle when he looked in the kitchen. Justin tipped it in her glass. Drowned the gin with orange juice. Put plain orange juice in his own glass. Took the glasses back to his bedroom with a grin on his face. When she'd finished the gin he was going to try again.

"Cheers, darling," he said.

"Where's the fag?"

"Everything in good time. Now, where were we?"

"You were buggering off up north. Dad thinks the Japs are coming in the war. Where your family go?"

"Mum and Dad went on the train to Adelaide. Her youngest sister's getting married. Two of the girls went with them. You haven't met my sisters. They're wild. The other two are likely fucking their boyfriends right now. It's an Australian sport, sport, don't you know? How's it taste, Frieda?"

"Lovely. Better not get tight or I'll fall off my bike."

"All downhill going home."

"Why's your dad's shop in the city, Justin?"

"Couldn't find one closer, likely. How do I know? Wasn't born. People in offices have jobs. Like your mum. They buy from us in the lunch hours. What Dad says."

"Does he make any money?"

"Not much."

"If you got me pregnant I'll never forgive you."

"Neither will I."

"You do know what you're doing?"

"Of course I do. We've got the bloody house to ourselves."

"When are you going to take me out?"

"When I've got some bloody money, Frieda."

Half an hour later, lying on her back, Frieda had tears on her cheeks, her soft eyes looking up at Justin full of puppy love.

"That was lovely," she said. "Can we do it again?"

She was a natural. When the tram went by outside, metal wheels on metal rails, neither of them had heard a thing.

"You'd done it before, hadn't you?" said Justin.

"Course I had. I'm sixteen, Justin."

"Said you were a virgin. Why'd you stop me the first time?"

"I never fuck on the first date."

"But this is the first."

"I know. I've been pretending it's the second. Isn't it lucky we live so close? Uphill when I'm strong. Downhill when I'm weak."

"You really are a sport, Frieda."

"Do you love me?"

"Of course I do."

"Then do it again. Like you said, we've got the house to ourselves."

"What about your dad?"

"He's drunk in the boozer right now. Met my mum in the boozer. She was the barmaid. Young and pretty."

"Be a sport, Frieda? Don't ask me to marry you."

"I wouldn't marry you in a fit... Give it to me proper."

Soon after the third time Frieda got on her bicycle and went down the hill. Justin saw her off at the door. He thought she was being sensible not to spoil her chances with her father by staying any longer. Both of them had nothing to say to each other. Someone had put an envelope under the door. It was a cable addressed to his father. Justin put the envelope on the letter tray on the half-moon table in the hall unopened. For a while he had opened his father's letters in the morning to give him something to do. He was twelve. They were always giving him things to do. Some customers were given drugs without paying on the understanding they sent his dad the money when they were able. Some of them paid. Some of them sent their money to his father's home address. Usually friends. Once he had taken half the money as the letter didn't say how much money was in the envelope. Justin got a good thrashing when his father met his friend and found out how much was in the envelope. Ever since, Justin left the mail untouched. Going down the driveway to see if Frieda was really going home down the hill he could see her back, her feet off the pedals, as the bike careered down Darling Street.

"Too much gin in the orange squash. Women!"

He watched her down to the bottom, expecting a spill that did not happen. He took the mail from the letterbox on the pole by the gate and walked back through the small front garden. He had promised his father to mow the lawn on either side of the crazy paving path. Justin hated pushing the mower. The lawns were still uncut.

Back in the house he closed the front door with the back of his foot. The letters in his hand he put on the letter tray. The letter box had been full. He was hungry and made himself a cheese sandwich. The bread was stale. He was meant to get fresh bread for the next day when his parents were coming home. In the kitchen, he put some water in the empty gin bottle and put it back in the cupboard. Usually his mother did not drink. Feeling satisfied with himself he turned on the radio, found only news about the war in England and turned it off. Now, he had nothing to do. Getting bored, he went outside and walked up the hill to the top of Darling Street. There was a girl at the top who would not talk to him she was so shy. She always giggled when he grinned at her in the garden and ran inside the house. He was always more randy after sex. The next girl was always the most exciting. As usual he had no money and nothing to do. Had it not been for the chance with Frieda he would have gone to Adelaide.

When his family came back the next day Justin was pleased to see them. Making small talk with his sisters was better than doing nothing. Worrying about his mother's gin bottle half full of water, Justin had mowed the lawn and trimmed the edges. His father put a hand on his shoulder when he saw the cut lawn.

Half an hour later his mother looked through the letters on the letter tray. Underneath the pile she found the brown envelope someone had pushed under the front door.

"Brad, there's a telegram," she said in a small voice.

The two older sisters were still not back from staying with their friends. His mother had gone white in the face. His father took the brown envelope from his mother, slitting it open with his index finger. There was not a sound in the house. Everyone was holding their breath.

"It's all right," said his father looking from one to the other with a big grin on his face. "Trevor's been wounded in action."

"What does it say?"

"The Air Ministry regrets to inform you Trevor Hemmings has been wounded in action."

"How badly, Brad?"

"That's all."

"How do we find out!"

"We wait. He'll be out of the war now. Coming home. You'll see."

"I need a drink."

Justin went white.

"I drank the gin, Mum."

It took a whole month to find out how badly his brother was wounded. Then a letter came from a Group Captain Lowcock at RAF Abingdon, his brother's commanding officer. The letter had come by air in the diplomatic bag to Canberra where it was posted on to Melbourne. The letter was addressed in beautiful handwriting. Trevor's bomber had landed badly damaged. Trevor had landed the plane with a bullet through his leg. The rear gunner had been killed over Germany. The navigator and Trevor were the only two alive. The aircraft had burned on landing as the landing gear would not go down, the plane landing on its belly. There was no mention of the type of aircraft. Where the CO had mentioned the type of aircraft, the censors had erased the words. Trevor's face had been burnt badly. The ground crew had pulled Trevor and the navigator out of the burning plane when it landed on the runway at Abingdon. The CO said he was putting Trevor up for a Distinguished Flying Cross.

That night the whole family took a drink in celebration. They all assumed Trevor was out of the war. That he was coming home as soon as he got out of hospital. They still did not know how bad were the burns or the damage done by the bullet in Trevor's leg. They had gone to the pub down the road. Justin's father lied, saying Justin had turned eighteen. The two older sisters came with them. Frieda's father with the big pot belly was in the bar. Justin avoided having to talk to him. Everyone in the bar heard about his brother Trevor, making Justin's first visit to the pub a pain in his arse.

"I'm joining the RAAF," he told anyone who would listen.

6

On the other side of the Indian Ocean, close to where the Indian and Atlantic Oceans meet, Anthony Brigandshaw was sitting on Clifton Beach looking at the girls. He had finished writing his matric at the Diocesan College, better known as Bishops, and had nothing better to do with his day now the hard work was over, cramming night after night in his determination to obtain a good enough pass to get himself into Cape Town University where he wanted to study medicine. Groote Schuur was close to the university and the medical faculty. Anthony wished to become a surgeon.

Having worked on his tan every day for a week, his skin was a golden brown, his hair almost white, bleached by the sun. Playing beach bats on the sand had made him fit, running all over the place to hit the tennis ball with a wooden bat the same size but heavier than a ping-pong bat. Anthony was Third Beach champion, the subject of many looks from the girls he had been too busy to notice while still studying at school.

With the burden of guilt lifted from his shoulders, sitting around on the beach was a pleasure. The sun was hot, the cool breeze off the Atlantic welcome, the sea icy cold when he went every half hour for a dip to cool down from the burning African sun. Each time he came out of the water, Anthony covered himself in baby oil, the schoolboys' cheapest suntan lotion. On his nose and cheekbones he layered a white cream that was meant to stop the skin peeling. By the time Christmas came in two months' time, the sun would be too hot to sit in for long at lunchtime; for now it was bearable for Anthony right through the day with the help of his dips in the sea.

Some of the lads were out on the waves, surfing their long boards, making Anthony jealous of their seemingly easy skill. Both the beach bats and the surfing were new to Cape Town's beaches. Some of the girls had learnt to surf, mostly the same girls who hung around the life savers' hut on First Beach. Even though he thought of Tinus Oosthuizen, Anthony doubted anyone on the beach was thinking about the war. The worst of their worries were the sharks lurking out in the sea off the five beaches, demarcated by giant granite boulders that dominated the sweet curve of white sand in the bay, where the sea was blue, the ozone pure, and black-backed gulls noisily scavenged the high line of the tide.

Higher, much higher, marched the Twelve Apostles from the east side of Table Mountain. For Anthony it never mattered which way he looked. Out at the ocean, up at the mountains, wherever he looked in Cape Town it was always beautiful. His days were perfect but for two things that he missed: his father's company and the chance to fly John Woodall's Tiger Moth.

That morning, before leaving the house in Bishopscourt on his bicycle for Clifton Beach, his mother had made him his favourite sandwiches and a flask of tea with a plastic cup screwed to the top. Egg and mayonnaise sandwiches were his favourite. The big tin box was full of them. When the girl with the body dived into the waves, Anthony opened the box that he had strapped on the small carrier at the back of his bicycle, counted how many were left and ate another, the mayonnaise trickling down his chin. There were still enough to get him through the day.

Wiping the mayonnaise off his chin, Anthony licked his finger clean as the girl came out of the surf, walking straight towards him.

"They look good."

"Want one?"

"No thanks. You English?"

"How'd you know?"

"Accent. Pommy. Not South African. The water's freezing."

"Don't tell me."

Lying back on his towel, his eyes shut, Anthony Brigandshaw went off to sleep while the tropical sun burned his skin. The same girl woke him five minutes later.

"Did it once. For half an hour. Couldn't take a shower for three days the sunburn was so bad. What's your name?"

"Anthony Brigandshaw."

"Eleanor Botha."

"Afrikaans?"

"Mother's English. 1920 settlers."

"My dad's from Rhodesia. My grandfather went up before Rhodes hoisted the Union Jack."

"So you're also African."

"Sort of a split personality."

"Coming in the water?"

"Why not? Where'd you live?"

"Sea Point. In a flat on the waterfront. I prefer Clifton Beach."

"Who doesn't? Bishopscourt. Came on my bicycle."

"Walked from Sea Point along the coast road. Are you rich? Wow! Bishopscourt. That's money. What's your dad do?"

"Works for the Air Ministry in London at the moment. Sent the family to Cape Town to get us out the way. His grandfather was rich, left Dad his money."

"Wish I had such a grandfather. Mine farms sheep in the Karoo."

"My brother Dorian wants to farm Elephant Walk."

"What's Elephant Walk?"

"Our farm in Rhodesia."

"You do get around. Can you surf?"

"Not yet. Want a game of beach bats?"

"You're on. First a swim. The sun's burning hot today."

"Then you can have one of my mum's sandwiches."

It was another perfect day.

Beth was home when he got back which was surprising. With their father in England Beth did what she liked. His mother shouted at her every now and again which made it uncomfortable for everyone. After one screaming match Mr and Mrs Coetzee resigned. They had had the house to themselves for too long to put up with being ordered around by Anthony's mother. He thought the screaming match debacle was an excuse for the caretakers to demand and get six months' salary which wasn't going far after living on ten acres with six servants at their beck and call.

Anthony hoped they had found something suitable. Beth had said it wasn't her fault. His mother had stopped shouting at Beth, giving up when she ignored the curfew and stayed with her friends. Some nights she didn't come home. Beth was turning sixteen in January which wasn't far away. The boys liked Beth. All of them. It was better not to think of Beth when you were the older brother. Anthony doubted Beth would pass her matric when it came to her turn. She never studied at night. Never talked about schoolwork. Only boys. Her school was co-ed, her second school in South Africa after a classic yelling match with their mother. The first school had been a convent.

Frank was with him at Bishops. Dorian was coming next year when Anthony would not be able to help. Frank had his own gang at Bishops, already making money. It was similar to a protection racket. No more sophisticated. The priests at the school, most of them teachers rather than practising priests, could not believe what Frank and his fellow bullies were up to and turned a blind eye.

Most of the boys were day boys or weekly boarders going home for the weekends. Frank had demanded he be a full-time boarder which made no sense to Anthony, the house being so close to school. There were no shouting matches with Frank. Total silence was his weapon when he wanted his own way. Silence with menace. The whole house suffered. Frank became a full-time boarder so he could run his gang and make sure no one was cheating him out of money. It was all stupid to Anthony. If Frank needed more pocket money he only had to write to their father in London. For some reason Frank would not write.

Anthony had left him and his bully friends alone. He was too senior in the school to have anything to do with his younger brother. They did not like each other. No one said so. Anthony feared for Dorian when he went to the big school. He was going to be a day boy so Frank would have less chance to bully his younger brother. Kim had the right idea. Kim was ten years old. Kim sailed through life not noticing the rough and tumble, his head in the clouds. Kim said he was going to be a poet, or a vet, or he was going to the moon. Anthony had asked him once how he was going to the moon.

"On the front of a rocket, stupid."

The boy had given him such a nice smile, Anthony had not felt quite so stupid. Kim was good at maths. There were still many years for him to decide what to do.

Putting his bicycle in the wooden shed at the end of the garden, putting on the padlock to make sure Frank did not go off with the bike, a habit that wasn't necessary with Frank boarding at school, Anthony had gone to look for his mother in the flower garden. In the evenings his mother liked to walk round looking at the different flowers, so many of them she had not seen growing in the gardens of England. She missed their father. With five children and a house full of servants Anthony's mother was lonely.

"Did you meet anyone, darling?"

"I did as a matter of fact. I fell asleep on my back in the sun and a girl woke me up before I burned. We're meeting again tomorrow. I gave her one of my sandwiches."

"Supper is nearly ready. Just look at all these flowers. They're so beautiful."

"Why's Beth home so early?"

"Had a fight with her boyfriend."

"Which one?"

"Don't ask me. Let's go and walk round the garden together. I had a phone call from your father. Cut us off after three minutes. The bombing's got terrible. The docks. He's sleeping on the platform in the underground at night. Charing Cross tube station. The German bombs can't penetrate that far. I told him to come out to South Africa. Then they cut us off."

"If I pass my school certificate, I'm going up to the farm."

"Which farm?"

"Elephant Walk."

"You've never been there."

"Oh yes I have. I was born there."

"You were still in the pram when we went to England."

"What's for supper?"

"Kingklip."

"My favourite."

"Every food is your favourite, Anthony Brigandshaw. Are you going to bicycle to Rhodesia?"

"I thought I'd take the train. Two and a half days. See the countryside. See the rest of Africa. The train goes through the Bechuanaland. Real elephant country."

A month later, after spending every day on the beach with Eleanor Botha, Anthony arrived in Salisbury on the train. Ralph Madgwick met him at the station. Ralph was the manager of Elephant Walk, having run away with Rebecca Rosenzweig. Anthony's father had told Anthony the whole story.

"Jews marry Jews. Especially rich Jews. The Rosenzweigs have been bankers across Europe for two centuries. The Rothschilds and the Rosenzweigs. Sir Jacob now lives in New York where he can't use his title but can hold on to his money. The Germans confiscated the bank's assets in Germany. The bank started in Berlin, I think the story goes. Berlin, Paris and London. Now New York. A real love match, Rebecca and Ralph. His family lost most of their money in the '29 crash. When you get to Africa and find a chance, go up to the farm. You were born on the farm. They've three children Sir Jacob has never seen. I suggested to her father when I was in New York with Tinus that he should go to the farm for a holiday. Too many business problems. Once they leave the tribe of Israel they don't get asked back. Ralph does a good job. You'll like him. He's trying to complete the dam on the Mazoe River with a local contractor whose biggest construction so far is the strip road out of Salisbury. Five miles of tarred strips twice the width of a car's tyre. Now that's driving. Makes Tembo keep his eye on the road. If you let the car fall off the strip it gets exciting."

Ralph Madgwick was wearing a brown bush hat the size of a Stetson. A bush hat, shorts, khaki shirt, long socks and a grin on his face. He was tanned the colour of mahogany.

Ralph proposed they have lunch in the dining room of Meikles Hotel.

"We all have lunch at the Meikles. Farming tradition. Get to know what the other chaps are up to. Very colonial I'm afraid. Punkahs on the ceiling. The old Zulu on the door has been there longer than anyone remembers. Your grandmother would have come to the station, Anthony, but Tembo drove her off the strip nearly into the ditch so she stays at home now. Your Aunt Madge has her hands full. They call me the manager and pay me a manager's bonus but Madge is the real boss. Not really, I suppose. When it comes to the labour force, Tembo rules the roost. Princess rules Tembo. Bit of a circle really. Works well enough, which is all that matters. We live in our compound. The blacks live in theirs on the river. They like it that way. If I want to go into the black compound I have to ask Tembo. We all keep our privacy. I hope you don't mind roast beef in ninety degree temperature. It's Thursday. Roast beef and Yorkshire pudding. Welcome to Rhodesia, Anthony. They'll all want to meet you. Brigandshaws are a bit of a legend in these parts. Your grandfather and old Tinus Oosthuizen hunted elephant under Lobengula. Had to go to Bulawayo every trip up from the south and ask the Matabele King's permission to hunt elephant. With the money they gave him for the hunting concession the wily old bugger bought guns to keep himself at the top of the pile, so to speak. Robbed and raped the Shona for decades. The Shona are the main tribe in Rhodesia. Came up from Zululand did Lobengula's father. Africa is always changing. Tribes moving in on each other. So much space and so few people so it doesn't matter, provided you don't get in the way. Here we are, Meikles. Sort of a club, really. In the rains when it's bad and the rivers come up between here and Elephant Walk I spend the night in the hotel. Two or three nights sometimes, if the rivers don't go down. Pussy cat streams turn into raging torrents. You'll see. The main rains are about due. How long are you staying with us?"

"I begin medical school in February."

"Plenty of time. Your grandmother will love having you for Christmas."

They drank beer in the lounge, the punkahs going round and round over their heads, moving the limp air, cooling the sweat running down inside Anthony's open shirt. There were only Europeans sitting at the round tables, African waiters with round trays and red fez hats serving them. All the women seemed to be dressed in print frocks, the men in khaki shirts and shorts like Ralph Madgwick. Ralph seemed to know everyone. People came to their table for the odd word or two before going back to their drinks and wives. There were no young girls of Anthony's age. Tinus had said something about the lack of girls when he came back to England and joined the RAF.

"The pretty ones get snapped up quickly, Ant. If you want a varied love life don't go live in Rhodesia. Girls from England from good homes with no money go out to find husbands. Pretty ones are married in six weeks, pregnant in seven and never go home again. Live in the middle of nowhere like your grandmother for the rest of their lives. Some like it. Most don't. Suburban girls from Epsom used to typing in offices and chatting all day. Can't speak a word of Shona. Staff can't speak a word of English. Husband in the lands all day. They have lots of children. Not much else to get up to, the next farm an hour away over a terrible dirt road. Most of them take to drinking by the time they're thirty. Sundowners. Oh well, better than a thirty-year mortgage on a semi-detached if they were lucky, or a dried-up old spinster more likely. After the war there were too few men in England, the ones they might have met and married buried in France. So they go to the colonies to find a life, dreaming of a great country estate, not a thatched bungalow in the back of beyond."

"I thought you liked living in Rhodesia, Ralph?"

"Of course I do. It's a great life if you like a farm, one wife and six children. And a liking for whisky and soda. Life's never boring in Rhodesia. You make of life what you want. Hunting trips in the bush and up the rivers. Carving a bit of civilisation out of the bush. Sometimes I think the blacks look at us as nuts. 'What are they doing here?' Every black man I've known with a missionary education has gone to Salisbury or better still Johannesburg. To get out of the bush. Some of the smart ones like Tembo dream about a second chimurenga."

"What's a chimurenga?"

"War of liberation."

"Doesn't Tembo like working for us?"

"All men like to rule. You'll see. Of course he likes working for us. He'd just prefer to be the local chief with the real prestige and power that goes with it. Who likes to be told what to do by foreigners? Especially when the foreigner knows what he's doing and makes everyone money."

"Then he's jealous."

"Not Tembo. He just wants to be the king. Why I like him so much. A proud man."

"All sounds too complicated."

To Anthony, looking round the big room with the high ceiling and sash windows along the courtyard side from the floor to the roof and remembering his conversation with Cousin Tinus, the women in their summer frocks looked happy. Most of them were laughing and smiling. One woman was having trouble with her brood of children.

Two tables away a young man was holding the hand of a young girl. Neither of them were talking. The man wore a blue uniform with a single thick ring of a flying officer at the bottom of the sleeves. On the shoulder, at the top of the uniform arm, was the word *Rhodesia* in a slight curve. Anthony guessed the man was on his way overseas, the girl seeing him off. She was not what Tinus would have called pretty. The look she was giving her man forgave any outward appearance. Anthony could see the look of love in her eyes, eyes on the brink of tears, already pining her loss. On the man's chest, white and new, shone the wings of a recently commissioned pilot. The girl's look and the man's stoicism made Anthony feel guilty he was not taking the same journey. Then the two of them got up, still holding hands, neither prepared to let go. They turned round their table in the direction of the hotel dining room at the end of the long room opposite the hotel's entrance, the man's eyes catching Anthony looking at him. In the girl's eyes he had seen love. In the man's was stark fear. The man was only physically in the room, his mind already fighting the distant battle. Without thinking, Anthony gave the man a salute, making the man in the Royal Rhodesian Air Force uniform smile. They both smiled at each other while the pair went off to lunch, Ralph Madgwick following the interchange.

Both Ralph and Anthony were silent, thinking the same thoughts.

"Is the Handley-Page still in the hangar?" asked Anthony.

"Better ask Tembo. He was the last to fly in the plane with Tinus Oosthuizen. The tyres will be flat. I take it you fly? That chap was scared."

"So would I be."

"Is Tinus all right?"

"I hope so. I'll have a look at the Handley-Page."

"You're wise to keep out of the RAF."

"You never know. February is a long way away."

"Are you hungry?"

"I'm always hungry. Mum says I have worms."

"The RAF has a flying training school at Gwelo. Some of the chaps training there want to come back to Rhodesia after the war. It's a bit hot right now but generally the highveld climate is perfect. When the rains finally break it will cool down."

"That was thunder outside."

"Better have lunch and go back to the farm. Don't want to be caught between two rivers. Rebecca still worries about me. Took to Africa like a duck to water. Misses her father. Had her mother out. What a disaster. Mrs Rosenzweig and Mrs Brigandshaw both trying to rule the roost at the same time. We were married on the farm. Did I tell you that? Becky ran off from her father's apartment in New York to find me in England. I'd gone to Rhodesia, so she followed. Apart from my odd forced night in this hotel we have never been parted. The cynics say you can't love someone all your life. We have. Hope you have the same luck. Come on. I'm starving."

"Why don't they serve cold roast beef?"

"Don't be silly. Cold Yorkshire pudding is soggy and horrible. The kids are looking forward to meeting you. Be prepared for a million questions."

The only English thing missing with the lunch was a foot of snow on the ground outside the dining room window. The dining room was full. They ate the food and went home. When they left the man and his girl were still holding hands across their table. They both only had eyes for each other.

"Came in the truck. Hope you don't mind. Transport is expensive to Elephant Walk so I always fill the back of the truck up when I come into Salisbury. Despite the lunch we all hate coming into town. Once you've found your own peace and quiet you don't need people. Let's go. I have a surprise for you. For you and your father. Isn't he worried about the Blitz? Every night they are saying on the radio London docks are burning, every night. How do people live? Get used to it? Go about their ordinary lives?"

"Dad sleeps on the platform of Charing Cross tube station. Some sleep in between the rails. They turn the electricity off on the rails at night. The Germans only bomb at night. When you've been through what dad's been through in his life, what's a few German bombs? The night fighters don't do any good. Why the Germans have switched to coming over at night. When they tried hitting Fighter Command's airfields and radar stations during the day they were massacred. The Messerschmitt is no match for a Spitfire or a Hurricane in a dogfight. Some say it was Churchill bombing Berlin that changed Hitler's mind. The *Cape Times* thinks the Luftwaffe were losing too many pilots they couldn't afford. Some in the South African papers are saying the peak of the Battle of Britain is over. That Germany will not gain air supremacy over England. That trying to land the German Army on British soil will be impossible. London can take it. They'll have to if we want to win the war. The Royal Navy hasn't been touched. Why we were able to evacuate the British Army from Dunkirk. The Royal Air Force, the Royal Navy and every small boat that would float. A friend of Dad's went down in a small boat on his fourteenth trip. He'd spent Christmas with us. Flew with us to Romanshorn before the war. Phillip Crookshank was the only one on board the Seagull when it took a direct hit from a German dive-bomber. Dad wrote to me when he found out. The family are still on the Isle of Wight. A wife and two small boys. I don't know what I'd do if anything happened to Dad. His wife's name is Mavis. Frank had a fist fight with the eldest boy when they spent last Christmas with us at Hastings Court. It doesn't seem possible to me that Mr Crookshank is dead. He was so alive at Christmas."

"I'm sorry, Anthony. Even out here the war gets real and close. I was eighteen when the last war ended. Lost my small finger."

"I'm seventeen. By the look of it this one has just started. It's wrong being able to fly an aeroplane. I'll be eighteen in May. What the hell am I going to do? Did you see the look in that chap's eyes?"

"Just don't talk about it in front of your grandmother. Her son George was killed in the last war. What triggered your father to go to England in 1915 and join the Royal Flying Corps. Revenge. Keep the war out of it. Aunty Madge expects a cable every moment of the day. We may be six thousand miles away but the war sits right with us on Elephant Walk. My wife's Jewish. Just about her whole race has been rounded up in occupied Europe. Stories filter through the Jews are being systematically slaughtered. What makes people do things like that?"

"I'll avoid the war, Mr Madgwick."

"Call me Ralph, we're not so formal in Rhodesia."

For half an hour they were silent, thinking their own deep thoughts. Anthony had never known his Uncle George. There was no point in worrying about his father or Tinus. But, always, they were in his thoughts.

"There it is. What do you think of that, Anthony?"

"What's all the water?"

"The Mazoe dam."

"It's the size of a big lake."

"Will be after the rains. Why we had to build a high road to go round the water. Using a road contractor to finish the dam wasn't so stupid after all. Good old Rhodesian ingenuity. We can do anything in this country when we put our minds to it."

"It's beautiful. You could sail a boat on all that water. In the middle of Africa!"

"That's just the Mazoe. They have plans to dam the Zambezi and put a lake across Rhodesia almost to the Victoria Falls. Hydroelectric power. Irrigation. You'll be able to put an ocean liner on a lake that big. Biggest man-made lake in the world. All we need is time and money to bring southern Africa into the modern world."

"Do they want to?"

"Who, Anthony?"

"The blacks. I wouldn't want to change this. Water, yes, so you don't suffer droughts. The rest wouldn't be for me. Have you asked them?"

"I don't think so."

"Maybe you should. One man's idea of paradise isn't necessarily another's. This to me looks like paradise just as it is, wild animals, birds in the blue sky, very few people. Now that's paradise."

"You're wise before your time, Anthony Brigandshaw."

"And I haven't yet seen Elephant Walk with eyes that can remember. Babies don't remember anything. Can you imagine what Rhodesia must have been like when my grandfather first rode his horse through this country? Paradise on earth. Dorian's going to enjoy his life on the farm."

On the top of the hill Ralph stopped the truck.

"There it is down in the valley. When your grandfather first saw this view, so the story goes, it was during the great elephant migration up Africa. Legend has it the elephant migrate twice a century. Down there, head to tail, the trunks of the baby elephants holding on to their mother's tails, mile after mile of moving grey elephant. They were all walking slowly through the valley. Why your grandfather called his house Elephant Walk."

"Someone should write about it. Have the elephant been back again?"

"Not yet."

"You say the whole valley down there was full of walking elephant?"

"So the legend says. Come on. That was thunder again. Are you ready to meet your family?"

"Thank you for bringing me home in this way, Ralph."

Far away to the northeast the storm clouds were black. As Anthony stood for another moment outside the truck on a rock looking at where he came from the thunder rumbled. To his untrained ear the sound was going away, the storm abating. His mind marvelled. His father and one of his antecedents had ridden over this country. Hunting. Sometimes alone. He a part of them unknown. He felt the call of the bush, the distant thunder a sound of comfort rather than fear. Rain was coming. The rain that nurtured the bush and fed the animals. Anthony's mind ran off as he smiled at how much he had to discover away from the tarred roads and brick walls of England. Where people did not drop high explosives on their cousins. Where a small boy did not punch another small boy he had never before seen in his life.

"It's so wild," he said in awe.

"The thunder is moving away."

"I thought so. Does it get in your blood, Ralph?"

"Oh yes."

"Can it be born in your blood?"

"Tembo says it can. Why underneath his acquiescence he hates us whites for taking his land. Not a specific piece of land. His land with everything in it. He told me once. All the birds and trees. The animals. His land. His land where he came from. They don't think of ownership like we do. The tribe and the ancestors own the land. We English are so material. Buy and sell what we own. They never realised we wanted to own the land. Put a fence round our farm, own it like a cow. They don't see how anyone can own land that has existed from eternity. We humans come and go so how can we own something when we are dead? Land, like the air we breathe, belongs to everyone. Can never be bought or sold."

"What are you trying to say?"

"There'll be trouble in the end."

"There always is. Look at London. I'm only seventeen and I see trouble all round me. We are trouble. My teacher said at school every species becomes extinct in the end so your man is right. Why don't people enjoy the land? Not fight over it. Isn't what we produce from the land the only true value?"

"The wisdom of youth. Happy wisdom."

"You're going to plant orange trees all over the valley?"

"Every piece of ground that will succour a tree. Water will be sucked out of the dam through pipes. The valley will be rich."

"What happens when the elephants want to go for a walk, all of them together? They'll make a mess of your trees."

"We'll make them walk somewhere else."

"I suppose we will. Poor elephants."

"Progress."

"For whom? The elephants? I just look out there now and don't want to change a thing."

"We all like our comforts. It gets rough out there when Mother Nature doesn't give us rain. Can't have what rain we do get for a few months of the year going off down the rivers to the Zambezi River which, far away, runs our water out into the sea. Wasted. No good to man or beast. There will be big parks for the elephant with water all year round. They won't have to trek when it's all there for them. Every time in my life I answer a big question I find another answer the next day. Often they contradict each other."

"It's all so beautiful."

"I think what you see down there is why people believe in God."

They both got in the truck.

"I hope that chap comes back and marries his girl," said Anthony.

"So do I. There is nothing more beautiful in life than marrying the girl you love and living with her for the rest of your life. Now let's get to the farm down there before I turn myself into a sentimental idiot."

Anthony was smiling, looking straight ahead. Instinctively he knew he was going to like Mrs Madgwick. The heavily loaded truck began the slow grind down the winding road towards the valley. Far to the left, buffalo were grazing next to a herd of buck.

"What are those buck?" Anthony said pointing.

"Impala. They are slightly bigger than springbok."

The sun found a gap in the black clouds making Ralph pull down the front of the bush hat shading his eyes, the rays of light brilliant from a patch of blue sky that looked through to heaven.

PART FIVE

THE CYCLE OF REVENGE – SEPTEMBER TO
DECEMBER 1941

1

When Anthony Brigandshaw, accompanied by his friend Felix Lombard, climbed up into the American-built Dakota in Gwelo to be flown to Cape Town he was wearing the uniform of a pilot officer in the Royal Air Force, the new wings on his chest as white as snow. No one from the family saw him off. For months, Anthony had fought with his conscience before throwing away his career in medicine. The argument had gone back and forth on Elephant Walk until after Christmas.

"To be called a coward, Grandmother? You want them to call me a coward? How am I going to feel in the years to come? I would never be able to look my father or Tinus in the face, let alone myself in the mirror. I'm a good pilot. Getting through flying training will be a cakewalk. There are men ten years my senior fighting in the RAF right now with less hours than mine. I spent days at Redhill picking Mr Woodall's brains on how to fly in combat. I would never be able to face myself. Britain is not going to be defeated. Now the war goes to the Germans whether the Americans help or not. The Italians have been defeated in Libya forcing Hitler to send Rommel's Afrika Korps to save North Africa for the Axis."

"You'll get yourself killed like George. He was your age. You all think war is a game."

"It's not a game, Grandma. Men have been fighting in wars right down the centuries."

"Have you spoken to your mother?"

"She wouldn't understand."

"Your father?"

"I'll tell Dad after I join up."

The talk for weeks in the flying school had been the war in Europe. The pending invasion by Germany of England. The Blitz. The Americans still sitting on the fence. Now, looking out the window as the aircraft took to the air, Anthony sighed with relief. Whatever the outcome he had made the decision.

When the aircraft landed at Cape Town, Anthony had still not made up his mind what to do about his mother.

"Better go and see her, Ant. It's not the end of the world."

"It is for Mother. I'm her eldest son. If the war goes on long enough they'll take her precious Frank. Come with me, Felix. You'll love Beth. She'll love you in that uniform. The boat only sails on Friday. Three whole days to enjoy ourselves."

"You can see Eleanor. Have a party. You never know what they'll do for a young lad going to war."

"If you even try with Beth!"

"I haven't met her. She's probably ugly."

"She likes men. You can stay at Bishopscourt. Just behave yourself. Why the hell they couldn't fly us up Africa to England I have no idea."

"The Germans, Ant. They control the air space in the Med and most of North Africa."

"We'll find a taxi and surprise them."

The ride across Cape Town from the South African Air Force base took them half an hour. Most of their luggage had been sent to the boat by train two weeks earlier. They had a change of civilian clothes in their small suitcases, all they were allowed to put on the Dakota. It was spring in the Cape. The flowers were out along the side of the road. Seeing the sea again made Anthony smile. There was a bathing costume in his case. He would borrow a towel. He would give her a call. Suggest a game of beach bats on the beach in the sun, a twinge of regret and fear surging into his consciousness, a fear he was determined never to show anyone. Appearances were everything.

All through his life Anthony had done what people expected of him. Had done what they wanted him to do with a smile on his face, despite what he felt inside. Always trying to think of the other person to make them happy. Anthony hated scenes. There was going to be a scene at the house in Bishopscourt. He had thought his mother would be proud of him when he called from Elephant Walk to say he was joining up. Going to flying training school in Rhodesia and not coming home. Straight away she had flown off the handle.

"You're a damn fool. What's the point in all that education if you go and get yourself killed? Your father sent us to Africa to keep us out of harm's way. What about your place at UCT? They don't take every Tom, Dick and Harry to become doctors. You're being a fool, Anthony. You don't have to go. Medical training is more important than flying a warplane. They will never call you up into the army from medical school, why I encouraged you so much. You go to this place in Gwelo and you throw away your chances of ever becoming a surgeon. You'll end up like the rest of them, going through life aimlessly."

"It's what's expected of me."

"I expect you to become a doctor, Anthony Brigandshaw. If you go to that damn flying school instead of coming home next week and taking your hard-won place at university, I'll never talk to you again."

"You don't mean that, Mother."

"Oh yes I do. You will never grace my home again."

"You're just upset."

"Damn right I'm upset! Bringing up children isn't easy. Forget about the servants. Pointing you in the right direction was my biggest job. Now you want to throw it all away."

"They'd think me a coward."

"I don't care what they think of you. It's what I think that counts. Have you told your father?"

"Not yet. I'm going to write him from flying training."

"He hates war. Any man who has been through a war says it's crass stupidity. In the end proving nothing for either side. He'll be disappointed in you."

"I hope not. Are you disappointed in me, Mother?"

"Damn right I am. Call me back when you come to your senses."

For the first time in his life Anthony had heard his mother slam down the phone on him.

When the taxi pulled up at the house it was half past six at night. The gardeners were still tending the front garden. They lived on the premises. One of them was cutting the new spring grass with a motor mower. None of the gardeners recognised Anthony in his uniform. Being away nearly a year must have changed him as well.

"Hello, Dickson. Aren't you all working a bit late? Where's the family? Can you hear me over the mower?"

No one took any notice.

"They know what my mother thinks of me joining up, Felix. Never cross Mother is the name of the game in this house. Anyone crossing Mother gets the boot."

"Lovely house. Didn't know your family were rich."

"You should have seen Hastings Court before the war. Before all the servants walked out. Good. There's Beth. Now tell me, is she ugly?"

"Oh, I'm in heaven. She's beautiful. How old is she?"

"Going on seventeen."

Beth was smiling at her brother.

"Why didn't you tell Mother you were coming? You look nice in uniform."

"This is Felix."

"Hello, Felix."

"Where's Mother?"

"In the garden at the back where she usually is at this time of night. How long are you staying?"

"The boat sails Friday."

"I heard the taxi. Come on then. Put your head in the lion's mouth."

"Is she still that mad at me?"

"She doesn't even mention your name."

Frank came out of the house and shook Anthony's hand while Beth took a good look at Felix in his uniform with the snow-white wings on his breast. When Felix looked at her, he blushed which made Beth smile. Anthony saw she was quite in control of the situation. Beth was always in control.

"Grandma sends her love to you all."

"Does she? I only met Grandma once when she came to England with her father to bury him. That was weird."

"She's still our grandmother."

"I suppose so."

"How are you, Frank? How's the gang at school?"

"My gang's fine. Like the uniform. Now you really are the big brother."

"Is Mother going to bite off my head?"

"Better ask her. Saw you through the window. Called out you were home."

"She hasn't come running. I'm in trouble."

"Frank, why don't we take Felix for a walk round this side of the garden? You're on your own, Anthony. Smart uniform. Suits you. All the girls are going to go crazy. How's Eleanor?"

"I was going to give her a ring."

"I think you'd better. Someone has to send you off properly. I'm sure Felix knows what I'm talking about. Now, Felix, tell me how long you have known my brother."

Pleased that Frank had shaken his hand, Anthony walked into the house to look for his mother. There was no sign of Dorian or Kim. Only after sniffing him did the dogs wag their tails. One of the cats looked at him from the sofa without blinking, a long cat stare of complete indifference. Anthony wondered if the cat had the slightest memory of him bringing her up from a kitten. Probably. The cat had always been aloof once it had grown up.

"Don't stare, Ginger. It's rude."

Again the cat did not blink. He could see his mother in the garden through the window, the mountain behind. There was a white tablecloth of cloud on Table Mountain, spilling over down the slope towards the house. A southeaster would be blowing from the far side of Table Bay. His mother was bent over a flowerbed wearing her gardening gloves. It was going to be a row that neither of them could avoid. He was an airman of the king whether she liked it or not. Bracing himself, he went through the French windows into the garden.

"Hello, Mother. I was going to ring. Felix is here. Beth is showing him round the garden. How are you?" His mother had never heard of Felix. Anthony hoped Felix's presence would help.

Only then did his mother stand up slowly and look at him. When she saw he was in uniform she began to cry silently. It was far worse than a row. A row he could have taken as his medicine.

"When are you going?"

"On Friday. Three whole days."

"Who's Felix?"

"Chap on flying training with me. They send them out from England to Gwelo to teach them to fly. Safer I suppose. Jerry can't get at them when they are still learning. I'm sorry."

"Are you flying to England? Your father will be pleased to see you. He's lonely in London on his own."

"By ship in a convoy. The South African Navy are supplying the escort. We'll be all right."

"Do you go straight to your unit?"

"Yes."

"What are you going to fly?"

"Bombers. My reflex actions weren't good enough for fighters according to the instructor. Have you heard from Dad?"

"He also thinks you're an idiot. But underneath he's proud of you. Why are you in uniform?"

"Came right off the plane from the air force station. The taxi is still waiting if you want me to go. I'm not going to argue about this one. There's nothing to argue about. I'm sorry."

"We're all sorry when it's too late. You're thin."

"I've grown. I'm still growing. Some chaps grow up to the age of twenty. Where's Dorian? He'll love Elephant Walk."

"They went down to the beach on their bicycles. I told them no later than seven o'clock."

"Have you given away my bicycle?"

"It's in the shed. Everything else is in your room. You were only going for a few weeks."

"I got delayed."

"Give me a hug. You're quite handsome."

"Can't I have a kiss?"

"If you get yourself killed I'll never forgive you."

Then his mother was howling, sobbing on his new tunic, the floodgate of her tears fully open. Not knowing what to do, Anthony patted his mother's back.

When she was finished she pushed him away and looked up at him.

"That's better. Should have done that long ago. You'd better introduce me to this Felix. Are you hungry? There's roast beef for supper."

"I don't believe it."

"When did you last hear from your father?"

"They wouldn't let us take or make calls during the course. Dad couldn't have got to my passing out parade anyway. They worked us night and day. We spent more time at our desks being taught the theory than up in the air. Then they had to teach you to behave like a proper British officer. Which knife and fork to use in the officers' mess. You just wouldn't believe it. Even the ranks in the Chinese air force for some reason. They think the Japs are coming into the war. This Chiang Kai-shek chap is important to them. One of the instructors was stationed in Singapore before the war. Did you know the Chinese have been fighting off the Japanese since 1937? They'll never try attacking Singapore. The island is one big fortress."

"When did you last write to your father?"

"I think of him in London every day. Letters take weeks to get to England. By the time I wrote him a letter and explained the rules and received a reply I'd be over in England drinking a beer together. He always took Tinus to the Running Horses. Now I'm eighteen we can go together."

"They've bombed Hastings Court."

"What?"

"An ARP warden saw the attack. One German bomber. The RAF had scattered the daylight raid. The bombers couldn't get through to London. This one had turned round to go back. Dropped his bombs on our house to lighten his load. A deliberate bombing run, according to the warden's report."

"Is Dad all right?"

"He was in London. One of the bombs hit the old clock tower. High explosive and no fire. If it had been an incendiary bomb your father says the Court would have been burned to the ground. Another hit the stables killing the horses."

"Patterson? He lives over the stables."

"The groom had been called up at Easter. The dogs are all right. The warden said the German pilot was more interested in unloading his bombs than hitting anything. His fighter escort was in a dogfight. He was trying to get out. No one was killed. In all the centuries when the Court was a small castle able to defend itself before they built the manor house, the Mandervilles had never before been attacked by foreigners. Your father says he can't do anything about the damage until after the war. There are streets in London bombed out. Every day it goes on. Why doesn't he come here? It's all a nightmare."

"That's why someone has to fight. At least he didn't drop his bomb load on built-up London. Felix, old chap, come and meet my mother. Mother, this is Felix Lombard. He's a Londoner, aren't you, Felix? The bloody Krauts have bombed my great-grandfather's ancestral home. Where Grandmother grew up. Where I grew up. Killed all the horses. I never thought of the animals getting hurt until now."

Anthony watched his friend shake hands with his mother. Now he was annoyed. Now the war was personal. Now he knew for certain he had made the right decision. Like his father when they killed Uncle George, he wanted his revenge.

"Now I hate the bastards," he said to Felix.

"Yes, I suppose you do. As we bomb the Germans they'll hate us. My father says everything in life is tit for tat. Now you can go and drop bombs on Germany. Beth says she'll bunk school tomorrow and go to the beach with us."

"Oh no she won't, Mr Lombard. Where are the boys, Beth?"

"Battling the wind back from Hout Bay I expect. I told them it was too far to cycle with a southeaster blowing. If the wind's dropped tomorrow can I go after school?"

"If your brother flies an aeroplane I'm sure by now he can drive a car. You can take the car, all of you... There they are. Did you two get to the beach? Don't you recognise your older brother?"

Whooping, Anthony's two youngest brothers came at him in a rush, running straight into his arms.

"Felix, meet Dorian and Kim. Now you've met the whole family."

"Not yet; your father."

"Oh, you'll meet Dad. Everyone meets Dad. They only knocked down the clock tower and the stables. You'll come and stay at Hastings Court when they give us a spot of leave. There's still a skeleton staff. Do you like roast beef? We're having it for supper. Mum, are there any beers in the fridge? The first thing I'm going to do is change out of this uniform. Can Felix stay with us until we get the boat? We kind of took some leave hoping."

"The spare room is always ready. You both go and change while I get out of my gardening clothes. Before you drink beer I want you to book a call to your father. Probably come through tomorrow."

"I can book the call," said Frank.

"What's come over you all of a sudden?" asked his mother.

"Thanks, Frank," said Anthony. "I'll show Felix the spare room. It's just so good to be home."

2

The air-raid warning went off at half past six, the second that day, at the same time Frank was telling his brother the call was booked for eleven o'clock the next morning. Harry Brigandshaw had looked up at the clock on his office wall as the siren wailed.

He had a good ten minutes to get down to Charing Cross. What with all the interruptions, the papers in the tin tray on his right were piled high. Carrying on until he heard the crump of falling bombs, he picked up his bowler hat and rolled umbrella off the wooden stand where they both hung and moved to the door. At the first sound of the siren everyone in the office had complied with Standing Orders and gone down to the shelters. Only Harry preferred the tube station with the ordinary people who kept his spirits alive. Two daylight raids in one day and the best of the night to come, he thought philosophically. Harry considered himself too old to worry about being killed. Most of his life was fulfilled he told himself every time the air-raid warning sent him to a shelter.

Downstairs in the street Harry walked along Whitehall in the direction of Charing Cross. He could hear the sound of machine gun fire. There were ack-ack bursts over behind Buckingham Palace from a battery in the Royal grounds. The machine gun fire came from the Browning guns in the Spitfires attacking the German bombers. He could see vapour trails. The sky to the south was full of the sound of aircraft engines. Heinkel HE IIIs and Spitfire Mk Vs. Harry could tell every aircraft in the sky by the sound of the engine, the sound of the guns.

The bombs were dropping nearer as the sun went down. He could feel the explosions coming up from the pavement through his feet. The wind brought the smell of the explosions, a mixed smell of dust and old age as London shuddered, the old buildings coming apart. Determined not to run, the sphincter in his backside tightened as he forced down on his nerves. The streets were emptying fast. Only when he went down the stairs into the tube station did Harry's arsehole begin to relax, the walls now giving him protection from a blast on either side. Then he was underground.

The lights were dim, the power off on the railway lines when he found his place under the advertisement for Wrigley's chewing gum. His bedroll was still where he had left it. The first time had been a year ago. Propping his umbrella against the curved wall of the tube station, Harry took off his bowler hat and waited for his eyes to get used to the light. After the last of the sun his eyes took time to grow accustomed so he could recognise other shelterers. To Harry it smelt like half the people were smoking to calm their nerves. The explosion from above produced a soft whimper followed by a strained silence. Later they would all start talking. It took time to grow used to the violent change in their lives.

When the pupils in his eyes were big enough to see, Harry looked around for his friends. There was nothing else to do but talk to each other or go to sleep. It was too dark to read a book. No one had even tried a radio. There was only war news on it. All of them knew what was going on without having to be told. Everyone had their own smell. Stale perfume. Dirty bodies. One had bad breath, the same bad breath night after night. There wasn't a bathroom. They were lucky to still have flushing toilets. Six months before, the Germans had smashed the water pipes into that part of London making the tube station stink from the toilets for a week until the water came on again and flushed them clean.

Harry was tired and hungry. Most of all he needed a drink. A big, long drink. As usual, he sat down on his bedroll and took his mind away to sundowners on Elephant Walk with the crickets singing in the long grass. Sometimes in his half dream he found Lucinda St Clair, his first wife, shot dead on Salisbury Station. Harry thought it was sitting on a railway station that brought her back to him. Not to be disloyal, Harry made himself conjure a picture of Tina in the house in Cape Town. The effort, in the semi-dark, did not always work. His eyes were closed and his shoulders drooped as he went off to sleep with his back slightly curved with the wall, the war overhead giving way to his dreams.

"Harry! It's Mrs Coombes. You haven't eaten lunch again, have you? Here's a sandwich. Bit of a door stopper."

"You're very kind, Sarah." Harry, woken from his tumbling dreams, took the sandwich. Mrs Coombes always gave him a sandwich. She knew about his wife living in Cape Town but not about his money. The way he spoke made her comfortable, his Rhodesian accent belying his position in the social structure of life. They always asked him to talk about Africa when the bombs were coming down. Harry was their comfort blanket when it got bad.

"Any news from South Africa?"

"The lines are bad and Tina hates writing."

Harry knew it was better not to tell them the truth if he wanted to sleep at night among the people. The whole class structure in the Air Ministry shelter, despite its comparative comfort, put him off.

The truth from Africa had arrived on his desk by chance soon after Anthony turned eighteen. Squadron Leader Timothy Kent had gone off to fly aeroplanes the week after Dunkirk. The Air Ministry staff were now old. Some were older than Harry. All had had something to do with the Air Force in the last war. Harry was now in charge of keeping track of the sleepers recruited by Henning von Lieberman late in 1937. Potential security risks, like the British fascist leader Sir Oswald Mosley Bart, were locked up for the duration of the war. Fools like Rodney Hirst-Brown were just being watched. Taking photographs of London Docks at ground level was as much use to the Germans as an old map of London. It was what his friend's cousin had up his sleeve for the ex-employee of Rosenzweig Bank that interested Harry. The ex-bank clerk was more use to British intelligence out in the open. Behind bars, Harry had argued, Rodney Hirst-Brown would lead them to no one.

Vic 'Ding-a-ling' Bell had been given the physical task of watching Rodney Hirst-Brown. Ding-a-ling had been adjutant of 33 Squadron when Harry was the commanding officer. Major Harry Brigandshaw Royal Flying Corps in those days. Back then Ding-a-ling's job had been to keep the flow of whisky and ordnance on schedule, administering the paperwork of a fighting squadron in the field.

Ding-a-ling had been born with a club foot so they wouldn't let him fly. Being adjutant was the next best thing. Harry had got him the job at the Air Ministry when Timothy Kent was recalled to his squadron. After scouting the field, Ding-a-ling had made a friend of the landlord at the Crown having found out where Rodney spent his evenings. After that it had been a pleasant job listening and drinking beer. Deliberately never speaking to Rodney.

Ding-a-ling clumped his way into Harry's office at the Air Ministry once a month. Rodney was only one of his jobs. It was in May when the daffodils were out in the small garden outside Harry's window that Ding-a-ling now remembered.

"I was going through the list of new recruits for pilots, checking them off our list. There's a Brigandshaw, Harry. Flying Training in Rhodesia. Now is that a coincidence or something?"

"Is his name Anthony?"

"I'm afraid so. You didn't know?"

"Neither does his mother."

"They kind of put them in quarantine during pilot training. Not allowed off the station. No phone calls. That kind of thing. I'll keep you informed of progress. He'll be posted to England if he gets his wings."

"He'll get his wings. I gave him flying lessons with John Woodall as his sixteenth birthday present, six months before Tina took the children to Cape Town. Ostensibly to keep him out of harm's way. Went up to Rhodesia to look at Elephant Walk. Must have been side-tracked. Children are funny. Not a word. Spent his last year of school at Bishops in Cape Town. Top marks and an entry into medical school at UCT, University of Cape Town. Thanks for telling me. Anything on any of our friends?"

"Bugger all. Real sleepers."

"Be careful. This is the time to watch carefully with the war overhead. When's Anthony scheduled back to England?"

"End of September. They fly them from Gwelo to Cape Town and put them on a boat. Can't afford to lose pilots before they get into combat. Sorry, Harry. I'll piss off so you can read my monthly report. Is he any good as a pilot?"

"Funny how the law lets them fly a plane in the air but not drive a car on the ground until they are eighteen. They'll change that law one day. I suppose I could say this is my own bloody fault. Taught Flight Lieutenant Oosthuizen to fly. My nephew. Madge's son."

"The chap they just gave a bar to his DFC?"

"The CO put him up for a DSO."

"Well, I'll be off."

For months nothing had come out of Rhodesia. Then Ding-a-ling had put Anthony's schedule in front of Harry.

"You think you could get me a rail pass to Southampton, Vic? I'll teach my son to blindside his father."

"Won't he phone you from Cape Town?"

"Maybe. Why do I feel so bloody old?"

"We are a bit long in the tooth. Hirst-Brown was flush with money in the pub last night. Offered me a drink with the rest of the bar."

"Watch him, Vic. I hate people with chips on their shoulders."

"When he left drunk I asked the landlord, off-hand of course, where the chap got his money from. Henry, the landlord, said the man was probably a spy. We both had a good laugh. Why would the Germans pay a man for doing nothing? What's the worst a fool like Rodney could do?"

"Why don't you get into Mrs Leadman's house and have a look through his drawers? He still hasn't got a job. Where does he get his money? It's fools that worry me most. Men with brains are logical. Fools get themselves killed and cause a lot of damage in the process. Fools never make sense. You can't think in their heads. Why did I ever suggest to Klaus his cousin visit Janet Wakefield to cure his bloody stutter? Enemies then friends then enemies again. Now our families are back trying to kill each other. Klaus spent his honeymoon on Elephant Walk."

"He'll come out of it all right, Harry."

"I hope so."

Furious with himself and the stupidity of life, Harry began to eat his sandwich. There were always homemade pickled onions in Mrs Coombes's cheese sandwiches. The onions crunched as he ate as good a meal as any he had enjoyed in the Savoy Grill. Only when he began to eat did he find out how hungry he was. He had missed breakfast as well as lunch.

"It doesn't do your health any good not eating properly. Have another sandwich."

"Do you make more for me specially, Sarah?"

"Of course I do. Someone has to look after you. Clerks in the War Office, or wherever you work, have their bit to do for the war effort. That one was close! You mind if I hold your hand, Harry? Start telling us one of your stories. I hate it when the lights go out. Jerry must have hit the powerline. Another bloody bomb!"

"They drop them in sticks."

"How would you know?"

"Read it somewhere. Where shall I begin, everyone?"

"Tell us again your trip up the Skeleton Coast with your friend Barend looking for diamonds."

"You remember that one, Fred?"

"You do speak with a funny accent but my missus reckons you read the story in a book."

Harry settled back in the middle of an air raid to take their minds off the bombs. They were safe deep underground in the tube station.

"Every night we made a fire on the beach. You could hear the hyena scrounging for carcasses washed up on the sand. Sometimes they found a dead seal and went off with it back into the Namib Desert. The sharks get the seals. The seals get the fish. The hyena scavenge the seals. Now that's nature for you, everyone. Back then Barend and I didn't need electricity to see. Three layers of stars in the sky were so bright you could read a book by starlight. Moonlight was better but starlight with the waves crashing on the shore was just as good, if a bit hard on my eyes. I was younger then so it didn't matter. During the day, after the fog from the cold Atlantic Ocean had been eaten up by the hot African sun, we collected mussels off the rocks. You never saw mussels like the mussels in South West Africa. Longer than a man's hand and nearly as wide. The shells were bigger than the meat inside so you needed ten dozen to get a good meal. We were young and hungry, Barend and I. Sometimes we caught a big fish fishing off the rocks, standing all day. Collecting mussels was quicker. Then we had the time to look for the diamonds."

"Did you find any, Harry?" asked a voice from the dark, down on the rails. They could all hear the aircraft directly overhead, there was so much noise in the night sky.

"Seven. We found seven diamonds. One the size of a chicken's egg."

"Blimey. Must have made you rich."

"Never sold it. As I said before, my dad had an old house on a farm, if you could call it a farm. Dad was a hunter. The Great Elephant killed my dad. So I built that diamond into the fireplace for a rainy day. It was still there last time I looked, before I came to live in London. My old mother and my sister still live on the farm."

"Why'd you come back?"

"My wife didn't like Rhodesia. The bush. Too wild for Tina. Now she's in South Africa and I'm here with you, dodging bombs. You'll hear the all clear quite soon. They're going away. Now, just look at that. The lights are on again. Jerry missed the powerlines. No, I'm wrong. I can hear another wave of Heinkels."

"How you know them is Heinkels, Harry?"

"By their engines."

"How you know about engines?"

"By listening, Fred. It's going to be a long night again."

"What did you do in the last war, Harry?"

"Not much."

Everyone fell silent. With the dim light now on it was not so bad. They could all hear the ack-ack battery start up from the grounds of Buckingham Palace. The searchlights would be looking up in the dark for the Germans. Harry had told them once two searchlights found an enemy aircraft, the aircraft was caught. Then the guns could fire at a target. The crump of bombs started again. Mrs Coombes took Harry's hand, gripping it for all she was worth. The lights stayed on. The man on the far side of Mrs Coombes was praying. Harry picked up the whine of an aircraft coming down.

"We got one," he said, as a matter of fact.

The aircraft exploding when it hit the ground made a different sound to the bombs. Harry waited for the second, bigger explosion when the bombs went off that the German pilot had not unloaded before he was hit by the ack-ack. Harry hoped the pilot wasn't Klaus's son. Soon, very soon, Anthony would be over Germany doing the bombing. German civilians would then be praying for their lives. There was mayhem up above them. Safe in the bowels of the underground rail system, without thinking, he had eaten Mrs Coombes's second cheese sandwich.

Half an hour later they heard the all clear. Mrs Coombes got up and went to the ladies toilet to make tea. She kept a Primus stove permanently in there. They all had their own tin mugs in the group they had made of themselves when the bombing on London first started. They were now as close as people ever got to each other. Real people without all the show and all the lies. People Harry liked and admired as they tried to convince each other they were not afraid. Only when the lights went out did Harry tell them a story. It seemed to help. Not only the people but Harry himself. Had Harry his choice he would have chosen piloting his aircraft where he had the chance to fight back. Cowering in the dark was not his first choice.

When Mrs Coombes came back with the tea there was only condensed milk in a tin and no sugar. Sugar was rationed. It came from overseas, if it got past the German U-boats. Spending the war down below in the ground was the worst experience of Harry's life. When he went to Southampton in ten days' time he hoped the port wasn't in the line of fire. The chances were small. The ships ran from Cape Town at full speed, too fast for the slower U-boats. It would be good to see one of the children again.

"That diamond, Harry, was it the size of a chicken's egg?"

"Just a bit bigger. A perfect blue-white."

"Why didn't you sell it and live like a rich man?"

"I'd seen rich men, Fred. You can have all the money in the world and still be poor. One day, someone in the family will need that diamond. Sarah, thank you for the tea. After the tea and a bit of a wash I'll be getting into my sleeping bag."

"How do you sleep so well on the hard ground?"

"Practice," said Harry smiling to himself. "One day I'll tell you about the Tutsi in the Congo. How I was forced to live with them for two years as their captive."

"That's got to be a tall story, Harry. How did you get to the Congo from Rhodesia and not get lost on the way? The Congo is darkest Africa."

"It's a long story."

"We'll bet it is."

"Next time when the lights go out."

"Harry sure can sleep sound on the ground. Every bone in my body aches in the mornings."

In the morning when Harry went out the entrance to the tube station, the fires started by the night's bombing were still burning. An ARP warden in a tin hat, his gas mask slung across his chest, told Harry not to go down Northumberland Avenue where the noise of the fire was coming from. Harry could see the water from a fire hose dousing the flames a street away. There was an unwritten rule when they came above ground not to look at each other.

"See you tonight, Harry."

"Thanks for the tea, Sarah."

"Thanks for the sandwiches, Sarah. Tonight's my surprise."

With the bowler hat back on his head and walking his rolled umbrella, Harry began the short journey to his office. Once in the sleeping bag he had taken off his pinstripe trousers, obligatory for every clerk in London, folded them carefully and put them under his back. His jacket and waistcoat were easier to take off before he went to bed. They were his pillow. Everyone looked rumpled coming out of the public air-raid shelters and no one complained. The fires were half a mile from his office. The early morning was chilly, reminding Harry the winter was on its way. Once October came the weather changed in England and the sun went out.

Back in his office, looking at his desk and the tin tray spilling over with files, Harry asked himself what the hell he was doing.

"You're too old for this shit, Harry, my boy. Admit it. You should be on the farm tickling behind the dogs' ears."

"Good morning, Mr Brigandshaw."

"Did you hear that, Katherine?"

"Only the bit about the dogs' ears."

"How do you arrive a minute after I get in?"

"Practice. Coffee first then take your bath. Mr Bell wants to see you."

"Everything all right at your flat? I don't bother to go to mine during the week."

"They haven't hit us yet. How do you stop your trousers creasing?"

Harry smiled, said nothing, and drank a gulp of his coffee that tasted as if it had been made from acorns. The Kenyan coffee had stopped coming a year ago when the stocks in London ran out. The acorn coffee revived him. When Katherine was out of the room Harry looked at himself in the small mirror that surrounded the wall clock in its silver case. He looked worse than he felt. Going into the bathroom, his one luxury next to his office, Harry locked the door out of habit, ran the bath and took off his clothes. Katherine would be sending last night's suit to be ironed. In the bathroom wardrobe were two changes of clothes. The second change was for the weekend when he took the train to Leatherhead before walking the last part home to Hastings Court. The stables and the clock tower were still in ruins. Most weekends he went to the family graveyard to have a word with his Manderville grandfather to buck himself up.

Soaking in the bath at the office was the best ten minutes of Harry's day. Restored in body if not in spirit, he dressed himself properly and stepped out the bathroom door.

"Tell Mr Bell I'm ready, Katherine."

Harry sat down at his desk and started to work, mechanically going through his paces. Everything was done with five copies. Everything he did complied with a government rule. There was no point complaining.

It was the way it was done in the Civil Service. Rules. Rules. Rules. Quite quickly, Harry was bored out of his mind.

When Harry looked up Ding-a-ling Bell was standing in front of his desk. Mostly, Katherine left the door to his office open. The adjutant looked serious.

"Didn't you get any sleep last night, Vic? You look terrible."

"Thank you, Harry. Not much as a matter of fact. If I'd found nothing I was going to take the day off, or at least the morning. During all the nonsense last night I used a key given us by the Yale lock company. Fits most Yale locks for some reason. Mrs Leadman and everyone in the street had gone to the public shelters. Apart from Jerry up above the place was deserted. Having overheard Hirst-Brown in the Crown tell Henry he had two rooms next to each other at the top back of the house I used a torch to go up the stairs. Inside the house there wasn't a sound. There was nothing of interest to us in the bedroom. In the dark room I found a box full of what looked like small radios. Twelve of them. All exactly the same. Expensive-looking, which made me wonder what our Rodney was doing with them."

"Did you bring one?"

"Didn't want to leave a trace of my visit."

"If they come over again tonight go back to Mrs Leadman's house and take one. I want an expert to have a look."

"Is that all, Harry?"

"For the moment. Just don't get caught."

"It was bad last night."

"Yes, it was. We got one of them."

Vic Bell closed the door when he left, leaving Harry pondering, his mind searching for an answer in different directions.

"What does an ex-bank clerk want with twelve radios?" he asked himself.

That night Harry told them about the Tutsi. When the worst was over, Harry produced his bottle of whisky and shared it around. Mrs Coombes liked her whisky. Then he slept through the rest of the night, dreaming about radios. He was in a Tutsi hut listening to the BBC. In the morning the fires were still burning. The same ARP warden was on duty.

"Keep clear of Craven Street," he was calling.

"Thanks for the whisky, Harry."

"My pleasure, Fred."

"Where'd you get it?"

"My secret. Thanks for the sandwiches, Mrs Coombes."

As usual, Katherine arrived at the office a minute after he arrived.

"Mr Bell wants to see you."

"Good. Send him in the moment he comes. No, go down to his office. I had a bloody nightmare last night. Then I woke in a cold sweat."

"I'll get him. Enjoy your coffee."

Ding-a-ling Bell arrived in the office before Harry had time for his morning bath. The tube station smoke from the cigarettes had been thick enough to cut. Harry did not smoke despite Elephant Walk being now largely a tobacco farm. With the war, everyone wanted to smoke.

"They've gone, Harry. All twelve of them. Along with our friend's suitcase."

"Find out Mrs Leadman's telephone number."

"I have it here."

"Katherine! Try and get through to this number. Tell the operator I'm in a hurry. Ding-a-ling, for goodness sake sit down. You look absolutely worn out. No sleep again?"

"Couldn't sleep when I got home."

"You'll have to find him, Vic. Then you'll have to follow him."

"I've got your call, Mr Brigandshaw."

"Mrs Leadman? This is the police. Your tenant Hirst-Brown. Where has he gone?"

"Brighton," she said. "Paid me a week in advance. What's he done?"

"A close relative died in the bombing last night, we want to inform Mr Hirst-Brown."

"Didn't know he had any relatives."

"We all have relatives, Mrs Leadman."

Harry put down the phone. People were strange when it came to authority. Mrs Leadman hadn't asked how he knew Rodney Hirst-Brown was her tenant.

"Get down to Brighton with his photograph. Ask the police to check all the hotels."

"What's he up to, Harry? Why Brighton?"

"The Chain Home stations, radar, along the south coast. There are twelve of them. If the Germans can jam our radar before our boys get in the air, they'll have a clear run into London during the day. We won't be able to scramble the fighters knowing where and when to intercept."

"Do you think a radio device would work?"

"I don't know. Find those radios, Vic, and we'll soon find out."

That night and the next day, the radar screens at RAF Poling were snowed over, stopping the radar supervisor from giving his report to the Fighter Command operations room at Tangmere. There was a hole in the radar cover that was not due to bomb damage or any malfunction of the equipment. RAF Poling were out of commission.

When Vic Bell called Harry from Brighton, Harry was certain Hirst-Brown was involved.

"Get the RAF police to surround Beachy Head but wait for him. He's knocked out Poling. Beachy Head is the next VH unit down the coast. We're going blind, Vic. Catch the bastard and find those radios. What they do with him after that I don't damn well care. And it's all my bloody fault. Teach me to fraternise with the enemy."

"It's his cousin. Not your friend. We all have our jobs to do in a war. Can't they trace that radio at Poling and pick it up?"

"Probably."

"Then we don't have a problem. If it's jamming the radar, it's sending out a signal they can follow back to the source. Aren't radio signals two-way traffic?"

"Don't ask me. They'll have to search the surrounding area in my logic. It's got to be above ground to do the jamming. Did you get any sleep?"

"Last night as a matter of fact. Not one bleep from the air-raid sirens down here. Why do people turn traitor?"

"There's usually a personal reason. He thinks he lost his job at Rosenzweigs Bank unfairly. Some people can carry a grudge for years. He hates the Jews. The Nazis hate the Jews. Your enemy is my enemy. That sort of crap."

"We should have picked him up at the start."

"Can't arrest a man for doing nothing. We do that and we're as bad as them. Now we can hang Rodney Hirst-Brown for treason when you find him."

"You think they'll hang him?"

"Not for us to decide. We all prefer fighting an enemy we can see. I'm tired, Vic. You and I have been through all this once before. It's all so pointless. You see, no one will be a winner in the end. They never are. Just find the bastard."

3

*S*even days later, while Harry was waiting to greet his eldest son at Southampton, the Luftwaffe attacked the convoy from South Africa as the ships came round the Isle of Wight, just over forty miles from the radar station of RAF Poling. The South African Navy escort put up a blanket of shellfire as the Stuka dive-bombers came down to attack the ship carrying the newly trained pilots. Many were standing on deck in battledress uniform, life jackets strapped to their chests, berets on their heads, taking in their first close-up sight of home for months. Anthony watched, mesmerised, as his baptism of fire came straight at him, not sure whether to jump over the side and swim to the shore. One of the Stukas blew apart, a direct hit on one of the aircraft's bombs by the South African Navy. The ship's captain had turned his ship away from the flight of bombs that exploded in the water. As the Germans pulled out of their dive the pilots at the rail began to cheer. There was a different engine noise in the sky.

"Spitfires," said Felix Lombard, pointing to three aircraft coming out of the sun.

"How the hell did they know who we were?" said Andrew Bathurst, a fellow passenger. "They only went for our ship."

"There are people in South Africa who don't like the British," said Anthony, his fear subsiding. "My cousin Tinus who's at Tangmere had his grandfather hanged by the British for treason in the Boer War. Many of the Afrikaners still hate us British. Someone told the Germans we were coming in one ship. Poor sods. Don't stand a chance. They are good in a dive. Worthless everywhere else, according to Tinus. Up there just could be my cousin."

"I'll be glad to step on firm land. Why do they call it the Solent?"

"Don't ask me. The aircraft look so small up in the sky."

When Anthony saw his father half an hour later, standing by the dock, he was only mildly surprised. With Anthony in uniform they shook hands.

"Ding-a-ling Bell saw the roster. You're posted to RAF Boscombe Down. Near Middle Wallop. We have an hour before you get on the train. How's your mother?"

"Crying, last time we spoke. Beth's in love with Felix. Felix Lombard, my father, Colonel Brigandshaw. Don't be blindsided by the rank of colonel. Dad flew with the Royal Flying Corps."

"There's a cafeteria at the station."

"Did you see the attack? Not a scratch."

"Let me carry your duffel bag. Did it frighten the shit out of you? At least our radar was working. The Germans took it out for a couple of days but it would take more than a couple of souped-up radios to bring down those masts. Shows how desperate they are. The last thing they want is reinforcements of pilots. We're going to win. Last September was the turning point. Should have kept up hitting the airfields and radar. Hitler was a corporal. Churchill says it shows, that when he's in real trouble he can rely on Corporal Hitler to get him out of the mess. Makes the Führer as mad as hell so he attacked our cities to teach us a lesson. You'd better have breakfast with us, Felix. My daughter's a bit young for love. Nothing like a uniform! Did you stay in the house at Bishopscourt? When you get some leave you will be welcome at Hastings Court despite the holes in the clock tower."

"How are you, Dad?"

"Bored stiff. Little excitement last week but generally bored. They don't want me to fly again. You young chaps are in charge. At least it isn't raining. This island has the worst climate on earth."

Anthony smiled, watching his father swing the duffel bag. They all walked to an official-looking bar, with Andrew Bathurst following.

"Do you mind if a cadge a lift, sir?"

"Be my guest. I was lucky to get the car and luckier to get the petrol. We had a chap buggering around with our radar. Combined business with the pleasure of seeing my son. I want a full report on Elephant Walk when you get some leave, Anthony."

"The dam really is beautiful."

"That much you did tell me in a letter. Since you wrote, the price of tobacco has doubled. How is it some of us make money out of other people's adversity? The Tender Meat Company I bought in America. Half of it anyway. Best investment in my life. The Yanks are making a fortune out of this war. The radios we picked up to jam our radar we think were made in America. Shipped straight to England into the wrong hands. They didn't know, of course. The sooner the Americans realise which side of their bread is buttered the better. Cousin George thinks it's criminal letting us fight the war alone. That second farm in Virginia's making money. There's money in food and tobacco. Everyone get in the car. Good to see you, son. You've grown. Makes me feel as old as the hills seeing my eldest son in uniform. How's the rest of my family? Frank still a pain in the arse?"

"Dorian can't wait to farm in Rhodesia. There's a girl called Eleanor Botha."

"There's always a girl at your age, Anthony. Is she pretty?"

"A body to kill for. Played beach bats with her on Clifton Beach."

"Memories. Sweet memories."

"Yours or mine, Dad?"

"Mine, I'm afraid. It seems impossible for you now but once I was your age."

"What was her name?"

"Jennifer. Her name was Jennifer. We were both still at school. Oh yes. Clifton Beach. That place was something. Is the water still icy cold?"

"Freezing. Nobody cares. I love South Africa."

"They've given your cousin Tinus a spot of leave. Ordered him actually. During the height of the battle they were taking Dexedrine pills to keep them alert. Not good for the long-term health, ingesting chemicals. He doesn't know but they've taken him off the active duty list. Don't want him and the others who flew at the start of the war to burn out. When his leave's up he's going up to Scotland to be an instructor. I suggested Gwelo to a friend of mine at the Air Ministry. They don't want the veteran pilots that far away. They gave him a bar to his DFC."

"Are his fighting days over?"

"Depends on how long the war lasts."

"When do we go on active duty, Dad?"

"When you get to Boscombe Down, weather permitting. Lancasters. But you all know about Lancasters. Best bomber we have."

4

_____

For the first time in her life Genevieve was perfectly content. The green Morgan with the top down was still the best way to travel on an evening in late summer. They had both begged and borrowed the petrol coupons. Now, for both of them, the war did not exist. No one existed other than themselves. All their thoughts were in the present, driving the country lane, holding hands, Tinus with one hand on the wheel, the two-seater the only car on the road.

"Are you hungry, darling?" she asked.

"Only for you."

"We have to eat as well."

"I used to come here with Uncle Harry. There was always a pretty barmaid at the Running Horses. Never did I think I'd take a famous American actress to dinner."

"I'm English."

"I was going to tell you before we were interrupted for so long. You have an American accent. Do you know how long I've loved you?"

"Tell me again."

"Since the moment our eyes first met."

"What was her name?"

"Minnie. I think it was short for Minerva. Christmas 1933. That was the time I saw you first. At the Mayfair. I found out you were really nineteen. You said you were twenty-one. Something to do with attending the Central School of Speech and Drama when you were too young to be eligible. I was sixteen but our eyes said we understood each other. You were going to be famous then. I was just a schoolboy. Then those lovely years we kept meeting at Oxford. The three musketeers. I'm going to miss André for the rest of my life. You never make friends like that again. He was a year older than me. Same cricket team at Bishops in his last year. Watched him score 112 runs for Oxford against Cambridge at Lord's. You remember that time you came to visit me at Oxford with Gregory L'Amour. What is his real name?"

Tinus had found it better not to talk about André after he was shot down six months earlier over the hop fields of Kent, his aircraft exploding on impact. They were both silent for a long time thinking of André.

"Joseph Pott," said Genevieve after Tinus had wiped away his tears and blown his nose.

"Before we made love I was bitterly jealous of Joseph Pott. Wouldn't admit it to myself. You, my darling Genevieve, were beyond my reach. Now we will always be touching each other. With you it was the first time I ever made love. Before I was satisfying lust."

"I hope you satisfied that as well." She was smiling up at him, the moment with André in the past.

"I will never satisfy my love for you if I live to be a hundred."

"Two days in bed, Tinus!"

"Everyone left us alone. Wasn't that just marvellous? Uncle Harry knew you were coming down with me to Hastings Court. He drove past to go to Southampton to meet Anthony. Left us alone. How does he know so often how to behave?"

"All we've eaten was bread and jam."

"And love, Genevieve. Maybe I am hungry. Please God, Anthony comes through the war. So many friends. So many dead."

"Please, Tinus, no more war. Stop the car. I want to sit on that four-bar gate and listen to the birds. We can wait ten minutes more for our supper."

"I could wait for ever sitting with you on a four-bar gate listening to the birds. Will you marry me, Genevieve?"

"You'll have to ask my father for my hand. Mother likes you."

"I'm glad. So, what do you say? Not them."

"Have we got enough petrol to drive down to Dorset? My grandmother is going to love my marrying you, Tinus Oosthuizen."

"So it's a yes?"

"From that first look in the Mayfair it's been yes."

"I'd never seen a girl with eyes of different colours. Will our children have mismatched eyes?"

"I hope so. You will be careful, won't you, Tinus?"

"Stop crying. Everything is going to be just fine. The Americans will be forced to come into the war with all the noise from Japan about America stopping their supply of oil. You forget, Gregory sent me this rabbit's foot he found in the graveyard of my ancestors at Hastings Court. Had it put on this chain by a jeweller. I only wear the rabbit's foot around my neck in combat. I hope he finds someone to love him."

"He's a pilot now. We are friends. Good friends. Can you understand that?"

"When Harry gave me this talisman from Gregory I knew he understood I loved you. It was you I thought beyond my grasp. Do you want a leg up onto the gate? It's quite tricky balancing. You need to wind your legs behind one of the wooden bars. I never knew it was possible to be so happy."

"Neither did I."

Faintly on the wind from the direction of Leatherhead came the sound of the air-raid siren.

"It's back again," Genevieve said.

"It's never far away. The Germans are early tonight. Look. My hands are trembling. You'd think I was used to it."

"The birds are still singing."

"To them all the noise is just man. They don't hear the threat. We were lucky they didn't knock Hastings Court to the ground. Just the horses. The head groom had gone off into the army. I want this damn war to be over. Now I'm trembling all over. My nerves are shot to ribbons. It's not just me. Most of us are scared."

"Come here."

"I can't. I'll fall off the gate."

Then they were laughing. When they got down to drive on to the Running Horses, Tinus had stopped trembling. Far away they could hear aircraft in the sky. A breath of wind brought the sound of machine gun fire. As they got into the car they could hear the sound of bombs falling followed by the explosions.

"I'm all right now. We'd better spend tonight in the shelter. Harry's very proud of his shelter."

"Caught in the spider's web."

"Something like that."

"Let's get back on the fence."

Sitting on the fence proved difficult. It was not possible to grip the slat of wood and hold hands. They got off into the farm's field and went for a walk. Holding hands was easy. The idea of sitting down in a restaurant while people were being killed had put them both off their food. The Morgan was left in the road with the top down. No one drove cars during an air raid. Near the elm trees they felt the dusk. Together they were happy. What the world did to itself was no longer their business while they held hands.

Tinus was now quite calm. He only let his mind stay in the very present. The bombing north of Leatherhead was not part of his present. Or flying aeroplanes. If his life stopped now it had been fulfilled. They were joined in mind, body and spirit.

The birds in the trees and hedgerows went on calling in the dusk. The smell of wild flowers had become stronger. They walked right round the field and back to the car where Tinus had left it to get on the four-bar gate the first time. There was dew on the leather seats. Backing in towards the four-bar gate, Tinus turned the car around.

Back at Hastings Court they found a tin of baked beans in the kitchen cupboard and a bottle of Uncle Harry's best wine in the cellar. They ate the beans with a spoon out of the tin. Not finding the can opener Tinus had hacked the can open with a carving knife.

With the bottle opener he found in the cocktail cabinet in the lounge, Tinus pulled the cork from the bottle of Hock. The Hock was from Germany. From 1937. The wine poured into crystal glasses tasted good. By the time they finished the wine by candlelight outside on the back lawn they decided to sleep in the house. The lawn had not been cut all summer. There was no petrol for the lawnmower.

They heard the last two servants talking quietly, the only two that had nowhere else to go so they had stayed with his Uncle Harry. The servants were walking out the side door through the garden to the air-raid shelter Uncle Harry had built at the start of the war. The air-raid shelter was dark and damp. Under the duckboards were pools of water. Someone had peed with fright. The square box of concrete blocks cemented together smelled of urine like the toilets at the railway stations.

They were quite happy to die holding hands. They were at the end of the bottle of wine. Tinus opened a second bottle of the same vintage which was just as good. Genevieve found a box of digestive biscuits which they ate. The biscuits were stale and slightly soggy. Neither of them cared. It was strange not to hear the clock tower chime the quarter hour which neither of them mentioned. The rubble from the bombing had been left, though the three dead horses were buried in an old rubbish dump and covered with soil. They could still smell the dead horses when the wind was blowing the wrong way.

When they went to bed in the main bedroom reserved in the past for the Lord of the Manor, both of them were drunk. They made love and fell asleep. They were still clutching each other. Neither of them woke in the night. The dawn chorus of the birds through the open window brought them awake.

"My mouth tastes like the bottom of a parrot's cage," said Tinus.

"So does mine. Can we make love again?"

Afterwards, they went back to sleep, still folded in each other's arms for comfort.

There was no such thing as a normal day anymore. The servants left them alone. In the kitchen someone had thrown away the empty can of baked beans. On the lawn on the table were the empty bottles of wine.

They were taking it minute by minute, not hour by hour.

Genevieve's play had opened and closed in three weeks. After the bomb exploded in the Café de Paris, coming through the roof killing everyone in their fine clothes and jewellery, people kept away from the West End theatre despite what everyone said about a stiff upper lip. The play was not very good. As a comedienne, Genevieve knew she was not very good. Cameras close up on her face gave her the power to concentre the minds of the audience. The power was in her eyes, the beauty of her face. She was photogenic, they said. It was better to act in a theatre, more personal than acting for a camera. She just wasn't as good. She was twenty-seven years old. Maybe, she thought sadly, she was losing her grip. Once Tinus had satiated himself would he behave like the rest?

With the war still raging there wasn't the future to worry about. Everything they did to each other was intense, made so by the certainty of loss. She would always be able to tell herself when she was old she had loved just once. They had a whole week ahead of them before his leave came to an end. To when they were parted. They were right to sleep in the big four-poster bed. She wasn't frightened when they were together. For long periods they held each other without saying a word. They had their own world for a while. A world without people intent on killing each other.

5

---

hile Genevieve was wondering if love was worth the pain to come, when the magical bonds were broken as they always were despite Tinus proclaiming his love would last forever, Rodney Hirst-Brown was enjoying himself. Something he had not done for a long time. Since Aaron Rosenzweig fired him for stealing thirty-two shillings he was going to pay back. Easier for the banks to get rid of him once they found him a thief. A petty thief that as chief clerk might grow. Easier to kick him out. Never thinking him human. A man with feelings. A man to say sorry and mean what he said. Kick him out, they said. We don't need him anymore. Once a thief always a thief. When society ostracises him it's his own fault. His own fault no one will give him a job. Lucky we didn't put him in jail. Lucky just to lose his job. Who the hell was he anyway? So he fought the Turks in the desert. Years ago. Now he's a thief. Fire the man. Get rid of him. We don't want people like him working in our bank. To hell with him. We have more important things to worry about.

And to hell with them, smiled Rodney to himself sitting comfortably in jail in the Brighton police station. Now they were talking to him. Now he was not ignored. Now he was important. A man to be taken notice of.

"Why did you do it, Rodney?"

"I hate the Jews. They fired me for thirty-two shillings. They stole my life. When Hitler wins this war he'll exterminate the lot of them. That'll make Aaron Rosenzweig think when they send him to the gas chamber. I fought for this country. I worked hard for that bank. I had to have that thirty-two shillings at the time. Look what I got for it. For fighting. Working. No one even looks at a man out of a job. The bastard had no humanity. Now it's going to be his turn. Now he remembers Hirst-Brown his chief clerk. The poor sod he fired for stealing thirty-two shillings. You asked me why I did it, copper, now you know."

"I'm not a policeman, Rodney. I'm with MI5."

"All coppers are bastards. We used to sing that in the army. Before they gave me my commission. There was an officer in the Cairo officers' mess who ran off with fifty quid. His dad was a peer. You know what they did, copper? Bugger all. Told him to go home and leave the army. Me, the whole bloody lot of you ostracised."

"You don't have to swear. Now, tell me, what happened?"

"I don't care if you shoot me. Better than always being on my own. Being ignored. Mrs Leadman only talks to me when she wants the rent. Henry only talks to me when I buy booze at four times the cost of drinking alone in my room. Four times to drink in company where the landlord says a few kind words he doesn't mean just to get your custom. Or do they hang traitors? I'm a civilian. I suppose you want to hang me, copper. You all make me sick. Did the best I could with my life and look what you all did with me. Mr von Lieberman bought me a drink in the Savoy. He was nice to me. Interested in my problem with the Jews."

"What was his name again?"

"You heard, copper!"

"You don't have to be rude."

"I don't see bloody why not. Take me out and shoot me for all I care. When Hitler's finished the likes of Aaron Rosenzweig will be dead and forgotten. Their money given to people who deserve it. You think he'd have lent me a fiver. A bank so bloody rich, a family so rich. What do they do? Kick me in the gutter. Kick me out on my neck."

"How did you get the radios, Rodney?"

"Bugger off. I want my lawyer."

"This is wartime, Rodney. You don't get lawyers in wartime. Not when you aid and abet the enemy. How does it feel to be a traitor to your country?"

"Very good as a matter of fact. Haven't had so much company in years. People actually talking to me. Interested in Rodney Hirst-Brown.

His brother's now Lord St Clair, the Eighteenth Baron St Clair of Purbeck."

"Who, Rodney? You're getting me confused."

"The officer and gentleman who stole the fifty quid. The Honourable Barnaby St Clair. Kept tabs on that one, I did. Specially after I got fired. Do you know what it's like to be a forty-two year old bald, ex-chief clerk without a job that no one talks to? The last woman that looked at me was years ago and she was a whore. The system's not fair. Hitler's going to change the system. Now do you understand? I don't bloody care anymore. You can shove the whole human race up your bottom, copper."

When the man left him alone in the cell, the loneliness flooded back again. Then he cried. Feeling sorry for himself. Wondering what his life had ever been about. If they were looking at him through the little square window he didn't care anymore. Just didn't care. The whole damn lot of them could go to hell where they belonged. It didn't really matter if he told them. It was all so simple. At least he'd have some company if he told them the story right from the start.

Wondering whether he should have told them the name of Herr Henning von Lieberman should Germany win the war, Rodney reverted to feeling miserable. Then he called back his interrogator. They were going to shoot him anyway.

The food parcel had arrived from America on the Saturday morning. Mrs Leadman had answered the door. Mrs Leadman had a strident voice when she wanted to be heard.

"Mr Hirst-Brown. The Railways are here for you."

Expecting a package from a letter a month before, Rodney wiped the smirk off his face and went downstairs. A man from the Southern Railway Company was waiting for him at the front door, a large box in his hands labelled 'Food Parcel' in red letters. Ever since rationing, relations and friends overseas had been sending food parcels to England. The Americans were particularly good at it.

"Sign here, please. Lucky bastard. By the weight of it, got to be sugar. My wife's got a sweet tooth. Kids the same. Oh well, some of us have all the luck. Americans like to send us food parcels. My missus says it makes 'em feel better. Kind of not so guilty, safe in their beds far from the bombing. Real sweet tooth she's got my missus. You going to open it now?"

"Better not," said Rodney, knowing what the man wanted.

"All right, then. Enjoy your sugar. Some of us are just plain lucky."

Rodney had shut the front door in the man's face and taken the parcel up to his room where he counted the radios that had been made in Germany specially for the job, shipped to America, reparcelled and shipped to England as a 'Food Parcel' with the big red label. The damn man had wanted a pound of sugar! Rodney had given a small laugh at the irony. Everyone wanted something. The trick was to have something they wanted. The instructions as to where to put the radio devices came with the money under his door the night he bought the bar in the Crown a round of drinks as he was feeling so good. For the first time since getting the sack from the bank he was getting the chance to get his own back.

As instructed in the letter telling him the parcel was on its way he burned the box from America in the grate, putting the radios in a cardboard box he had taken for the purpose from Mrs Leadman's basement-well when he put out the garbage. Once a week it was his job to put the dustbin that stood in the well up on the street for the dustman to collect. He had seen the box in the corner under a shelf out of the rain, saving him from looking outside the shops where the shopkeepers threw away their boxes they didn't want. Rodney had put the radios in the old box, making them as inconspicuous as possible. The letter had said to keep anything that arrived for him out of sight. Inconspicuous. Like in an old, discarded box.

The morning after the air raid Rodney had carried his box to Holland Park tube station where he had taken the Tube to Waterloo and his journey down the coast as instructed in the letter with the money. The journey that had ended in his being nabbed by the police outside the wire fence that surrounded the big VHF radar mast at Beachy Head where he had placed one of the radio devices in the long grass at the bottom of the wire mesh fence, pushing down the switch that he was told to push down in the letter. Finding the mast at Poling outside Arundel had taken him longer. The first time for anything was usually the longest.

"What's that you got, Rodney?"

Even then they had known his name.

Hugging his own knees on the single iron bed in his cell, Rodney began to hope they would shoot him. There was something brave about a handkerchief over his eyes, the crack of guns the last sound he would hear in his life. Being hanged by the neck made him squirm. No doubt the police had found the rest of his German radios in the room of his

Brighton hotel. Only mildly curious, Rodney wondered how the radios worked. What the whole fuss was about. Why he was suddenly so much the centre of attention.

Feeling over his bald patch with the palm of his hand, Rodney began to sweat with fear. They were going to kill him whatever he said. When his revenge came he would be dead. Even dying wouldn't let him win. So it did not matter. While he spilled his guts out they brought him lunch. That was something. He hadn't eaten lunch with company for years.

Ding-a-ling went back to London the following night. Colonel Grant had repeated his interview with Rodney Hirst-Brown word for word. Colonel Grant had been an infantry officer in what they were now calling the First World War. They had eaten supper together in the Royal Hotel.

"If they'd got enough of those radios in place last summer, and they'd actually worked, the Germans would have beaten us already. We couldn't have fought the Battle of Britain without the radar. We'd have lost the war for thirty-two shillings. Can anything be more bizarre? Thirty-two bloody shillings!"

"Thirty-two shillings cost him his life. He should have stolen fifty thousand quid and gone to live in South America. Somewhere like Bolivia where they don't ask questions if you have money."

"You think if he'd known they'd stop him getting a job with any of the banks he would have stolen more?"

"Wouldn't you? The bank might just as well have cut his balls off. Emasculated the poor sod. Doesn't seem fair to me. It most certainly didn't seem fair to him."

"He stole money. Does it matter the amount?"

"St Clair got away scot-free. Look at him now. Rich as Croesus. What might he have done if society had turned its back? Life's difficult enough without an impediment. This damn club foot has been a drag on my life all the way through. What are you going to do with him?"

"What are we going to do about von Lieberman? Did the girl know she was helping a Nazi?"

"Unless you send in the commandos on parachutes and assassinate von Lieberman you can't do much. He's doing his job. Acting Lieutenant-Colonel Keyes tried to get Rommel on a commando raid in North Africa. Got right into the General's office in the General's headquarters before the Germans stopped him. Shot him dead. They're putting Keyes up for a posthumous Victoria Cross. I'll talk to Harry. He and von Lieberman's cousin are friends. Were friends. Spent time together in Africa. What put us onto Hirst-Brown. We let von Lieberman loose in London before the war and watched him. Now it's paid off. Bloody food parcel. Delivered the goods to his door. How often simple ways are the best. There are more sleepers on the list. Vigilance, Colonel Grant."

"He'll be shot."

"For stealing thirty-two shillings! My bet is he'd have put the money back. Life goes round in circles. Did you know Harry Brigandshaw's first wife was Barnaby St Clair's sister? Could have helped to shoot his brother-in-law if the stolen money situation had been reversed. Fifty quid! Couldn't do much then with fifty quid except drink it. Another bottle of wine, old chap?"

"Don't see why not. They haven't come over tonight."

"We put a spanner in their works."

"Hope so. Which do you prefer? Vic or Ding-a-ling?"

"Ding-a-ling."

"Call me Bennie, Ding-a-ling. To happy days."

6

By the time William Smythe came back from a tour of the Far East as an accredited war correspondent for the BBC in early December, Betty Townsend, his secretary, was getting desperate. Giving compassionate sex to war-ravaged pilots on forty-eight-hour passes was getting her nowhere, however much fun she was having. Betty wanted a future. At twenty-eight her clock was ticking out of time. Two of her beaus had been shot down and killed since William went off to report on the Japanese and Chinese situation, warning both England and America not to be complacent in his weekly talks from the island fortress of Singapore.

She had seduced William long before he took the tour for the BBC, again pleasant and satisfying but getting her nowhere in her quest to become Mrs Smythe, mother of his children, secure in a house and a future. Always, always, there was Genevieve.

The pilot the previous night had taken her to the cinema as a hopeful prelude to sex before he returned to his squadron at Tangmere. Right through the film, a replay of *Holy Knight*, the boy had held her hand as Betty watched her nemesis chase Gregory L'Amour up on the screen. Even the boy was besotted by the end of the movie, doing later to Betty what he really wanted to do to Genevieve. The boy was nineteen, already a veteran of the war. He had a small moustache so fluffy it tickled. After sex they sat up in Betty's bed drinking mugs of cocoa she had made in her kitchen. They had ignored the air-raid warning, the night's air battle sounding far away towards the East End of London.

"The docks," said Colin. "The East Enders have had a bad war."

"She's very beautiful, isn't she?"

"Who?" For a moment the boy had almost remembered Betty's name. Colin had been given her phone number by another pilot. The pilot had died the previous month. Colin had phoned to give her the news, hoping to get a date and some sex for himself.

"Genevieve. The girl in the movie."

"Everyone fantasises about Genevieve. She's a film star."

"Not my boss," said Betty, ignoring the reality of what she knew he had been thinking when they were making love. "He had a one-night stand with the damn woman years ago and can't get her out of his head."

"He had it off with Genevieve! Are you in love with your boss?"

"Yes," she said, thinking two could play the game and let out what was running through her head. "He won't marry me until Genevieve marries. They still meet on occasion. William thinks he still has a chance as long as she's single."

"Could he be brushing you off?"

"I'm not sure. Don't think so. He's obsessed with her. He's nearly forty. Why he's not in the army. William's a war correspondent. Coming back from the Far East on a Royal Navy ship tomorrow. First thing he'll do is look for Genevieve. She's back in London. Doing a new stage show. Her first one back from America flopped."

"Your boss is out of the picture now. The story goes at Tangmere she's marrying one of our pilots when the war's over. Flight Lieutenant Tinus Oosthuizen. You remember that World War One pilot who crashed his seaplane on a river in the Congo? Colonel Brigandshaw. Famous fighter pilot. It's his nephew she's going to marry. They took him out of active service and posted him to Scotland as an instructor. His nerves were shot to ribbons. They say after four tours you're either dead or finished. They won't let him fly in combat again. I'm only at the end of my second six-month tour at Tangmere. Can we possibly make love again? I've finished my cocoa."

William Smythe had gone to his flat on the Bayswater Road before going to his Fleet Street office to find the Germans had put a bomb through the roof of the building. There was nothing left that resembled it. The broken bricks that had made his home for so many years were dripping wet from the rain. The place was a shambles. The ARP wardens had long ago left the bombsite of rubble. There was no point in trying to clear it away. Each morning there were new piles of rubble.

"Lucky you were away," said the taxi driver. "Where've you been, guv? Nice navy duffel coat. Wouldn't mind one of them myself. Anything you want to look for?"

"Just my old life."

"Where you want to go now?"

"Fleet Street. I've still got an office."

"You can sleep on the floor. Got your navy bag and your duffel coat. You in the Royal Navy?"

"I'm a reporter. Freelance with the BBC. My name's William Smythe."

"Blimey. Remember you from the BBC Empire Service. Before the war."

The taxi driver went on talking as William tried to think. There was so much of his life lost in the rubble he would never find again. Familiar things, however trivial, were important to remember in life. No one ever collected bad memories to remember.

"I've been bombed out, Betty."

"Oh, good. You can come and stay with me. Who gave you that duffel coat?"

"The captain of the ship as a matter of fact. Don't I get any sympathy? There were six years of my life in that flat."

"I can give you a kiss if that will help? Welcome home, William. It's lovely to see you. Sorry about the flat. It must be awful to lose your possessions. Do you want to go through everything now? It's all up to date. The banking. Letters replied to. I'm good at forging your signature. On the letters, William, not on the cheques. Oh, one bit of news I heard last night, your old friend Genevieve is getting married."

"Who to?"

"Young Tinus Oosthuizen. They've grounded him. My informant says his nerves are shot to ribbons."

"Who's your informant?"

"We won't go into that, William. While the cat's away the mice will play. How was Singapore?"

In less than half an hour both parts of his life were shattered. His home and his dreams. Any other man's name would have meant nothing to William. Now it was finally over. Writing novels in Cornwall with Genevieve by his side could no longer even be a dream.

"Why are you looking so damn happy, Betty?"

"Sometimes the people you least expect do you the biggest favours."

"Who are you talking about?"

"The Germans... Thank God you weren't at home."

To William's surprise his secretary broke into uncontrollable sobs. Going across to her, William pulled her face against his chest. When it was over a tearful face full of love looked up at him. It was the same way Cherry Blossom looked at his cousin Joe in Singapore. Sergeant Joe Smythe, Royal Engineers. The look that back in Singapore had made him jealous of his cousin, something he had never been before.

THE NAME CHERRY Blossom sounded better in Chinese, a word William had been unable to get his tongue around much to the girl's amusement. Marrying a local and having two kids had made sure Joe stayed a sergeant. Joe had been in Singapore since 1937, on his second tour with the British Army, not bothering to go home on leave. His family in England were dysfunctional so there was nothing to come back for now his parents had sold their family home in Wimbledon where Joe had grown up with six siblings. The whole family had fought with each other.

"You're better off staying in Singapore."

"You don't think the Japs will enter the war? Have you seen my parents, Will?"

"Not recently, no. I'm not very good at visiting, sorry. You've got a beautiful life where you are."

"I don't suppose they approve, of course. The establishment. The Raj. Bloody stuck up, the lot of them. What makes me laugh is the hypocrisy. Half of them have Chinese or Malay mistresses. There's a whole damn school for their kids. They just don't mention their Asian family in polite company. One of the officers married his Chinese girl like I did. Threw him out of the Singapore Swimming Club. Don't be put off by that mundane name. The club's the place for the British. Only officers. No Chinese, Indian or Malay, of course. I often wonder if we know what we really look like. So you like my Cherry Blossom, Will?"

"She's gorgeous in more than looks. Your kids are as bright as buttons. If I could find a girl to love me the way you all love each other I wouldn't be such a miserable sod."

"Still no luck with Genevieve?"

"Don't be silly. She's a star. Film stars don't marry old has-beens like me. She's famous."

"So are you, Will."

"We're just friends. That's what she says."

"Horrible."

"So they won't let me take you both to the Singapore Swimming Club tonight to meet the rest of the press?"

"Don't be daft. They won't let me in, let alone my Chinese wife. I'm a sergeant. This is the British Raj, Will. Warts and all. Just don't mention you have a cousin here in the Royal Engineers. They'll want to know his name, rank and number and look down their nose when you tell them. Don't you want to stay with us while you are here?"

"Of course. Can't of course. Business comes first. We'll see a lot of each other, Joe, while I'm in Singapore. Why's the climate so sticky?"

"They say you can set your clock by the afternoon rain. Four o'clock. It rains every afternoon in Singapore at four o'clock."

"You're a lucky bastard, Joe Smythe. What you going to do after the war?"

"Stay out East with Cherry Blossom and the kids. Sounds terrible in English. I'm going to be a trader of some sort."

"Not coming back to England?"

"How can I? Imagine what the neighbours would have to say. British aversion to anyone not British isn't confined to the officer class. I'm going to be an expat for the rest of my life."

"Sounds good to me. The buggers at the Club have missed the point. The Chinese were civilised when we were living up trees. Quite rightly, they think us the savages. How's your Mandarin coming along?"

"Not bad. We want the children to be completely bilingual. English and Chinese. Stand them in good stead for the future. They'll never want to live in England if the empire lasts another thousand years."

"It won't. Mark my words. My sources say the Japs are up to something."

"Against the British?"

"Against the Americans."

"You've given us both the cold shivers. Cherry Blossom hates the Japs for what they are doing in China."

"Singapore will be all right. It's an impregnable fortress they all tell me."

"We can only hope. Good to see you."

"Good to see you too, Joe. Good to see you so happy... Why did they give it such an ordinary name? Singapore Swimming Club. Kind of thing you'd find in Battersea."

"Not when it was founded during the time of Governor Raffles. First swimming pool on the island. Very snooty. Couldn't have plebs in the same water, now could we?"

"There's a causeway now so it isn't an island."

"It's the longest one in the world, joining Singapore with Malaya. Railway line. Water pipes. Roads. Great feat of engineering."

"Couldn't the Japs invade over the causeway?"

"Not through the jungle."

"Better not. All the big guns are encased and pointing out to sea. The other way."

"You journalists have too vivid an imagination. Have a nice swim for me, Cousin William."

"I'm just going to talk and drink."

The only person William knew to talk to was Harry Brigandshaw. Having moved into his secretary's flat in North Kensington and made himself comfortable with his few possessions, William made an appointment with Katherine at the Air Ministry. Happily for a man with too many stories going through his head at the same time, Betty was as organised in her flat as she was in the office. Living with her would smooth out his entire day, not just the hours at the office. There was no argument when the lights went out and no complaints from William. There had been no women on board the fighting ships of His Majesty the King."

"Is it urgent, Mr Smythe?"

"It could be, Katherine. Hard to tell in the fog of war and diplomacy. More of a sinking feeling. I got back to Portsmouth last afternoon and found my flat a heap of rubble."

"Where are you staying?"

"With my secretary."

"Convenient. I'll go and ask Colonel Brigandshaw. Hold the line."

William was having a late breakfast now he could work with Betty and not have to rush to the office. The telephone in her flat was for business and paid for by himself. Betty said being on call twenty-four hours a day was not worth a free phone.

"William? Harry. Come right on over. Sorry to hear about the flat."

When William finished the call he finished his breakfast.

"I like that man. None of the usual bullshit about being busy to impress. Can we still get taxis, Betty?"

"The Tubes run during the day. They're quicker. What's the problem?"

"Japan. Japan's the problem. My years at trying to be a journalist tell me the Americans are being complacent. They're pushing the Japs on oil, to put a spanner in the works of the Japs' war with China. The Americans are stopping oil shipments from the Middle East reaching Japan. The Japs are being cornered. Harry can't do anything himself. He knows people. Can put a word in the right ear. I'm probably wrong but the Chinese I met in Singapore say the Americans are prodding the tiger."

"How did you meet the Chinese in Singapore?"

"My cousin's wife. Joe is married to a Chinese girl. Two kids. Never seen a happier family. The last thing we need is a war in our Far East possessions. India is politically vulnerable. Gandhi has stopped his nonsense for the duration of the war but it's still dangerous. Gandhi's just as frightened of the Japs now they've conquered half of China on his doorstep. Needs the British Army. It's Singapore and Hong Kong I worry about. They are too isolated from help if the Japs attack."

"You think the Japs are going to attack us?"

"Cherry Blossom's father thinks they have no option. They can't fight a war without Middle East oil."

"Who's Cherry Blossom for God's sake?"

"My cousin-in-law. Her name sounds better in Chinese. Damn fine breakfast, Betty. You'll make someone a good wife."

"I hope so."

"Kids always want their mothers to be good cooks above everything. You should have tried Cherry Blossom's cooking. Got to go. Harry's waiting."

"I hope so," said Betty with a smile after the door closed with William on his way to the Air Ministry in his Royal Navy duffel coat. Then she made the decision to beard the lion in its den and picked up the phone to book two tickets to the theatre. She wanted Genevieve to tell William in front of her when they went backstage after the show. She rehearsed her smile and what she was going to say while the phone rang at the ticket agent.

"Congratulations, Genevieve, on your forthcoming marriage to Flight Lieutenant Oosthuizen."

She just hoped Genevieve would be nicely stunned and not ask who had told her the good news. Poor Colin. He'd never forgive her. Explaining to William how she knew Colin would scupper her campaign before it started. The breakfast was a good sign. Men liked being pampered. No wonder the cousin liked his Chinese wife. Right through history Chinese women were renowned for pampering their men.

Then she did the washing up, dressed in a suit and went to the office to start her day.

The worst part for Harry Brigandshaw was not knowing. Listening to the news left Harry in a state of panic. It was always the same at the end of the bulletin describing the RAF's latest bombing raid on Germany. 'Aircraft attacked the heart of Germany's industrial might last night destroying factories and German morale. The raid was successful. Three of our aircraft failed to return.' The last part caused Harry's panic by failing to answer his question: 'was Anthony flying one of our aircraft that failed to return?' It was a BBC euphemism for 'three of our aircraft were shot down. There were no survivors. The pilot, navigator, middle gunner and rear gunner. Families will be informed.' It was always 'missing'. As if the crew had landed other than at home base, or baled out of the aircraft. Sounded better. Better for British Morale.

By the time Harry finished listening to the ten o'clock news, William Smythe was shown into his office giving Harry something else to think about. They had known each other a long time, ever since the press came into his life when he returned to England from his journey out of the Congo, much of the trip still a blur. William had found him at the Hospital for Tropical Diseases in Bloomsbury.

"Come in, William. Remembering how we first met at the hospital. Do you know, Will, that was ten years ago? Sit yourself down. For a chap who's just found his home bombed out you look damn chipper. Like the duffel coat. Did you steal it from the navy or did they give it to you?"

"The captain gave it to me. How are you, Harry?"

"Worried stiff every time I listen to the news."

"It's not that bad. Not as bad as September 1940 when every fighter in the RAF was committed to the battle."

"You've been away. Anthony's flying a Lancaster over Germany with his squadron. It's the bit at the end of the bulletin that gets me. Three of our aircraft failed to return. You chaps in the BBC have a way of putting everything so it doesn't affect British morale. It was better in the last war. At least I knew what was going on. Now I just wait. What's up, William?

You never do anything without a reason. Do you know I sleep every night on a platform underground? Made myself some friends. You make your best friends in life in adversity. So, what's up?"

"The Japs are getting up steam to attack America. No one will listen to me. Cherry Blossom's father has a network of contacts in the Far East."

"Who's Cherry Blossom?"

"My cousin's wife."

"Start at the beginning, Will. I'm listening. What do you want me to do?"

"Tell someone in Whitehall who will listen."

"They've got enough on their plate without worrying about rumours."

"It's not a rumour, Harry. The Japanese navy with aircraft carriers is getting ready to sail into the Pacific. If they haven't sailed already. It's been a long voyage from Singapore."

"There's Glen Hamilton in Denver. He'll be interested."

"The papers report, Harry. This is intelligence information. Why I came straight to you. No one else would listen to me in Singapore. They still drink cocktails and dress for dinner as if Japan isn't at war with China right next to them."

"Do you have specific proof? Other than this Chinaman's word. Just because he's somehow related to you won't wash in Whitehall. There were three aircraft missing last night. Bomber Command is building up its strength. Now it's the turn of the Germans to get a bit of their own medicine. I like telling them that at Charing Cross Tube station every night. You should come down and spend a night with us. Mrs Coombes makes me cheese sandwiches. Thinks I'm as poor as a church mouse."

"What's wrong with the Air Ministry shelter?"

"Wrong people. I've made some real friends in the underground. But I'm digressing. Don't forget the Japs were on our side last time. The Russians are having a bad time. We're sending them fighter aircraft through Murmansk when that part of the sea isn't frozen. Round neutral Sweden. The route to Leningrad is in German control. Now the Russians are our Allies. Before the war, those that knew said Russian communism was worse than German fascism. At least fascism has a strong element of capitalism in how they run an economy. Any port in a storm, I suppose. Ha, ha. You're meant to laugh, William Smythe. Before you start and I shut up I'll have Katherine bring us in some tea. What would we British do without tea? Now if your Japs conquer India and cut off our supply of tea we'll all be sunk... Katherine, my dear. Could you rustle us up a pot of tea? There isn't any sugar, of course."

After William left, to visit their mutual friend and William's fellow journalist Horatio Wakefield, Harry got on the phone. After an hour it was clear no one was interested, or if they were, they showed no concern to Harry. Some of the people he spoke to were short with him.

"Nice of you to call, Harry. Aren't you with the Air Ministry? There's a real war right here in Europe."

The inference was plain. It was none of his business. When Ding-a-ling made his daily report he heard William's Japanese story.

"Why would they want to warn the Americans, Harry? Even if it was anything to do with us. The Civil Service likes to keep it in compartments. Even in wartime. You only worry about your own house burning down. They've decided not to hang Hirst-Brown. The bit about the thirty-two shillings must have got to someone."

"What are they going to do with him?"

"Leave him in jail."

"How long for?"

"Who knows. If the Japs attack the American fleet they'll have to declare war. Then they're in. They'll declare war against Japan's ally Germany. No wonder they've been giving you the cold shoulder. They're all hugging themselves, hoping the Japs go in. When Hitler did it for us in Russia by breaching their non-hostility pact and attacking the Soviets, Churchill did a jig. If you can imagine that. He won't cry if the Japs bring America into the war. I didn't realise until the other day Churchill's mother is an American. Roosevelt says he drinks too much."

"I'm always suspicious of people who don't drink."

"So am I. Damn unsociable. Maybe if you phone the Prime Minister he'd warn his mother's family in America."

"Even I can't get through to Churchill. For some reason he never takes my calls."

"Have you ever tried, Harry?"

"Of course not."

"I heard Anthony was on that raid last night, by the way. Glad he landed safely."

"Oh thank God."

"You didn't know?"

"Why do we worry about our children more than ourselves?"

"They are all we leave behind that lasts. Money gets spent or stolen.

If the kids have their own kids, you go on. Basic human instinct. We want to survive on this earth. It's the only certainty we have. Unless we blow up the world."

"Won't the Japs attack India if they attack America?"

"They want to control the Far East. The way Hitler wants to conquer the whole of Europe. You mark my word, that chap Gandhi will let us British defend India against Japan and then throw us out."

"So you believe William's story?"

"If the oil bit is true they don't have a choice. Do you have any more of that Scotch?"

"Not a drop. The last drop went down Sarah Coombes's throat, bless her heart."

"She has her eye on you, Harry."

"I'm married."

"Tina's far away. Do you miss her?"

"All of them. More and more. Your own family is the only sanity in this world."

"You want to run a story on Japan about to attack America? Mr Glass will never go for that without proof, William," said Horatio Wakefield.

"I phoned Glen Hamilton at the *Denver Telegraph* from Harry's office. Got straight through after only ten minutes, just shows where the priorities lie. He also wasn't interested. Sounded a bit on edge. Won't run the story. Told me to stop spreading rumours. He was even quite sharp on the phone for Glen. I've done my bit. I'm staying with Betty."

"You can always stay with me and Janet. If you can put up with the noise of the kids. I want them to go to Cornwall. Janet says we're all in this war together. The idea of foster parents for the kids doesn't appeal. The school's closed down. Janet's teaching Harry and Bergit at home."

"He was a spy for the Nazis, Horatio. Harry's confirmed it. One of Henning von Lieberman's sleepers did something Harry won't explain to the press."

"Janet won't believe you. Said he was such a gentleman."

"They often are."

"Did you get enough details for a story?"

"I was told just enough to let you know."

"How long are you staying with Betty?"

"Who knows. The flat's comfortable. The girl can cook. And she's organised."

"Sounds perfect."

When William came backstage that night with a bunch of flowers, Genevieve was surprised to see him. He had a girl with him which made it easier. They should never have had their one-night stand in New York when she was feeling lonely and homesick. She had used him which wasn't right. Having casual sex with someone who cared was wrong, even if at the time she was unaware of the intensity of William's feelings. Afterwards in England she had tried to explain. Explaining made it worse. If he had come alone with his bunch of flowers she would have had to tell him what was going on with Tinus and hurt the poor man again. Why couldn't men be just friends, she asked herself shaking hands with the girl. The way the girl looked at William made Genevieve smile.

The play had been running a week, Genevieve taking a cameo part to relieve her boredom with Tinus in Scotland teaching young men how to fly. Her whole life revolved around his odd days of leave. The play was a trivial drawing room comedy about a shiftless young man trying to win the heart of a sports-mad heiress by pretending to be an Olympic athlete. It took people's minds off the war, relieving the permanent tension. It was not, in her opinion, a very good play but served its purpose.

There was talk in Hollywood of making a movie. Gerry Hollingsworth phoned her every week telling her to come back to America. One of his boys had been killed in North Africa by Rommel's Afrika Korps. Genevieve had not known what to say. She had once met David in London when Gerry Hollingsworth was Louis Casimir and Jewish. David, she was told, was a lieutenant. Gerry had not told her the name of his regiment. He had been crying down the phone. The sickening feeling in the pit of her stomach at the thought of Tinus going back on active service had stopped her saying the right words, like 'no man should bury his own child'. Everything was personal. David to Gerry. Tinus to her.

"Congratulations on your forthcoming marriage."

"What did you say?" she asked the girl quickly, glancing at William. In his eyes was the look of total loss.

"Your marriage to Flight Lieutenant Oosthuizen. You're wearing an engagement ring."

"Oh, this. Well I suppose you could call it that."

"On the right finger." The girl was looking self-satisfied.

"Was it your idea to come backstage, Betty?"

"Yes, I'm sorry. William won't believe me."

"And you love William. I hope you enjoyed the show. Not my most spectacular part. We are getting married, William, but only after the war. Tinus won't marry with the war hanging over our heads. Why we've told no one other than close friends. How did you find out, Betty? It is Betty? Won't you both sit down if you can find some room? This is a small dressing room. You see, this time, I'm not the star. Tinus is up in Scotland. He's a flying instructor. His nerves are shot after four tours so they pulled him off active duty. I suppose you know someone at Tangmere. Pilots talk to each other sitting waiting to be scrambled into action. They say things they normally wouldn't, not knowing if they will be alive in an hour's time."

"Will you have dinner with us, Genevieve?" asked William.

"Not tonight, William. I try and make a call to Tinus from my hotel room. Mostly I don't get through. Just another girl in love with a pilot. I'll put your flowers in water. They are pretty. How are you, William?"

"Bombed out. Literally. The whole damn building came down while I was in Singapore."

"I'm so glad you were lucky not to be in your flat. Have you seen Harry Brigandshaw recently?"

"This morning."

"Give him my love."

"Does Harry know?"

"Not officially. We want to be married from Hastings Court and go and live in Rhodesia. As far as possible from all this madness."

"You'll give up your career?"

"We give up everything for love, William. Where are you now staying?"

"With Betty. Betty's my secretary."

"Ah, that Betty," said Genevieve with a soft smile. "How convenient. I hope you'll both be very happy. These are lovely flowers. So difficult to get fresh flowers at Christmas."

"Goodbye, Genevieve."

"Goodbye, William. Have a good life. You're a good man. Look after him, Betty. Good men are hard to find."

The bombs did not come for three days. For three nights Janet did not take the children to the air-raid shelter under their house in Chelsea. Horatio had had the roof of the cellar reinforced with one-inch steel at the start of the war. There was an outside stairwell to the cellar. The door to the outside had been reinforced with a steel plate. Only a direct hit through the three storeys of the house with the bomb exploding at the bottom was a threat. Horatio had not explained to Janet how they could all be killed. If the house caught fire they would escape up the stairwell into the street. It was better than sleeping in the subway if not so safe. There was always the risk of getting to the underground tube station before they were safe. There were hurricane lamps and a paraffin heater which warmed up the small room in winter. Horatio wanted Janet to take the children to Cornwall which wasn't being bombed by the Germans.

Her speech therapy practice had stopped. People had bigger problems to worry about than cleft palates, or stutters, or speaking the King's English without a provincial accent. Janet would not go without Horatio, the foreign correspondent at the *Daily Mail*. Except that with the war raging overhead all his reporting came from London. All of it about the war. Everything in their lives was concentrated in the war, in the present, which included Herr Henning von Lieberman.

"He was such a nice man. Spoke beautiful English. How can such a nice man do such terrible things? Without radar, William says, the Germans could bomb London into the ground, day and night. Why? He was so friendly when I helped his stutter. What's gone wrong with the world, Horatio?"

"According to Harry Brigandshaw it happens slowly. At first you think you are doing the right thing."

"I think the children are asleep. If the air-raid siren hasn't gone off by now they can stay in their beds all night. I hate that shelter. Never sleep properly cooped up in a dungeon watching the children toss and turn by candlelight after you turn off the hurricane lamp."

"Go to sleep, my love. They're not coming over tonight. Billy Glass thinks the tide has turned in the air war. That the generals in the German high command have realised they can't invade England across the Channel without command of the air. Even if Hitler won't believe them. Mr Glass thinks we're over the worst in London. Now it's us bombing Berlin and Cologne."

"And if the Japs come into the war?"

"Don't let's think about it. I'm going to have a look at the children."

When Horatio came back to tell Janet they were asleep, she was breathing softly. Horatio kissed her gently on the forehead, not wanting to wake her up. Of all the things he had done in his life, marrying Janet had been the best.

Instead of going to sleep, Horatio lay on his back thinking of his conversation with Harry Brigandshaw when Horatio had congratulated Harry on his twenty-three kills in the last war, the start of what Horatio thought would be an easy conversation. The exchange had been at the very beginning of what became a lasting friendship of mutual trust.

"It was murder, Mr Wakefield. What's the difference? Thou shalt not kill. Under any circumstances. When they asked Socrates in the Plato Dialogues if it was right to kill a man if the man had a knife to his throat about to kill him, you know what Socrates said?"

"No, sir."

"Then you should read Plato before congratulating me on shooting down twenty-three enemy aircraft. Thank God Klaus von Lieberman survived."

"I'll read Plato, Mr Brigandshaw. What did Socrates reply?"

"The man might change his mind. Killing him was still murder. The crews that died by my guns were murdered by me, Mr Wakefield. I have to live with that every day. Men with families who still remember them and I didn't even know their names. Saving Klaus from the flames of his crashed aircraft was the only good thing I did in the war. Revenging the death of my brother George was only compounding the wrong. Making the whole damn thing go round again. If I knew who they were I'd find every member of those families and go down on my knees. Thou shalt not kill. Under any circumstances. Plato explains the complete certainty of that rightness better than me."

With the night sky outside their bedroom still quiet, not even a roaming searchlight in the sky, Horatio realised once again the rightness of Harry Brigandshaw's words. In the children's bedroom young Harry and Bergit slept. His son was named in honour of Harry Brigandshaw who had called Klaus von Lieberman when Horatio had been abducted from Berlin to the countryside by the Nazis before the war while he and William were on assignment as freelance journalists to report the rise of Hitler. His daughter Bergit was named in honour of his saviour's wife. The goodness of Harry's words was not lost on Horatio. Without Harry saving Klaus, he would likely have been dead, his two children never born. Now Harry's son Anthony was bombing the Germans, Klaus's son Erwin blitzing the English. Man's stupidity once again in its eternal repetition.

Sometime after the moon stopped shining through the bedroom window, Horatio fell into a restless sleep.

When he woke in the morning it was still quiet outside.

"Good morning, my darling. Did you sleep better last night? Bergit and Harry haven't made a sound. Go back to sleep while I go downstairs and make us some tea. My word, it's chilly this morning."

"Did you sleep all right, Janet?"

"Like a log. Won't it be nice when the war is over?"

7

The call came through from Glen Hamilton in Denver, Colorado, ten days later. Horatio was in a meeting with Billy Glass, the editor of the *Daily Mail*. William Smythe was sitting on the leather sofa in Mr Glass's Fleet Street office. The call had been redirected from William's office by Betty Townsend. Horatio picked up the phone after a nod in the phone's direction by his editor. Mr Glass believed in delegation right from the start.

"William?" said a distant voice. The line was bad.

"Horatio Wakefield of the *Daily Mail*."

"Glen Hamilton. It's not yet on the wire. William was right. The Japs have attacked Pearl Harbor in a surprise assault from aircraft carriers. Devastation to our Pacific Fleet. Roosevelt is about to declare war on Japan. Probably Germany a couple of days later. Thought I owed that to William for not listening."

"He's right here."

The line suddenly went dead leaving Horatio staring at an empty phone.

"Who's right here?" asked Billy Glass, taking in Horatio's expression of surprise, quickly followed by relief, followed by a broad smile.

"My friend William. The Japs have attacked the American Pacific Fleet at Pearl Harbor. They're in the war. We're not on our own anymore.

We can win. That was Glen Hamilton from Denver returning William's favour."

"Then get off your arse down to the newsroom. Talk it straight to Jimmy on the press. Stop everything. We can get this into the London streets first."

"What about me?" asked William as Horatio ran for the door.

"Bugger you, Will," said Horatio over his shoulder. "Every man for himself."

"Do I get my usual fee, Mr Glass? Sounds like Betty redirected my call from Denver."

"Your freelance cheque for top information as usual, William Smythe. What would we at the *Mail* do without you? Now this does put the cat among the proverbial pigeons. They'll attack Hong Kong and Singapore next. A small price to pay for America coming into the war."

"Not if your cousin is stationed in Singapore and the Japs invade overland down the Malayan Peninsula. My cousin Joe is a sergeant in the Royal Engineers. Married to a Chinese girl. Cherry Blossom's father was the one who tipped me off. Sometimes I don't like being right. They have kids. Now this bloody war is right on their doorstep."

"Have a drink with me, Will. It's six o'clock. We'll have the paper on the street corners by dawn. Got hold of a bottle of Scotch from a lady that owed me a favour. This means victory."

"Not if they sank the American fleet."

"Singapore is a fortress. The Japs won't get in there. That port controls the seas of Asia. But you know all that."

"Cherry Blossom's father said..."

"Is he a military man?"

"He was right last time. Is it real Scotch?"

"All the way from Scotland. I'm so glad Horatio took that call. Now you and I can drink in comfort while he does the work. It's two weeks since Jerry last hit London. Oh yes. Now we are going to win. You know my guess, William? We'll win the war and lose the empire. Isn't America's wish for the British Empire to dissolve part of a pet theory of yours? Empire out one door. The dollar in the other. There's always a price to pay. Whatever we do, with or without the Americans, our two nations are joined at the hip. Lose a bit of money in the colonies. Make it up in joint American British trade. Half the bloody colonies cost us more money to administer than we get from trade. Or am I quoting back your own words, William? Let Gandhi have India and see what they do with it.

In the end they'll still be speaking English like the Americans. The educated Indians. Met a few of them in London. Jolly good chaps. We'll export more railway rolling stock than ever. You don't want soda in your Scotch? Of course not. Ruins the aroma. Have a cigar. Last box. This is big news."

"I'll just phone Betty. Say I'll be home a little late."

"How nice. She really has sunk in her claws. I have a new mistress even my wife doesn't know about. Chop and change to keep on top's my motto. Makes me feel years younger. Now just smell that malt whisky. Some Sassenachs say there are only two good things out of Scotland: the road out and the whisky. For myself, I'm rather partial to the Scots. My new lady is a Scot. Ministry of Information. Not sure if she wasn't planted but who cares? She doesn't. Asked her once. You know what she said? 'Who cares.' Lovely girl."

"Did she get you the bottle of whisky, Billy?"

"How on earth did you know?"

William waited for a moment as his call went through.

"It's me, Betty. Back a bit late. Thanks for Glen's call. No, I won't be too late. Billy Glass has found a bottle of whisky... Yes, I'm sure you can. Bye... She's coming over."

"Clever girl."

"She is rather."

When Glen Hamilton phoned Freya St Clair she was sitting in front of the fire in the lounge of Purbeck Manor. As Freya Taylor she had been Glen's personal assistant at the *Denver Telegraph* before marrying Robert St Clair. She was the first to read *Holy Knight* in 1928. Her son Richard, just turned eleven, was sitting next to her reading a book, quiet for once in his life. Outside the long sash windows rain was pelting down. Merlin St Clair, the Lord of the Manor and her brother-in-law, had moved the phone from the hall to the lounge. It was better than talking in a draughty hall that was often cold in summer. Four-year-old Chuck had gone off to find his grandmother. Lady St Clair always found time to alleviate Chuck's boredom. Chuck was mostly bored in the old manor house living with the old people. There were no young children for miles.

Merlin St Clair had unsuccessfully offered the house as a refuge for children from the East End of London. They could see Poole Harbour from the top of the Purbeck Hills behind the manor. The Germans had bombed the harbour since the start of the Blitz. The London children had been sent to Cornwall and up to Scotland, some as far as Canada. Every acre of the old family estate was growing crops to help the war effort. Most of the labourers were land girls, the men having gone off to war.

Upstairs in the old manor, her husband Robert was trying to write a book, his head full of the war and getting nowhere. Trying to write a book about medieval England when the island was under attack was proving too difficult for Robert's imagination.

When Freya picked up the phone the last person she expected was her old boss in America. Barnaby St Clair was coming down with a girl from a band.

"Is that Barnaby?" asked Freya, her mind elsewhere.

"Hello, Freya?"

"Glen! Why this is a lovely surprise."

"We're in the war, Freya."

"What do you mean?"

"Roosevelt has declared war on Japan and the German Axis. We were attacked by carrier-based planes. Half the Pacific fleet is burning in Pearl Harbor. Dreadful devastation. Nothing on your radio?"

"Merlin won't let us turn on the news."

"Wise man. Are you all right?"

"They bomb the harbour. We can see the flames at night. Nothing too bad in the country. Poole Harbour is beyond the back of the hills behind the house."

"So here we are again. How's the heir to the St Clair Barony?"

"Reading a book next to me on the sofa in front of the fire. Why did you phone?"

"I felt lonely. You were with me in the last war. It's the boys. Glen Junior is turning eighteen. Can't wait to fight the Japs. Alwin's a year younger. Samantha's in a real state while the boys are jumping with joy. Gregory L'Amour, hero of the films, is finally going to get his wish to fight a real war. America's at war, Freya. That's a real bitch. You be careful."

"You too, Glen."

"Why does the world always want to destroy itself?"

"Human nature passed down to us by our ancestors, most of whom were the survivors of wars. Darwin, Glen, survival of the fittest."

"Are you writing?"

"Given up plays. Robert's struggling. Surrounded by war there's little else to think of. Give my love to America."

With so much to say in so short a time, both of them had said little when the three minutes came to an end. Her connection to her country, America, was cut leaving Freya bewildered.

"What was that all about, Mum?"

"Go back to your book. Nothing, thank God, that affects you, Richard. I'm going up to see how your father is getting on with the book. The fire needs some more wood."

"I want to be a writer when I grow up."

"I'm glad. Being a writer you can live in nice places."

On the way up the stairs to Robert's old bedroom he was using as a study, she met Merlin coming down the other way past the old, dark family portraits that lined the stairs.

"Glen Hamilton just phoned. America's in the war. Japs attacked Pearl Harbor."

"I know. Listened to the news."

"But you won't let us! Do you always listen to the news?"

"Always."

"Why didn't you tell us?"

"You can't do anything. Just upsets everyone. It's better not to know bad news when there's nothing you can do about it. Now we are going to win."

"That's good news."

"But not for a long time. A lot of people are going to die across Europe and the Far East before this is over."

"Have you told Robert?"

"He's having enough trouble with the book. I'm going out to shoot us a rabbit or two."

"It's pelting with rain. Poor little rabbits."

"When it's stewed you'll eat it just the same. There's a war on."

While Freya was powdering her nose in their bedroom, sitting on the stool in front of her mirror before going up to her husband's study, Robert from his study window was watching his brother Merlin walk out of a side door into the rain. Robert smiled, knowing what Merlin was up to. Under the oilskin cape there would be a loaded doublebarrelled shotgun. A 12 bore, as Merlin preferred to call the antique, hammer-head weapon that had belonged to their grandfather. Merlin was going hunting. Most likely for a brace of rabbits. Something was on his brother's mind.

With his train of thought taken out of the book he was trying to write with absolutely no success, Robert got up from the chair of his desk that gave him a view through the window over the family estate and put some wood on the fire in the grate.

When they had first arrived from America fifteen months earlier, Robert had begun chopping the firewood for the winter so the logs dried out. The children had joined them when they decided to stay in Dorset and not with Barnaby in London. Richard had been made a weekly boarder in a small private school not far from Purbeck Manor. After the long summer of 1941, the wood was bone dry, the split elm logs burning nicely in his old bedroom grate, the room he had made into his study. Everything was perfect for writing.

Day after day Robert sat at his desk or in the armchair he had brought up from downstairs. Nothing happened. His mind was crammed with the war. For the first time in his life Robert was unable to write, unable to leave the real world to go with the people in his book. Into a world he made himself to his liking, not the world of people forever discontented with their lot, arguing with each other to get their own way. In Robert's books, everyone except the villain was nice to each other. Loved each other. Cherished each other.

"You can come in, Freya. Heard you coming down the corridor on tiptoe."

"How's it going?"

"It isn't. And won't. Until this bloody war is over. Are the children all right?"

"Richard's reading a book. Wants to be a writer. Chuck's gone off to find his grandmother. He's bored."

"Wants to write? That's a turn-up for the books, no pun intended. I'll talk him out of that idea. Writing is wonderful when it works. Agony when it doesn't. This last year has been agony. What's on Merlin's mind? Gone off with a gun under his oilskin in the rain. Merlin only goes for a tramp in the rain when he has something on his mind."

"America's come into the war."

"Have they? Why?"

"The Japs bombed Pearl Harbor. Glen just phoned. Merlin had heard it on the news."

"He doesn't listen to the news."

"Apparently he does. In secret. Now the whole world's at war with each other."

"In the olden days the wars were local. Still, everyone was fighting each other somewhere. Just no one knew about all the other wars. Come and sit on my knee by the fire. I just put on a nice dry log. My poor mother, Chuck is a handful when he's bored."

"She loves it. Takes her mind off the death of your father. Gives her something to do."

"I suppose so. The star of *Holy Knight* now has his chance to fly in combat. We humans really are a mess."

"It'll be over quickly now. Last time it took America a year to win the war."

Robert smiled at his wife as she sat on the side of his chair. There was no arguing with the Americans. They had won the war. That was that. Pulling his wife down onto his lap they fell silent, happy with each other's company. For the first time in years his right foot began to itch. The right foot he had left in France in 1916. The one the German shell had taken away, never to be found.

"My missing foot's itching. Memories. I'll just scratch it mentally so the itch goes away."

"Mad as a hatter. You English are as mad as hatters."

"Probably."

"One brother shooting rabbits in the rain. The other scratching an invisible foot. Tell me about the book."

"All my characters have buggered off. None of them want to talk to me. I love this old house. It's in my bones. I imagine my ancestors sitting right here. Getting up and looking out of that window. Putting logs on the fire. Shooting rabbits in the rain. Pestering their grandmother. Right down the centuries."

PART SIX

ONLY GOD KNOWS WHY – APRIL TO
JUNE 1943

1

The row had started at Christmas the following year. Gerry Hollingsworth in Los Angeles wanted Genevieve to play the lead of a nurse in love with an American soldier. The soldier was Gregory L'Amour. The picture was propaganda. It was important for the American people to be united with Britain in the war against Japan and Germany.

The same day Genevieve told Tinus she was contemplating a film offer from America, Tinus was on his way back to active duty in command of a wing at RAF Tangmere, reducing Genevieve to a flood of tears. The RAF had developed a system of concentrating three squadrons of fighters on enemy formations simultaneously, giving them not only superior aircraft in the Mark IX Spitfire, but superior numbers in the air. The newly promoted Wing Commander Oosthuizen DFC and Bar was to be one of three pilots leading the new wing formations at Tangmere. Over England, the RAF were in command of the air. The German High Command had abandoned Operation Sea Lion to invade Britain having failed in its attempt to shoot the RAF out of the skies.

"Then we get married now," said Genevieve the moment she learnt Tinus was going back on active duty; they were arguing in Genevieve's small flat in Hay Street, close to the theatres.

"But you're going to America."

"I won't if you marry me. I can live on the station at Tangmere."

"Haven't you forgotten the third of the three musketeers?"

"I very often think of André. Why I want to be Mrs Oosthuizen before it's too late. I want something to remember if anything happens to you. If you won't marry me now, I'm going to America."

"To Gregory L'Amour, I suppose. They won't let their precious film star fly in combat. Far too valuable as the hero in a propaganda movie."

"Propaganda has always been part of wars. I'll be doing something if I can't be the wing commander's wife. We can have a child before it's too late."

"And leave him without a father? I said right from the word go when we became engaged we would marry the day the war was over. It's not fair on you and certainly not on a child. I know what it's like to go through most of my life without a father. What I would have done without Uncle Harry I don't know. You and I don't have brothers. The child would be all on its own with no one to help."

"The child would have me, Tinus. I'd have the living memory of you. Don't you want to leave something of you behind on this earth?"

"I'm not going to die! The experienced pilots survive."

"Then let's get married."

"No, Genevieve. If I'm killed you will still have your own life to live. What is so important now is soon forgotten. Ten years down the line with three kids from some famous actor, you won't even think of Tinus Oosthuizen. I'll be a vague smile in the back of your memory."

"Don't say things like that!"

"Go to America, Genevieve. It'll be better. You'll have something to do and think about other than the war."

"When do you go back to Tangmere?"

"I'm on my way now. Had to change trains in London. When did you hear about the film with Gregory?"

"A week ago. I was going to write."

"Do you want to go?"

"Not if you marry me."

"Just look at the time! The taxi's waiting outside. How do you like the new uniform with three thick rings on my sleeve?"

"Very smart, darling. Now go. I'm about to blub. I'd never forget you with ten children. Please be careful."

They had fiercely hugged each other, parted and gone their separate ways.

When Tinus reached RAF Tangmere, he found her engagement ring with its small diamond in his pocket. She had slipped it in his pocket when she hugged him goodbye.

A week later in his room he read about her going to America in the paper. It was headlines. With a picture of Gregory L'Amour. There was no point in crying over spilt milk. He had to concentrate to survive or the Germans would get him the same way they got André Cloete. He left his room with the photograph of Genevieve by the side of his bed and went across to the officers' mess. Standing at the small bar he ordered himself a pint of beer from the mess steward. They all had problems. There was no point showing them his. If their leader was an emotional mess, it would affect his pilots.

Keeping a grim smile on his face at the thought of Gregory L'Amour again touching Genevieve, even if it was only on the set of a film, Tinus prepared to live what was left of his life on his own. In his stomach it was empty. Hollow. Everything good in his life had gone. They had to finish the war before going back to normal life with family and kids. 'Life,' as Uncle Harry so often said to him, 'was never easy.' He had a job to do. Being sentimental about André had never helped. Thinking constantly of Genevieve would not help either. He needed a clean, clear mind. Later, when the war was finally won, they would have their children, children with a father to cherish them through life.

Tinus looked around with a smile on his face. He was again under control.

In the bar was the Polish pilot who had visited Hastings Court with his Polish girlfriend before the war.

"Janusz! I'll be blowed. Tinus Oosthuizen. You visited my uncle's house from Poland before the war and again at the start of the war. Have you got the other wings?" Tinus could see Janusz Kowalski was wearing the same uniform with the three thick rings of a wing commander on his sleeve.

"They've broken up the Polish Squadron. Not enough of us left. I heard you were coming to join us, Tinus. Just back myself from a spot of leave."

"How's Ingrid, I think her name was?"

"Not a word since the war started. Nor of my family. How've you been? I still remember that Christmas at Hastings Court in '39. When I escaped from Poland and joined the Royal Air Force. What were the names of those two girls who played in a band?"

"Fleur and Celia."

"Are they all right?"

"Never better. When you and I get some leave we'll go up to London together. Nice to see a familiar face."

"Yes, it is. Gets less and less I'm afraid. Come and tell me what you've been up to apart from fighting the war."

They were both looking at each other in mild shock. Both were thinking the same thing about the other. They were both thinking the other looked ten years older than the last time they had met at Hastings Court.

When the cameras finally rolled on the worst script Genevieve had ever read, England was a long way away. In the four months she had been in America Genevieve had moved into a small, two-roomed apartment close to Gerry Hollingsworth's studio. The fact the script was terrible did not matter. It was all about America's brave soldiers winning the war with the help of the air force and marines. Patriotic Americans would flock to see the movie. The film would make a fortune, which was Gerry Hollingsworth's sole intention when it came to making them. Everyone was in a hurry to get the movie into the cinemas as soon as possible. Every now and again they tried rewriting the crass dialogue as they went along, Gregory, like Genevieve, cringing at the things they were meant to say from the script.

"Whoever wrote this script must have swallowed the book of clichés," said Gregory L'Amour after a week. "It's terrible."

"There's a war on," said Gerry Hollingsworth without taking offence.

"Are you sure you didn't write this yourself, Gerry?"

"As a matter of fact I did, or some of it. The idea was mine."

"And half the dialogue."

"Something like that. I asked Robert St Clair to write a script, and his wife, Freya. Wouldn't budge out of England. Their boy's in a good school."

"Did you send him your idea, Mr Hollingsworth?" asked Genevieve.

"Yes, I did. Please, Genevieve, Gerry. I hate that Mr Hollingsworth."

"Then he's still laughing, Mr Hollingsworth." Getting a rise out of the producer was always fun for Genevieve.

"The public will love it. It's so rich in sentiment and patriotism."

"That's what worries us. Never mind. We're all doing our bit to win the war even if our contribution isn't as much as General Montgomery."

"It's the Pacific theatre that worries Americans. Why my film is set in the Solomon Islands where our brave forces are launching a major offensive against the Japanese right now. The papers are full of it. Our film will show the public what's going on through the eyes of an ordinary soldier and a young nurse."

"We shall persevere. Can't you find a proper scriptwriter?"

"They're all in uniform."

Genevieve being flippant didn't help. They were all going through the motions numbed by their own pain. She knew that. How could Gerry Hollingsworth concentrate on writing a good script with his son David buried in North Africa? Even Montgomery's victory at El Alamein in November had not brought Gerry Hollingsworth any consolation. His son was still dead.

His daughter Rachel's fiancé, a regular officer with the Royal Navy, Pangbourne College and Dartmouth, had gone down with his destroyer a month after David had died fighting in the desert. Why, in Genevieve's mind, they should have been married. Now Rachel was thirty and likely to be alone with nothing to look forward to forever. No children to watch growing up. Nothing of importance to do for the rest of her life.

Genevieve had not heard from Tinus since giving him back his ring. She was not even certain if he were alive. Who would tell her? Maybe Uncle Harry, but should Tinus be killed and with Anthony flying raids three times a week over Germany, Harry Brigandshaw would have other things on his mind to worry about. She was cut off. Despite her temporary fame, she was going to die an old maid.

She had tried using the phone but the British Post Office were unable to put personal calls through to RAF Tangmere in time of war. She needed some kind of clearance. Asking Uncle Harry would tell him something was wrong between the two of them after all the excitement when they both told him together they were engaged. Now, that day seemed a lifetime ago. All she could do was hope the war came to an end before he was killed.

It was something she was unable to talk to Gregory about, miserable at his own inability, despite all the bluster, to get into a uniform that did not come from a film studio's wardrobe. To Gregory, acting the part, as he had told her in one of his depressions, was like a man trying to make love without his balls.

"I'd rather be dead than make this movie, but they won't let me join up. I tried at the recruiting office downtown. The charade lasted five minutes lined up in the queue. Then someone pointed, 'Isn't that Gregory L'Amour.' Pandemonium broke loose. When I asked the sergeant if I could sign up as a private he laughed in my face. Within a minute some captain was wringing his hands, fawning all over the place and me in particular. Bloody circus. When I said I was Joseph Pott not Gregory L'Amour and showed them my identification papers, that really set them off. Next I was drinking coffee with the colonel in charge of recruitment. The air force had chased me away soon after Pearl Harbor when I first tried to join up. They all just smile at me. Say how good my films are for morale. Now look at this load of shit, Genevieve. If I ever have kids they'll laugh at me. I'm not even a real person anymore. I envy Tinus more than you can imagine. He's a real man. No wonder you want to marry him and not me. I'm just an image on a screen that people think is a bloody hero. I'm not real."

"He won't marry me either. Not until the war is over. Now I've given him back his ring in an attempt to force him to the altar he doesn't even write."

"Then he's a fool."

"You don't know what it's like."

"I know I don't."

"Gregory, come here and give me a hug. At the end of this stupid film you'll still be alive. Tinus likely will be dead."

"Will you marry me then, Genevieve?"

"That's just horrible."

"Wasn't meant to be. Just remember I love you."

"Poor Gregory. The most eligible bachelor in America. Why can't you find yourself a girlfriend?"

"There are always girls. I just love you. He'll be all right. He's a great pilot. He still loves you. I can only imagine what he's thinking in combat. It's better for him not to be thinking what you said in your last letter. You have to concentrate to fly a plane, that much I do know. No distractions. Especially when the Germans are trying to kill you."

"Come round to my apartment tonight and we'll try and do something with this script. That last bit hurt."

"I'm sorry. Truth hurts. I'd love to come round to your apartment. Don't worry. I'll behave myself. That's about all I can do these days with you, Genevieve."

Genevieve had made the supper. They were seated opposite each other in the small lounge. Outside the open window, seven storeys below, they could hear the traffic. With oil in abundance in America, petrol was not rationed. Except for the patriotism, all the flags, all the brass bands playing the American national anthem, the average person's life in Los Angeles had seen little change. Only those with loved ones overseas knew what the war was all about. Like Genevieve's mother back in London.

The letter from Esther had been in the morning mail. Esther hated writing letters, putting her thoughts down on paper in a hand that was barely legible to her daughter. It seemed from the letter Esther's biggest problem in wartime London was how difficult it was to buy booze. Half the letter was a plea to her daughter to set up a free flow of good gin from America to England. There was no mention of Genevieve's father in the letter. There never was. Since Merlin had become a hermit in Purbeck Manor, living with his mother and brother Robert, Genevieve doubted the two of them ever saw each other or spoke on the phone. All they had in common to talk about was her. Going to live in America had removed their only reason for communication.

They were reading through Gerry Hollingsworth's script scene by scene, silently. After each appalling scene they made suggestions. Mostly their suggestions made it worse.

"How do they do it?" asked Gregory. "Like your uncle. All of *Holy Knight* came out of his head, even if it was based on fact. All those ancestors of his and yours had been dead for centuries. They couldn't help."

"Oh, but they did. Uncle Robert said they were in his head talking to him all the time. Even when he wasn't writing down the book. They followed him everywhere."

"Well, no one's following me now."

"It doesn't matter. It's gooey and sentimental. There are people who talk like this, we just have to make it sound real when we act the parts."

"Couldn't Bruno Kannberg help?"

"Probably. He's in New York. War correspondent for the *Daily Mirror*. Given up writing memoirs for film stars, as he frequently likes to call us."

"Give him a ring. He owes us."

"Now? What's the time in New York?"

"Just give him a ring. I brought the number of his apartment. Thought you and I would come unstuck trying to be writers. We're performing artists, not creative artists."

"You want him to fly to LA?"

"That's the idea. It may have all the right goo and sentiment but this dialogue is going to make us a laughing stock. We need help, Genevieve.

Without our friendship Bruno wouldn't be in the States. He'd be in the British Army with the rest of them. Now there's a man who doesn't want to fight."

"And there's a sensible man. I'll call him. Do you want him to bring his wife?"

"Why not?"

The leer on Gregory's face was unmistakable.

"You haven't! You dog."

"She wanted to come up in the world."

"Does Bruno know?"

"Not unless Gillian told him."

"So you do have a secret girlfriend?"

"A lay, Genevieve. Just a lay."

"Poor old Bruno."

"Don't think he cares a damn. Met his editor out on a visit from London, Arthur Bumley. According to Arthur, Gillian refers to him as Art the Bumley. Arthur doesn't care what she calls him. Nice guy. Says Bruno's besotted by the woman and needs his eyes opened. It was Arthur who suggested I make a pass at Gillian. She has something that's very sexy. The way she looks at you. Goes straight to your balls. Social climber. Wants all the money. She'd love the papers to blast us across the scandal pages."

"I'll give Bruno a ring. You dirty, sly old fox. Was she any good?"

"Brilliant. One of the best fucks I've had."

"Good for you."

"Aren't you jealous?"

"I'm in love, Greg. People in love only think of each other."

The telephone was in the bedroom by the side of her bed. Genevieve closed the door and dialled the long distance operator, giving him the number of Bruno Kannberg's apartment in New York.

"Hold on please."

Sitting on the bed waiting for the connection Genevieve wondered why she had shut her bedroom door. Was it to keep out Gregory or was she annoyed he was having an affair? Like so many things she had done in her life it was easier to do than be done by. The fact it was Bruno's wife committing adultery was not part of her disquiet.

"Gillian Kannberg," came a voice from a long way away.

"It's Genevieve. Can Bruno come to Los Angeles to help with a script? Greg and I think it's terrible. We've tried to do something about it but neither of us can write. Gerry Hollingsworth wrote the script which should explain the problem. He's a film producer. Not a script writer."

"We can fly down for a couple of days. Bruno's going to cover the war in the Solomon Islands next week so it's on his way so to speak. Maybe I can stay on and help? I learnt a lot when we wrote your book, Genevieve. Do you remember that two weeks at Hastings Court? Do you ever hear from Harry Brigandshaw? I heard his wife took the kids to South Africa."

"Would Bruno mind?"

"Of course not. Why should he?"

"Can I speak to him?"

"You don't have to. We'd love to come down. April in New York is wet and cold. He can tell his London editor he's on assignment, which he is in a way. Film people are always news."

"I'll book you a hotel. Ring me when you know your flight. You're very helpful, Gillian."

"We English have to stick together. Isn't the war terrible? Is Gregory with you by any chance?"

"He is, matter of fact."

"That is nice. Art the Bumley will never find out. We'll pay our own expenses in Los Angeles."

"Of course you will, Gillian."

"Bruno's always wanted to get into film. With the new offensive he says the war in the Pacific will be over in months. Then America will go for the Germans. I'd love to live in Hollywood when the war's over. This is exciting. I'll tell my husband the moment I get off the phone."

"You don't have to ask him first?"

"Of course not. Bruno does whatever I want or I keep him short."

Genevieve heard the girl's giggle all the way from New York.

"Is that how it works?" said Genevieve.

"It's the only weapon we women have got and it's powerful. It's so lovely to have you back in America. How's your fiancé? Are you going to live in the States after the war? Doesn't Tinus have a cousin in Virginia? His Uncle Harry owns a big share in the Tender Meat Company I remember. See their products everywhere. What fun. Tinus will be rich. So looking forward to seeing you. Just give me your address and phone number. Life really can be fun. I just love the unexpected."

After Genevieve gave the information and put down the phone she sat silently on the bed, her mind going back through the conversation.

"Anything wrong, Genevieve?" called Gregory through the closed door. "Why did you close the bedroom door?" he asked.

"A girl needs her privacy," she said opening the door and going back into her lounge. "That girl is a real bitch."

"I know. Isn't she lovely? So she's coming I gather?"

"Oh yes. She's coming, Greg. Probably for too long. Bruno's off to cover the war in the Pacific after staying over with us a few days."

"You think he can sort out this movie?"

"Just don't tell Hollingsworth. If the changes come from us he won't be so upset. Diplomacy. Why don't we go out and get some supper? I'm hungry."

"What's the matter?"

"She was talking about Tinus. A right little know-all. How can you possibly screw someone like that? She's not even pretty."

"It's called a dirty fuck."

"That's disgusting."

"Not when you're doing it."

"I hope he's all right. I just hope he's all right."

"What time is it in New York?" Gregory had waited a full minute before changing the subject.

"I didn't ask her. Any more than she asked Bruno if he wanted to visit and help with the script. Do all men do what their wives tell them?"

"Not all. Some. Makes life easier. My guess is Bruno Kannberg has a girl or two on the quiet. Fool if he didn't. Only young once."

"You can go off people, Gregory L'Amour. Did you know that?"

"I think you are jealous."

"Don't be ridiculous. What I really don't understand is how Sir Jacob Rosenzweig gave Mr Hollingsworth the money to make a film from such a lousy script."

"Now there's a scandal story for the papers. The old boy's wife found the London bombing too much for her nerves and pitched up in New York. They'd been separated for years. Kicked the young mistress right out of the apartment. If you won't marry me, Genevieve, I'm never getting married. Just look at all the shit you have to go through to have kids. And some of the kids turn out just like their mothers, boys or girls, doesn't matter, they want someone to look after them financially. It's all about money."

"Not with me. Tinus doesn't have a penny. Oh, and you are a patronising swine, for the record."

"But his uncle does."

"Harry Brigandshaw has five kids. I think there's a scandal there somewhere. Frank looks just like my Uncle Barnaby. The family have been pussyfooting around that one for years. Not mentioned in polite society. I love my Uncle Barnaby but he is a rotten sod."

"What did I tell you? I think we should eat Italian tonight. With a nice big bottle of Italian wine now America has invaded Sicily. This war is crazy. Half of us Americans are Italians."

"Then you're doing them a favour deposing Mussolini. There are always two ways for looking at anything."

"Except you of course. There's only one way I will ever look at Genevieve," said Gregory with a lecherous grin.

BRUNO KANNBERG HAD BEEN LISTENING to the phone call from the bedroom where he was trying to calm his nerves at the thought of living for a week on an American destroyer off the American landing grounds on the islands in the South Pacific. This time, whether he wanted to or not, he was going to war. The thought of incoming shells and torpedoes sent him into a funk. Being the *Daily Mirror*'s foreign correspondent in America had given him a job far from the sound of the guns. How his father had fought with the Whites in the Russian revolution was beyond his comprehension. He was a coward. He was afraid. Lying on the bed fully clothed, thinking of where he was going, sent him into a state of cold shivers, sweat soaking the inside of his clothes. If the rumours were true and Gillian was having an affair with Gregory L'Amour, it did not matter at the moment. The pain was less than the imminent prospect of going into a war.

Before the assignment Bruno had written the word 'petrified' many times in his dispatches to London. Only now did he know what it meant. He was going to die. Of that he was certain. 'To hell with Gregory L'Amour,' he said to himself, shutting his mind to the telephone conversation going on in the lounge even when it was over.

"Darling, we're going to Los Angeles. They have a problem with the script. You're going to write a film. Isn't that exciting?... Are you all right? Bruno! Did you hear me? I need some money to pay for my flight. You can do a stopover on your way to Honolulu. Genevieve just phoned. Can you rewrite a script in a couple of days? If you get it right we can live in Hollywood after the war with all the rich and famous. Gerry Hollingsworth has made a muck of the dialogue. Genevieve and Gregory don't know how to fix it. You owe them that after the success of their books and all the money we made. Are you listening, Bruno, or am I wasting my breath? They are going to give you your uniform as an honorary American officer in Hawaii. You only need a small suitcase. I can stay with Genevieve after you've gone so I won't have to be alone after all. Isn't that wonderful? You wouldn't want me sitting here alone now would you? Will you book the plane tickets or must I? You don't even have to tell Art the Bumley. When the tickets are booked and paid for you and I can have some real fun. You'd like that wouldn't you? Bruno! What are you doing? Answer me."

Even the thought of having sex with his wife could not pull him out of his funk. The very idea of being in the uniform of a foreign country made his stomach flip. Instead of going into the lounge to join his wife, Bruno lurched his way into the bathroom where he was violently sick, his head half down the toilet bowl.

By the time Bruno Kannberg left with his camera for the South Pacific on board an American Air Force Dakota, the dialogue made sense. Bruno had worked nonstop for forty-eight hours, drinking so much coffee his eyes felt they were popping. By the time the taxi delivered him to the designated air force base, in what looked like desert to Bruno, he no longer cared. About his life. Or about his wife. If they killed him it would all be over, the world no worse off. He had no children. Despite all his pleading Gillian had managed not to give him a child. He was thirty-five years old and childless without any purpose to his life. Fixing the lousy script so it talked all right had been the first pleasure in his life for months.

If his wife screwed her brains out with Gregory L'Amour it didn't matter. After the vomiting he couldn't make love. Something of a relief rather than a frustration. When she found out in the bedroom she couldn't get him aroused, the woman changed. There was a hint of fear in her eyes. The recognition that at the age of twenty-six she might be losing her power to bend his will to whatever she wanted. From power to panic in half an hour, watching his wife made Bruno conscious of the fickleness of life.

Inside the base they took his small suitcase and told him where to go. He tried on three uniforms, one of which seemed to fit. There was no rank or insignia. Looking in the mirror, the eyes about to fall asleep looked back at a stranger. His eyelids were half closed.

"That'll do, Mr Kannberg. The corporal will call you when the plane is ready to take off. Get some sleep. You look terrible. You reporters are always up to something looking for a story."

"You won't forget me?"

"How could we? You're in the army by the look of you. Just don't forget your camera. Shots of our marines wading ashore on Japanese-occupied islands is just what the American public want to see. And the same goes for you British. I'll be your press liaison officer right through the trip. Captain Delany. You can call me Johnny. Funny name, Kannberg. Where is it from as it ain't English?"

"Latvia. My father fought for the White Russian Army against the Red Army in the Russian Revolution."

"Then you know all about war. When did you last get some sleep?"

"Three days ago. I was rewriting a film script for Gregory L'Amour and Genevieve."

"You met them! Now he's a real American hero. The All American Man, they call him. Now I am impressed. Do you mind if I call you Bruno? I'd give just about anything to get that girl into bed."

"Why am I not an officer? There's no rank on this uniform that I can see."

"Well, Bruno, first you got to be a soldier. Then you got to go to Officer College. Then they put a rank on your uniform. We don't want photographers and newsmen in suits on our destroyers. Looks untidy. Bad for discipline. We want you to blend into the war, Bruno. When you go ashore, wading with the troops, you got to look right. But no rank I'm afraid."

"I'm going ashore!"

"Of course you are. Don't get your camera wet. Only bigshot war correspondents get invited. *Daily Mirror*. Popular paper. Spent a week in London when I was twenty-one. Just out of college. Did a stint with the *Denver Telegraph*. Denver, Colorado. I'm also a newspaper man, or was until I went into the army two days after the Japs bombed Pearl Harbor. You'll still see our ships sunk in the harbour. Bastards didn't even declare war. Now is that honourable? Is that the honour the Japs talk about when they despise their prisoners of war for being captured and not fighting to the death? After the fall of Singapore and the surrender of the British Army they're making the prisoners build a railway line across Burma on a handful of rice a day, according to our information. Your troops are dying like flies. Don't worry. Uncle Sam's going to teach the Japs a lesson and save those British prisoners."

"I hope so. My friend's cousin was captured in Singapore. Not a word from him since. Chinese wife and two kids and William doesn't know what's happened to any of them. Are you sure about what you heard?"

"Get some sleep now. The aircraft is noisy. No frills in the army. When they come for you I'll have them bring a mug of strong coffee. On the plane I want to hear all about Gregory L'Amour and Genevieve. All our information is correct, Bruno. Who would make up such a story?"

2

When Gillian asked to stay a few days, Genevieve agreed. There was a small bedroom with a single bed that was never used. She was lonely. Being famous often made it worse. To have another Englishwoman to talk to when she came home from the studio would stop her brooding over Tinus. Whether she liked the girl or not it did not matter, or what Gregory L'Amour was up to on the side. Ever since Tinus had given her the ring with the small diamond she had not so much as looked at another man. When Gillian, Bruno and herself were finishing off the book on her short life that had sold so well on both sides of the Atlantic, they had got on well enough. There were so many twists and turns in life.

The moment Bruno was seen off in the taxi at the start of his journey, Gillian had moved into the seventh-floor flat in downtown Los Angeles and Genevieve had the feeling her guest would remain until her husband came back from the war.

Genevieve had given her the spare key and a note to the downstairs security desk. She had also told Jim to expect a friend who was going to stay in her flat. When Genevieve came home after the day's shoot and opened her front door, the smell of steak and kidney pudding wafted over her. Instantly her mouth watered. Steak and kidney pudding done in a white bowl with a saucer on top of the suet pastry, wrapped in a white tea-towel and boiled in a pot of water was the cook's favourite dish for them when they stayed together at Hastings Court. It was Genevieve's favourite, something she could never find in America; steak and kidney pie, but never steak and kidney pudding. Her guest was in the kitchen wearing Genevieve's apron when Genevieve followed the smell of the cooking to its source.

"That smell, Gillian. It's so English. Makes me so homesick."

"He's gone. Poor Bruno is scared to death. I thought men strode off to war with a smile and a whistle. So much for the big brave husband."

"André Cloete threw up every time before he got into his aeroplane. Before and during the war. There's nothing wrong with being afraid of dying. Tinus says he shakes from the moment they are scrambled to their aircraft in full flying kit and a parachute on his back. Once in the cockpit of his Spitfire his teeth chatter uncontrollably. Only when he sights enemy aircraft does complete calm come over him. Every fibre of his body comes into focus. Tinus says a man's a fool if he thinks he's not going to get killed. That most of the gung-ho types get themselves killed in the first two weeks of combat. My father said it was the same in the trenches in the last war. Uncle Harry told Tinus what to expect and not to be frightened of fear. Uncle Harry says it's fear that concentrates a man's mind. Makes a good pilot in war and in peacetime when something goes wrong. Don't knock your husband, Gillian. You missed the Blitz. If I may be so rude to say, you don't know what you're talking about. Just pray Bruno comes home. He's a good man. Uncle Harry once said good men, truly good men, not those who make themselves out to be good, are as rare as hen's teeth."

"I'm sorry."

"Don't worry. I'm also on edge. All the time not knowing what he's doing. The pudding makes up for everything. Now we can worry together. How about a gin and tonic? My mother's favourite. Did I ever tell you my mother was the barmaid in the Running Horses at Mickleham during the last war?"

"It was in the book."

"Of course it was. How silly of me."

"Why aren't you full of yourself, Genevieve? You're famous. Your dad's a lord."

"My mother says we all look the same under a bus. You want too much, Gillian. There's only so much we can have in life. All the baubles, however expensive, never count. They never change us, change who we are, however rich and famous we may become."

"How's the film?"

"Much better now we're not talking garbage. He's good, Gillian. Bruno's good. Very good. There's a big career waiting for him in films."

"I'm going to enjoy staying with you."

"So am I. I get lonely. Big gin or small gin?"

"Big one."

"Good. Then we'll open a bottle of red wine with the steak and kidney pud. No filming tomorrow. It's a Sunday. We can get a little drunk and have a good chinwag. I haven't had a good chinwag with a girlfriend in years."

"Neither have I."

Impulsively they both hugged each other before going into the lounge where Genevieve opened her cocktail cabinet and poured them both a stiff gin. Then they sat down.

"Tomorrow it's my turn. I'll take you out to dinner."

Vida Wagner recognised Genevieve from her first dinner party at Abercrombie Place with Harry Brigandshaw and Robert St Clair. Everyone else in the restaurant knew Genevieve too. It was a game in Los Angeles to go out to famous restaurants looking to spot famous people. Vida waved. To her surprise, Genevieve waved back and walked across towards her table.

Life since running out of New York had been good to her. So far as she knew Jacob Rosenzweig, her 'old goat', had not found out where she lived despite her promise to still be his mistress on the quiet now his wife was back in his life and living with him in New York. She had his money from the trust fund which was what counted. In most people's eyes she was rich.

The man holding her hand under the table and stroking her knee was ten years her junior. The poor boy had tried the movies where his good looks got him in the door. Unfortunately he could not act. Without money, away from his roots in the mid-west, the only alternative to going home or joining the army was rich, older women. The army thought he was thirty-two, which was a lie to avoid conscription. Nathan Squires was twenty-eight with not an ounce of fat on his beautiful body, and he knew how to 'sing for his supper'. She would dump him when she was bored. For the moment he made her feel good. Attentive men always made her feel good. Like the large sum of money old Sir Jacob had placed in her trust fund to pay for the last bit of fun in his life before he died.

Rich in LA was the perfect combination. Going back to Berlin, with her Germany no longer winning the war, had slipped out of her mind. She was having a good time. All her plans had come to fruition. So long as no one found out her story, that her papers were false, nothing could go wrong. If they found out, she had money. Her own money. Coerced but not stolen. Anyway, she always rationalised with herself, old Rosenzweig had enough money for everyone. Priorities for Vida had changed. She had the best of both worlds in America pretending she was Jewish, not Lebanese where both her families came from, mother and father, her Arab ancestry as anti-Jewish as the Germans, whatever her family's religion.

"Hello, Vida. Gerry Hollingsworth wondered where you were. Do you still keep in touch with Sir Jacob Rosenzweig?"

"His wife ran away from the London Blitz and came to New York. I had no idea he was married. This is Nathan. Nathan, meet the famous Genevieve. You want to join us?"

"I'd like to. You met my Uncle Robert who wrote *Holy Knight*, and Harry Brigandshaw I like to call Uncle Harry. That was some dinner party you put on. I think you know my friend, Gillian Kannberg? Her husband's gone off to cover the war in the South Pacific. We're consoling each other. You remember Tinus from that party? We're engaged. He's a fighter pilot in the Royal Air Force. Being German Jewish you won't mind that will you? Are you also in film, Nathan?"

"I've been trying."

"Keep trying. You never know. Can we sit down, Vida? Your boyfriend financed the movie I'm making."

"He's no longer my boyfriend."

"I suppose not. You did something for him, Vida. First time I ever saw him happy that night. Max Pearl said the same. That's the most precious gift you can give anyone. Happiness. What else is life all about?"

"What's your new movie about? Gregory L'Amour. I read about it."

"How America is winning the war. Morale booster. Since Gillian's Bruno rewrote all the dialogue it's going to be good. Certainly make money. Sir Jacob will make a lot of money."

"Same old story. Money makes money."

"Only if you look after it, according to Uncle Harry. They have lovely fresh oysters, Gillian. Gillian cooked last night. This is my treat. With filming tomorrow I just can't drink. Cameras have an uncanny way of finding the hangover deep in the back of my mismatched eyes. Gerry Hollingsworth's son was killed. Gerry was also at your dinner party."

"I'm sorry."

"You're lucky to have got out of Germany. Hitler's final solution for the Jews is appalling. The things mankind does to each other in the name of religion. We have the same god but that doesn't seem to matter... Thank you, Pablo. You can tell François I don't need my table reservation. He can give it to some lucky person. This is my favourite restaurant, Vida. They look after me."

"So I can see. Thank you for joining us, Genevieve."

"It's my pleasure. You knowing Tinus makes me feel closer to him. You'll have the lobster, Gillian? Good. Oysters to start. Put this table's food on my cheque, Pablo. And whatever else the people have tonight."

"Not at all. Sir Jacob left me well provided."

"If you insist. Looks like a free supper for me tonight, Pablo.... Now tell me what you've been up to, Vida?"

Smiling to herself, Genevieve watched Gillian plunge into conversation with Nathan, her eyes sparkling. By the time the oysters arrived she had Nathan's complete attention.

"You don't mind?" she asked Vida, raising her eyebrow.

"Plenty more like that where he comes from," whispered Vida close to her ear. "It's only money."

"Ah. Yes, well I suppose it is. Never looked at it that way. Maybe I should. You look happy, Vida."

"I am."

People came and went to and from the table. A photographer, with Genevieve's permission, took a photograph. Most people knew each other. Getting a table at the Oasis without first knowing François was virtually impossible. A lucky shot like the party of four sitting next to Genevieve's table, looking around like children at their first fair, gawping at the people they had only seen before in the newspapers. Genevieve couldn't hear one word about the war. It was all about showing off and talking rich which for some was a career in itself. At least her grandmother in Corfe Castle would laugh at her now sitting with Vida Wagner in François's restaurant.

When they found out they lived just one street apart, Vida in an expensive apartment five storeys up from the traffic, it was the address that counted, like being seen having supper in the Oasis. For Genevieve being seen and smiling was part of her job. In a roundabout way what she was paid for by Gerry Hollingsworth. Good individual press for the stars was as important as a good critique for the film. Everyone fed off everyone else, the money going round and round. The trick, Gerry Hollingsworth said to her, was to make sure the money never stopped going round.

Gillian said nothing more about Nathan Squires when they reached Genevieve's apartment. They both went straight to bed. When Genevieve went to work in the morning Gillian was still sleeping in the small room with the single bed. The phone had not rung and no one had slipped a telegram under the front door. It was the small envelope under the door that Genevieve feared most.

Confident that Tinus was alive, she did a good day's filming. All of them on the set said how well the dialogue was sounding.

"Who did it, Genevieve?" asked Gerry Hollingsworth.

"You won't be insulted?"

"I'm in this game only to make money. Getting my back up never makes me money."

"Bruno Kannberg. On his way to the South Pacific. When the war's over he wants to be a scriptwriter."

"You mean if I give him an idea he can write a script like this? Perfect. What's he doing in the South Pacific?"

"Trying not to get himself killed. Accredited to the marines on a US destroyer. They want him to land on the beach with the troops and take photographs. Stanley, his photographer on the *Mirror*, taught him how to use the camera. They only want one newsman from a British newspaper on the destroyer. Something about space and security."

"This war never stops."

"No, it doesn't."

Gerry Hollingsworth put a comforting hand on Genevieve's shoulder and walked away. Both knew what the other was thinking without having to say.

When Genevieve went home early she could smell the sex as she opened her front door. The afternoon shooting had not required her character. The word 'nymphomaniac' for Bruno's wife came to her mind. Neither of them said a word. Nathan Squires must have left minutes before she opened the door. She would have to have a word with Jim at the security desk. The man must have tipped off Gillian by phone when Genevieve entered the building.

Going straight to her window she looked down onto the street seven storeys below and waited. He had to still be in the building. When he came out soon after and hailed a cab Genevieve was not sure whether to clap her hands or be annoyed.

When Gillian appeared, Genevieve was still looking down onto the street. What other people did in their lives was none of Genevieve's business. In a way it was like putting horns on Gregory L'Amour, making Genevieve feel better about Gregory's infidelity with another woman that wasn't her. Human emotions were indeed strange. She was as bad as the rest of them with no right to get up on her own high horse. The one-night stand with William Smythe came to mind, along with the consequences for the poor man. She just hoped he would stay happily married to his secretary. That when they met again the pain would have gone from William's eyes. Uncle Harry had written Betty Townsend, now Betty Smythe, was pregnant with their first child. That Uncle Harry had been asked to stand as godfather. In that strange roundabout way they would all be related for the rest of their lives.

"He's gone," said Genevieve. "No matter. Gregory sends his love. My part didn't have to shoot this afternoon. Go back to your nap. I'm having one. I always take a nap when I get the chance."

Gillian said nothing which for both of them was the right thing to do. As they said so often, there was a war going on. During wars the rules for some reason were different. Genevieve thought it was likely the primal instinct to procreate when the species was threatened. That if the men died the women would still have their children to carry on the human race. Tinus was wrong and she was right. Unlike Betty Townsend she had been a fool not to get herself pregnant by Tinus when she still had the chance. Then she made up her mind. When the film shoot was over she was going to England to get herself pregnant. Tinus would never have to be told it was deliberate. That way, whatever happened, she would not spend the rest of her life on her own.

3

The word reached Horatio Wakefield in London before it reached Gillian Kannberg in Los Angeles. Bruno Kannberg was missing in action. Billy Glass, the editor of the *London Daily Mail* had heard the news first from Arthur Bumley at the *Mirror* and called Horatio into his Fleet Street office. It was the last week in May and the trees in London parks and along the side streets were green with the new leaves of spring. Life was renewing itself after the cold, bleak winter.

"You're a friend of Kannberg. Doesn't look so good. Went ashore on one of the islands near Guadalcanal and hasn't been seen since. Heavy fighting. Japanese soldiers don't believe in surrender. Fight to the end. Honour before life or some such tripe. Amazing how you can indoctrinate the average sod to lay down his life for his country which isn't his anyway. Only the buggers at the top gain. The troops are fighting nine times out of ten for the privileged who never hear a gun fired in anger. All tied in with religion. For God and country. Bullshit. For the people with the money and their cronies. Brainwashed. The whole damn lot of us. In Africa they sent the missionaries first. When the locals put the missionaries in the pot to boil them, we sent in the troops. If the missionaries didn't end in the pot they told the locals to kneel down and close their eyes. Whichever way they opened their eyes they found the Union Jack flying above them in the name of Western civilisation. Just a fresh approach to man's eternal quest for conquest. No one's ever satisfied with what they've got. Anyway, the empire's finished. The moment we lost Hong Kong and Singapore to the Japs, the empire was finished. Once you're seen as vulnerable and lose face you never get back on top. No one believes you are invincible anymore. They're not frightened of you. Even if we win the war India will want independence. And why not? Like the Chinese, they were civilised thousands of years ago when our ancestors were still climbing trees. Poor Kannberg. Another sacrifice on the funeral pyre of empire. After Asia, Africa will want to break its colonial shackles. The Americans can't wait. All those lovely new markets just waiting for American business and the mighty dollar. Do you know, we just had to pledge the Bahamas for those defunct and out of date destroyers the Americans gave us on lend-lease. We haven't got a bloody dollar left in the bank. Were it not for Rhodesian tobacco, none of us could get a smoke. The Yanks want to be paid in dollars for their tobacco. Can you believe it? A poor sod can't even have a smoke. They only came over here in droves to protect us because we owe them so much money. The old story. Borrow twenty quid from the bank and you've got a problem, Wakefield. Borrow a million and the bank's got a problem if you can't pay it back. After this damn war's over the Americans will have to get Europe's economy going again or they'll never get their money back. We'll all be working to pay back the Yanks for the next fifty years."

"With respect, Mr Glass, you sound like William Smythe."

"His secretary just had a son."

"I know, sir. I told you. Maybe Bruno Kannberg will come out of the fog of war. I liked him. We sent two hundred and twelve bombers over to Berlin last night. The American Flying Fortresses have gone over again this morning. The Germans have to break some time."

"We didn't. They're all underground. You'll only kill a few when you knock down the buildings. There's a lot more to go in this war, Wakefield. We're fighting our way down Burma now. Jungle fighting. Man to man. The Japanese are going to find out what we British are made of."

"Is there any point if the empire's doomed?"

"Pride."

"Mr Glass, you just said the Japanese were brainwashed."

"That's different."

Shaking his hand, Horatio left his editor's office. Bruno was the first friend he had in newspapers to go missing. For years he and Janet had envied Bruno and Gillian living in America out of harm's way.

Back in his office, Horatio began to mutter behind his closed door.

"Must have been given the boot by his latest girlfriend. His poor wife. At least I didn't get the usual diatribe on the virtues of Karl Marx and communism."

Then Horatio picked up the phone to give William Smythe the bad news about Bruno and hear about the new baby, Ruth. Once again, as he waited for the call to come through, Horatio thanked his lucky stars for being happily married. With the daily bombing of London a thing of the past, some of Janet's patients were coming back again. Her appointment at Harrow School had been renewed for every Tuesday in the afternoon. Chuckling to himself in the certainty the boys would no longer spit cherry pips at his wife, as they had done on her first day before the war, Horatio leaned forward to get a cigarette from the wooden box on his desk.

"What are you chuckling about?" came a voice down the phone line. "Have you heard about Bruno Kannberg?"

"I'm phoning you about Bruno, Will. He's gone missing on one of the islands in the South Pacific."

"There, but for the grace of God, went I," said William Smythe.

"Can we have a drink together? It's made me feel hollow."

"We'll have a wake."

"Don't tempt fate. He's only reported missing. I'll meet you in the Duck and Drake at five o'clock. How's Ruth?"

"She's fine. Just fine. Do you know, Horatio, I'm actually happy."

Across in Whitehall, while Horatio was putting on his overcoat to go out against the bitter east wind despite the month of May, Ding-a-ling Bell was giving the same news to Harry Brigandshaw in his office at the Air Ministry.

"You know that young reporter who found you in the Tropical Disease Hospital when you got back from the Congo, Bruno Kannberg? Gone missing in the Pacific Islands. Waded ashore from a landing craft with the US Marines and hasn't been heard from since. That was days ago. Fierce fighting. The Japs are holding on to every small island with grim determination. Whatever you think of them for abusing our chaps in Burma, they are brave men. The Americans are having to go in with fixed bayonets to winkle them out of their foxholes. Fine, well-trained soldiers, the Japanese. Very old tradition."

"Is he dead?"

"No one knows. Nothing. A Captain Delany lost sight of Kannberg in the surf, according to my source. Delany is the press liaison officer."

"Did Kannberg have a gun?"

"That's where the muddle starts. The Japs held their fire until the marines were clear of the landing craft and opened fire with well-placed machine guns in the dunes above the beach. Delany says men went down in the surf all round Kannberg. Some dead, some getting down to make smaller targets. Everyone who got up after that and stormed the shore was carrying a rifle. Kannberg was not armed when he left the landing craft making Delany think he died in the surf. Delany for some reason stayed with the navy on the landing craft. Said it was difficult to pick out who was who from the distance to the shore where the marines took out the enemy machine gun nests. The idea was for Kannberg to take close-up pictures of the troops landing and get back to the landing craft with his pictures. Why Delany stayed on board, I suppose. Once the marines overran the machine guns they carried on into the interior of the island. Each island had to be cleared out one by one, man to man, often using hand to hand combat. There's one hell of a fight going on in the South Pacific. They never found Kannberg's body in the surf when the firefight died down."

"So he might have picked up a dead man's gun?"

"Delany said Kannberg was terrified before he went ashore. That he had never been in any kind of military situation."

"Shot pheasants with a shotgun at Hastings Court. My staff said he was a damn good shot. They were writing a book about Genevieve. I lent them the Court for a couple of weeks. A 12 bore has a kick worse than a rifle if you don't pull it into your shoulder. He could shoot all right. When people start shooting at you things change inside your head. Adrenaline pumps and the whole body goes on survival mode. At that point fear's the last thing you are worried about. You want to kill the other bastard before he kills you. Basic instinct of man is to survive. No one wants to die. What happened to the marines?"

"Some were picked up by other units to hit the next island before the Japs could prepare another defence. They rolled on. Those Yanks can fight, Harry."

"Then he could be alive. Has anyone told his wife in America?"

"I've no idea. Thought you'd like to know. We hit Berlin again last night. Two hundred bombers plus. Like the Americans, the RAF are starting to drop incendiary bombs to fireball the German cities."

"Makes me sick."

"Not if it makes Hitler stop the war."

"Still not right burning civilians. Aren't we meant to be civilised? I'd like sometimes to phone Klaus von Lieberman and see if his family are all right. Just because Hitler exterminates Jews in concentration camps doesn't make our case for burning civilians alive. Poor sods are cowering underground like we were in the Blitz. I hate war. It's always the same. Tit for tat, getting worse and worse. We're all a bunch of bloody savages. Is Anthony still grounded?"

"His leg is still a mess."

"Thank God."

"The CO has put him up for a DSO for getting his aircraft back to Boscombe Down."

"I didn't know."

"Was going to tell you when it was confirmed."

Vic Bell saw visible signs of relief on Harry Brigandshaw's face.

"I took an interest in Bruno Kannberg when he kept his word not to give me away to the press before I got out of that Paddington hospital," said Harry. "Keep me informed. Are you coming down to Hastings Court for the weekend? Gets lonely on my own. My nephew is back on active service at Tangmere. Haven't seen him or his Polish friend in weeks. I think they slip up to London on their forty-eight-hour passes. They have mutual friends in the theatre. I wish he had married Genevieve and not waited. Girls are girls in London, especially in the theatre. Everybody grabs what they can while they can. Oh, well. What can an old man do? I miss my wife and children."

"I'm sure you do, Harry. I'd enjoy a weekend out of London. We can go and get happy in the Running Horses. Always have such pretty barmaids."

"You should have got married."

"Oh, you know how it is. Too late now."

"Never too late to put on the old ball and chain. Those were good days at 33 Squadron. Despite the war. The last war still had a spark of chivalry. These raids over Germany are mass murder."

"It will likely get worse. The Americans are developing an atomic bomb."

"So are the Germans."

"God help us."

"He never does in war. Whose prayers should he answer? Ours or the Germans'?"

When Katherine, Harry's secretary, came in with a fresh pot of tea with two cups they sat back separately looking into their pasts. Katherine always brought in a fresh pot of tea when Harry had a guest. It was the nearest he got in London to domesticity.

"Went round to have a cup of tea with Sarah Coombes last night. Fred was there. Like old times. Why do we bind much better in adversity? When everything goes smoothly again we're back at each other's throats. Arguing. Sometimes being rude to each other."

"She still doesn't know you have money?"

"Would spoil it all. People don't like the other person to have more than them. Makes them feel uncomfortable. Why do possessions make so much difference to our perception of people? Most rich people have stolen their money, inherited it like me or got lucky."

"You had to work hard at holding on to your money. You had to come over and run Colonial Shipping."

"That I did. Strange, isn't it, everyone wants to get rich. All I wanted was to be a tobacco farmer in Rhodesia. Live in the bush among nature. Subsist off the farm if necessary. The old African has the right answer. A hut by a river. Patch of vegetables watered by the river. Couple of cows and some goats and three wives to look after him. Now that's living. You don't get your knickers in a twist living that kind of life. Peace and quiet in the African tranquillity. Now that's a perfect life. All this bustle and scheming is for the birds. We all want too much. Strange part is, when we get it we don't want that either. A river full of Zambezi bream, a cow to give you milk and as much meat as you can eat on both sides of the river when the game comes down at night for water. You don't live so long in Africa without modern medicine but the years you do live are sweet.

"I envy Sarah Coombes and Fred. Both of them are happy with their lot. Look forward to those cups of tea. Like this one with an old friend, Vic. Both times war brought us together. As it did with me and Klaus von Lieberman. I hope they all make it through our bombing. At least Anthony out of action won't be asked to drop fire bombs on women and children. Get me a full report on that leg from the doctor when you can. Anthony doesn't like me visiting the hospital too often. With luck, they'll invalid him out of the RAF. He can stay with me at Hastings Court or go back to his mother in South Africa. Probably South Africa. He has a girl there he's been writing to. Eleanor Botha. They met on Clifton Beach before Ant was on his way down from flying training in Gwelo. First loves can stick. Become permanent."

"The youngsters build up love in letters."

"What does an old bachelor know about love, Vic Bell?"

"You'd be surprised. We were all young once. Idyllic. Full of hope. Full of optimism."

"What was her name?"

"I forget now."

"What was her name?"

"Sandy. We wrote for three years when I was in France."

"What happened?"

"Married another guy. Last I heard of Sandy she had two kids by him. Married him the day he was demobilised from the army. Hope she's been happy."

"No one else?"

"Not really. You know how I am. How I look. Some say it's better to grow old alone than with a bickering wife."

"Next time I visit Sarah Coombes you're coming with me."

"Don't be bloody silly. Why?"

"Because you are both nice people."

"What happened to Mr Coombes?"

"Like Phillip Crookshank, he was killed at Dunkirk. They couldn't have children. When the war's over I'm going across to the Isle of Wight to see Mavis Crookshank and the children. They spent Christmas with us at Hastings Court in 1939. Their Paul and my Frank had a fist fight. Phillip and his wife were so happy together. So often the good marriages end in tragedy when one of them dies prematurely."

"How old is this Sarah?"

"Why don't you ask her? Just be humble."

"Haven't got much else to be."

"Another cup of tea?"

"Always a pleasure. I'll lift my cup to old friends. Present and departed."

"So many faces from 33 Squadron have faded from my mind. Sometimes I can't recall their names. When I do, I can't see their faces anymore. That's how we all die out in the end. Fade out of the memories of everyone we know on earth. Do you think they are all right in Cape Town without me?"

"Of course they are. You had to make a choice. If those bombs had hit Hastings Court in a stick you could have lost your entire family. They are safe in Cape Town. When the war comes to an end they will still be there safe and sound to live through their own lives. To have their own families."

"There'll be another war."

"I hope not."

"There always is."

4

The whole building had gone that morning when Melina von Lieberman had come up from the Nazi Party shelter close to her flat. She had gone to work in the clothes she had tried to sleep in. All night long the Royal Air Force had crossed and recrossed Berlin dropping high explosive bombs. Everything she owned had gone up in the attack.

"Where was the Luftwaffe?" she screamed at her cousin Henning von Lieberman who had placed her in the secretarial college in 1941 when she left home. Afterwards he had given her a job in the Party Headquarters. "The ack-ack was only intermittent. The English were flying over Germany at will."

"Most of them were shot down on the way home."

"Why not before they blew my flat to pieces! I haven't got any clothes other than these."

"Many were shot down on the way to Germany."

"Didn't sound like it to me."

"Keep your voice down, Melina. You know I don't like it."

"The door's closed. They can't hear outside. I know what you do like, Henning. I know just what you do like. Are we by any chance going to lose this war? Around about lunchtime the Americans will come over dropping more bombs. In broad daylight. For God's sake, their bombers shoot down our fighters, they have so many gun turrets. Box formations.

We can't get inside the American box formations, according to Erwin. What happened? We were winning!"

"The Americans came into the war," said Henning almost under his breath. "It's better. You can stay with me. I'll buy you some more clothes."

"I'm going home to Bavaria. That's what I'm going to do. How can I work here with no clothes and nowhere to stay?"

"I've said. You can stay with me."

"And my father finds out? You're his first cousin. He'll kill you, Party or no Party."

"Calm down."

"How can I? The damn British have demolished my home. It was fun in Berlin in the beginning. All the parties. All the lovely attention. This now is a nightmare. I'm going before I have to walk. Before the RAF take out our railway marshalling yards and the trains stop running. You got me into this. You must get me out of it. Please, Henning. Your dream of a master race running a disciplined world full of law and order sounded so wonderful at the beginning. Let me go. Please let me go. I won't say a word. Promise. Not to anyone. Not a word to my father or mother. Not a word to Erwin."

"So you want to run away when the going gets tough?"

"It's going to get tougher. The Russians have liberated Stalingrad. Some say they are advancing through Poland. The Americans have invaded Italy, deposing Mussolini. The British are back in control of most of North Africa. They almost murdered Erwin's godfather. General Rommel wasn't at his headquarters for some lucky reason. How many times can we be lucky? There's talk of France being invaded from across the English Channel. The Japanese are being pushed back into the South Pacific. What's going to happen to us? Working here in intelligence, I know what I hear is right. That's what frightens me. I can't believe in the propaganda anymore. I don't believe we shot down the British air force last night. Get me a rail pass. I want to go home. Please. You owe me that much for what I've done for you. I'm only twenty years old. I don't want to die! My whole life is still ahead of me!"

Without a word, Henning slapped her face. Twice. Hard.

"You're getting hysterical. Shut up. I am a senior member of the Party. Have some respect. I'm not frightened of your father. You will move into my underground apartment and officially become my mistress. That's an order, Melina!"

"I'll tell your father."

"He knows. Getting you under my thumb was his idea. The same way the Party took control of your brother Erwin. A fine pilot. A fine officer. A fine member of the Nazi Party. We shall still rule the world."

"I don't think so. Go on, hit me again. Only cowards hit defenceless women."

"Where are you going, Melina?"

"None of your business. Keep your hands off me. Whatever you were, I always thought you a gentleman. The Party has twisted your mind."

"Careful, Melina."

"What are you going to do now? Shoot me, Cousin Henning?"

For the first time since Melina left the family estate, Henning von Lieberman was speechless. The more he tried, the less he was able to utter a word. The impediment he thought Janet Wakefield had cured before the war was back with a vengeance. His face contorted. A tic appeared in his left eye. The man now looked his age. Not the ten years younger that people congratulated him upon. The black uniform looked sinister. No longer romantic to Melina. Drawing upon every ounce of her strength not to burst into tears, she controlled her fear and let herself out of his office. Quietly. Looking back over her shoulder before closing the door, she looked into his contorted face, the larynx trying to perform its task. The eyes spoke more than any words. She doubted her cousin had ever hit a woman before. She felt sorry for him, no longer afraid of him or the Party. In that mutual look of understanding, they both knew it was the beginning of the end of the Third Reich. Of Henning von Lieberman's dream of an ordered world without war or argument. Where the Party told the people what was good for them instead of the mess they made of running their own lives.

Two hours later, when the rail pass was put on her desk by a clerk, she heard the warning siren blaring outside the windows. Picking up the rail pass, she prepared to go down into the air-raid shelter deep under the building where they were safe from the bombs. It was almost lunchtime. Far away to the west of the city she could hear the American aircraft. The menacing sound of multiple engines. The ack-ack fired sporadically. There was the sound of distant machine gun fire as she went down the stairs. She felt much older than her twenty years.

Before the RAF came over in the night, Melina was safely on a train out of Berlin, headed for her family estate in Bavaria. They had not even said goodbye. She wondered if she would ever see him again as she sat looking at the black curtain over the window from the dim light inside the railway carriage. Her rail pass let her travel first class. In the carriage were three old men and a girl. No one said a word as the steam engine slowly pulled the line of carriages through the darkness away from Berlin. Later, Melina could hear aircraft overhead.

"Every night," said one of the old men.

"And every day," said one of the others.

It was cold in the carriage. Melina pulled the rug she had found on her seat up to her chin. The rug was the last expression of first class travel. She was still wearing the same clothes from the previous day. She felt dirty, the smell of her perfume too strong. Deliberately she had splashed on too much. Closing her eyes, she tried to go to sleep. Somewhere in her dreams far away she heard the bombs dropping. When she briefly woke all she could hear was the rhythmic clack of the wheels on the rails.

They would be surprised to see her. All she wanted to do was bury her head in her father's chest. Feel his arms round her tight. Making her safe, as he always had done when she was growing up as a child. In those days people were always smiling. The little girl was asleep, rolled up in the opposite corner. Melina wondered which one of the old men in the carriage was the girl's grandfather. They were far too old to be her father. She was hungry but did not care. She had got away. Smiling with hope, Melina went back to sleep. She slept through the night, her young body exhausted from the tension of the previous day.

When she woke there was a thin light in the carriage from the breaking dawn. One of the old men or the young girl had pulled aside the blackout curtain. Outside the fields and trees looked normal. The girl gave Melina a shy smile. Not wanting to talk, Melina looked away, out at the countryside running slowly past the train window. The wind was pushing white smoke from the engine back over the line of carriages. There were too many carriages for the one engine which was why they were going so slowly. Her mouth was dry and her stomach empty. She tried to go back to sleep.

"No luggage?" said the old man next to the girl, now awake huddled in the corner.

"Bombed out. All I have." She moved her hands to include what she was wearing.

"You have a rail pass?"

"Yes, I have a rail pass."

"That is all you need. Hilda is my great-niece. My name is Hillier. Hillier, not Hitler. Are you going home?"

"Yes. I hope so. My last stop is Ravensburg but I have to change trains. I'm not sure how many times."

"I can help you. You were not at home when you were bombed out?" The old man was very polite. Melina kept on her guard. There was something sinister about him. The girl did not touch him with any part of her body.

"In the air-raid shelter."

"It was during the day. They were all killed except Hilda here. She was under the stairs. I am taking her to my sister. My sister is her grandmother. She will be safe until the war is over. The Americans. They come over during the day. Where do you stay in Ravensburg?"

"Ten miles away. The von Lieberman Estate."

"You work there? I have heard of the place. Fifty, maybe sixty miles from my sister."

"I am a von Lieberman."

"But you don't have any luggage?"

"I was bombed out yesterday, as I said. Left my job with the Party. No time to buy anything."

"Of course. The rail pass. The von Liebermans are powerful. General Werner von Lieberman. Very powerful. I am also a member of the Party. Heil Hitler."

To Melina's surprise the old man stood up and gave a stiff-armed salute, almost touching the naked light bulb in the ceiling of the carriage that was still burning with a soft red light. When the girl caught her eye she was giggling. Melina managed to stop herself from giggling. Hillier had a big pot belly that stuck out when he gave the Nazi salute.

"I will tell you when to change trains," he said when he sat down. The girl instinctively gave him more room. Melina, attuned to the atmosphere in the Party Headquarters, thought the girl's giggle had come more from fear.

"You are very kind," said Melina.

"I am honoured. May I offer you a sandwich? That big wicker basket on the luggage rack is full of food and flasks of coffee. We are all friends in Germany. What is mine shall belong to everyone." The old man was being magnanimous.

"You are most kind."

"I am honoured to give food to a von Lieberman. Are you by any chance related to General Werner von Lieberman? He is a personal friend of Field Marshal Rommel."

"So is my father. From when they were boys. General von Lieberman is my father's uncle."

"You will have some coffee?"

"It will be an honour."

"Maybe now is the time for everyone to introduce themselves. If these other two gentlemen are going as far as we are we all have a long journey to complete. The dining car is not available on this train. We all have to make sacrifices for the Fatherland. Heil Hitler."

Again, the old man stood up though he did not salute. The girl whose name was Hilda giggled out loud nervously and put her hand over her mouth. It seemed everyone was afraid of her great-uncle Werner. The girl seemed to know his name. Melina thought the old man knew she was a relation of the General right from the start. There was always a list in the new Germany. A list of everyone. On or off the train. No one was anonymous. Everyone had a name known to the Party to keep them all under control. The sandwich when it came was delicious, she was so hungry. So was the coffee. It was still hot from the flask and served by the old man in a paper cup. Melina and the young girl smiled at each other as if they were friends.

Melina was lucky the bomb had come during the night. The idea of going on to Switzerland and her schoolfriend Françoise came to mind. They could go sailing on the lake in Monsieur Montpellier's yacht and stay at the Romanshorn Hotel. The Swiss had been sensible and stayed out of the war. She would be out of danger. Monsieur Montpellier would not mind. Most men did not mind if she stayed close to them. All three of the old men had given her the look. Each in their turn. Men did not change whatever their age.

Later, she found the small ladies toilet on the train and had a wash. Every clack of the wheels took her further from Berlin. She felt better. The fear had gone. Back in the carriage she smiled at each of the old men in turn. It was going to be a jolly journey thanks to the young girl. Together, neither of them had anything to be afraid of.

5
_____

*M*elina had been in the same clothes for three days when the train pulled into Ravensburg Station. With the old man's help the journey ended without mishap. There were taxis at the station but no petrol. Like her brother Erwin, when he stormed out of the house in 1937, she had to walk. She had been wearing her walking shoes in the air-raid shelter when the bombs hit and the sun was shining. The contrast of the birds singing and the bombs falling made her want to run home to her parents. It was better to walk in on them. Give them a surprise. She had no luggage to carry. She could see the snow on the Alps in the distance across in Switzerland.

Without being recognised by the staff at the station she began her walk through the countryside. The war was far away. Like Henning von Lieberman. They had finished the food in the picnic basket the night before. It was too early for blackberries in the hedgerows. She had bought a small meat pie in the village. The pie was freshly baked and delicious. She began to sing. The birds sang back. She was not going to die. Whatever happened to Germany, she was not going to die. If he hadn't slapped her face and seen what he had done she would not have been given the rail pass.

When she saw the old house through the trees she began to run, skipping as she went. One of the farm workers in the field by the road recognised her and waved. Melina waved back. Her feet hurt. The pain was pleasant.

At the front door, Strauss stood with a look of surprise. He was a Nazi as she knew his instructions came from Henning to report on her father.

"Mr Henning von Lieberman sends his regards," she said with a smirk to let him know what was happening. Servants spying, or 'looking after' as General von Lieberman preferred, stuck in her craw.

"Your mother's in the garden."

"Who is it?" came her mother's voice, drifting lazily through the old house. The house was quiet, letting her mother's voice travel.

"It's me, Mama. Melina. I'm home."

When Klaus von Lieberman rode back from the fields an hour before sunset they were sitting by the fire. A cold wind had come up from the direction of the snow-capped mountains. All the windows in the house were closed. He had rubbed down the horse and left her eating hay in the stall, the soft brown eyes watching him with love. They had known each other a long time.

In the small room with the log fire Melina jumped up and ran to him, putting her head on his chest. She had not buried her head in his chest since she was twelve. The last time he had seen his eldest daughter was at the railway station when he drove her there in the trap on her way to secretarial college in Berlin. Klaus put his arms round his daughter and held her tight. Gabby, his second daughter, was watching them. It was difficult to tell as a father which was the prettiest of the two girls. Keeping his arm over her shoulder they walked towards the warmth of the fire.

"It's damn cold for the end of May. They've finished ploughing the ten-acre field. Tomorrow we plant it out with cabbages. I'm quite the farmer," he said looking at his daughter. "To what do we owe this privilege, Melina? How did you get from the station?"

"I walked. Took us three days in the train from Berlin. My flat's been bombed out. These are Mama's clothes. Lost everything in the bombing."

"Did the Party let you go? I am surprised."

"Cousin Henning got me a rail pass."

"Good for Cousin Henning." In better times, Klaus would have had more than words with his cousin Henning for seducing his daughter. An old friend from the war had written him a letter congratulating him on his daughter's luck on having a boyfriend so high up in the Party. In case his letter was read and reported to the Nazis, he had suggested no criticism. "Your mother's clothes suit you. Your mother was younger than Gabby when I married her."

"I'm not exactly on the shelf, Daddy," said Gabby. "Melina says an old man on the train had a basket of food. There wasn't a dining car. What has first class rail travel come to in the brave new Germany?"

"There was a blanket," said Melina. "At least there was a blanket."

"Did you find out this old man's name?" asked her father.

"He gave me sandwiches and hot coffee from the flasks. There were four of them. He was coming to his sister's with his great-niece. Her parents had been killed in the bombing with her brothers and sisters. We parted at Neuberg. He was very helpful but gave me the creeps. I don't think the girl was really his relative. His name was Hillier."

"Did he say Hillier not Hitler?"

"How did you know?"

"He was making sure you went where you said you were going, Melina. Hillier not Hitler shopped young Horatio Wakefield in 1934 when Harry Brigandshaw asked me for help. He's a diehard Nazi."

"Did the stiff-armed salute in the carriage."

"He's an associate of Cousin Henning, I should think. And Uncle Werner. They don't let us out of their sight in case we get up to mischief."

Taking his arm off his daughter's shoulder, Klaus strode back to the door. When he opened the door and looked into the hall there was no one there.

"Don't mention him again."

"Who was the young girl?"

"Not his sister's granddaughter. Hillier's estate is in Prussia. The Nazis gave it back to him for services to the Party... Now pour your father some tea. At least we learnt to drink tea from Harry... A pawn, Melina. Hopefully you will never know who she was."

"Her name was Hilda. She was frightened of him."

"Had good reason, I expect. He's a dangerous man. That kind of man only thinks of himself and the Party. Did he tell you when to change trains? Of course he did. You arrived safely. What's for supper, Bergit?" he asked his wife.

"A goose. I asked Strauss to kill a goose."

"Very appropriate. Hope he killed a fat one."

"I'm very hungry," said Melina. "All I've had is a pie at the station."

"Now, tell me what really happened, Melina. You haven't run into my arms since you were twelve. What's the matter?"

"I want to go over to Switzerland. Stay with Françoise in Geneva."

"I'm sure that can be arranged if you are prepared to ride a horse. You can take Gabby out of harm's way."

"We're going to lose the war now the Americans are fighting."

"I know we are. But I still have to grow the people food. Whoever is in charge of the government, the people still have to eat."

In the morning the wind dropped and the sun came out. Sleeping in her own bed had given Melina a good night's sleep. The depth of the sleep, without the undercurrents of worry and fear, left her refreshed and confident. Her mind was thinking clearly. She was no longer negative, caught in a trap with no way out. She hoped Henning had slept as well in his privileged, underground apartment. Something she doubted. To be 'lucky' to live away from natural light summed up her feeling of the war. The regression from arrogant certainty had come to them all bit by bit in Berlin, most of it unnoticed at the time. Henning was now living in a bunker whichever way he looked at it.

Her father had put his finger over her mouth when she tried to talk about Berlin in front of the fire after they dined on roast goose. There was more food in the country than she had seen for a long time. The war had not yet reached their part of Bavaria.

After a good breakfast her father suggested a walk. The two of them alone. Her mother was going off to help a sick tenant and Gabby did not like walking unless it was with a young man. Gabby found any talk of politics boring and was glad to see them go. She knew what her father wanted to talk to her sister about.

"You two go," she said. "I'm going to play the piano. Are you going into the fields later, Father? You are becoming quite the yokel farmer riding around in old clothes on a horse."

Father and daughter smiled at each other. Melina could see the 'yokel' farmer was an old joke between them.

Her father said nothing until they were far away from the house. Then he looked around at the trees and the clumps of bushes.

"Have you seen Erwin?" he asked.

"Not for months. They transferred him to fighters. Messerschmitt Bf 109s. Says they're a match for the Spitfires and the Hurricanes any day. Why are you so cautious?"

"Strauss, and a few others like him."

"Erwin's disillusioned. What he believed at seventeen he doesn't believe anymore. He says it's like being stripped naked in a crowd.

Everything he had on has been taken away from him. Many of his fellow officers think the same. He mentioned his namesake General Rommel. They all think the war can't be won. They think the Americans, if not Churchill, will do a deal. That way they'll still be better off than under the Versailles Treaty."

"What do you think, Melina?"

"I agree with him. Henning and I fell out. I told him we were losing the war and he shouted. The information coming into Party Intelligence is obvious to an idiot. They don't want to believe what's in front of their noses. Prefer to believe in Party propaganda. Unlike Erwin, they are not the ones fighting the war."

"Don't ever say this out loud again."

"Don't you believe me?"

"Of course I do."

"They think German science will come to their rescue. The new flying bombs they're planning will put the British on edge again just when our bomber squadrons are not flying over England. There's also some kind of new bomb they all talk about that will win them the war in a day. Just the threat of dropping it is meant to win us the war. Then Britain and America will sue for peace. If you ask me they're clutching at straws. Just more propaganda. They get more and more cocky at Party Headquarters, which is never a good sign. Do you think I can cross into Switzerland?"

"They'll come for me and your mother if you do. Strauss will tell them you've gone from the house. You girls go, Melina. Better to save two of my family than lose all of us. Your mother will agree with me. For hundreds of years von Liebermans have made sure the next generation survived."

"You think they would?"

"I'm certain. Frightened people are dangerous. From what you tell me about Berlin, most of them know what's going on at the fronts. They should be more scared of the Russians after what we did to them. Let's walk. A good walk with the dogs and my daughter will make my day. Come on."

Everyone they met or saw in the fields either doffed their caps or waved to her father. All of them were employees or tenants. They all knew they depended on her father. None of it was ingratiating. Trying to get in his good books. If her father left or was killed the estate would fall apart. He was the glue that held it all together, each of them doing their job in the larger jigsaw puzzle managed by him. In every society, so far as Melina had seen, someone had to lead. The hope for everyone was a leader who knew the difference between right and wrong and acted accordingly. She had listened to that lecture many times from her father and never believed a word until now. She had thought it was his way of explaining why the family was so privileged. Had so much of everything and more than the rest. Looking at them now, as she passed, their eyes pleading, the people needed her father more than he needed them.

"You know more about Hilda, don't you, Father?" she said when they sat down together on an old bench that looked for miles towards the snow-capped mountains over the lake.

"Not Hilda specifically. There's a boarding school in Neuberg for young girls run by the Nazi Party. They take children of recalcitrant families and put them in the school. Young minds are easily moulded to the Party's agenda. Why the Nazis have the Hitler Youth Movement which brainwashed Erwin. Turned him against the authority of his father for the protection of the Party. Every political movement with the purpose of maintaining power for a long time has a youth movement, some more evil than others. With everyone marching in step, the leaders of the Party can control everyone. Anyone stepping out of line is ridiculed by the others. Sent to concentration camps if they don't immediately step back into line. Their children taken as hostages to schools like the one Hillier was taking the girl to in Neuberg. My guess is he was doing two jobs in one. Seeing the girl into boarding school while making sure the von Liebermans toe the Party line. When things start going wrong for undemocratic rulers they become paranoid. Very dangerous. Be careful, Melina. The months ahead are dangerous for every German. Tell Erwin to keep his nose out of other people's business. You used to write to each other. Didn't Strauss deliver his letters? When we are young, we imagine we can change the world. By the time we get to my age we know we can't. That life is just a repetition of what happened before. It looks different but it's just the same. There are many influences trying to govern the progress of mankind. Religion. Party politics. A few good men and women with optimistic ideas. A lot of bad men and women using whatever means for their own end. Bribery. Fear. War. Patriotism. Racism. The list is as long as your arm. My father said it was the nature of the beast. That the beast was man. Talk to me again in thirty years if we are both still alive. But I'll take on one bet, sometime in the future you'll be having this exact same conversation with one of your own children who will be thinking just as you thought when you went to Berlin. That the Party was going to solve all the people's problems. We all like being part of a gang. A group. We like being part of something. Makes us feel we are wanted. Not alone. Not on the outside. Man, like animals which we are, like to herd together. This war and the Nazi Party will all be over one day. We'll look back and hope it never happens again. But it will. In some other form that at first we don't recognise. Somewhere else, probably. Another continent. Man and woman can never change. It's in our ancestry. What we inherited in our bodies from our mothers and fathers. The good and the bad. Just don't lose hope. You'll find a nice young man your own age and settle down."

"You know about me and Henning?"

"Of course I do. I'm your father. It's my job to know what's going on in my family."

"But you said nothing."

"There was nothing to say. You had to find out for yourself. Part of growing up. Part of learning about life. Every father says it but we all have to make our own mistakes. And don't only blame Henning. Blame his father. Unless he too is playing a game with the Nazi Party. Nothing would surprise me. We von Liebermans have changed sides a few times in history when it was necessary for our own survival as a land-owning family. Uncle Werner once said he had my best interests at heart. I just hope so. When the war's over maybe we'll all find out, Melina. I'm going to pick your mother a bunch of wild flowers. Will you help me?"

"That poor child."

"Yes. I wonder what will become of her?"

"Do you think her name was Hilda?"

"Probably not. Not, anyway, the name her parents gave her."

6
_____

The bunch of wild flowers was worth more to Bergit von Lieberman than any expensive jewellery. Gabby was playing a Chopin prelude in the music room with the door open. Bergit could see her seated behind the grand piano, the wild flowers in a vase on top of it. Gabby never put up the lid of the piano when she was playing music for herself. Klaus had got back on his horse to ride into the fields they had ploughed yesterday to supervise the planting of cabbages. Underneath where each seedling was planted, the field hands would dig in manure with a small trowel. The individual manure for each plant was her husband's way of ensuring a good crop of big cabbages without wasting valuable horse manure mixed with old hay. It was all in the detail, her husband liked to say. Nothing slipshod. Always better to appraise the job before rushing in.

"If you think it out first, you save time and money, Bergit," he would say. "Brains make money. Not brawn. You have to think through the process in your mind. If it doesn't work in your mind it certainly won't work in practice. Why some people get ten times more out of the same piece of land than another. Think it out and follow it through. Something I doubt the Nazis have bothered to do. They want only what they see in front of them and to hell with the consequence."

Seeing his flowers on the piano, hearing her daughter faultlessly playing Chopin, remembering her husband's words, Bergit wondered how it was possible for her family to be so close to the abyss. She was sitting in the bay window of her sewing room, next to the music room, both looking out on the garden in spring. The lawns had not been cut. There was no petrol for the lawnmower. Klaus had said using the hand mower was a waste of labour better put into growing cabbages. The yellow flowers of the dandelions made the lawns look quite as pretty as when the grass was cut in straight lines. The weeds in her flower beds were competing with the perennial flowers. The chaos had its own kind of beauty.

Gabby had switched to Beethoven as Bergit watched a blackbird digging for worms among the long grass and dandelions, pulling out a three-inch long worm with its beak. Quickly the bird gobbled the earthworm and returned to its digging. With another worm the bird flew off with the twisting morsel in its beak. Food for the nest, thought Bergit. Nature at its best and worst. Life for the nestling. Death for the worm.

"Penny for your thoughts?"

So absorbed with the blackbird, Bergit had not heard Melina come into the sewing room. The doors to the hallway and the piano room were both open.

"Life and death."

"Sounds heavy."

"Not really. The blackbird feeds its young. The worm dies."

"She's much improved," said Melina, nodding her head towards her sister at the piano.

"You've been away a long time. In better times she would go to the Conservatory in Berlin. Such a shame to see so much talent go to waste."

"She can still go when the war's over."

"Should have gone two years ago but your father rightly said no. Another price we pay for going to war. Which was more important, any of the kaisers or Ludwig von Beethoven? A silly question. Beethoven and war. We Germans are good at producing both. The finest of music and the worst of hell on earth."

"Wasn't his grandfather a Dutchman? Van Beethoven. Not von."

"Does it matter with music like that? Maybe her children can become concert pianists." Bergit was smiling at Gabby still playing, oblivious of their conversation.

"She'd better find a husband who can play the piano, who's musical. Where's Papa?"

"Gone to plant his cabbages. All ten acres. Lots of sauerkraut. Are you all right?"

"I am now. Calm has returned, as they say. For the time being."

"What are you going to do now?"

"I have absolutely no idea. Does it matter? Maybe I can help Father supervise the farming. In England they have land girls after the men went to war. That's it, Mama. I'm going to be a land girl. To hell with bashing a typewriter. I've got to do something to pay for my supper at my age."

"That I've got to see," came floating in from the piano room with the notes of music. Her sister had been playing and listening.

"You can help me, Gabby."

"You've just got to be kidding."

"You can help me darn some socks," said her mother. "I never thought my embroidery would come down to darning people's socks. You can't buy socks for love nor money. The wool goes to make clothes for our soldiers on the Russian Front. Your father says many froze to death in the winter. These grey socks were your father's in the last war."

"Give me a pair. These are not Father's."

"Strauss doesn't have a wife anymore."

"Strauss!"

Her mother gave her a sharp look. Melina had never before darned a pair of woollen socks.

"Whose are these?" There was a wicker basket full of clothing ready to be darned.

"Erwin's. He left them with me on his last leave. On Wednesday you can help me with the pool... Gabby, please don't stop. I'm so enjoying the music."

The piano played again, music Melina had not heard before.

"What's that?" she asked.

"Her own. Gabby's composing her own music. That one is *Opus Number 6*, I understand. Sounds very grand. It soothes my nerves. On Wednesdays the village people and the tenants bicycle to the house bringing clothes they don't wear anymore. Mostly children's clothes the children have grown out of. Gabby and I sort through what they bring, label everything with a price and the name of the seller which we keep in a book. The previous week's clothes and what's left over are displayed on the dining room table. It's better than swapping. My decision on price is final or they can take the clothes they brought away.

We've kept our tenants and many from Ravensburg clothed during the hard winter. Nothing goes to waste. It's the fairest way of exchanging clothes."

"Only clothes?"

"It's not a jumble sale. I take the money, enter the sale in the book and give the seller their money. Mostly the money goes back in the system to buy someone else's clothes."

"I'm impressed, Mama."

"It's made a lot of friends. We give them tea. People talk to each other round the fire in winter. In the garden at this time of year if the weather's fine. Lifts everyone's spirits, including mine. We all get to know each other from all walks of life. It will be the one part I will miss after the war. People are very nice. I hear all sorts of things you would never believe. They confide in me so I won't divulge one word." With her glasses perched on the end of her nose Bergit finished darning the grey sock.

Having found the right needle and threaded the wool, Melina spread the sock over her fist to display the hole and started to darn.

"Do it across and then across the other way, Melina. You'll get the hang of it."

Surprised her father had not mentioned Erwin coming home on leave, Melina concentrated on her darning.

By the time her father came back from the fields Melina had comfortably dropped back into the life of her family. Despite there being no men to flirt with, Melina was content.

On the Wednesday, when the clothes were pooled on the antique dining room table, there were only women milling around in the room. Tea was served on the lawn among the long grass and the dandelions with the pigeons calling from the surrounding trees. With so many people, the dogs behaved, to Melina's surprise.

When, at the end of June Erwin came home for the second time on leave, Melina was hopeful she had heard the last of Henning von Lieberman and the Nazi Party Intelligence Service. No one had come anywhere near them since she walked home from the railway station.

Her father had driven the horse and trap to the Ravensburg railway station to collect Erwin. Expecting to only see her brother, Melina was surprised to find Jürgen Mann sitting on the wooden bench behind her father. Jürgen was dressed in civilian clothes. The sleeve that would have covered his left arm was pinned to his shoulder. Erwin was in uniform with faded insignia on his shoulders. The last time Melina saw Jürgen she had seduced him, losing her virginity in the process.

They were all smiles. Jürgen's look suggested to Melina she should not mention his disability. The missing arm was likely the reason he was not in uniform. Flying aircraft in combat with one arm was difficult if not impossible, Melina supposed.

They all went inside. Strauss took the horse by the head and led it away towards the stables. The dogs barked happily, Jürgen bending down to pat the dogs in turn with his one hand. Her brother saluted her. When Gabby ran out of the house she was surprised by a second salute. Having made the right impression, Erwin hugged the two of them in turn. Then he saw his mother standing in the doorway of the big house smiling down and ran up the steps.

Melina was left standing next to Jürgen and the dogs. All the dogs were wagging their tails.

"How are you, Melina?" said Jürgen with a wry smile.

"So nice to see you."

Melina found it hard not to giggle. After her stay in Berlin and what went on with the men in the Party, she was sure Jürgen had also been a virgin. Very quietly he slipped his hand into hers, walking just behind her father up the stairs into the house.

"How long are you staying?" asked Melina.

"As long as you'll have me. I'm out of the air force. Mother is still running the family estate. Papa hasn't improved. His mind is never with us. I told them if I could no longer fly an aeroplane I'd be a farmer. The Reich needs food so they let me go."

"Why didn't you contact me in Berlin?"

"Silly. You were working for the Party. Erwin warned me about your cousin. What happened?"

"He slapped my face. Twice. Hard. I made him give me the rail pass home. Since then, not a word."

"How long?" Behind Jürgen's smile Melina could see the disquiet at referring to the Nazi Party.

"A month ago. How long's Erwin's leave?"

"Two days. They've put him in fighters. Short of fighter pilots."

"It's a lovely day. Why don't we take a picnic basket to the lake? Like last time you were here."

"Hans Bengler was killed when I crashlanded. He was my navigator. You remember Hans?"

"Of course I do. He came on the picnic."

"I was lucky. With a little more luck I'll survive the war. Erwin wishes he'd also lost his left arm. Fighting a losing war is no fun. This is only the beginning of the end. Your brother's been posted to the Russian Front. Why they gave him two days' leave. It's bad on the Russian Front. He'll come through. You'll see. Experienced pilots survive."

With the cloud of war once again hanging over the von Lieberman estate, they all tried to make the conversation as normal as possible. Jürgen had a limp that went with his missing left arm. The twenty–year-old Melina had first met three years earlier looked like a man with a heavy weight on his shoulders. There were lines on his face, an intermittent twitch under his right eye. His eyes had the distant stare Erwin had talked about, a stare that afflicted most of the pilots after a while. To Melina it looked as if both men had lost their youth ten years earlier than they should have done.

"You youngsters go off to the lake and enjoy yourself," said Bergit wiping her tears. "I want to make sure tonight's supper is perfect. We'll eat in the dining room."

"What about the second-hand clothes?"

"They can be moved, Melina. This is a celebration. For the first time in a long time I have all my children under one roof. I'll make you some sandwiches to take to the lake. Take the dogs and let the horse take you at his own pace. The pull from Ravensburg was a long haul for that old horse. The young stallions are used to pulling the ploughs through the fields. Without petrol we've dropped back half a century. It's rather nice. I much prefer the neighing of a horse than the angry sound of a tractor's engine. The tractors have a nagging, intrusive sound that never goes away."

Everything was done in a hurry, as if to pack as much into two days as possible for Erwin. For all of them, the words 'Russian Front' were hanging over them, a cloud of dark, unspoken menace just above their heads.

By the lake it was no better. The conversation turned to the war. The beauty of the distant Alps, the call of the water birds, her mother's egg and homemade mayonnaise sandwiches could not stop Erwin talking about what was uppermost in his mind. When Melina thought of stopping him, trying to change the subject, Jürgen lifted his hand in a gesture that said it was best to let him go on. Erwin wanted to talk. When he talked it was as if he was talking to the faraway mountains in the neutral country of Switzerland where the citizens did not have a war to worry about.

"We should have won the war in 1940. Before we had to fight the Russians and the Americans. September 1940. Field Marshal Goering wanted to go on hitting RAF Fighter Command. Shoot the RAF out of the sky. The airfields and radar stations were our targets. For political reasons, after the RAF bombed Berlin, we attacked London with our bombers. Knocking down buildings rather than shooting down their fighting aircraft. We know now the RAF had run out of reserves. Another month and the *Blitzkrieg* that had conquered continental Europe would have crossed the Channel. Without air cover the Royal Navy would have been naked against our dive-bombers. The Stukas are deadly provided the enemy can't attack them from the air with their fighters. Now we have to suffer British and American bombing on our industry night and day. Our armies are fighting the Russians in the east and the Americans in Italy and the British in North Africa. We can't win anymore. It had to be one at a time. Not all together. The Japanese are only concerned with Asia so they won't help us in Europe. The Americans and the British are going to invade France any time soon and there is little we in the Luftwaffe can do about it. The Americans will soon be pouring men and equipment into Europe. If it isn't too late to make some kind of peace, we are finished."

"What about the secret bomb?" said Melina.

"We don't have it yet. The Americans are also trying to make an atomic bomb."

"So what do we do?" said Gabby.

"Pray to God."

"Will he listen?"

No one answered.

"I want to go for a row on the lake before it's all too late," said Erwin.

"Will he give up?"

"The Führer? Of course not. They are fanatics. You should know that, Melina."

"What made you change your mind?"

"I grew up. It all sounded so glorious at the age of seventeen. The Third Reich ruling a world without war. With order. With industry for the benefit of the people. Each with their own small car. Their own small house. Always enough food. Medicine for everyone. New medicine to conquer disease. A world where man's energy is properly put to work for the benefit of mankind."

"That's what they told you and me," said Melina. "I thought it was all for the benefit of Germany. It wasn't. It was all for the benefit of the Party. The ruling junta of the Party. The perfect dictatorship if they got away with it. In history the longest periods of peace have been under dictatorship... The Greeks liked a benevolent dictatorship without everyone bickering over power. Democracy has its problems."

"It's easy to believe when you wish to believe. When you are seventeen. You don't know enough to question." Erwin was looking at his sister. They both knew the dream was turning into a nightmare. Again, no one said a word, hoping the conversation would go away from something they could do nothing about.

"I can man the tiller," said Jürgen. "Let's go out on the lake."

"Better to get to the bigger lake," said Melina bitterly. "Lake Constance as the Swiss call it. Cross into Switzerland. All of us alive."

"Mama and Papa? The people on the estate? My fellow pilots? There's no way out, Melina. We can all just hope we survive. That the peace won't be worse than the last one when the French tried to starve us to death. Will you play for me tonight, Gabby?"

"Of course I will. I wrote something especially for this weekend. A sonata. So far, I've only finished what I like to call the first movement."

"Lovely. First a row on the lake. To hell with war. For two days I'm going to enjoy myself."

Letting the old horse out of the shaft to graze on the summer grass on a long rein, they walked down to the boatshed on the jetty. The wooden jetty pushed out thirty yards into the small lake. At the disturbance, the ducks swam away trailed by little rows of ducklings behind their mothers. There was a smell of wood smoke drifting down to shore from a house half hidden among the trees.

"Mrs Gottlieb baking I would guess," said Erwin, lightening the mood. "We'll call in on Mrs Gottlieb when we come back from our row. I'll do the rowing."

"What's wrong with us?" said Gabby. "I want an oar: Melina can row the other side."

"In unison!"

"Let's try."

For half an hour squeals and laughter drifted over the water as the girls tried to dip their oars in the water to pull back at the same time. The old clinker-built wooden boat had gone out in a zigzag for the first hundred yards. In the middle they shipped oars and drifted in the light breeze. Melina had felt Jürgen watching her as she rowed. Once she turned and smiled at him, sitting pensively at the tiller.

"You have to pull the boat straight or we'll go round in a circle," he had said.

Everyone was trying to be gay. Trying to forget the harsh dissertation from Erwin. They could see the horse, head down, grazing the lush grass. The picture was beautiful.

When they came ashore Mrs Gottlieb was waiting.

"Can we buy some of what you've been baking?" said Erwin who, like Jürgen, was now dressed in civilian clothes. The small conversation with Mrs Gottlieb made no mention of war.

The horse played up before Erwin put it back in the shaft. The basket that had brought the sandwiches was now full of Mrs Gottlieb's small cakes.

"You gave her far too much money, Jürgen," said Melina.

"Does it matter? Are there any fish in the lake?"

"Never caught one. There's a river nearer the Swiss border," said Erwin. "There you can fish. Melina will show you when I'm gone."

"That's the day after tomorrow," said Gabby. "Far, far away. She's a lovely old lady. She only had girls. Lucky. None of the girls are married! Old Mr Gottlieb works for Dad in the fields. They've lived in that house all their lives. Like his father. And his father before him. Such a pretty house. I'd like a house like that with a piano and never let my children out of my sight."

"Doesn't work like that," said Melina.

"It did for Mrs Gottlieb. What a lovely day. Why do horses only eat grass? You'd think they wouldn't get enough nourishment."

"They eat oats," said Jürgen.

"That's grass seed. Well, a sort of grass. If he goes any slower he's going to stop."

"Doesn't matter," said Gabby. "Dinner's only at eight o'clock. Mama wants us all to dress for dinner. I like dressing up. If you don't have evening clothes, Jürgen, you can borrow from Erwin. After dinner I'm going to give a little concert. Isn't this all fun? In the old days the big house was full of young people. Papa says before the last war they had weekend parties every weekend. With every bedroom in the house full of guests. That must have been fun. Can you imagine? All those people having a good time together. Papa says they sometimes had a very small orchestra to play for them sent down from Berlin. Before the family ran out of money and had to borrow from that Jew in New York. Papa still says he's going to pay Sir Jacob Rosenzweig back one day. I hope he does. It's not right to borrow money and not pay it back. Mama says you always have to do the right thing in life. I'd like to go to New York when the war's over."

Bergit had found some paper hats from before she was married to Klaus. They were in the cupboard with the Christmas decorations she packed away carefully every year. They had been bought by old Mrs von Lieberman before she drowned herself in the lake when they told her about her husband. Klaus had said his father was far too old to have gone to war. His death had started the von Lieberman slide towards bankruptcy. When his mother walked into the lake and sank below the surface, never to come up again alive, her children were away. The girls were married, the boys fighting in the war. Except for Klaus, who inherited the estate, none of the children came home to live after the war. Except for her funeral, none of them visited the estate again. They had been a happy family. Their mother was the glue that held them together. After her funeral none of them could face their memories. Bergit hoped she would be able to face her own memories if they came to say Erwin was dead. Which was why she dug out the paper hats. To remind herself that whatever happened, life went on. That she should be thankful for what she had had in her life.

She had cooked a leg of lamb to be served with a mint sauce from the herb garden. Fresh peas and new potatoes. Sauerkraut as a side dish. Clear fish soup to start with. The lamb followed by an apple strudel cooked with cloves she found at the back of the kitchen cupboard. The cloves were as old as the paper hats. Cloves came from the East. Impossible to buy in Germany.

They all tried their best. Had it been a funeral nothing would have felt any different. They were all preoccupied despite the laughter and the talk. Her children looked grand in their evening clothes. Happily Jürgen had fitted into a suit of her husband's. Old-fashioned but somehow appropriate. She remembered Klaus wearing the same evening dress when they came home after their honeymoon in Africa when they had stayed on the Brigandshaw farm in Rhodesia.

The visit to Harry Brigandshaw had come at the end of their trip. Erwin, smiling now and doing his best to make a party, had been conceived on the Brigandshaw farm. If they had stayed another nine months her son would have been born British, like Harry Brigandshaw, in the British Crown Colony of Southern Rhodesia. She remembered their journey and the smell of the bush. There were plants growing she had smelt nowhere else in the world. Harry had said the smell was of wild sage. One day she wanted to find that scent again. He was going to be all right, she kept telling herself, trying not to cry.

When Gabby played her music in the music room where they had all gone after dinner wearing their paper hats, elastic under their chins to keep the conical hats on their heads, Bergit cried. The new sonata was sad. Erwin shifted in his chair. Jürgen looked at Melina with an unobtainable longing Bergit remembered from the looks given her by Klaus before they were married. Jürgen wanted her daughter. For Melina, a good match of similar families. They would have a life like hers on a country estate, bringing up their children in peace, away from the harsh bustle of the cities. Bergit wondered if Melina knew.

When Gabby finished playing her own composition they all clapped. They drank small glasses of dandelion wine made by Mrs Müller, one of the tenants' wives. It was as good as any liqueur from France, they all said. It was strong, the second glass going to her head. They had drunk a red wine with the lamb from a nearby estate that was still making wine despite the war. Provided it was local, they could have what they wanted. Only in the cities there were terrible shortages of everything. Bergit drank a third glass of the dandelion wine at Erwin's insistence. Then they sang songs. They were all a little drunk. Jürgen kissed Melina on the cheek right in front of everyone. Melina turned and kissed him gently on the lips. It was a dinner party they were all going to remember, Bergit said to herself.

Like all time it was soon gone. Quicker than usual but gone. Instead of waiting for her son to run up the steps from the driveway, Bergit was standing alone looking down, the last feel of him still in the sinews of her arms where she had hugged, not wanting to let him go. He saluted her from the bottom of the steps, the big black officer's cap overshadowing his lean face. Klaus was already up on the trap, reins in hands, waiting. The girls were shouting at the dogs, the dogs barking in excitement. Erwin patted each dog in turn before getting up next to his father. Klaus had made sure there was plenty of time to get to the station. There was only the one train for Erwin to start his journey back to the war.

The old horse took up the weight of the trap. Slowly the trap moved forward, gathering pace down the driveway. Erwin turned once and waved. They all waved back except Jürgen who saluted despite wearing civilian clothes. They watched the backs of the men and the horse until they were right out of sight. Bergit was crying. The girls were crying. The dogs, sensing something was wrong, kept quiet. Loneliness came upon each of them. It was over. His leave was over.

"You'll stay a few more days, Jürgen?" said Bergit. "It will be nice."

"He'll be all right, Mrs von Lieberman."

"I know he will. Will you excuse me? I'm going up to my room to lie down. Maybe tonight, Melina, you can take charge of the food?"

"Of course, Mother."

"I've never been able to get away from these damn wars. First your father. Now Erwin."

"He'll be all right, Mama. Papa came home."

"Thanks to Harry Brigandshaw. I hope Anthony's all right, and his nephew Tinus. It's all so damn crazy. Excuse me. I'm not myself."

"I'm going to play the piano," said Gabby. "I have it in my head now he's gone. The second movement is always slow and very sad. Take her for a walk, Jürgen. I'm so glad for Melina you are staying. With an oar each on either side of the boat you can go for a row on the lake. It's still a lovely day. Papa won't be back for a couple of hours. Papa made sure they would be an hour early for the train."

By the time Jürgen and Melina had put on their walking shoes and gone for a walk with the dogs barking at their heels they could hear Gabby's music coming through the open window of the music room. They were holding hands, Melina on his right, instead of the left where she normally walked next to a man.

"She plays beautifully," said Jürgen.

"She needs a bigger audience than herself and the old house."

"One day she'll find her audience. Oh yes, she'll find it. That music is making me want to cry. Captain of a bomber and I want to cry."

"Why don't we both cry together?"

"Will you marry me, Melina?"

"Don't be silly. In total we haven't known each other a week."

"We made love quick enough."

"Don't be naughty."

"What do you say?"

"You'll have to ask my papa when he comes back from the station."

"You won't mind a man with one arm and a limp?"

"Why should I ever notice?"

PART SEVEN

IN THE LINE OF DUTY – JUNE TO DECEMBER 1944

1

_____

The following summer, Squadron Leader Trevor Hemmings was waving the Australian flag, standing on the Leatherhead roundabout as the convoy of British armour passed by heading for the Dorking bypass and the road to the south coast. Next to him, flying goggles hanging from his left hand, stood Harry Brigandshaw, cheering along with the boys from the nearby prep school. To the side of the boys were the girls from the convent in their school uniforms. All the boys and girls were waving at the smiling troops, with the soldiers, their heads and shoulders out of the turrets of the tanks and armoured cars, waving back. Harry and his weekend guest at Hastings Court had ridden their motorcycles to the designated spot.

When the cheers from further back towards Ashtead increased they all craned their necks.

"He's coming," shouted Trevor. "The bloody beauty's coming. Harry, give that small kid a hike up on your shoulder. Poor little bastard can't see from down there. This is history in the making, mate. Bloody history. The blokes back home will want to know all about this. Timed it perfect, we did. Who told you?"

"My old adjutant, Vic Bell."

"Hope Jerry doesn't know Monty's schedule like you do."

"Shot in the dark, really. Vic said stand on the roundabout at lunchtime and you'll get a surprise."

"What a bit of luck on my leave. Tinus will be pissed off to miss this. That's him, isn't it? With his head and shoulders out of that armoured car. He's the only one wearing a beret. Wave, kids. That's the man who took the Eighth Army to victory at El Alamein. Yes, that's him. He's waving back."

The excitement was quickly over as the convoy passed on down the road.

"Now I need a drink to celebrate. Can we call at the Running Horses on the way back, Harry? Have they still got the same barmaid?"

"She got married to an American GI. There's a new one."

"Is she pretty?"

"Not for me to say at my age."

"You old fox. I'll bet you can still get what you want."

"I'm married."

"When did you last see your wife?"

"Four years ago. I talk to her and the children on the phone."

"That's what I call being faithful. Don't think I'd be that good after four years."

"You're younger, Trevor. Anthony would find out. Can't teach your children bad habits. We can have a pint in the pub if that's what you want. I'll give John Woodall a ring from the Running Horses. I'm sure he'll like to see you again. He'll probably want you to tune up his bike. 1938 when we first met at Redhill Aerodrome seems like a century ago with what you've all been through since. You're going to miss Anthony and Tinus if you go tomorrow. Want me to wangle something with your CO?"

"Course I do."

"I'll ring Ding-a-ling."

"Who's Ding-a-ling?"

"Vic Bell. He has a way of getting what he wants. Favour for favour, that kind of thing. He can give Air Commander Lowcock a ring. Strings, Trevor. It's all about pulling strings. We must just hope German Intelligence doesn't know where the Allies are going to land. Churchill wanted to go with the troops. The King said he'd go too. They've compromised. Neither of them are going. Just a rumour at the Air Ministry. Vic picks up everything. Thank God the war's going to be over soon."

"The Germans will fight."

"Hopefully not to the death. It's all so bloody futile."

. . .

THEY DRANK two pints of bitter in the Running Horses. There was no reply from John Woodall's telephone at Redhill Aerodrome. Harry noticed the Australian drank his beer using two hands to keep the pint steady as it came up to his lips. To help, the man bent forward to drink. Harry knew the feeling. The men had been in combat too long. The barmaid tried to flirt with Trevor. The bar was half full. Most were old men, too old to fight. The only young man in the bar was Trevor Hemmings. Trevor told everyone Field Marshal Montgomery had waved to him. He was like a small boy with his first bicycle. The afternoon quickly went flat after the story at the roundabout.

They rode back to Hastings Court on their motorcycles, through the leafy lanes and hedgerows. Trevor's brother had been killed in the Pacific at the age of nineteen, he had told Harry. The words had been blurted out leaving Harry with nothing to say. Justin Hemmings, Harry learnt, had been with the Australian Army. Later in Trevor's stay at Hastings Court, Harry expected to hear the full story. Over the four years of the war, Harry had taught himself to be a good listener. To wait. In the end it all came out. It was a beautiful day for riding through the English lanes on a motorcycle.

In the driveway sitting in a RAF car was Vic Bell. Harry's stomach sank when he saw his old adjutant. Carefully, trying not to panic, Harry leant the bike on the rest he pulled down with his left foot after turning off the engine. Vic got out of the car.

"It's Anthony, isn't it?" The words were pinched in his throat.

"I'm afraid so, Harry. Last night. Part of a thousand-bomber raid over Berlin. One of the chaps said it was a lucky shot from the ground. Before Anthony had dropped his bombs. Hit the open bomb bay with a full load of bombs, they think. Exploded in mid-air."

"Thank you for coming, Vic. For not using the telephone."

Trevor Hemmings had gone to the rose bed where he was being violently sick at the news.

"We've mourned them before, Harry."

"They were not my son!" shouted Harry. "You don't have a son. You don't understand."

"There's still Frank..."

"He's not my bloody son. Barnaby St Clair poked my wife when I was on the farm in Rhodesia. They were lovers before I married her. I got her up the pole with Anthony on the boat out to Africa. She followed me to the farm. Why I married her. That was how I started my family... No one baled out?" he said, looking at Vic hopefully.

"The explosion tore the aircraft apart. I'm sorry, Harry. Do you want me to go back to London now?"

"Of course not. Oh my God. Oh my God. My son. My son. I've lost my son. Why did I bloody teach him to fly?... Does his mother know?" he said after a long while, by which time Trevor had wiped his face with a handkerchief.

"Not yet. We thought..."

"Of course. I'll phone her right away. Come in, Vic. This is Squadron Leader Hemmings. We were going to ask you to fiddle some leave for Anthony. They first met when Anthony was learning to fly at Redhill. Before the war. Trevor's just lost his brother in the Pacific. I should go to Cape Town. To be with her. Can you arrange to get me there?"

"I'm sure we can."

"Will you tell Tinus? I couldn't phone two of them now. No man should outlive his children. I'm going for a walk. Go inside. I have to walk and think or I'm going to die. Why didn't he stay in Rhodesia?"

"Are you going to be all right, Harry?"

"Of course I'm not. I just want to be alone."

Both of them were gone when Harry came back from his walk. Both of them had left letters of condolence. Trevor said he could not stand losing any more of his friends. The shadows were long on the lane. Evening was approaching. Everyone left him alone. The pigeons were cooing from the elms across the back lawn. The clock tower had still not been cleared of rubble. Harry doubted now he would ever clear away the mess until after the war. The stables would stay in ruins. The grass would stay uncut. There was nothing Harry could think of to do. His mind was not strong enough to phone Tina in Cape Town. However their marriage had taken place in his life she was just as much Anthony's parent as he was. More. A mother mourned her lost children, they said, more than the father. Harry could not see why.

When the phone rang from inside the house he was sitting on the lawn in the gloaming. Harry took no notice of the ringing. He could hear Anthony talking in his head. The young, confident Anthony with his whole life in front of him.

"You'll like her, Dad. She's Afrikaans. Like Tinus's father. It will be nice to have a family with deep roots in Africa. I want to run Elephant

Walk. Eleanor and I have discussed it in our letters. Mum doesn't want to live in Africa. Dorian can help me. He wants to be a farmer. We'll buy more land and turn the whole Mazoe Valley into one big citrus farm now you've built the dam. I think we should give Ralph Madgwick a share in the company I plan to form to run the estate. There'll be much more than farming so we need a company with distinct sections. A manager for each section. A marketing division for selling our orange juice. Another for exporting the oil we extract from the orange skins to the perfume factories in Europe and America. There's so much to do. Eleanor is going to be a qualified nurse. She wants a big clinic on the farm so she can help Aunty Madge. Grandma Brigandshaw will love Eleanor. Everyone loves Eleanor. She wants a dozen children. The Afrikaners are ones for big families. I can't wait for the war to be over so we can be married. I'll be twenty-one in June. That's not too young to get married when you love someone. We met on the beach. Clifton Beach. We played beach bats together for hours in our bathing costumes and bare feet. The sand at Clifton is so soft. The water's so cold. Freezing. You must have gone to Clifton Beach, Dad, when you were at Bishops?"

"It's for you, Mr Brigandshaw," called Mrs Craddock. "Long distance. It's your wife. You better come inside."

"Does she know, Mrs Craddock?"

"She says the British High Commissioner in Cape Town came to see her this afternoon."

"I'm coming. Tell Tina to hold on."

When Harry reached the phone in the old house, Anthony's voice had gone from his mind, leaving his head empty of all thought.

"He was shot down by German flak, Tina. Vic Bell came down from London. I'm so sorry for you. I was about to call you. Anthony must have given them both our names as next of kin."

"I'm coming home, Harry. With the children. They break up at the end of July. All of us."

"Why, Tina?"

"I can't stand it here any longer. He would have turned twenty-one on Wednesday."

"I know."

"Are you all right, Harry?"

"No, I'm bloody well not. He was my son."

"He was my son too."

"I'm so sorry... Are you going to fly? I was going to come out to you."

"Flying home will be quicker."

"Hug the children for me. How are they?"

"None of them have stopped crying from the moment they heard."

"I hate bloody wars. Always the best get killed. He was going to marry his Eleanor. Did you know that?"

"She's a nice girl."

"You'd better go and tell her."

"I don't know where she lives. I'll find out. They're cutting us off, Harry."

The phone went dead. For the first time in his life Harry had no idea what to do. He wished he could cry. Like the children. Instead he was numb.

Mrs Craddock, the old cook, took him by the arm and led him through the house to her kitchen where she cooked him bacon and eggs with a cup of cocoa. She stood over him while he ate.

Afterwards Harry went up to bed. All night he lay awake. All night he lived with his ghosts.

Later that day in London, Vic Bell went to see Sarah Coombes in her flat off the Charing Cross Road. The church bells were ringing for matins. Harry had phoned his flat to say Tina was bringing the children back to England.

"You don't have to get me on a flight, Vic. Anthony must have given both our addresses as next of kin in case something happened to me in the bombing."

"Are you coping?"

"We all cope one way or the other." There was a long pause on the phone. Vic suspected it was while Harry gained control of his voice. "It will be nice to have Tina and the children in the house," said Harry, back to his normal voice.

"Adversity brings people closer together."

"I hope so. I'll see you in the office tomorrow. What did you do with Hemmings?"

"He wanted to get drunk. I left him in Soho. I'm having a word tomorrow with his CO. They must take him off active duty. Half his friends are dead including his younger brother. The mind can only take so much before it breaks. You always think of other people. No, maybe not. Air Commanders don't take kindly to Air Ministry personnel telling them what to do."

Sarah Coombes's small flat was over the tobacconist's. They met twice a week for a cuppa as Sarah liked to call it. Her husband had owned the tobacconist's before he was killed at Dunkirk. Sarah ran the shop on her own. The shop was closed on Sundays. They were a great comfort to each other.

"What's the matter, Vic?"

"Harry. His eldest son's been killed."

"Was he in the army?"

"Pilot of a Lancaster."

"I didn't know."

"There are lots of things you don't know about Harry."

"He grew up on a farm in Rhodesia, so far as I remember from those nights hiding underground from the bombing. Clerk in the Air Ministry."

"I suppose you could call him a clerk. He's my boss, Sarah. His wife's coming back from Cape Town. Did you know he had a wife?"

"Yes, that I knew. I want to go and see him. Poor man. Was his son a sergeant pilot?"

"Flight lieutenant. Harry was a colonel in the last war. Royal Flying Corps. I was his adjutant."

"Never said nothing to us in the underground. Told stories about Africa. We all thought he was making them up to keep our minds off the bombing."

"His father owned that farm in Rhodesia. Harry owns it now."

"Come on, Vic. We'll go round to his room. Said he had a room nearabouts."

"He's not there now."

"Where is he?"

"At Hastings Court near Leatherhead. I went down yesterday to tell him the news about Anthony."

"He's rich, is he? Is that what it's all about? Didn't want to blow his trumpet with us ordinary folk. You never know people do you, Vic? I always believe what they say. Take them at face value. Poor Harry. He was so good helping everyone. And I made him sandwiches thinking he had no money. What's Hastings Court?"

"A mansion he inherited from his family. Been in his mother's side of the family for centuries. Better not to go down today, Sarah. He wants to be alone. They had grown close since Anthony came back alone to England from Africa to join the RAF. Harry taught him to fly. Harry has his own plane in Rhodesia. I'll take you and Fred down later in the summer. We'll go for the weekend. When Tina comes back. She'll like having guests."

"Is she la-di-da?"

"Quite the opposite. Grew up in a railway cottage in Corfe Castle. Her father's the stationmaster of a one-horse town."

"I'll be buggered. What made him marry her?"

"She was pregnant with Anthony."

"Drink your tea, Vic. Now you've started I want to hear everything. This beats his stories during the Blitz. Was he ever in the Belgium Congo? With a tribe of savages?"

"Yes he was, Sarah, for a number of years. He finally walked out of the jungle and found his way back to London. Back from the dead, so they said in the newspapers."

"I'll make us another pot of tea before you start. Poor Harry. He's such a nice man. I miss my Tom, Vic," said Sarah, bursting into tears.

"I know you do, Sarah," said Vic putting his arm round her shoulders.

Janet Wakefield heard about Anthony from William Smythe. Horatio had been sent down to the south coast by Billy Glass, the editor of the *Daily Mail*.

"What can be so secret on the south coast?" Janet had said to Horatio before he went. "Everyone knows there's going to be an invasion. There are more Americans in England than English. Certainly seems like it. They're everywhere and loud. Why can't they talk without shouting?"

"Most of them are very charming. I'll be away a while, Janet. Look after the kids."

"I always look after the kids. What's the matter, Horatio?"

"It's going to be dangerous."

"Why?"

"I can't tell you. I'll call soon as I can."

"Why can't you tell, Horatio?"

"You'll find out soon enough. In the *Daily Mail*."

"If you're trying another Berlin on me with William, I won't have it. We're married. We have kids. What about young Harry and young Bergit?"

"I have a job to do. We all have a job to do."

"Oh, my God! You are going to be part of the invasion!"

When William came round to see her with the news of Anthony she was with a patient.

"I'm with a patient, Will. Can't you see?"

"Anthony's been killed. Harry Brigandshaw's Anthony."

"Mr Makepeace, will you excuse me?"

There was one advantage of her profession thought William, as he watched the man struggle to get out a reply without any success. Harry had asked him to write a piece on Anthony for the newspapers. They both knew the papers would pick up on the story. Harry and his family were news on both sides of the Atlantic. William had not wanted Janet to hear about Anthony from the papers.

"Where is Harry?"

"In his office, I expect. Trevor Hemmings was with him when Vic Bell drove down to Hastings Court to tell him the news. This is my article for tomorrow's papers. I've cabled it to Glen Hamilton in Denver."

Janet read the story, tears coming down both sides of her face. Mr Makepeace left without her noticing. She gave the article back to William and wiped her eyes.

"Poor Harry. Anthony was all he had in England."

"Tina's flying back with the kids."

"I'm glad... Is Horatio in any kind of danger?"

"Not at the moment, Janet."

"What is that supposed to mean?"

"He told me to tell you when he was gone. So you wouldn't throw a tantrum. He's going on a British ship with the invasion fleet."

"Will he come under fire?"

"No one knows, Janet. Maybe the Germans will withdraw from the coast. The RAF and the American Air Force have command of the air."

"It's Berlin all over again. Why didn't you go, William? You always liked to be in the thick of it."

"Ruthy, Janet."

"I'll wring his bloody neck when he comes back."

"Horatio said you might."

"Then why did he go?"

"Billy Glass asked him. Someone had to go from the *Mail*. I'm freelance. Can choose my jobs. Horatio can't. He didn't want to put the others in jeopardy. They're all married with kids. He said it was his responsibility."

"First Bruno Kannberg. Now my husband. Just for a bloody story. Where's that Mr Makepeace?"

"He left. He was trying to say something."

"When's the invasion?"

"No one knows exactly. Moment I hear anything I'll let you know. I've managed to filch some petrol to go down to Hastings Court on Saturday to be with Harry. Do you want to bring the kids? I thought they'd help. Young Harry in particular."

"Anything to take my mind off Horatio. When's this damn war going to be over?"

"Soon, we hope."

"If anything like that happened to young Harry I don't know what I'd do. Poor Harry."

"Let's hope young Harry never has a war to contend with."

2

_____

*B*eing a father had changed William's life. From being a self-centred hedonist taking from life what he wanted, everything was now about Ruthy.

"Marrying an 'old man' does have its compensations," Betty had said to him six months after Ruth was born. "She'll grow up into a bitch with all this attention. Please don't let me stop you. I won't be marrying her. Some poor man down the line is going to have to start running after her where you left off, William. By the by, when the war's over we're moving out of my flat. I want a couple more kids to keep you on your toes. Can't have just one demanding child, now can we?"

"Where do you want to go?"

"I don't mind North Kensington. We need a bedroom for Ruth. She can't spend much longer sleeping in the bath. It's the howling noise. I don't mind the poo. I don't mind being sicked all over. I just want my sleep."

"I always get up."

"You do, Will, but she wakes me up. I'm all alert. Motherly instinct. Then I can't get back to sleep. Listening for her next sound. When she's dead quiet I wonder if she's got her head in the pillow suffocating."

"I'll start looking. Better to buy now with the war still on. The doodlebugs are getting on everyone's nerves. After the invasion the army will knock out the launch sites the RAF haven't found. We've still got money, if that's what you're asking. You never ask me about money. Most women do."

"I'm your secretary. I do the banking. I never wanted much materially. Just to be comfortable and eat plain good food. Do you still miss Genevieve?"

"Not for a minute. When we saw her last film I didn't even bat an eyelid."

"Is it me or Ruthy?"

"Both of you, Betty. Not only are you a damn good secretary, you're a damn good wife."

"Is that a backhanded compliment?"

"Whatever made you think that?"

"Didn't you really get a twinge when you saw Genevieve's film?"

When William reached the small flat after visiting Janet in Chelsea, his wife had the supper ready in the oven, with Ruthy bathed, the bath dried, and Ruthy's bedding back in the bath.

"We're going down to Hastings Court with Janet and the kids on Saturday."

"Poor Harry. He must be feeling terrible. You were a long time."

"She's worried about Horatio."

"Thank God you didn't go."

"Is she asleep?"

"Out like a light. Putting her down in the bath was your best idea. Don't wake her up. Want a cup of tea before supper? You'll want to listen to the news."

"Yes, we'd better listen to the six o'clock news."

Looking down, Tinus Oosthuizen could see the landing craft, all heading for the shore. At fifteen hundred feet he could see the first rays of the morning sun rising from German-occupied Europe. Down below on the sea the first light was full of moving shadows, the wakes of the blunt-nosed landing craft running back in straight phosphorescent lines. All other thoughts left his mind.

"They'll be coming out of the sun, chaps," he said over the radio.

"Bandits one-five to the northeast."

"Tallyho."

Adrenaline pumping, Tinus led his wing to the northeast, scanning the sky for the glint of sun reflecting off metal.

"I see them. I count ten bandits, 109s. Here we go."

Within minutes the sky above Normandy was filled with dogfights while German artillery on the ground opened fire on the incoming landing craft. Quickly the 109s were breaking away, overwhelmed by the three squadrons of Mark IX Spitfires. For half an hour, Tinus patrolled above the landing beaches.

"Tinus, you can go back for fuel," he heard from the incoming wing.

"They didn't know we were coming, Janusz, or they don't have enough aircraft. Not so good down below. Going home for fuel. Good hunting, my friend."

All day the fighters left RAF Tangmere, Tinus flying six sorties before the dusk came and night shielded the troops on the beaches. Only the Americans on Omaha beach were held up by German artillery and machine gun fire. By nightfall the British and Canadian armies had reached the sand dunes and beyond. In the British sector the Royal Air Force had control of the sky, their overwhelming numbers preventing the Luftwaffe from attacking the ground troops.

In the officers' mess, while the maintenance crews worked on the spitfires, Tinus stood with one elbow on the bar surrounded by his pilots.

"It took the Yanks longer than everyone expected. They were right to build up overwhelming force. The Germans don't have the aircraft to fight on two fronts. The Americans will break out tomorrow. Equipment will be hitting the beach all night. Pratt, give everyone a drink and put it on my card."

No one mentioned the pilot they had lost during the day until the round of drinks was in their hands."

"Fisher," said Tinus raising his glass. "At eighteen I hope his life was fulfilled."

"Fisher," said the other pilots.

When Janusz joined him at the bar, Tinus was not thinking of the youngest pilot in his wing. He was thinking of his cousin Anthony as he had been for days.

"Sorry to hear you lost Fisher. It's always the novice."

"The old hands among the Germans can see the inexperienced pilot and single him out. I was watching Fisher. When I got to him it was too late. He was going down in flames. Did you lose any pilots?"

"Not today, Tinus."

"Anthony was just unlucky. Bomb bay open to drop his stick and a shell hits the bloody load. Fluke. Lucky shot. He was coming to live in Africa after the war. Had it all planned. Had a girl to marry. Well, he can't do any of that now. You never heard a word out of Poland since you fled the country after the German invasion?"

"Neither my family, nor Ingrid. Not a word. Now, instead of being ruled by the Nazis, we're going to be ruled by the communists. I wonder why I worried."

"You can stay in England."

"On my own? I'm a Pole, Tinus. The same way you are an African. You love Africa. I love my country. Except there isn't one now."

"The Russians will let you go home."

"To what? Communism confiscates the land. Gives it to the people to run as a commune. Well, I suppose that is good for some if they know how to farm. I was educated to be a lawyer and run the family estate one day. Father was a judge. All those jobs are defunct under communism. In Russia they shot their aristocracy. Going back to Poland after the war claiming I'm Count Kowalski will get me shot. No, there's no comfort for me after the war. Even if I find my family alive."

"You could come out to Africa. There's plenty of land in Africa that is not being used. The population in Rhodesia is sprinkled among a few rural villages. The wild animals roam over most of Rhodesia."

"The Americans won't let you keep your empire once they've won your war for you. India will be first to get independence. The Americans are already talking about a free world under democratic rule. Colonialism will be a dirty word."

"They need us to develop Africa. Without our knowledge the black man will starve as they multiply. With modern medicine we've cut the child mortality rate in Rhodesia by eighty per cent in the last fifty years."

"They won't remember that. They'll want their land back. Like the Russian peasants. People always want what they haven't got. They don't see hard work and knowledge as a prerequisite for making a success of their lives. When the politicians say they are going to give them what they want the people think it's a handout. That they'll have everything for doing nothing. We should go to America. That's where we should go. You know the old saying, if you can't beat them, join them."

"Genevieve has suggested the same. She's also worried about the future of the white man in Africa."

"Doomed, I'd say. When this is over, go to her in America, Tinus."

"I might just do that. You can come with me... First light tomorrow. The CO says we'll be flying six sorties a day for the next week. A few more drinks and I'm getting some sleep. It's the beginning of the end,

Janusz. The invasion of Normandy is the beginning of the end of the war in Europe."

"For the British maybe. I don't think so for the Poles. We'll be no better off under the Russians than under the Germans. All of us. Not just the aristocracy."

3

Sarah Coombes held his hand when Harry Brigandshaw went round on the Wednesday for his weekly cup of tea. The Air Member for Personnel suggested he take a week's leave. Vic Bell pussyfooted around his office every morning with the daily situation report. Everyone, as Harry put it to himself, was so damned nice while all he wanted to do was scream from the top of a hill. There was nothing anyone could do. He had to sort out his own mind. Stop the recurring picture of the exploding bomb bay, Anthony turning round from the cockpit as he recognised in a second before death he was going to die. The worst curse for Harry was a vivid imagination, with each time his inability to stop what was about to happen.

In deference to Air Vice Marshal Healy's suggestion, Harry put in a formal request for leave which was instantly granted. Going down to Hastings Court on the Thursday night from London a day early, Harry took the 770cc BSA motorcycle from the shed. The same bike he had owned for nearly twenty years. In the flying coat he had worn in the First World War, flying goggles to keep the wind out of his eyes, Harry began the long ride to Corfe Castle and the Purbeck Hills where first he had screamed at the loss of Lucinda St Clair, his wife killed by Mervyn Braithwaite while Lucinda was expecting Harry's first child. Soon after the war had ended, Braithwaite, out of his mind from all the killing he had endured in the war, had felt the urge to go on killing his imagined enemies, friends turned to foes in his paranoid mind. Riding the bike at full throttle, Harry hurled himself through the English lanes seeing nothing that was not in his mind. For four years all Harry had seen of his family was Anthony. Anthony back from flying school in Gwelo. Anthony in his officer's uniform, new wings bright on his breast. Anthony at Hastings Court, the two of them walking the estate, talking, always talking. Of the future, of what his eldest son was going to do with the rest of his life, the excitement, the hope, the golden future of a perfect life seen through the eyes of youth before the warts set in and reality came down to the facts of life. Eleanor, the perfect girl, never to argue with in his life. Harry, seeing the excitement in his son that made life worth the living, even though Harry knew most of what his son wanted was the basis of fiction.

Except for petrol, Harry did not stop until he reached Purbeck Manor and looked up at the Purbeck Hills. Without seeing anyone, Harry left the flying coat and goggles draped over the bike. Looking at the spine of the Purbeck Hills in the middle distance, Harry began the long walk. Over the small stream, up the paths he had walked so long ago with Lucinda until he reached the top. Harry knelt down first and prayed to all the gods. Then he stood up and screamed at the heavens, the sound echoing down into the valley, the birds taking little notice, a rabbit scurrying away, a cock pheasant lifting out of the bushes to fly down into the valley empty of people. Then he was finished.

When Harry walked back to the Manor house and his lonely motorbike parked in the drive, Robert St Clair was waiting. Neither said a word. They hugged each other. Then Harry looked up to the second floor landing of the old house and saw Lady St Clair, who once had been his mother-in-law. Maybe she still was. Later he would ride to see the Pringles and tell them the news they likely knew already. Maybe losing a grandson for Old Pringle was as bad as Harry losing a son. Harry did not know.

Merlin St Clair came down the steps from the long terrace that ran the length of the house and shook his hand. Mrs Mason, the cook, was standing just outside the gothic front door of the house.

"I'm so sorry, Harry," he said. "If anything ever happened to Genevieve I don't know what I would do. How are you coping, Harry?"

"Went up on the hills over there and screamed at the heavens."

"You did that, I remember, when you came back from Africa two years after Lucinda was killed."

"Somehow again it has made me feel better."

"How long are you staying?"

"Back in the office on Monday. With the war going on, we have to go on for the ones that can't fight anymore... I need the distraction."

"Judging from last night's six o'clock news, the invasion has been a success. You likely know more than us tucked away in the country. Old Mrs Mason will see you have a room. You remember Mrs Mason? She's still the housekeeper and the cook. She and Mother are a comfort to each other. He was such a lovely boy. Why does God always take the best in a war? We weren't so lucky either, Harry. Lost Frederick, then Robert lost his foot, which wasn't so bad for a writer. A writer doesn't need two feet to write a good novel. But you know this... Robert has a new book on the way. Freya said she was going into Corfe Castle for something. For Chuck. Why do Americans call Charles by the name of Chuck? Never did understand. Richard's at school. Well, you know all that as well. How long are you staying?"

Smiling at Merlin's forgetfulness, Harry followed them into the old house. When he reached the lounge, Lady St Clair was waiting to give him another sympathetic hug. Harry wondered if she knew Frank was her grandson, Barnaby's son, not his. The thought of his family coming back from Africa made him suddenly smile.

"Nothing like a good scream," he said, accepting the glass of dry sherry Robert put in his hand.

"To absent friends," said Robert raising his glass.

"To absent friends," they all said in reply.

For Harry, it was good to be among old friends who had shared so much of his life. Through the open door, Harry could see Mrs Mason going off with his old flying coat to make him up a room. For the first time in many years he could feel the presence of Lucinda, dead for so long. Outside the window, looking out from the back of the house, the lawn was uncut, like the lawns at Hastings Court, for lack of petrol to drive the lawnmowers.

"Why do we bother to cut lawns, Harry?" asked Robert following the direction of Harry's gaze. "We could trim everything and bring it into line. Does that make it any more beautiful? We like to impose our will. Silly. All of nature is best left alone. You think we've lived too long, Harry? Is there more in the past, for the likes of you and I, than the future? Oxford. Where you and I met. All that enthusiasm to change the world. All that energy expended to get our degrees. Did we ever use our degrees? Did we ever learn anything?"

"We learnt to think. That was all it was about. Now I'm thinking too much. All I do is think of him. Will it fade? Will his face fade away by the time I'm very old? Is there anything left of this life when we die? The world only exists when it is seen in our own minds. Without our minds creating the picture there would be nothing... Are you going back to America when the war's over? Won't be long now. Months rather than years. All that death and destruction. What for? We all have to rebuild what we knocked down. The Americans are talking about rebuilding a new Europe with some kind of an economic plan. To stop us all squabbling. There will always be disagreement. Human nature. To kill and be killed. Darwin and his bloody survival of the fittest. Anthony was one of the fittest. So was André Cloete, South African friend of my nephew Tinus. Only the living talk. The dead stop where they died, soon forgotten. Sorry, Robert. I'm just feeling sorry for myself; the most pointless act of mankind. What's the point of feeling sorry for oneself? Makes me achingly sad. The children coming back will help."

"And Tina?"

"Four years is a long time. I never ask her on the phone what she's up to. If it's bad, I don't want to know. If it's good, I hope she will tell me. It's only ever about the children. Never about us. We need the children more than they need us. Does Freya miss her parents, I wonder? Not as much as they miss her. What I'm going to do to amuse myself after the war I don't know. Right now, Tinus is giving air cover over the landing beaches. Once the army have secured the German airfields he'll fly his wing to France, I suppose. He's survived so much. Just a few more months. How does Merlin see Tinus as a son-in-law?"

"Never talks about it."

"I suppose he wouldn't. Fathers can be jealous of their daughters, so I am told. How's the new book coming along? Whatever happened to the mother? Esther, I think, was her name. Barmaid at the Running Horses at Mickleham. Strange, Merlin should meet her so close to my ancestral home. These things happen in times of war."

"Like the rest of them. In the end they get written. People read them. Just another business really, Harry. Another way to make money. She's drunk most of the time, to answer your question. Genevieve keeps in contact. Drunks live solitary, lonely lives."

"There must be more to it than that, writing a book."

"Sometimes. The publishers get excited. Max Pearl in America likes money. His whole life has been focused on money. Why do people want more and more money when they've got enough?"

"Feelings of insecurity. As hunters and gatherers our ancestors always searched for more. Even when they had enough food. Wired into us, I suppose. Barnaby can never get enough. Do you think she knows?" said Harry, looking at Lady St Clair where she sat talking to Merlin on the deep settee.

"Probably. My mother would think it rude to talk about something like that. 'Some things, Robert, are best left alone,' she would say to me. Frank's birth is one of those subjects."

"He must know instinctively he's different to the others. Always fighting. Always on the offensive. Always on the outside is Frank."

"He'll grow out of it."

"I hope so. For his sake. And everyone else's. Do you believe the sins of the father are visited on the son?"

When Harry looked up, Lady St Clair was looking straight at him. A look of admonition he remembered from his own mother. Lady St Clair must have heard what they were just saying.

"Have another sherry, Harry."

"I'd better. What a strange life it has been for all of us."

"Where are you going to live after the war?"

"Who knows? Tina will want to live in England. I want to go home to Africa. My mother would love to fuss over my children on Elephant Walk. Do we ever get what we want? I don't think so. Even when we get what we think we want. The human race is never satisfied. No wonder we are always fighting... Will the bike be all right in the driveway?" They could both hear a car outside.

"I expect so. Sounds like Freya and the children. Let's go out and say hello. That look my mother just gave you was so sad behind the disapproval."

The next day after breakfast Harry took the footpath along the stream in the direction of Corfe Castle. The previous evening Mrs Mason had made them sandwiches for their supper. No one had wished to sit down to a formal dinner. Halfway to Corfe Castle, Harry knocked on the door to the railway cottage. The walk had softened his mood. Mrs P, Tina's mother, opened the door. Old Pringle was in the shadow behind his wife, the morning sunlight blinding Harry at first as he went inside. No one said a word. In the kitchen, on the mantelpiece over the wood-fired stove, was a photograph of Anthony in his officer's uniform, the peaked hat at a jaunty angle on his head. The photograph took in the head and shoulders with the RAF wings on Anthony's uniform prominent. Next to the photograph was the picture of a young girl. Mrs P began to cry. Old Pringle put his arm through hers and took her to a comfortable chair near the kitchen table where he sat her down. On the stove, the kettle was just on the boil. Harry had never visited his in-laws without finding the kettle ready to make a pot of tea.

"Who's the pretty girl?" asked Harry.

"Eleanor Botha," said Mrs P looking up through her tears. "They were going to be married and live in Rhodesia."

"When did he last visit you?"

"A month ago. Said not to say. Worried you were always on your own in that big house over the weekends. Every third leave he visited us, Harry."

"Tina phoned?"

"She's coming home with the children. There's a telephone at the railway station. Mr P's still working. Doesn't want to stop. Are you staying at the Manor with Lady St Clair?"

"Do you mind?"

"You were Lady St Clair's son-in-law first. What are we all going to do, Harry, without Anthony?"

"Remember him as he is in that photograph. Now he'll never grow old."

"Your nephew all right?"

"Yes. They would have told me. I always leave a number when I'm not in my London digs or up at the Court. I was so selfish to think I was the only one feeling pain."

"All we leave behind are our children."

"I'm glad Anthony came to see you two often. You will always have those memories."

"Yes. He was our favourite grandson. Mr P always said Anthony was the only one in his family ever to be given a King's Commission. Our grandson the officer, we used to say. We were so proud of him."

When Harry left the cottage after drinking his tea, trying to find a subject to talk about other than Anthony, he walked slowly back to Purbeck Manor. Most of the time they had drunk their tea in silence. There was nothing more he could do for them. They all had to live their different lives the best they could.

"You are good people," he had said as he left. "I have not been able to say that truthfully many times in my life. Tina will bring down the children when she comes home."

"You don't mind about Frank?"

"The truth? Of course I do. Except for one part of the mess, Frank is a living part of Lucinda in my house."

"Of course. She would have been Frank's aunt. God has strange ways of compensating our follies."

"The one I worry about most is not myself, Tina or even Barnaby. It's Frank."

"Does he know?"

"Nobody has told him. What he does know is that he's different. Different to the rest of the children."

"She loved Barnaby so much. From a child. We never saw it coming, you might say. Let them play together as children. Barnaby never married. All about class. Him from the big house, us common people."

"It's how we behave that counts."

"Don't be hard on her. Wasn't her fault. Never could say no to Barnaby. Whatever he wanted she did for him."

"She gave me five lovely children."

"*You* include Frank?"

"Of course, Mrs P. I have always treated him as my son."

How such a deep chasm had come between two families living five miles apart for centuries was beyond Harry's comprehension, as in Frank they had to be related. Not once but many times. If the truth of the family trees were known, they were likely one interlocking family of cousins, distant and not so distant.

As he walked back under the trees near to the river, some with their branches under the water, Harry thought of a distant conversation he had had with his father before he left Rhodesia to go up to Oxford. His father had been explaining why there was no difference between his own father, the Pirate, and Harry's mother's father, Sir Henry Manderville Bart with a written pedigree that went back to the time of William the Conqueror.

"You can usually be sure who is your mother, Harry. Never your father. The origin of your father you take on trust. We are all the same. Some are luckier than others to have the man they call their father with enough money to send us to Oxford."

"Are you really my father, sir?"

"Of course I am. Your mother said so."

"She was married to your elder brother when I was born."

"A little too soon after the marriage, son. No, Harry, it was me. In the grotto at Hastings Court, your grandfather's ancestral home. She only ever loved one man. That was me. Why, when I knew the date of your birth I came back to England, put a ladder up to your mother's bedroom window and ran off with the three of you."

"Who was the third?"

"Your nurse. The wife of Tinus Oosthuizen, my mentor and friend when I first arrived in Africa. Long before Cecil Rhodes sent his column to Fort Salisbury and hoisted the Union Jack."

"So you are my father?"

"Of course I am. Mark my word. One day Madge will marry Barend. The Brigandshaws, Mandervilles and Oosthuizens will then join to create one African family. Madge swore to marry Barend on her sixteenth birthday. One happy family, my son."

"General Oosthuizen was hanged by us British for treason. For going out with a Boer commando from the Cape."

"Something I tried to stop. With every fibre of my body. Not for going out with his fellow Boers. For us British hanging an honest person."

"It's all so complicated."

"It'll get more complicated as you go through your life."

"Is it all worth it?"

"Only you will be able to answer that question Harry. Have a good life. It's the only one you are going to get, despite what my Reverend Uncle Nat the missionary might have to say about it. One life. Make the most of it. You never know how short it is going to be. Uncle Nat says a lot of things he's not quite sure about. All part of increasing the empire, I suppose. Make them all Christians and they'll behave themselves."

With the tall chimney pots of Purbeck Manor now in his sights, Harry came back in his mind to the present, worrying about Wing Commander Tinus Oosthuizen, Royal Air Force, old General Oosthuizen's grandson.

4

Seven weeks later when Tina Brigandshaw brought the three youngest children back to Hastings Court, Betty Smythe put the morning mail on William's desk. On top of the opened letters was an envelope.

"Thought you'd like to see the envelope first. Indian postage stamps. Can't read the postmark. The return address on the back in Singapore. From your cousin-in-law. My guess is she got the letter to India in a bigger envelope. Someone then posted this letter to England."

"You'd better go look at Ruthy. She's making noises."

"Your servant, sir."

"Go on then."

"I want to know what's inside. Ruthy's gurgling to herself. She's going to be a singer. They all start singing in the pram. The good ones. Go on, Will, open the bloody thing. It must have something to say about Joe and the children."

Carefully, having peered at the stamps, William slit the envelope open with a letter opener. Inside were four sheets of pale blue paper.

"It's in English."

Watching her husband read the pages, Betty saw his face light up as he read.

"Joe's in Changi jail. The Japs brought his unit back from building the Burma railway line... The RAF have bombed Singapore naval docks from Rangoon... Wavell's Chindits have pushed the Japs halfway down the Malayan peninsula. It's all here. The Royal Engineers are trying to rebuild the docks under Japanese guards. We've sunk some of their ships in the harbour. Joe's going to come out alive. I don't think Cherry Blossom wrote this letter. It's been dictated more likely. All the spelling and grammar are correct. Somehow, Cherry Blossom, or her father, have contact with Joe in prison when the work detail is over for the day."

"Or Chinese friends in the docks."

"There's a PS. She says there's a British journalist in Changi with the rest of them... That Joe says I know... She says his name is Bruno Kannberg, from the *London Daily Mirror*. Where's Horatio right now? Well, I'll be buggered."

"How must I know? Don't be vulgar. Someone will hear."

"Do we have Gillian's phone number in New York? She never came back to England. Go and phone Arthur Bumley at the *Mirror*. Bruno must have been captured by the Japs right at the start of the American attack on Guadalcanal. The Japs found out he was British and sent him to Singapore with the rest of the British prisoners."

"Calm down, Will!"

"Why should I? This is the first good news to come out of the bloody war."

"Did she say anything about the kids?"

"They're fine. I'm going to phone Harry Brigandshaw right now. Cheer him up. Isn't his wife due back from South Africa this week? She had to wait to get the kids out of school at the end of term. Why weren't we told the RAF have bombed Japanese shipping in Singapore harbour? Get your shorthand pad. We'll get this story out before Arthur Bumley. We can wire it to Glen Hamilton in Denver. News, Betty, what news. Even in Asia we have the enemy on the run... It's Bombay. The postmark is Bombay."

"Don't you want me to check Ruthy?"

"She can wait."

"Men and their priorities," said Betty sarcastically.

"Money, Betty. You want new furniture for the house."

"Are you going to mention Bruno by name? It'll be big news in America. He went ashore from an American boat."

"He's still a Japanese prisoner."

"If the Japanese know we know he's alive they'll be careful. They know they are going to lose the war. People change their minds when the boot is on the other foot. Prison guards in particular."

"We'll make it front page news across America."

"You're more excited about Bruno than Joe."

"Of course I am. Bruno's famous. Bruno's news."

"Joe's your cousin."

"She says he's all right. The Japs need a sergeant in the Royal Engineers to repair their docks. What a bit of luck."

Smiling to herself, Betty went out of William's office to get her notebook. Ruthy was still sitting up in the pram, gurgling.

"You're wrong," said William through the open door. "Joe's important. Of course he is. He's my cousin. He has children. What would happen to Ruthy if I couldn't look after her? If you couldn't look after her? Children need both their parents."

Getting up on an impulse, William walked into the smaller room where his wife did the typing. Bending down, he kissed Ruthy on the forehead.

"It's going to be one of those days," he said, patting his wife's bottom on his way back to his desk.

When Betty went back to take shorthand notes, William was staring at the ceiling.

"When the war's over you are going to become a housewife," he said.

"Whatever for? I'd be bored stiff. I could think of nothing worse than staying at home looking after the children."

"Who said anything about children in the plural?"

"I did."

"You can't have two kids in the office once they are running around. You'd better have a boy."

"At your service, sir."

"Come here and give me a kiss. Do you really want another child?"

"We can't have just one, can we? Ruthy will be lonely. In the new house we haven't yet bought, we'll need lots of children. I always wanted to be part of a big family."

"Be careful what you wish for. My mother called me Cocky Alljaw."

"Why ever for?"

"I suppose I was cocky even then."

"She had you pegged. 'Alljaw' for a journalist!"

"It'll pay for that new house and furniture."

The Duck and Drake was full of newsmen all talking at the same time. Betty had taken Ruthy home in the pram to give her the nightly bath. William had arranged to meet Horatio in the pub. Arthur Bumley of the *Daily Mirror* and Billy Glass of the *Daily Mail* were to join them. Horatio had told a friend before William walked in the door. The whole pub knew Bruno Kannberg was alive in a Singapore jail.

When William joined them at the bar, his fellow newsmen put up a cheer.

"You'd think I'd saved the bugger single-handed."

"Where's Betty?"

"Bathing Ruthy. She wants to go on working when the war ends."

"The holes we dig for ourselves. After three phone calls I caught up with the dutiful wife. She was in Los Angeles. A man answered the phone. When I told her Bruno was alive in a Japanese jail she didn't say a word for ten seconds. Caught her on the hop. All those time zones in America make phoning from England a problem. If I had to guess, the once-upon-a-time widow was in bed when I rang. With the young man who answered the phone. She liked to keep Bruno short to keep him on his toes. Poor boy was besotted. At the *Mirror* we were very generous when Bruno was taken from us. The widow's pension was the equivalent of forty-five years' loyal service. Looked good in the paper when we told our readers. Everyone's patriotic in time of war. Showed the paper cared. Now the pension stops. Bruno gets his weekly pay. I'll have to look into a refund."

"You mean she was getting more from a dead man?" said Horatio Wakefield.

"More than double. The merry widow. In America they love money, especially when the men don't have to do any work for it. Instead of holding them by the balls with her sexuality, our Mrs Kannberg had them over the barrel with her money. Probably more than a barrel. Looks fade. Money lasts. Poor old Bruno. All that time in a nasty foreign jail and nothing to show for it. Chances are, after a couple of years he won't fancy her when he gets out of Changi. Can't be long now."

"So she wasn't pleased?" said William.

"Not really, if you ask me."

"He can always find another wife."

"And who's going to pay for the first one?"

"Hopefully Bruno will write a bestselling book about his time in a Japanese jail. People read that kind of stuff. Some poor sod worse off than they are. You think her young man will walk out on her?"

"Wouldn't you? The husband won't be his problem. My stopping the pension will stop the attraction. She's thirty next year, according to our pension department. Poor girl. What a disaster. She was better off with him dead."

"You don't think she loves him?" said Horatio.

"I don't think so. Had her bum in the butter... Here comes the man from the *Mail*. Come over here, Billy Glass, and buy us a round. It's a celebration we don't get much of these days. Good old Bruno. He'll be all right. Not quite so sure about his wife."

"She'll get herself pregnant when he comes back," said William from experience.

"Good thinking. A journalist's salary is better than nothing. All this might make Mrs Kannberg behave herself. She was having an affair with Gregory L'Amour they say. Oh well. All good things have to come to an end. Like my mistress. She met my wife by accident and liked her. Buggered the whole thing up. At least my wife isn't talking to me. Would you have given the grieving, or in this case, the not so grieving widow such a generous pension, Billy? Would Wakefield's wife with two kids have got what our man got for getting himself killed as we thought? You were lucky, Wakefield, to get back alive from Normandy. For the sake of your children. The *Mail* would never have been so generous as the *Mirror*."

"After all these years, won't you call me Horatio?"

"You know what she calls me behind my back? Art the Bumley. The longer version, I should think, of Bum Fart. People are so unkind."

"Have you told her the pension stops?"

"I'm sure she's worked it out on her own. She'll find out next month when the cheque doesn't arrive."

"You're damn cruel, Arthur," said Billy Glass after ordering the round. "Of course we would have looked after Janet. Bruno's alive. That's what's important. I give you a toast. To our fellow newsman. Very much alive. Bruno Kannberg."

When each of them had bought a round of drinks they all went home. William was not smiling. The truth of being a freelance journalist had struck home. What he now needed was lots of insurance for Ruthy and Betty if anything should happen to him.

"What are you grinning at?" Betty asked him when he opened the door to her flat.

"You and Ruthy. Some men have all the luck."

5

In the end Tina Brigandshaw had taken the boat. The extra two weeks was better than flying up Africa to the Mediterranean where the air war was still raging. The ship had sailed from Cape Town to Bristol on the west coast of England. With the battle of the Atlantic mostly over there was no need for an escort. For Tina and the three children the journey was dull, stopping only at the British islands of St Helena and Ascension.

Mr and Mrs Coetzee had moved back into the Bishopscourt house at Harry's suggestion. Both of them had smirks on their faces when they arrived in a taxi with their suitcases to take up their caretaker post for the second time. Tina had not bothered to ask them what they were doing in the time after she had fired them in October 1940; some things were better unsaid. In Tina's mind there was no way she was coming back to Africa so what they did with the house did not matter. She was going to tell Harry to sell the place now the war was coming to an end.

Harry had come on board at Bristol to see them off the boat. His family having once owned the shipping line that brought them back to England had made going on board a simple request. They hugged for a long time, both glad to see each other. Living on their own had been lonely for both of them. Then he hugged the children in turn.

"Where's Frank?" said Harry looking around.

"In the Zambezi Valley I should think by now. All your talk of the

African bush had sunk into his mind. Went with one of his bully friends from school. They took the train to Victoria Falls from where they were going to camp in the valley."

"Whatever for?"

"He's nineteen in December. Didn't want his head blown off. Says he may or may not come back to England when the war's over."

"What's he doing for money?"

"I gave him some. Brian Tobin's father has a cattle ranch outside Bulawayo. They took guns. Going to live off the land like you did with Barend on the Skeleton Coast. Had it all worked out. I think he wanted to escape being called up when he turned eighteen by disappearing into the bush."

"You're probably right. He's a strange one, Frank. Where did you find all this luggage?"

"We're coming home, Harry. Didn't want to leave anything behind. Are you pleased to see us?"

"You have just no idea how much. So Frank's gone his own way?"

"Looks like it. How is Hastings Court?"

"The lawns are overgrown. The clock tower and stables came down in the bombing. We don't have any servants. Otherwise, the old house is still perfect."

"Have we lost our money during the war?"

"Matter of fact, we haven't. The Tender Meat Company declared record profits right through the war. I went down to see your parents in Dorset. Anthony visited them his every third leave."

Only then did they both clutch each other as the pain surged back in both of them. When Harry looked over Tina's shoulder through his tears, Beth was crying. Dorian and Kim had gone up on deck.

"I miss him, Daddy," said Beth.

"We all do, darling. Give your father another hug."

When William Smythe phoned Harry to tell him Bruno Kannberg was still alive, Hastings Court was returning to normal. With feminine zeal, Tina had gone into the village looking for staff to work in the house and the garden. The back lawn had been cut, the dandelions rooted out of the grass. Windows, that had not been cleaned for years, were clean, the rubble round where the clock tower had stood was now being cleared. Everything for Tina was a frenzy. A frenzy, Harry knew, to stop her thinking of Anthony. Instead of staying in town during the week,

Harry caught the train to and from Leatherhead, using his motorcycle to get to the station.

When Tinus Oosthuizen came on leave from France at the end of September Harry was able to talk of Anthony without the choke in his throat. Life, he told himself, always went on. The regime of an ordered house had returned, with meals served exactly on time. Dorian and Kim had been put into private schools. Beth had stayed at home whilst considering what to do with her future. Looking at Tinus in the deck chair on the newly cut lawn, Harry hoped the horror of war, the pain of loss, was almost over.

"You want to talk about the future, Tinus?" Harry asked his nephew.

"Why not? It's nice to see there is one."

"How's Genevieve?"

"Lonely."

"Would you like to live in America? Fact is, I have a pile of accumulated money. The deals we did with Clint Granger and Cousin George were better than either of us imagined. I need someone to run my affairs in America. Someone like you with a degree in economics, if you haven't forgotten what they taught you at Oxford. We need to reinvest our profits. Diversify. Or do you still have too much of Africa in your bones? Now Tina is home I don't want to leave her and the children."

"Where's Frank, Uncle Harry?"

"In the Zambezi Valley. Didn't want the army calling him up. Will you go to America for me? Genevieve can continue her career. Europe's going to find the peace as difficult as the war. We're knocking it down now but afterwards we'll have to clear away the rubble and start over again. It will be years before Europe is back on its feet."

"We have to bomb the Germans into submission."

"I know. I've been under the bombs in the Blitz. Poor Klaus and his family. It's far worse for the Germans. We're setting fire to their cities."

"When do you think we'll be in Berlin?" asked Tinus.

"After the Russians. And they want revenge. America's going to be the place after this is all over."

"Not Africa?"

"Do you really think we will have the strength to hold on to our colonies? I don't think so. We've promised Gandhi independence. The rest will fall like dominoes. We must get out without leaving a mess.

Without leaving a vacuum of power. The world's very different to what it was before the war."

"America. I never thought of living in America. Do I need a permit to live over there?"

"Not when you marry Genevieve. She's the right to American citizenship. In that last film she was talking with an American accent that sounded to me quite natural."

"Why don't you come and live in America?"

"Tina loves England. She can have whatever she wants after Anthony."

"I've lost so many friends," said Tinus getting up and walking away. "What was the point of it all, Uncle Harry?" he said without turning round.

"I want to ask Klaus von Lieberman that same question next time we meet."

"Any news of him?"

"Not a word."

"Wasn't his son a pilot?"

"Yes, he was."

"They've taken a terrible beating among their pilots."

"So have we. Just be careful."

"We're taking over the German airfields. As they retreat, we move in. Once we ate their dinner in the officers' mess. The food was still hot. The chaps had left before the cook could put the food on the table. Even the cook had left. Like eating a dead man's banquet."

"You know that chap Bruno Kannberg that disappeared in the Pacific? Wrote the book on Genevieve. He's alive. They've found him in Singapore. William Smythe found out and gave me a ring."

"That is good news. His wife will be so happy. She's in America. Gillian and Genevieve see a bit of each other. Two English in a sea of Americans."

"I'm sure she'll be delighted. Both of them. Will you go to America for me?"

"Why not? But what are you going to do about Elephant Walk?"

"Leave it as it is. Ralph Madgwick does a good job. He's happy to manage the farm and receive a good bonus. Do you know Sir Jacob Rosenzweig has still never set eyes on those grandchildren? I suggested he come for a visit. Must be strange to have grandchildren you have only seen in photographs. The tobacco crop is making the money. For the moment the Mazoe dam is a nice place to sail a boat. We've put in some of the citrus trees around the perimeter of our side of the dam. No point in bottling and extraction plants until after the war. People want basic food at the moment. And tobacco to calm their nerves. Fruit juices and perfume will have their place in a more prosperous age. We're supplying oranges to the Salisbury produce market.

"Later, after sorting out our assets in America, you can take another look. Dorian will need a career in the not too distant future. They become men very fast. He's sixteen. Still can't believe it. When I last saw him he was a small boy. My mother is the one that worries me. Your grandmother, Tinus. She and your mother live in each other's pockets. Have done ever since your father was killed. They won't come back to England. I have suggested they come back now Tina has made it plain she wants to stay in England. Your sisters and their children are a big draw for them to stay in Rhodesia. Mother's getting frail. I'd like to be closer to her but you can't please everyone. Do you know in the old days here in England people never moved ten miles from where they were born? Families stayed close together giving each other support. The modern age, with the English spread round the world, has ruined our family unity. I think we've lost a lot of what is good in life. The most important people to us are our extended families. It's not only financial support we can give each other. Moral support is just as important."

"Won't Frank want a job on the farm?"

"Very much doubt it. Frank will either make a fortune on his own or end up in jail for shady dealing. He's far to like his father."

"What do you mean, Uncle Harry?"

"Frank's not my son. He's Barnaby St Clair's. I thought you knew. Lady St Clair was too well mannered to mention it. Tina had grown up with Barnaby. Not in the same house, of course. Lovers long before I came on the scene. The snob in Barnaby wouldn't let him marry a Pringle. The Pringles have been living five miles from the St Clairs for centuries. Always subservient. I was away in Africa. These things happen, Tinus. You just have to live with them. You've been through enough by the age of twenty-seven to know what I'm talking about. I treat him as a son. Who knows, one day Barnaby may accept him as a son. What else is Barnaby going to do with all that money when he dies? Our Barnaby isn't the type to leave his money to the cat's home. He doesn't have any more children as far as we know. The world goes round in strange ways. Never what it appears to be. Like what we think in our heads and what we say. To be polite in society the two are often very different. No, I correct that. They are always different or we'd be fighting like cats and dogs. It's often wiser not to tell the truth about someone to their face."

"Does Frank know?"

"I haven't told him. Neither has his mother. She's taking the children down to Dorset tomorrow to see her parents. They'll be surprised to see our Beth. When she left England she was a gangling, awkward fourteen-year-old. Now she's a woman. I'd like you to meet the Pringles one day. You don't meet many genuine people these days. They've been in the same railway cottage all their married lives. He works for the railways. There's a brother in Johannesburg who made a fortune in mining. Never comes home. He has, unsuccessfully, tried to give his parents money which I appreciate. You see, there's family all over the damn place. The price of spreading an empire round the world."

"I came back to England on leave with Janusz Kowalski. You remember him? Dropped him off at Fleur and Celia's. Do you know they've still got the same flat in Paddington? I don't ask too many questions. No one does when there's a war going on. Hasn't heard a word from the love of his life since the Germans invaded Poland. You met Ingrid here. It was the first time I met Janusz. Must have been at the end of 1938. Not a word from anybody in his family. He thinks Poland under the Russians will be no better than under the Nazis. We owe a lot to those pilots who made it to Britain after Poland collapsed."

"And to the Australians. Trevor Hemmings paid me a visit back at the start of June. Waved to Montgomery from the Leatherhead roundabout, the day I learnt of Anthony's death. Trevor's kid brother was killed. His face is scarred and he walks with a limp. They gave him the DFC for landing the plane without undercarriage. Plane was full of holes. Can we ever repay them? The Poles, the Australians, the Rhodesians. A few years after the war is over they'll forget them.

"Vic Bell thinks Churchill will be booted out of office after the war. When he's won them the war and they don't need him anymore. Attlee's socialists will get into power. A free pair of spectacles more important than saying thank you. Vic says Attlee's Labour Party are going to bring in a welfare state. Sounds good on paper but who's going to pay for it after we pay back the Americans what they loaned us to fight the war? When the danger's over people think differently. They become selfish. The party that promises the most in a democracy is the one that wins.

Promises, promises. They don't care if they can't do what they promise when they get into power. All Churchill promised was blood, sweat and tears. Then we didn't have an alternative. The truth was obvious. So was the need for good leadership. Vic says Labour will borrow money they can't pay back and leave the mess to a Tory government when the Labour Party in turn get kicked out of power. You wonder if any good comes out of changing the government. Trouble is, if you leave them in power too long they think they are God and can do what they like. We've never found a proper way of governing ourselves."

"At least it won't kill anyone if Labour gets in."

"Don't you be too sure if they ruin the economy. Revolutions always start on an empty stomach. Then some opportunist shouts his mouth off. Always keep out of politics, Tinus. It stinks. How are Fleur and Celia?"

"The band's as popular as ever. Barnaby has signed up every top musician except Vera Lynn, according to Fleur. He's made another fortune out of the war. Someday a very young girl will see him coming. Make him marry her. That's where his money will go. To some flighty eighteen-year-old."

"It's his money."

"What do you do with all that money, I ask you. It's never made him happy. Everything he does is for the moment."

"Just maybe Barnaby is the clever one. That there isn't a future. Only the present. A whole lot of nows that make up our lives when we look back. Why, when we get old like me, we look back on the past with nostalgia."

"You're not old, Uncle Harry."

"You want to go for a walk? Stretch our legs?"

"This old place is very beautiful."

"Yes, it is. But still not as beautiful as Elephant Walk. There you are, you see. The nostalgia. We never know we've got what we want until it's all over."

"I didn't want this war. I'll be glad when that's over. America. I never thought of America."

"Canada to the north. Mexico to the south. What more could a man want? I wish I could make your Aunt Tina happy."

Wisely, remembering the words of his uncle earlier on, Tinus kept his thoughts to himself. All he hoped for in his own life was to make Genevieve happy. With her face foremost in his mind, Tinus whistled for the dogs and followed his uncle in the direction of the trees.

It was wet under the trees where the sun had not been after the morning shower. Pigeons were calling to each other. When they passed the cedar trees that guarded the ancestral burial ground of the Mandervilles, Tinus tried not to look. The dogs had raced off ahead, barking at each other. Among the tall cedars were the yew trees cut in the shape of boxes before the war by the gardener, before he went off to war to join Dent the chauffeur in the Royal Army Service Corps. They had fallen into silence, Tinus walking behind his uncle along the path that led through the trees. Uncle Harry turned into the old burial ground where some of the older tombstones had half sunk into the ground. The place was untended, the old, moss-encrusted headstones difficult to read. Going in among the graves of his ancestors made the hair stand up on the back of Tinus's head.

"It's as if they are watching me," said Tinus.

"You're watching yourself, the living bones from those buried in the ground. I can't bury Anthony among his ancestors but I can put up a monument with the words 'Flight Lieutenant Anthony Brigandshaw DFC, great-grandson of Sir Henry Manderville, died fighting for his country three days before his twenty-first birthday'. Even if the Mandervilles will never again own Hastings Court, or the Brigandshaws in all likelihood if Clement Attlee gets his way and taxes the old families out of existence. Future Englishmen passing this way should understand what a young man did for his country with little reward. I like that idea. I like the idea of young hikers passing this way a hundred years from now on their way to Headley Heath. Stopping. Seeing the small monument. Pausing in their own passage through life. Seeing one life cut short in its prime. By then fascism will have a new word, a new meaning, but that won't matter. Maybe one of them will mutter a short prayer for my eldest son. Somehow, that gives me comfort. I'm going to put the small monument next to the grave of my grandfather. What do you think, Tinus?"

"I think it's very lovely. Anthony would be proud." Thinking of his old schoolfriend André Cloete, Tinus hoped old Mr Cloete had done something for André in the Cape.

Then they walked back to the path that led them to the ancient oak trees, the trunks of the oak thicker than the outstretched arms of three grown men holding hands in a circle around the tree. The roots of the trees pushed out of the ground for many feet in all directions, thick green moss growing in the space between the roots.

"You want to sit down under this oak. Don't sit on the moss, it's wet. It's rather special to me, Tinus. It was near to here that I was made."

"I don't understand."

"When your grandmother brought the body of her father back to Hastings Court for burial we took a walk down the same path we have just taken. Mother and son. She took my hand as if I were a child and sat me down under this tree. Then she talked very quietly. I had the feeling she was really talking to my dead father."

"It was near to here, Harry. The grotto where you began. I was sixteen, your father a year older. Pure love overcame both of us and in the making of that love the seed of you, my son, was born. I have never loved a living soul the way I loved him. There was nothing but beauty on the soft green moss. It's not all death, Harry. There's life as well. The pure joy of living. I'm going back to Elephant Walk because there I still feel the presence of my husband. Your father. You don't mind. Daddy's come home so now I can go home to Rhodesia."

Watching his Uncle Harry remembering his mother's words, Tinus sat silently under the tree until the sadness seemed to seep out of his uncle's body. Feeling uncomfortable, Tinus got up to look for the dogs. There were some things better not put into words, he told himself. How strange, he thought, his own grandmother making love, something he could never have imagined in his wildest dreams.

They walked for half an hour in companionable silence, thinking their separate thoughts. There was no one to be seen on Headley Heath. They found the witch's circle of logs with the old, flat sitting stone in the middle. The logs looked new, cut recently and placed in a circle.

"Who did this?" asked Tinus.

"I wish I knew. So far as anyone in the family can remember there has always been some kind of a ring round the flat stone. Each log is placed to seat one person looking at the sitter on the stone. No one ever admits to placing the logs. No one has ever dared move them. Grandfather told my mother the druids kept the place for their ceremonies. No one ever saw a druid as far as I know. Those logs have been placed recently. You can see by the soft gum oozing from that one. Legend says the stone was as tall as a man when it was first put in place. Century after century of sitting upon wore it down to that flat stone. Maybe it was pushed down in the ground or sank. Nobody tried digging them up. Why don't you go and sit on it Tinus? Ask the circle to keep up your good luck. Can't do any harm."

"What do I say?"

"'Bring me home in one piece to my love' should fit the bill."

"You actually believe this circle is magical?"

"Been there a very long time. Has to be there for some reason. Can't hurt. I asked the circle for help at the start of the First World War. I'm still around. Just sit on the stone. You don't have to say it out loud. Go on. The dogs have put up a hare. That should sort them out. Go on, Tinus. Sit on the stone. Think of it as a wishing stone. That's the stuff. Just look at that hare run. Now there's an animal built for speed. Do you still wear the rabbit's foot Gregory L'Amour found under the cedar trees and sent you on a chain as a lucky charm?"

"Every time I go up. Every time I make enemy contact I rub the fur of that rabbit foot. There's not much fur left. Whatever he meant to Genevieve, I'll always remember Greg for that charm. They were once lovers but why can't we all be friends? Every man and woman has their own private history."

"Then sit on the stone and ask the ancients to help you marry her. I'll be silent."

With Uncle Harry watching, Tinus sat on the stone, his knees up to his chin. Then he closed his eyes and prayed to the gods. When he opened them Uncle Harry was smiling.

"That's better. Now I feel much better. Where are you getting married?"

"Probably in America. They're going to make a big fuss."

"They always do with film stars. Gregory never got to fly in combat."

"He was lucky. What's so glamorous about killing a man you never even knew?"

"Kill or be killed, Tinus. Since time immemorial. Like that poor hare if it can't run fast enough. Oh, good. The dogs are giving up. Good for the hare. Ran them right into the ground. The perfect example of the fittest surviving in a war. And for the hare that was war, make no mistake."

"You're feeling better, aren't you?"

"Yes, I am. Let's go home and drink a cold beer. How the English drink it warm I never know. A good Rhodesian always drinks from a bottle that has frost on the outside. Feel like a beer, nephew?"

"Lead on. You're right. Those dogs are blown. The hare's stopped running and looking back at them, no longer afraid. Are you sure that wasn't a game?"

"Quite sure. If those dogs had caught that hare they would have eaten him."

"Or her."

"Nature at its best, or its worst. Take your pick. How's your mother? Have you heard from her recently?"

"We write to each other every week. Sometimes it's easier to say what you are really thinking in a letter. I've got every one of them. Mum says she's kept mine. That one day when the war's over they should be chronicled into a book. She wants to call it 'War from the Cockpit'."

"I can ask Robert St Clair to look at them. Better still, your friend Bruno Kannberg now we know he's alive. He's the chronicler. Robert's more a storyteller. Or so he says. The way I see it the book should be titled 'Letters to a Mother from Her Son'. Bruno will have to incorporate Madge's letters to you. Anthony hated writing them. Whenever he could he phoned Tina in Cape Town. She never writes either. Never had one the whole time she was living in Bishopscourt. Must be some kind of record."

"Gillian would be pleased if the book sold. Genevieve says she likes money."

"Never fall in love with possessions, Tinus. They don't know how to love you back. Give Genevieve lots of good memories, not diamonds. Oh, and children, or Merlin will never forgive you. He never had a son so he wants a grandson. He told me so last time I was at Purbeck Manor."

"He's happy with the idea of me being his son-in-law?"

"Very much so."

"The day the war ends I'm writing him a formal letter asking for the hand of his daughter in marriage."

When they reached the house there was a message for Tinus calling him back to his unit. The Germans were putting up more resistance to the Allied advance than expected. Janusz had phoned for him to go to RAF Tangmere, their old station, from where they would be flown back to France. The brief moments of respite were over.

"I'll drive you to Tangmere on the motorcycle," said Harry. "Less petrol. How's Janusz getting to the aerodrome?"

"It's easier to round up the chaps in London. Four other pilots are on leave. They're driving to Tangmere in one car. We thought the bad days were over. With the daily pattern bombing of German cities Hitler would give up. Worked the other way by the look of it."

"Amazing what a man will do when his back is to the wall."

The tension came back to both of them. Everything else but getting to Tangmere was forgotten. The children no longer laughed when they heard Cousin Tinus was going back to war in a hurry.

"We thought the war was over," said Beth.

"It will be soon," said Tinus giving her a big smile. "Enjoy the rest of the summer holiday before you go back to your new school."

"Are you going to teach me to fly when the war's over?" asked Kim. "Dad says he won't teach me. I want to be a pilot."

"Maybe when you are older."

"I'm fifteen. The boys who don't go to public schools leave school at fifteen and go out to work."

"Say goodbye for me to Dorian. Where is he?"

"Went to see a friend in the village. She's a girl. Her brother's fifteen and got a job on a farm. I hate school."

"Kim, we all do. It's just nice to get a good education and go to university. Won't you want to play cricket at your new school?"

"Of course I will."

"Good. When I come back next time I'll coach your batting."

"It'll be winter."

"Then we'll kick around a football. Look after your mother and father for me."

"Please come back, Tinus."

"Of course I will. I was just sitting in the magic circle asking to come back soon."

"Where's the magic circle?"

"The one on Headley Heath."

"Oh, that one."

Uncle Harry appeared in his old flying coat carrying his goggles.

"You can pick up your stuff next time. The weather looks fine. Nice day for a ride through the countryside. Do you know, this motorcycle is twenty-five years old and still goes like a dream. I'll drive. You get on the pillion. Back in a couple of hours, kids. Wave to your cousin."

6

*W*hile Tinus Oosthuizen was hurtling through the Surrey countryside on the pillion seat of a motorcycle on his way back to war, Genevieve was sitting at her desk in her flat in Los Angeles writing him a letter. It was quiet in the room with the window closed as she collected her thoughts to put down on paper. Every time she wrote to Tinus with the idea of coming back to England he wrote back telling her to stay in America until the war was over. There were no ifs or buts; according to Tinus, nothing could be done for their relationship until the war was ended. She wanted to tell him about Bruno Kannberg being heard from after going missing in action but did not wish to chance her luck in case it backfired on Tinus.

Gillian Kannberg, living in Los Angeles, having not gone back to New York after seeing her war correspondent husband off to war on the West Coast, was in a flat in the same block living comfortably from the generous widow's pension sent to her every month by the *Daily Mirror*. The survival of her husband had come as a shock to Gillian in more ways than one.

"You don't think they'd dare to cut off the pension," she had said to Genevieve the day after receiving Arthur Bumley's phone call from London telling her Bruno was alive. "I'll never be able to afford this flat, or apartment as they call it in America. We only just lived in that tiny flat in New York with the help of royalties from the books. Now that's stopped. People are reading war books, not books about film stars. What am I going to do? I'd have asked Bumley on the phone if he wasn't so snooty. Nathan answered the phone as I didn't want to get out of bed. Newspapermen can pick up the story down a telephone line without having to see it. Well, you know, Genevieve. With Bruno dead I wasn't doing anything wrong. Not by then, anyway. What will I do if they chop off my money? Nathan will walk out on me."

"Shouldn't you be thinking of what Bruno says when he comes home and finds you living with another man?" Sometimes Genevieve was inclined to lose her patience with Gillian.

"He's not coming home now is he! The war isn't over. He's in a Japanese jail in Singapore."

"What did Nathan say when you told him your husband is alive?"

"Nothing. Gave me one of those faraway looks, as if he was thinking ahead."

"He still hasn't landed a part?"

"No, he hasn't. But he will. I know he will. He's so good looking."

"You still have to be able to act. Gillian, you should be thrilled. Your husband is alive."

"I know I should be, but what am I going to live off? I live up to the last cent as it is."

"You could always go back to being a shorthand typist."

"Don't be ridiculous. I haven't typed in years. The last big job was retyping your script for Mr Hollingsworth. What am I going to do?"

"Kick Nathan out the door and be thankful."

"What if Bruno doesn't like me anymore?"

"He's your husband."

"I suppose I'll have to get myself pregnant."

Writing down what she wanted to say to Tinus was more difficult than saying the words with a smile or a gesture. Writing was harder than acting. When she acted they were distracted by her looks in every sense of the word. An intense, sexual smile could not be written in words. Genevieve looked at the blank sheet of paper on the green blotting pad in front of her. Once again her mind went blank. Talk of Gillian Kannberg was trivial to a man daily fighting a war. Life or death were right in front of him, not the whims of a stupid woman with sawdust for brains. As much as she liked the company of Gillian in her loneliness, the flightiness of the woman was absurd. Nathan wanted a free billet while he tried to break into film. The moment he had a part worth anything he would dump Mrs Kannberg like a hotcake, straight on the floor.

There had to be more between two people than money and sex. To love a man with the passion she displayed on the screen was the wild first expression of youth. Before reality and life got in the way. In Genevieve's experience, young love was perfect and lasted for a short while, not happily ever after as depicted in her movies. The minds of men and women met then left each other the same way their bodies followed their separate paths after sex. She wanted to live with Tinus for the rest of her life, accepting his moods, being looked after when she was sick, when the world, like Gillian's, wasn't going her way. There was never a constant level of happiness. Companionship and love. Love and companionship. Respecting each other. Wishing to be nice to each other. Not wishing to hurt the other's feelings. Above all, she wanted to be Tinus's companion on their journey through life.

At a loss for the right words to give Tinus the right picture of what was in her mind, Genevieve had put down her pen and picked up the phone. Over the phone, she sent him a telegram to his last known airfield in France. 'I love you' was all she could say without getting into a muddle. Tinus was better at writing letters. She was better at portraying what was inside her mind with the way she looked at a person.

Then she turned on the news to hear of the new German offensive in Europe, the terrible battles still raging in the Pacific, the war going on and on.

"When's it all going to be over?" she said to her lonely room.

To get out of her dark mood, Genevieve decided she would go and visit with Gillian on the third floor. Despite all Gillian's nonsense there was always a sympathetic ear for other people's problems. She was not sure what she would do without Gillian. With luck Nathan Squires would be out as usual, hunting for a part, or, as Genevieve was sure, hunting something a little younger than Gillian Kannberg, a woman with too many selfish wants in her life for her own good.

They were going to make a new film. Gerry Hollingsworth had bought the film rights to a book on the war in the South Pacific. Genevieve had read the book. This time there was a story. More than heroics and soppy love duets that always ended the same. Once again 'The All American Man' was going to play opposite Genevieve. In the film, Gregory L'Amour was going to win the war for America.

When she knocked on the door, Gillian answered the knock. She was crying.

"He's buggered off. Nathan has gone and left me."

"About time," said Genevieve smiling. "Go and get dressed in your glad rags, Gillian. We shall dine together at the Oasis. My treat. Likely we'll both get ourselves a little drunk. When did he go?"

"This morning."

"Why don't you move into my flat until the war is over?"

"Will you have me?"

"Without rent. We want you in good shape when Bruno comes out of prison."

"You're a darling, Genevieve."

"I know I am. Back in an hour. Both of us dressed to the nines. Us girls have to stick together."

"Do you think there will be any single men in the restaurant?"

"There'll be dozens. All rich and famous."

"You're kidding."

"I hope so. Did they cut off your pension?"

"Yes. I phoned Mr Bumley when nothing appeared in my bank account. He was very polite. Said we should talk of all the overpayment since they gave me my pension that wasn't due. They've deducted Bruno's salary from what they paid me. I owe them one hundred pounds and some change. Right now I am penniless."

"They won't sue you."

"They won't send me any money either."

"Tell the other papers."

"Bruno's not dead. He's not a war hero. No one will care for a penniless girl after she finds out her husband is still alive. People are meant to live on love. Bumley found out about Nathan. One minute so nice when Bruno went missing. The next minute cruel."

"I'm glad I asked you to move in before you told me this. You know my offer's genuine."

"I'll go and get changed."

"And I'll do the same. The war news in Europe is terrible. I feel miserable."

"My poor darling. One minute I was down in the dumps. Now I'm on top of the world. Do you think he's lost weight in prison?"

"Most probably, Gillian. The Japanese don't like prisoners. They think a true warrior should fight to the death or fall on his sword. Now let's get a move on. I need a drink and I never drink on my own."

When she phoned François, the owner of the Oasis restaurant, he effused over the phone. He could only charge the exorbitant prices if his place was littered with faces everyone knew. In the world she now lived in, everyone fed off everyone else in more ways than one. It was all part of the game, she told herself smiling at how charming François could be, even over the phone.

"I don't have a separate table, Miss Genevieve but I can place you with a party."

"Who's coming tonight, François? We wanted to be on our own. I'm bringing a guest."

"Of course. How indiscreet."

"It's a woman, François, and you know my reputation from before I was engaged so don't get any wild ideas."

"How is the pilot?"

"Alive, I hope. I just sent him a telegram."

"Your producer is here as usual. With a guest from New York. His wife is not coming. I don't think his wife likes our food."

"I'm sure Carmel likes your food. It's Mr Hollingsworth's friends she likes to avoid. Especially the pretty ones."

"A woman of great culture, Mrs Hollingsworth. Can I put you at his table? I'm sure he will be delighted. I've often heard him say how fond he is of Genevieve."

"Probably because I'm the only one he never laid."

"Oh, my goodness. I would never have allowed that thought to enter my mind."

"Two of us, François, if that's how it is. You are most accommodating."

"Always a pleasure for someone so beautiful."

"You old flatterer. Her name is Mrs Kannberg."

"But it is true."

"How many so far in Mr Hollingsworth's party?"

"Eight, it will be, with you and Mrs Kannberg. The table is booked for eight o'clock."

Soaking in the bath, knowing Gillian took her time to get dressed, Genevieve smiled at the thought of Gerry Hollingsworth. Mr Hollingsworth, as she liked to call him to his face, especially in company. It must be over ten years, she thought, since they had met at Elstree Studios when he was running Drake Films. So much time and trying and still he had failed to lay a hand on her.

"You're the only one that got away," he had said to her again only the previous week when she signed her new contract.

"Doesn't Carmel mind your philandering, Gerry?" They were alone in his office.

"A sensible wife lets her husband do what he wants provided he doesn't embarrass her. One day we'll sit in rocking chairs opposite each other. Just the two of us. When all this nonsense is over. We have the children. We both miss David unbearably. We have a lot of history together. If I have a little on the quiet to prove to myself I'm not getting old it's all part of our strangely working marriage. It's how we humans are made. None of us can change our make-up. You have to accept the good and the bad. The man goes off because he can. The woman, mostly, doesn't because she can't. Some take a king's ransom in alimony and live the end of their life alone. Sir Jacob Rosenzweig's wife is more sensible. We understand each other. Sir Jacob is finding his Hannah quite therapeutic. Says he's over Miss Vida Wagner. Says he's more tranquil. Mostly they eat at home on their own, Hannah doing the cooking. Talking of the times when they were young together. You can never make conversation about your past without someone who knows your experiences. If you do talk about your life to a semi-stranger you're a bore, Genevieve. Don't judge a book by its cover. Terrible cliché but true. Now, when are we two going to make love?"

"Get out of here, Mr Hollingsworth."

"Oh, Genevieve. You don't know what you're missing. I see you are still not wearing his ring."

"You don't have to flash diamonds to show you are loved by someone."

"What do you do with all your money in that minute little flat? You should show off. You never seem to spend any money."

Soaping the top of her body, Genevieve slid deeper into the bath, just the warm water coming up to her chin. She had picked up the new contract from Gerry Hollingsworth's desk, vetted by her Uncle Barnaby, and gone home to her small flat. The new airmail between America and England made it possible for her uncle to control her financial affairs from London. Despite his past reputation she trusted him implicitly. There was a lot of herself in the life of her Uncle Barnaby. He too had had one love, he had told her. Drunk. The truth so often coming from the mouths of drunks.

"I'm the real bastard, Genevieve. Not you. Tina and I were part of each other from the time we were children. From before I became a snob. You see, we are snobs, the St Clairs. Ask your father. Could you ever imagine your father, the Eighteenth Baron St Clair of Purbeck, being married to your mother, the barmaid from the Running Horses at Mickleham? Of course not. A bit of nooky and here you are. Both people had their fun without any commitment."

"They didn't even love each other. For my mother it was the best way to go and never have to work. Father still pays her bills diligently without some lawyer telling him what to do. I respect them both for their own reasons. It was my luck or I wouldn't be here."

"But I was a fool. I loved her. Never found anyone to love after Tina. Harry's lucky. He grew up in Rhodesia where if you are white that's all that matters. There's no class distinction among the whites in Rhodesia whatever their social position back in England. I followed her out to Africa when she went to live with her brother Bert in Johannesburg. Bert had an elocutionist teach her to speak English with an upper-class accent. She was all right so long as she stuck to the colonials. Ever since she married Harry I've jumped from one girl to the next. None of them last. I get bored too quickly. Lucky for you we found out you were my niece. I'd have had a go at you."

"What a terrible thought."

"Don't laugh at it. I'm a full-blown lecher. I even make money out of the singers and musicians that join my label for God's sake. A lot of them have done well out of a roll in the hay with Barnaby St Clair."

Thinking back on that conversation, Genevieve was glad she had kept her trap shut. For a moment she thought her uncle was going to spill the beans and admit he was Frank Brigandshaw's father. A nasty piece of work in the making if ever she'd seen one. Turning on the hot tap with her toe, she let the bath warm up, swishing the water around with her hands. She liked her Uncle Barnaby. Of all the members of the St Clair family, except for her father, she liked him best. He was honest. He did what he wanted, never hiding his intent. Apart from the fifty quid gossip said he had swindled in the army during the First World War, no one said anything bad about him in business. An opportunist, but never a crook. A womaniser but with single women.

"She was mine first. I didn't even borrow her from Harry. He borrowed her from me."

So often their conversation was either about money, her money and what to do with it, or about Tina. Looking from the distance of her warm bath it was all quite sad. The poor man had everything and nothing at all. If Gerry Hollingsworth knew how much money she had he would be utterly amazed. Gerry was both good at making money and spending it. Except for building her assets to pay for a large, well-educated family, Genevieve had little interest in money. For a moment it made her laugh out loud in the bath. It had not been her intention when she asked Gillian to the Oasis but it wasn't going to cost her a penny. Once again, a man would pick up the bill. This time Gerry Hollingsworth or whoever else was sitting at the table trying to make a point.

All the money she earned flowed into her bank account with very little coming out, except to pay Uncle Barnaby in London when he made her investments. They had a trust fund together. Genevieve owned ninety-five per cent for putting in the money, Uncle Barnaby the rest for making the investment on their fund's behalf. It seemed coming from an ancient family that had held onto its money for centuries had more benefits than blood.

"Any fool can make money if he's lucky, Genevieve. Keeping hold of it for your kids is another thing."

Her uncle's latest plan with the proceeds of her new film contract was to buy up bomb sites in London where the owner wanted money while the rent stopped coming in. Not only were they buying land cheap, they would be compensated after the war for the bomb damage. Genevieve had a portfolio of investments she had not shown Tinus in case he changed his mind about marrying. They both knew her fame would dwindle and not get in their way. What he would find out once they were safely married was the increasing accumulation of her wealth. There had been investment mistakes but very few. Tinus, with his degree in economics, would be just right for guarding her money for their children.

When Gillian rang her front doorbell, it was she who was not ready. They both had a laugh at the boot being on the other foot.

"Come on, Gillian. Let's go and have some fun. Dressed to the nines. Only way for two girls to go out on the town."

There were four men, all over fifty, sitting at the table. The two pretty girls looked to Genevieve as if they had left school the day before. The dew was still wet behind their ears. Max Pearl, her publisher, was at the table and the first to stand up.

"What a lovely surprise. The beautiful Genevieve with the beautiful Mrs Kannberg. Gillian, you have no idea how happy I was to hear about

Bruno. I want to make him a famous author. I hope he's been writing in prison. This is a lovely surprise. We only found out from François when we walked in the door. Your young pilot still well, I hope?"

"Yes, Max. We both had the blues and wanted a night out to get over our sad moods. They didn't have a table. Hope you don't mind, Mr Hollingsworth."

When they sat down, with François fluttering at their elbows easing them into their chairs, only the two young girls were not smiling. The other two men Genevieve had not seen before and quickly forgot their names. The girls were only introduced by the oldest of the men by their Christian names. Genevieve gave them both her best smile of sympathy, breaking the ice. To be confronted by four old men and a famous actress in one night was an ordeal by the look of the girls' expressions. Even Gillian looking at the four men immediately lost interest and gazed round the room. Gillian looked good, Genevieve thought, with her carefully applied make-up in the soft, flattering light of the restaurant.

The old man who seemed in charge of the party had his eyes glued to Gillian's cleavage. All men were the same whatever their age, she thought, giving him a wink when he looked up into her knowing face, the old boy for a fraction of a second looking guilty at being caught in the act of a voyeur.

"Mrs Kannberg's husband has just been found in a Japanese prison," she said sweetly. "This is our night out to celebrate. They are so in love with each other you have no idea."

Gillian, still checking the rest of the field in the restaurant, didn't seem to hear what Genevieve had said. Something was going on under the table as the old man suddenly swung his lecherous gaze to the young girl on his left.

"Mr Hirschman is financing the film," said Gerry Hollingsworth. "Jacob Rosenzweig is out of the movie business for some reason."

"His wife, Gerry," said Max Pearl. "After the German girl, Hannah Rosenzweig is being very careful. He doesn't go out at all. They never throw dinner parties. New York will never be the same without Vida Wagner. She's now quite well off. Living somewhere about, I believe. Lucky girl. Lucky Jacob. A sunset romance. Hope it happens to me, I should be so lucky."

"It will be my pleasure financing a movie that stars the famous Genevieve," said the old man, switching his gaze to Genevieve's cleavage.

Carefully, deliberately, Genevieve placed a table napkin between her breasts. The man was making her feel unclean, soliciting a look of 'be careful' from Gerry Hollingsworth whose main job in life was raising money to make his movies. Having got across her message of 'don't touch', Genevieve gave the old man one of her famous looks that hit men straight in the crotch, leaving the poor old boy bewildered. Then the wine came and the evening began, the conversation staying top surface and trivial. Genevieve felt sorry for the two young girls until the youngest told her the truth in the loo.

"We're whores, darling. The old man has to be amused. Mr Hollingsworth hired us. There were going to be two more."

"So Gerry knew I had phoned François?"

"Must have done."

"Play your cards right and you might get into the film. You're pretty enough. Both of you."

"Is that how you started?"

"Not quite. The trick was to keep them on the hook without giving it away."

"We all have to start somewhere. Working the cash register in the shop down our road in Kansas City was not my idea of fun. So here we are. What's Hollingsworth like?"

"A nice man under all the talk. We've known each other for many years."

"I liked your films."

"Thank you. I'll ask Gerry for you."

"Will you?"

"I can only try. My best advice is not to sleep with him until after you've got the part."

"I'm a whore, darling."

When they came back from the loo, the look Mr Hirschman gave Genevieve said he now expected more than just sexual suggestive smiles. Gerry Hollingsworth must have spoken to him. Many times she and Gerry had played the same game to keep the customers happy. With the conversation going back and forth over the table she began to enjoy the evening. The two young girls had ordered the most expensive items on the menu. Gillian had done the same. François was particularly attentive to Mr Hirschman now he knew who was going to pay and add the tip to the bill. The two waiters did the same. For a moment Genevieve tried to mentally count how many restaurant owners she knew were called Francis or François.

Genevieve ordered an omelette but let the wine waiter fill up her glass when it reached half empty. After a few glasses of good Californian wine she hoped Mr Hirschman would look more inviting. It was better to like someone to give them genuine conversation. She at least wanted to make the old voyeur think he had a chance. Some of her friends liked to act in front of the camera with a glass of booze in their stomachs. It made them less inhibited. Thirty years ago the chances were Mr Hirschman was a smasher. He still saw himself as the same, especially now he was rich.

Somewhere after Genevieve finished her omelette Gillian left the table without a word to anyone. Genevieve thought she had gone to the loo to repair her make-up. When she saw her at another table surrounded by young men, Gillian waved. By then she had eaten her expensive meal. Letting the conversation drift between the men, all about business which bored Genevieve stiff, with the help of half a bottle of wine, she got up and left the table. She had done it before. Gerry Hollingsworth would understand. By then she had the dirty old man nicely on a string that she now stretched right across the restaurant. Mr Hirschman was getting drunk and more confident. For all of them she was better out of harm's way. They had come uninvited and left uninvited. The whore from the loo had given her a forlorn look when she saw Genevieve had left the table and wasn't coming back; even whores had grander ambitions, especially when they were so young. Genevieve felt sorry for the girl.

The young men at the new table were more drunk than Mr Hirschman. Gillian was tipsy. They drank, smoked and joked for an hour. When Genevieve slipped away, Mr Hirschman had started to wave to her from across the restaurant. Waving her to come back. She hoped Gillian had the price of a taxi which she likely didn't need. Poor Bruno in his prison, thought Genevieve.

Back in her lonely flat she sat down on her sofa and had a good cry. Not only was the war killing her friends, it was killing the time of their youth together. The time she and Tinus would have made so many wonderful memories. Then she went to bed, the wine letting her fall straight asleep.

When Gillian moved into the flat a week later neither of them mentioned the evening in the restaurant. Genevieve doubted Mr Hirschman remembered making a pass at her. For everyone, nothing had happened. The show would go on. If it was any good, Mr Hirschman would make his money instead of making the leading lady, the money more beneficial, more lasting. There was still no news from Tinus in France. Sometimes she hoped never to hear a word until the war was over. No news meant he was still alive. Harry Brigandshaw was certain to let her know if anything happened to his nephew. In England Harry Brigandshaw was Tinus's next of kin, the first to be advised if anything went wrong.

Then they started shooting the new film and Genevieve absorbed herself in the work, trying not to think. At home, the chatter from Gillian helped. There was no sign of Nathan Squires, or any of the young men from the Oasis. What the girl did all day when Genevieve was away at work, she had no idea. It was better than living alone and thinking what could be happening to Tinus. Gregory L'Amour, once Gillian's lover, had the brains to keep well away from the flat. And from the war.

During the long weeks of waiting, as the Germans and Japanese were pushed further back towards their respective homelands, Genevieve talked some sense into Gillian.

"We won't hold them with our sex appeal forever, Gillian. Better to make a good friend of Bruno when he gets back from the war. Living with a good friend is as important, more important in the end, than having good sex, or finding the sexual stimulation in a row of affairs. One good man. Bruno's a good man. Tinus is a good man. That's what counts in the end. Bruno doesn't have to know what happened while he was presumed missing. Don't tell him. What the eye doesn't see the heart doesn't grieve about. When he comes home, give him some love. Yes, give him a baby. More than one. I want you to be one of my friends who lived happily ever after. It's your only chance."

"You're a good friend, Genevieve."

"I hope so. You've helped me through the weeks with Tinus still fighting. We need friends in life. Going through bad times together makes good friends. I'm not going to stay in the movie business all my life. You are not going to want to chase every good-looking man you see. Just don't bugger up your marriage, Gillian."

"I'll try. It's all so difficult. If you're nice to them all the time men get bored. They start the roving eye."

"Just hope it doesn't happen to you. Have a family. That always helps cement a marriage. The war's not going to go on much longer, God willing. Then our men will be coming home."

PART EIGHT

LIGHT AT THE END OF THE TUNNEL – MAY 1945 TO MAY 1946

1

When Harry Brigandshaw looked up from his paper-littered desk at the Air Ministry, Vic Bell was standing in front grinning like a Cheshire cat. Harry had a bad habit of leaving the door open.

"Sorry to barge in, Harry."

"Now what's happened?" said Harry leaning back in his chair, stretching his back. "No man should ever be confined to a desk. What good can I possibly be doing shuffling paper?"

"It's all over, Harry. The Germans have surrendered. The Russians are saying Hitler has committed suicide in his Berlin bunker. All hostilities will come to an end in Europe at midnight tonight. We should walk down to the gates of the Palace. Every Londoner is going to be out in the streets."

"Do I have to finish this bloody paperwork?"

"Not now. Come on. The others are going. Katherine has put on her coat. The phones are jammed so you can't phone Tina. There they go. The church bells. Just listen to them pealing."

"So Germany is split in two?"

"Looks like it. The Russians have agreed to stop where they are. Do you think the king will come out onto the balcony? He'll have summoned Churchill to the Palace. They may come out onto the balcony together."

"Is it cold outside?"

"Put your overcoat on. Early May is a little chilly."

"We're getting soft, Ding-a-ling. In France you and I ate supper standing in mud up to our ankles. What about the Japs?"

"Still fighting. Unless the Americans do something drastic the Japanese will fight to the death. The Emperor will never surrender."

"He might not fall on his sword like Hitler? So Berlin is to be part of the Soviet zone of occupation. You solve one problem and start another. Before we make happy fools of ourselves mingling with the crowd I have a better idea. I have a bottle of Scotch in my drawer you purloined for me. The glasses are in the filing cabinet. Second drawer. Be a good chap and ask Katherine to come into my office."

By the time Katherine had removed her coat Harry had the whisky glasses on the top of his empty desk, the papers swept on the floor both sides of it.

"Just one good slug before we brave the streets. I give you absent friends."

"To absent friends," they chorused.

"You'd better stay in town tonight," said Vic Bell. "You'll never get on a train even if they are running. The pubs will stay open all night."

Only when he followed his friends down into the street did Harry realise his job at the Air Ministry, which had started so tenuously at the start of the war, was over. There was nothing now left for him to do. So far as he was concerned, the papers strewn on the floor could stay where they were to eternity.

The church bells had not stopped pealing from all over the capital. Everyone was smiling. Strangers were shaking hands. Outside the gates of Buckingham Palace the crowds were singing *God Save the King*. After half an hour the king and queen came out on the balcony and waved. The crowds of people were running far back from the palace gates down The Mall. The leaves on the trees were lime green, the young shoots of spring. Many in the crowd were arm in arm, drunk from the patriotic singing.

"Twice in my life," said Harry.

"What do you mean?" asked Vic.

"I was here at the end of the last war. Came to look through the gates at the palace. The war to end all wars. How long will it be before we start all over again? This time, instead of fighting with the Russians against fascism we'll be fighting the Russians against communism. The same old fight for power and territory with a different name. Do you think Sarah's in the crowd somewhere?"

"Never find her in this lot. Here he comes. The man of the hour with a bloody cigar between his fingers. Harry, just listen to that cheer. It's louder than the one for the king. They're all screaming 'Winnie'."

"Churchill always looks bigger in an overcoat. He's brought us all a long way. He's loving it. Look at him loving it. The crowd's going berserk. Why don't we find a pub before the others have the same idea? I don't do it often but tonight I'm going to get drunk. I'll go home tomorrow with a hangover. You're right, Vic. Who wants to struggle for a train tonight?"

"What about the papers on the floor, Mr Brigandshaw?" asked Katherine.

"Leave them. I'll come in Monday and formally resign. Then we'll tie up the loose ends."

"Will I be out of a job?"

"I'll need you, Katherine. My private affairs have been left to stagnate through the war. I'll need an office in London. My nephew will be joining us before I send him to America. Drinks are on me. What a day. What a night. This is one we'll remember till the day we die."

When Harry reached Leatherhead railway station the next day his motorcycle was still standing in the rain with the tarpaulin over the top tied to the wheels. Trying to kick-start the machine with his right foot over the saddle ended in frustration. Harry was suffering from what he termed 'a creeping hangover', the longer the day went the worse he would feel, the patriotic, drunken fervour of the night coming home to roost. He felt terrible. Most of what happened after dark he could not remember.

Having flooded the carburettor, Harry sat on the bike in the rain, both feet on the gravel. There was always a price to pay for everything, even the pleasures of victory. Most of the people off the London train had gone on their way. One old woman was looking at him waiting for her lift under the overhang of the ticket office. There had not been a taxi at the station since the second year of war. Seeking redemption for his abandoned revelry, Harry put the cover back on his bike and began the walk to Hastings Court, his long raincoat pulled up to his chin. Thinking of Africa and walking for miles through the bush among wild animals, he began to enjoy himself. His circulation returned, his hands warmed. After ten minutes the drizzle stopped and the sun peeked out from behind a cloud. Harry began to whistle. He was thinking of Tinus as his mind walked through the African bush in his imagination. When he walked up the driveway, Kim was coming down on his bicycle.

"Where's the motorbike, Dad?"

"Wouldn't start. What are you doing home?"

"They sent us all home. What are they going to say on the news now the war's over? Did you walk all the way from the station? Beth's home. You'd better go and explain to Mother."

"What must I explain, Kim?"

"Why you didn't come home last night."

"You want the facts, son? I caught myself up with a nice crowd of drunks. The trains weren't running, so they said. Everyone was celebrating. I saw the king and queen at the palace. And the prime minister."

"Aren't you working today?"

"Questions. Always questions. I'm resigning. My job's finished."

"What are you going to do with yourself? Mother says she's bored."

"Not with you three home. Where are you off to?"

"Questions. Always questions. Have you got a hangover?" Kim was grinning all over his face.

"The worst of my life. They'll find something to say in the news. It's not over yet in the Far East. We still have to defeat Japan. There's going to be a general election I should think."

"Dorian's gone into the village to see his friend. The girl."

"What's her name?"

"Won't tell anyone. Mum's up at the house. Good luck."

Harry shook his head, smiling to himself, and trudged on up the long driveway to the old house where the builders were repairing the bombed-out stables. For the clock tower they needed plans to be passed with the council before the men could start building. His home was almost back to its pre-war state. Poor Tina, he thought. The worst thing in life was to be bored. To have nothing to do. Nothing that was interesting. He would tell her they would go to America for Tinus's wedding. He would put her in charge. Most women liked planning for a wedding.

When he almost reached the house the dogs came hurtling down the steps, barking. When they reached him they all jumped up and put their dirty paws on his raincoat. Somewhere, an aircraft was flying in the direction of Redhill Aerodrome.

"Thank God, Harry, it's over," said Tina coming out onto the terrace to look down to where he was patting each of the dogs in turn.

"Did you hear the church bells? London was chaos. Walked down The Mall and back to Charing Cross. Then we all crawled from pub to pub. Even the bobbies were drunk. One lost his helmet and didn't seem to care. No one cared. It was over."

"Are you hungry?"

"Starving. The bike wouldn't start. Had to walk from the station."

Then they walked inside the old house holding hands, both of them thinking of Anthony and the new memorial among the cedar trees at the back of the house.

When Tinus came home to Hastings Court he had taken off his RAF uniform for the last time. The war in Europe had been over for two months. As a Rhodesian he was one of the first to be discharged, along with the Canadians and the Australians who had ended up in the RAF at the start of the war. In his pocket was a very nice letter, he thought, from Lord St Clair saying how delighted his Lordship would be if Tinus married his daughter. And no, with his mother ailing from old age he wouldn't come to America for the wedding. If Harry Brigandshaw was going, Merlin suggested in the letter in reply to Tinus's formal request for Genevieve's hand in marriage, Harry could give away his daughter. 'She calls him Uncle Harry as he was married to my late sister.' There was nothing immediately wrong with Lady St Clair. Tinus imagined his future father-in-law did not like travelling. If Esther came to the wedding his lordship's sense of decorum would likely be out of joint.

"What are they going to do when they have grandchildren?" he said to his Aunt Tina while they were discussing the wedding.

"It's all the photographers, Tinus. All the newspaper nonsense. I'd love to plan your wedding. I'll need a good month or so in America to learn the ropes. If Cousin George wasn't so far away from Los Angeles we could stay with him. Maybe after the wedding. When you lovebirds have gone to your secret honeymoon. Where are you taking Genevieve for your honeymoon?"

"She wants to go to a desert island with no one around."

"Have you found one?"

"Not yet. You really don't mind all the work of planning a wedding?"

"Do you know what it's like to be bored?"

"Not recently. Janusz has gone back to Warsaw to look for Ingrid and his parents. His father, the judge, is nowhere to be found. The Russians called on him after Germany surrendered and he hasn't been seen since. He was advocating elections in Poland. To elect a government after the German occupation. Now the Russians want to occupy Poland. Not getting any sense on the phone, he's gone to look for himself with special permission from the Air Ministry. They've allowed him to wear his uniform. They think the British uniform will give him protection so they must know something is wrong. Everything's very fluid on the east side of the Russian front line. The Russians are never going to let go of the territory they won from the Germans. Right of conquest, to hell with what the countries were before the Germans marched in. He's a trained lawyer. Can't practise law in the States with his Polish degree but he can give me legal advice when we look at expanding in America. He can join the firm of Brigandshaw Oosthuizen Inc. That's what we are calling the consulting firm. Once I'm married I'm to stay in America with a full-time job with Uncle Harry."

"Won't you miss your friends in the RAF?"

"All of them, Aunt Tina. The living and the dead... Oh, I'm so sorry, that was terribly insensitive."

"I miss him so terribly. Every day I go and look at that damn memorial among the cedar trees. As if that will do any damn good."

"Seeing me come back alive doesn't help."

"Of course it does, Tinus. What a terrible thing to say."

"Give me a hug. Why don't we both go and have a look together? Uncle Harry showed me the moment I got to Hastings Court. I should like to see it again."

"Would you?"

"He was your son. He was also my first cousin and a fellow pilot. Do you know, I think of André Cloete nearly every day. We called ourselves the three musketeers. Me, Genevieve and André. We were so young and innocent in those days. Feels like a hundred years ago. Then we can talk more about the wedding when we've paid our respects."

On the way to the ancient burial grounds of the Mandervilles, Tinus picked wild flowers from the side of the path. Beneath the cedars and next to the smaller yew tree, Tinus placed the flowers on the small plinth below the cross. The monument Harry had had built by a stonemason was small, no bigger than the others, in deference to the many of Anthony's ancestors who had died fighting for their country. Only the lord of the manor was entitled to a mausoleum if the family was rich at the time. Sir Henry Manderville, buried next to the monument to his grandson, lay in a small grave, the headstone the same height as the cross. On the cross, people would read the words down the years of a young pilot killed in action. What was so big in his aunt's heart, the poor woman crying without hiding her tears next to Tinus as they stood silently looking at the simple inscription on the cross, was the same pain so many women had endured down the centuries. There was nothing more Tinus could say to a woman who had lost her son, the first born, the one he was told was always the most precious to a mother.

Taking her arm, he walked with her away into the afternoon sunshine, away from the deep shade of the cedar trees.

"Thank you, Tinus, for not talking. Sometimes it isn't easy... You were saying about the wedding?"

"Like my esteemed father-in-law to be who will not be at his daughter's wedding, neither will my mother be at her son's. Like Lord St Clair, she won't leave her mother alone on the farm. Grandmother could easily go to one of my sisters but mother won't hear of it. She's frightened, I think, of America. Of the whole big wide world outside Elephant Walk. To get my mother in the frame of mind to drive into Salisbury is an exercise all in itself. She doesn't like leaving the farm where she feels safe. She doesn't like strangers. She's been as far as Cape Town. Seen the sea, believe it or not."

As he prattled on to distract his Aunt Tina, they walked back to the house. On the newly cut lawn on the side of the house away from the terrace that ran down the length of the front of the house, Uncle Harry was waiting for them at the wrought-iron table, the tea tray ready, the cosy on top of the pot to keep the tea warm while he waited for them. The children were away at school. Mary Ross had brought the tea tray and smiled at Tinus as they passed. Mary Ross from the village, he remembered, had worked part time at the Court before the war. With her brother Herbert. She was going to be married about the same time as Tinus. Her wartime job at the Goblin factory had come to an end. She was saving every one of her pennies, she had told Tinus, for her wedding. They had had quite a conversation about her fiancé. Apparently there wasn't much money to be made as a private soldier, even in time of war. In peacetime, the private was a plumber, a man, Tinus was told later by Uncle Harry, on his way to getting rich. Uncle Harry said lawyers and plumbers made about the same money.

"Why don't we give her a wedding at the Court?" he asked his uncle. Uncle Harry had stood up as his wife approached to pull out a chair.

"Before I go to America. Aunty Tina can use it as a dry run for my wedding in Los Angeles. She'd like that. Her brother Herbert worked here part time before he was killed."

"Why don't you suggest the idea? She just gave you a beautiful smile."

"That's what prompted me. We actually had a long conversation about her boyfriend this morning."

"Amazing what a woman can get with a smile," said Uncle Harry, ignoring his explanation.

"I'm about to be happily married."

"Tea, nephew?"

"Thank you, Uncle. Milk and no sugar. I've got used to drinking my tea without sugar during the rationing."

"Lucky for you. There isn't any sugar. It's still rationed. They say in the village there'll be rationing for years. During the war we couldn't get it to the island. Now we don't have the money to pay for luxuries. It's a strong point in the Labour Party manifesto, sugar. Labour promises sugar. What a smart way to get votes. Churchill is still promising them a hard time until the country gets back on its feet. If he doesn't try some of the Labour Party bullshit he's going to lose the election. If you want to win in politics, don't tell them the truth. I have written to Klaus and Birgit von Lieberman in Bavaria, to make sure they are all right. For weeks I've waited for a reply. Posted a third letter this morning. If we can't get sugar, can you imagine what's happening in Germany? I've got a mind to go back to Romanshorn and enquire of them across the lake. It was the big industrial cities we knocked to the ground with the help of the Americans. Heard from Ding-a-ling the Americans are threatening to drop an atomic bomb on Japan if the Emperor doesn't surrender. Vic's still at the Air Ministry. Says he wants to stay. He's going to marry Sarah Coombes."

"Doesn't she own a tobacconist's? Why doesn't he get behind the counter? Expand the business. Turn it into a corner shop. The Air Ministry in peacetime must be boring."

"I'll suggest your idea though I doubt you're being serious. They're still young enough to expand the shop. Maybe we should look at it if they need capital. A chain of corner shops. How does that sound?"

"From selling a few packets of cigarettes, not bad. When do I start my new job?"

"After you get married."

"I'm getting bored."

"There's that word again. I don't even know if Klaus's family came through the war alive. We can take the train to Romanshorn and make our enquiries. Fly to Zurich and take the local train. Or whatever."

Tinus smiled to himself. His uncle was on a roll.

"See if they reply to your third letter," he said. "Have you tried phoning?"

"The post office say there isn't such a number. The only one I have is from before the war. When I phoned Klaus about Horatio Wakefield. Horatio is the one who asked me to find out. Janet wants to know. She says without his help she would never have had a family. She has so many patients now she doesn't know what to do. People came back from the war with stutters brought on by fear."

"When do you want to go to Romanshorn?"

"Give today's letter a couple of weeks. I've asked Klaus to phone me his new number."

"Why do you call him Ding-a-ling?"

"It's better than Ding Dong. Tina, will you pour the tea? You are much better at it than me. This time you will come with us to Switzerland. If the children are home they are quite old enough to look after themselves. Kim's turning into quite a cricketer. Must run in the family. Have a piece of cake. Why don't you go and ask Mary Ross?"

"You mean, now?"

"No time like the present. The tea won't go cold. The sun's shining. We can use the Great Hall. Ask Fleur and Celia to come down. I feel like a party."

Both of them just looked at him. Then Tinus got up and went to have a word with Mary Ross.

"Do you really want to throw a wedding for Mary Ross?" asked Tina.

"Why not? Show solidarity for all of us putting our backs to the war effort. Be a chance to invite all the tradesmen. They all know each other. I'm going to invite Sarah Coombes and Vic to the Court for a weekend. Vic's told her I'm not quite as poor as she thought I was in the bomb shelter. You'll like Sarah. Now that is a good idea. All our friends together... What did Mary say, Tinus?"

"She was a bit overawed by the violins and the Great Hall. She'd like something a little simpler in the garden."

"There you are, Tina. Not as bad as you thought."

2

_____

William Smythe's new house in Chelsea was three doors away from the three-storey house of Horatio and Janet Wakefield. He had bought the house at rock-bottom price a month before the end of the war. Next door was a bomb site. The house had taken a direct hit from a doodlebug at the end of 1944. The rubble had been cleared away. Weeds were growing out of the open foundations which was why their house was so cheap. Other people thought the foundations of William's new house had been damaged by the blast. He didn't care. At that price he could dig in underneath from the outside and pour concrete to cement the old foundations. Like Horatio's house it was three storeys high with an attic. The attic was for Ruthy's playroom. It was a house William had thought he would only afford in his wildest dreams. The river, not far away, was within an easy push for the pram, with trees overhanging the water. When Betty said she was pregnant with their second child, William's happiness went on a trip to the moon. Even the invitation to Genevieve's wedding in Los Angeles made no difference to his euphoria. She was all in the past. He was going to write Tinus a 'Can't make it. Have a good life.' note and with it send a cut crystal wine decanter, not mentioning the invitation to Betty.

"Are we going? I saw the invitation."

"Does it matter?"

"Not to me."

"Are you still jealous, my darling? Joe's going to be home soon. The Japs can't last much longer."

"Will his house be here or Singapore? Won't he stay out East? His children have as much Chinese blood in them as English."

"He'll have to come home to England to be demobbed if he wants to leave the army. In the army, you go where they tell you. Joe's a regular soldier."

"Why don't we all take a trip to America? When I see you two together I'll know. I want to be certain there's nothing deep in the back of your mind to haunt us later on. People do weird things if they don't lay their ghosts. We can go by ship. We never took a honeymoon. You can visit Glen Hamilton in Denver. Mix business with pleasure. I'm not too pregnant to travel. Janet will look after our house."

"You really want to go down that path, Betty?"

"I insist, lover boy."

"Why not? Maybe I can syndicate the story of the wedding and pay for the new furniture. Do you think Horatio has had an invitation?"

"Why don't you ask them? They're not exactly far away."

"We can put Ruthy in the pushchair."

"Silly. She can walk. It's all of three doors. She can run there and back quicker than you."

"It's so nice having friends close by."

When Trevor Hemmings picked up his invitation to the wedding at the Royal Air Force Club in Piccadilly, he was at a loose end. With only the prospect of the chemist shop in Collins Street as a way to use his degree in pharmacology, he was not inspired to catch the first boat home to Australia and face the boredom of wearing a clean white coat for the rest of his life. His sisters would fuss all over him after his kid brother's untimely death. They had lost one brother. He had lost his brother and most of his friends. Anyway, he thought, as he opened the invitation standing in the lobby of the club where the doorman had handed him his mail, no woman would want to marry a man with a face scorched like his.

Being away from the blokes on his terminal leave from the RAF did not help his mood. He was on his own. Why he came to the club. Hoping to see a familiar face after so many years among all the male family of the squadron. He missed the banter. He missed the company. He even missed the war. At the moment of reading the invitation to a film star's wedding in America he had no purpose left in his life. He was empty.

Drained of excitement. He didn't even want to get drunk. Certainly not among strangers. Certainly not alone.

"Well, I'll be buggered. My mate's marrying a bloody film star. Now there's an idea."

"Pardon, sir?"

"Don't worry, Jim. I'm just an uncouth Australian. You ever been to America?"

"No, sir."

"Neither have I. Anyone in the bar?"

"I haven't looked, sir. There are usually a few gentlemen in the downstairs bar at this time of the day. The ladies' lounge upstairs is not open until six o'clock. Of course the ladies you bring to the club must enter through the Park Lane entrance. The back entrance so to speak."

"Of course. How silly of me to forget," said Trevor, his sarcasm going over Jim's head. "Can you book me a room in the club? Instead of going straight back to Australia on the next boat, I'm going to hang around. Take a boat through the Panama Canal to the west coast of America. It's halfway to Australia. Tomorrow I'll go see Cook's. They've got a shop off Piccadilly Circus."

"Very good, sir. One single room for Squadron Leader Hemmings."

"Thank you, Jim. Suddenly I feel much better. The old fox. Tinus marrying a film star. I'll be buggered."

When he looked back over his shoulder on the way down the wide corridor to the bar, Jim was back at the pigeonholes sorting out the members' mail, the man unfazed by his Australian habits. On both sides of the corridor, right up the walls, were pictures of aircraft, mostly from the First World War.

"How Harry Brigandshaw flew those things is beyond my understanding. Stretched parchment. Wood. Held together with piano wire."

At the long, mahogany bar a man he had met at RAF Abingdon in 1940, just before he crash-landed his plane on return from a raid over Germany, was standing on his own, a half-drunk pint of beer in front of him.

"Wally Chapman. This is a pleasant surprise. Trevor Hemmings. Abingdon. 1940. You feel like getting drunk with an old friend?"

"Trevor Hemmings! What a pleasant surprise. What can I get you?"

"The same you're having, Wally. You discharged like me?"

"Once it's over it's over. No point hanging around. Even if they'd let you. Back to civilian life for me."

"What are you going to do?"

"No idea."

"Join the club. What did you do before the war? Where did they post you after Abingdon? Are you staying at the club? Just booked myself in for a couple of nights. Taking a slow boat back to Australia via America. You ever see an actress called Genevieve?"

"Of course. Everyone has seen her films."

"I'm going to her wedding. Have a look at this."

"I'll be buggered," said Wally reading the invitation.

"Tinus Oosthuizen was Fighter Command. Met him before the war. They've known each other for years."

Esther was drunk when her invitation came in the afternoon mail. The postman opening the hard-sprung lid attached to her front door caught her attention, followed by the sound of the envelope dropping inside the cage. Her friend Joan had come from Lambeth to Esther's flat in Chelsea, the lease on the flat paid for by Merlin. They had been drinking gin since lunchtime, Esther with nothing to do with her days for most of her life. With the formal, printed invitation purportedly from the Eighteenth Baron St Clair of Purbeck requesting the pleasure of her company at the marriage of his daughter to Wing Commander Martinus Oosthuizen, son of Mrs Madge Oosthuizen and the late Barend Oosthuizen of Elephant Walk, Mashonaland, Rhodesia, came a handwritten letter from Genevieve which she read and handed to Joan before pouring them both a stiff gin. While Esther was reading the letter, Joan had read the fancy invitation after a struggle in her handbag to find her reading glasses. Joan was a few years older than Esther.

"Well, ducks, are you going to America? Who's the relative who's going to do all the arranging and going with you on the aeroplane?"

"Not Merlin. He won't go. Given some reason. Didn't send the invite neither. Men know how to get out of things they don't want to do."

"You haven't answered my question, Esther."

"Of course I am. She's my daughter."

"You'll have to keep off the gin."

"I only drink gin for something to do. During the war Genevieve sent cases of gin from America when we couldn't get it. Weren't we lucky?"

"There's still a war with Japan."

"One o'clock news says they've had it. Weeks they said. Now the Japs will have to do what they're told. They'll be run by the Americans."

"Don't know nothing about that. What's the boy like?"

"Bit younger than Genevieve. She's had her eye on him since the lad was seventeen. He's twenty-eight. She's thirty-one."

"Long time to wait."

"He wouldn't marry her when the war was on. In case he got killed. Came right through the war from the very beginning. Battle of Britain. His uncle taught him to fly."

"I thought she was going to marry Gregory L'Amour? So tell me, Esther. Who's the bloody relative she's referring to?"

"Her Uncle Barnaby runs her money. He has a bastard son. Must have found his conscience. They do you know."

"Come off it. Would you have married Merlin?"

"Don't be daft. Mind you, he's been good to me, Merlin. He's been good to Genevieve. Stick me away in the countryside, no thank you. Anyway, they'd never have let us. Even for the kid. Turned out all right."

"She wants you to live in America."

"Saw that. Have to behave myself. Here I can do what I like. No one to boss me around. I like my flat. What would I do without you, Joan? Want another gin, love?"

"Haven't finished this one. Aren't you frightened of going up in an aeroplane?"

"Why should I? My future son-in-law's a fighter pilot."

"Does he come and see you?"

"Never seen him in my life."

3

Six weeks later, Gerry Hollingsworth was sitting on his porch at Long Beach, California, looking at the sea as workmen erected a marquee on his lawn. The previous day an American bomber had dropped an atomic bomb on the Japanese city of Hiroshima, obliterating most of the people and buildings. If the Emperor did not surrender they were going to drop another one according to a man Gerry knew in the army. The Pacific was blue, with no indication of the holocaust inflicted on the other side of the ocean. Three people were walking the beach in the hot sun, others were swimming in the sea. Further out, a man was fishing from the back of a moving boat. To all intents and purposes, there was peace on earth. When Gerry called to his wife inside the house there was no trace of a British accent in his voice. To the outside world, Louis Casimir and his Jewish religion were gone forever, like his son David killed in the war. Inside his heart, his son still lived along with his religion. When Carmel came out from the house she sat in a chair. Together they contemplated the ocean.

"Now the war's almost over, don't you think it's time we went to shul?" said Gerry. "We don't have to pretend anymore. In Europe they are putting the Nazis on trial for war crimes. Never again will they massacre the Jews."

"You want to be Jewish again, Gerry?"

"I've never not been Jewish. Just kept my mouth shut."

"Do we have to change our name back to Casimir?"

"That doesn't matter. I'm too well-known as Hollingsworth in America. People don't like to be confused. They've nearly finished the marquee. Do you want to have a look inside?"

"Where do we go to shul?"

"Can you find out? How many guests are actually coming?"

"Two hundred. Maybe more. The press are inviting themselves."

"Is this too much of an intrusion in our home?"

"Not for Genevieve. You owe her a lot."

"She owes me a lot. She won't go on much longer."

"Why do you say that?"

"She's got a lot of pretty actresses ten years her junior snapping at her heels. If she has kids she'll want to retire. She's worth more than me. Did you know that? Spoke to the Honourable Barnaby St Clair. Her uncle runs her financial affairs through a trust to avoid tax, clever chap. Bought up dozens of bombed out sites in London dirt cheap. They're going to sit on them. Wait for the economy to pick up. Then build with the money they got from the British government for the bomb damage. To look at him you wouldn't think he was rich. The old aristocracy don't have to show off. There's nothing like old money or an old title. Not that Barnaby's money is old. Made it all himself. Took the risk on the stock exchange with good information and came out top. Got out before the '29 crash. Had friends inside the companies giving him information. They're going to make it illegal in the States. Insider trading. Trick is to find the loopholes before they block them."

"What's she going to do with all that money?"

"What do people do with money, Carmel? They show off."

"Not Genevieve. You forget. She's old aristocracy from her father."

"Then she'll send all her boys to Harrow or Eton. Tinus went to Oxford. On a Rhodes Scholarship. Forget all the stuff about the decorated fighter pilot and the Battle of Britain. He's got a top economics degree. Good cricketer. Played cricket for Oxford. She's picked the right blood in Tinus. If his Cousin George went to England he could call himself Sir George Manderville, Bart, Harry Brigandshaw told me. By the luck of the draw, Harry owns the Manderville family seat in Surrey. That's what George wants. The family manor house. Anyway, they're now in business together. George is going to grow cigar wrapper leaf on his tobacco plantation in Virginia. Told me so. Calling his cigars Mandervilles with a knight in armour on the box. There are tobacco merchants in London selling 'Churchills'. Not a bad marketing idea. Said the idea of the name came from Tinus. One smart lad."

"Where are they going to live?"

"Haven't said. Tinus prefers the West Coast. After growing up in Rhodesia in the African sun, he doesn't like the cold. Look at that, Carmel. That chap's caught a fish. Look at it leaping out of the water on the end of his line."

"Poor fish."

"You still eat beef. Someone has to kill the cow."

"You want tea or a drink?"

"A drink. Can you imagine what that lawn is going to look like on Saturday? I've hired six buses to bring them from LA. Instead of them driving all the way back."

"It's so nice under this tree."

"Isn't it? The Pacific Ocean is so blue. None of the Rhodesians have come to America for the wedding. Not even his sisters."

"Maybe they can't afford it. Do farmers in Rhodesia make any money?"

"You know the old saying. Plough it back into the land. Probably short of ready cash. Shall I call Mrs Mendez, or will you? She can bring out the drinks cabinet with lots of ice in the bucket. I like America. Even the drink cabinets have wheels in California."

They were married by the Reverend Jethro Thackeray of the Methodist Church, a compromise between Genevieve's Church of England and Tinus's Dutch Reformed Church, the church of Tinus's Afrikaans ancestors. Tina had chosen the Reverend Thackeray, impressed with his nickname of 'Priest to the Stars'. A second bomb had been dropped on the people of Nagasaki, ending the Second World War. The Emperor had surrendered. The clear blue Pacific Ocean was untroubled as they vowed to be man and wife until one of them died.

Against his wishes and with special permission from the Air Ministry in London, Tinus wore his uniform, drawing the line at including his medals. Any one of the British at the Long Beach wedding could have read the ribbons on his chest. A Distinguished Service Order and a Distinguished Service Cross with a bar on the ribbon. After the ribbons for bravery on his chest were a small row of campaign ones. After much argument from Tina who wanted a brand new outfit, Tinus had worn his old uniform, the wings on his chest dulled by the years of war. One of the cuffs was slightly frayed. Janusz Kowalski was his best man.

Janusz, also in the same kind of faded uniform worn by Tinus but with the word 'Poland' on the shoulders, stood next to Tinus as his fellow pilot. The ribbons on his chest were exactly the same. Looking distracted, Janusz's mind was elsewhere.

After he spent a week in Warsaw searching for any trace of his previous life, the RAF had been told by the Russians to send him out of the country. Uniform or no uniform, they would have him arrested. Ingrid he had found the first day of his visit.

"Where did you spring from, Janusz? I'm married, you know. What were all these messages you kept leaving for me? We were children, you and I, before the war. Just children. My husband is a leading member of the Polish Communist Party. Take my advice and go back to England. We've won the war."

"You mean the communists. Not Poland. Where did they take my father?"

"To some nice cold place in Russia where he won't be a nuisance."

"My mother and sisters?"

"I have no idea."

"I've been asked to go to America."

"Good riddance. Unless you are a communist you have no place in Poland."

"Goodbye, Ingrid. I kept your pretty face in my head all through the war."

"Then you were a fool. Before the war you were a count. Now you are nothing."

"I'm still a count."

"Tell that to your friends, the Americans, and see how far you get."

As Janusz gave Tinus the ring, he forced himself to only think of the present and the crowd of people seated in chairs on the lawn overlooking the sea. At least he had a job and a temporary permit to live in America. Three of the bridesmaids were well known in the cinema. One of them smiled at him as he took a pace back. The Reverend Thackeray, who it seemed liked the sound of his own voice, went on, extolling everyone's virtues. Janusz had heard the Reverend's enemies considered him a frustrated actor unable to get a good part in a movie.

Janusz smiled back at the girl who had starred in a movie. All the girls in America smiled at the men. Unlike in England, it meant nothing. The polite way to behave in a society where everyone said they were equal. It was going to take him time to adjust to a life in the New World where every second émigré called himself a count in a pronounced, un-British accent. Genevieve was going to let him live in her flat now she was married and going to live in a house. Gillian Kannberg, who shared the flat with Genevieve, was about to go and look for her husband. William Smythe, the well-known newspaper and radio journalist, was taking her to Singapore once the country was liberated and returned to British rule.

Across to his right, the bomber pilot from Australia gave him the thumbs up, giving a nod and a wink towards the bridesmaids. Next to him was Harry Brigandshaw who had given away the bride and a strange-looking woman in a pink dress Genevieve said was her mum. It was one extreme to another. From the rubble and political uncertainty of Poland to the rich, ordered opulence of America dressed up for a movie. When the party was over and Janusz got back on the chartered bus that would take him to his flat in Los Angeles, it would start the beginning of a new life with all its fear and opportunities. Then he smiled. It was good to be alive.

Three rows behind Harry Brigandshaw, sitting between his wife and the man they called Cousin George from Virginia, Betty Smythe was watching the new bride and groom with a smug grin on her face. The ghost was laid. The skeletons in her husband's cupboard had been rattled into silence, the final curtain coming down in front of the Reverend Thackeray, a fraud if Betty had ever seen one. The ghost-laying had begun when they met each other, Betty standing back to have a good look. Genevieve had smiled with her mismatched eyes, the one almost the colour of smouldering coal, the other a bright, intense blue. She had expected her husband's knees to buckle, but nothing had happened. The chemistry for William had gone. Instead of the face that haunted his dreams was the face of a friend, a friend who quickly talked of old memories, friend to friend, no glimmer from either of them of lover to lover. For Genevieve there may well have been nothing but a roll in the hay. For William, whatever it had been that had taken him in so wholeheartedly, it had gone. Now Genevieve was safely married to Tinus Oosthuizen, no longer a thorn in Betty's imagination every time William mentioned Genevieve in passing. Or they went to the cinema and watched her up on the screen.

Feeling slightly nauseous, sitting in the sun under a picture hat decorated with yellow daisies, she hoped Ruthy was not running riot among the rest of the guests' children in the big room at the top of the house Mrs Hollingsworth had given over as a crèche. Two of Mrs Mendez's cousins from Mexico had the job of watching the children.

"I love Ruthy, Will. Don't get me wrong. But this is bliss. We have three whole hours to ourselves. Having the money to pay a nanny is something I dream about."

"All in good time. When we get home, we'll employ a nanny and you can come to the office on your own."

"What about Ruthy?"

"She's all right now, isn't she?"

"She'll be all right. It's the other girls' pigtails I worry about. Who's the woman in the pink dress with an inch of make-up covering her face?"

"Don't be rude. That's Esther, Genevieve's mother. As a young woman when she seduced Merlin I'm told she was a very striking woman."

"Didn't he seduce her?"

"I wasn't there. Have you ever seen so many people at a wedding? Lucky they have a big garden. Where's young Harry and Bergit? They're not with Janet and Horatio."

"I believe they were taken to the beach, under supervision. Said weddings were boring. Isn't America wonderful? The climate. The people. All the money. Everyone here looks stinking rich."

"They are, darling. I'll have to mingle at the reception. If you get lost tag on to Harry and Tina. The more story I dig up on the wedding the more money we make."

"Don't worry about me when you want to work. Never stop a man working, I say. It's all the familiar faces. Familiar from screen. Never seen any of them in the flesh before. This has been the best honeymoon of my life."

"You're only meant to have one."

"Then I'll treasure it to my dying day, lover."

Gregory L'Amour watched the proceedings with the same emotion as William Smythe; he was over her. The girl he had brought to the wedding, trying hard to get her face in every photograph, was ten years younger than Genevieve. One of Gerry Hollingsworth's rising stars. With all Gregory's heart he hoped the bride and groom would be happy for the rest of their lives. They had had a good chat, as Tinus called it, the previous day. Genevieve had gone off with Tina Brigandshaw to the shops for something.

"It doesn't end here, Greg," Tinus had said. "I never once flew in combat without your talisman. Each time we made contact with enemy aircraft I rubbed the rabbit's foot. Look, you can see there's very little fur left."

"I'm glad. Back then I was jealous, buddy. Jealous of the way she looked at you. Jealous of you as a fighter pilot. Now I know I was lucky not to go to war. Too many people didn't come back from Europe and the Pacific. What was it really like?"

"Frightening. Sad. Yes, sometimes exciting. Like a boxer when they hold up his hand. Except the opponent gets up off the floor in a boxing match. You never forget killing someone. My cousin died in a Lancaster. So many friends in a war that stretched over five long years. As terrible as the bombs on Japan seem now, they will save lives. If America has to invade the Japanese islands, millions will be killed. American and Japanese. Somehow man has got to find a way of arguing without losing his temper and using his fists. Once we were the three musketeers. You remember André Cloete when you came with Genevieve to Oxford? I miss him so much. School. Cricket. Oxford. Rowing on the Thames and the Isis. Janusz is going to be best man tomorrow. I asked him not to mention André in his speech. Once I sat on a stone inside a magic circle on Headley Heath and asked all the gods for protection. Just to be safe. All the time I was holding your rabbit's foot. Please remain friends. You will always have a big part of our hearts. Find a good girl who loves you, Greg, and not your fame."

Then the ceremony was over. People rising from their chairs, moving towards the marquee and the drinks. Flash bulbs going off a few feet from his face temporarily blinding his eyes.

"Did you love her, Greg?" asked the girl, surprising him with her perception.

"Oh yes. I loved her. You can't fool the camera lens all of the time. Now I love her as a friend. She's giving up the movies. Maybe stage acting after she has had her children. They are going to have three, so she tells me. What we have left, she and I, is our chemistry on screen which will last forever if they replay old movies. They're going to live in New York when they come back from Mexico. For their honeymoon Tinus has found them an island off the coast with just one thatched house and no other people. Won't tell anyone where. She wants to be Mrs Oosthuizen, no longer Genevieve."

"Does the press know she's retiring?"

"They don't want to make a fuss. Just let it happen. The orchestra is striking up. Anything over twelve instruments, I'm informed, is an orchestra not a band. I call it a swing band. Let's go and dance."

With a certain amount of self-satisfaction, Tina Brigandshaw watched the proceedings sitting at the top table, a long series of interconnected tables covered in one long, white tablecloth, two away from the groom. From where she sat, the dance floor was swinging, the guests glad to get out of the sun and shake a leg. The fact the wedding she had planned so carefully cost a small fortune had never entered her head. Harry had paid for the wedding with a small fraction of the profit he made from the Tender Meat Company supplying tinned food to the Allied armies around the world. She had stinted on nothing. The best florist for the flowers. The best caterer for the food. A wine connoisseur recommended by Gerry Hollingsworth for drinks. The smart little wedding they had given Mary Ross and her plumber on the lawns of Hastings Court paled into nothing compared to the raucous opulence in front of her.

For the first time in years, Tina felt she was doing something worthwhile, glowing in the warmth of all the attention, the reflected attention, she admitted to herself, directed at the star of the show, Genevieve. William Smythe had promised to mention her by name as the well-known Mrs Brigandshaw from Hastings Court in the English county of Surrey who planned the sumptuous wedding attended by so many Hollywood stars. For the first time in her life, Tina felt she had personally arrived. If only her children, left at boarding school in England, could now see her sitting with the stars.

Even the upset of watching Tinus and Janusz in their RAF uniforms had lasted through the Reverend Thackeray's ceremony, a man of God who impressed her immensely. Never before had Tina met a famous priest, one as equally recognisable to the press as the stars. With all the publicity in the English papers, the old families in Surrey who looked at her down their noses would have to think again, accept her in English society despite the fact she was raised in a railway cottage, her father a porter at the time she was born. Now, with the biggest wedding in America for many a year swirling around her, she was satisfied.

"Isn't it all wonderful?" she said to Cousin George sitting on her right, Harry on her left smiling more than she had seen him do since Anthony's death.

"Mixing with the rich and famous, I'd call it. My wife never seen nothing like this before. You done a job fit for a queen. Pity her father didn't come. Like to have shaken hands with a real-life baron. Never done that before, despite me being a real life baronet under all my American. This band can play real swing. Where'd you get them, Tina? Come on Thelma, you and I are going to dance."

Getting up, moving back his chair, Cousin George bowed from the waist to his wife, pulled back her chair and offered her his hand.

"Can you dance, George?"

"Let's go find out. There are still things you don't know about George. All these young, good-looking people make me feel a young man with his beautiful wife."

"What's got into you?"

"The wedding, Thelma. Weddings make me smile."

Harry Brigandshaw, watching with pleasure the happiness between Cousin George and Thelma, was thinking how different his life could have been had his great-grandfather come to America instead of his younger brother. That way, Harry surmised, he would have been an American. Had he been twenty years younger he might have considered living in America, a compromise between England and Africa for Tina.

"Would you have liked to live in America, Tina?"

"Oh yes. There's none of the class nonsense in America."

"I think there is. Here it's just money, not who your father was. People always drift into company where they feel most comfortable."

"What would we do with Hastings Court?"

"Or Elephant Walk?"

"You're not harping back on that one, Harry. We've been through all that."

"It's always in the back of my mind. It gets into your blood."

"Never got into mine."

"Seems to have got into Frank's. The war in Europe's been over for months and not a word from him. Last letter from Ralph Madgwick said Frank's hunting in the Zambezi Valley."

"I read the letter, Harry."

"Sorry, darling. Just it doesn't look like he's coming home in a hurry. Do you mind?"

"The children should live their own lives, whatever we say. Can you imagine us as grandparents? Beth's going to be married first. She's very beautiful. They grow up so quickly. She was a bit torn in coming to America but I think staying at home and having a bit of freedom from us was really what she wanted. Dorian and Kim will be out of boarding school before we can blink."

"What does Beth want to do? I've asked her. All she says is to enjoy herself. Twenty-one next year. Key of the door. So many of the men she would have married died in the war."

"Please, Harry. Don't remind me."

"I'm sorry. Would you like to dance, Tina? Just look at Cousin George. There's more to him than meets the eye."

"Would you live in America, Harry?"

"If it would make you happy."

"And make you miserable. Hard enough to keep you in England. Come on. Let's shake a leg. I hate the speeches. Do we have to have them?"

"You are lucky not to have to give one. Just me. Janusz as best man. Tinus as the groom. It's called tradition. They both look nervous."

"Do you like giving speeches?"

"No one does. Especially at weddings. The trick is to make them laugh once and sit down. Barnaby's enjoying himself."

"Of course he is," snapped Tina. "The place is crawling in young girls. Just look at him. That one's young enough to be his daughter."

Sighing to himself, having brought up two subjects he should not have done, Harry put out his hand to his wife having pulled back her chair. Then he led her onto the wooden dance floor in the middle of the marquee.

They all had a small table to themselves next to the third pole that held up the tent. William and Betty Smythe, Horatio and Janet Wakefield, Gillian Kannberg playing the part of the lone dutiful wife waiting for her husband to be released from a Japanese prison. On Tina Brigandshaw's scale of importance, William thought, none of them ranked very high. There were so many newsmen at the wedding, two more from England made little impression.

Arthur Bumley of the *Daily Mirror* in London had asked William to report on the British prisoners to be released from the Japanese prisons. And take Mrs Kannberg with him; a human story of the *Mirror* looking after its own would be good for circulation. As in Europe, there was going to be a tribunal to charge the Japanese Prime Minister Tojo with war crimes, especially for his handling of allied prisoners of war. Stories of atrocities building the Burma railway line with British troops had been circulating before the atomic bombs were dropped on Japan. For some reason the Emperor was above the fray.

William's commission was to interview released British prisoners on how they had been treated. According to Arthur Bumley, the British public were entitled to the truth and with the truth, retribution. If Englishmen had died like dogs under a Japanese whip, someone was going to pay, the *Mirror* calling the fouls. In William's personal opinion, one he would keep out of his dispatches to London, there was going to be a witch-hunt in the Far East, similar to the one taking place in Germany. To the victors the spoils and the righteousness; to William the job of digging up dirt. The fact that Arthur Bumley had not so much as mentioned William's cousin Joe in Changi jail, said something for Arthur Bumley's priorities.

"It's like Versailles all over again if we're not careful," Horatio had said to him before they left their small hotel in Long Beach for the wedding. "Don't we ever learn? Hanging a few poor sods won't change what happened. We flattened Cologne and Dresden with the help of the Americans. The Yanks just flattened Hiroshima and Nagasaki on their own. What do you think the Germans and Japanese would have done with Truman and Churchill had they won the war? Our kids will have to live in the same world as their kids. With this new bomb we can annihilate each other, entire countries in one day, not cities pounded into the rubble week after week. Hatred. All they think of is hatred. What can the likes of us do, Will? Janet and I are staying a few days after the wedding before flying home. The kids want to play in the sand and swim in a warm sea. They never knew the sea was warm before. Do you know, this is the first holiday we've taken as a family? What are we going to write about now the war's over, William? They won't listen to a lecture on the stupidity of war."

"Don't you worry about that. There's always a story the public want to read. The big one from our side of the pond is the end of the British Empire. From now on America will call the shots. We've won a war and are about to lose an empire. Like Churchill. The opinion of those in the know says Labour will win the election by a landslide. Take from the rich and give to the poor. Wonderful politics. Especially when the poor voters outnumber the rich by ten to one. Oh, we'll have plenty to write about. My pieces on Genevieve are paying well. People want to know the intimate details of the famous."

"There's no dirt on Genevieve."

"Of course there isn't."

"Gregory says she's pulling out of film now *Pacific War* is on the circuit."

"When you've made your money what's the point of making more? Give the next lot a chance."

"How are you getting to Singapore?"

"The American Air Force are flying us. Big press detail. You know the Americans. Like to do everything big. They also want the dirt on the Japanese to show the public why it was imperative to drop the atomic bomb. Betty's looking forward to the wedding. Tina's organised a crèche in the house. Give Betty some peace from Ruthy. As you know, they're demanding, young children. In the old flat Ruthy slept on a mattress in the bath. Only way we could get any sleep with the door closed."

"When's the new one due?"

"January."

"Good luck."

"Do you know, I like being married."

"So do I."

"We'd better find the women and go to this wedding."

"That's why we came here."

Looking across now to Horatio and Janet dancing like lunatics on the dancefloor brought so many memories back to William. From the days they were both cub reporters on the *Daily Mail*. The almost catastrophic trip to Berlin before the war.

"Would you and our son like to dance, Mr Smythe?"

"Thought you'd never ask. How do you know it's going to be a boy?"

Then the thought of meeting Joe and Cherry Blossom in the days ahead made William smile with the pleasure of expectation.

Tinus Oosthuizen had listened to his Uncle Harry's speech with tears in his eyes, the pain of losing his father flooding back to him as Uncle Harry talked about his friend Barend, Tinus's father. Uncle Harry read out a letter from Tinus's family in Rhodesia. Another one from Lord St Clair and his mother. Genevieve's Uncle Robert St Clair stood up among the guests at the mention of his name, having brought his American wife to the wedding with their two children. Janusz Kowalski made them laugh as the best man. Then it was his turn in front of the guests and the press. Remembering every word his Oxford tutor, Mr Bowden, had told him about speaking in public, Tinus began without any notes. Everything he wanted to say about his new wife was firmly in his head.

For a moment he had the soft-hearted ladies among the guests looking for their handkerchiefs as they soaked up every sentimental word; when he looked at Genevieve there were tears in her eyes.

"No, I'm not going to thank you all individually for coming to our wedding. I'm not going to say the names of my friends who will never be able to go to a wedding. We have waited long years through the war for this moment, Genevieve and I, God bless you all."

Pulling out her chair from the back, Tinus having stood behind his own chair for his speech, he helped Genevieve to her feet. Then they moved together among the guests, all of them standing and clapping as they passed. On the dance floor, Tinus took Genevieve in his arms.

"Where'd you learn to speak so well in public, my darling?" asked Genevieve.

"Oxford University Debating Society. Are you happy?"

"Of course I am. It went off without a hitch. How soon can we make a duck? Mother's getting quite tiddly."

"Barnaby has promised to look after her. You can't worry about everything."

"After this dance I'm going to change. How are we getting out of here?"

"On the back of a motorcycle. Compliments of Uncle Harry. Parked at the back of the house near the path down to the beach. The press will never think of that one. Give it an hour. Then we'll be off on our own."

"Don't we have to say goodbye to everyone?"

"By the time the last guest leaves this marquee most will be beyond caring. We can write them nice little letters of thank you for their wedding presents. How does it feel to be Mrs Oosthuizen?"

"Wonderful. At last I have a surname. Hold me, Tinus. Hold me very tight."

4

Ten days later the DC-3 took off from its base outside Los Angeles en route for Singapore. On board were William Smythe, Gillian Kannberg and seven Allied journalists. In charge of the press detail was Major Johnny Delany, the army press liaison officer. In the flat in Los Angeles Janusz Kowalski had been left on his own waiting for Tinus and Genevieve to return from their honeymoon. Betty and Ruthy had flown back to England via New York. The DC-3 was to refuel along the South Pacific islands and Northern Australia. It was going to be a long, hot, noisy journey, according to Major Delany.

For once in her life Gillian was not trying to flirt with the men. She was to William subdued, brooding on the reception she would receive from her husband. Briefly, William had spoken to Joe and Bruno separately by phone on the 15 September from America, three days after Singapore was liberated. They were both alive, unwell, but alive. They were both recuperating in the same hospital.

Three days after leaving America the plane landed in Singapore. William and Gillian drove to the hospital. When they found Joe on the third floor his hand was being held by Cherry Blossom. Soon after Gillian found Bruno on the second floor and burst into tears. His face was the colour of yellow parchment, his eyes sunk in the back of his head.

An hour later William and Bruno found themselves alone. Gillian had gone to the shops.

"You want to tell me your story, Bruno? Arthur Bumley wants a sob story for the *Mirror*. My cousin Joe's on the floor above."

"How's Joe?"

"Buggered. Like you. They tell us the body picks up quickly with proper food. What did the Japs feed you on?"

"Rice. Just rice. Sometimes water from the cabbage they cooked for the Japanese soldiers. It might have been better for Gillian to let me get well first. Going to the shops to find me some fruit was an excuse."

"Maybe not. She wants to find a place and nurse you back to strength herself."

"Gillian!"

"We all change, Bruno. I'll ask Cherry Blossom. If there's room you can come to Joe's house. The Japs had commandeered it but they've got it back. It's a mess. Her father lives with them. During the occupation they all lived in one room, Cherry Blossom, her father and the two kids."

"Would Joe mind?"

"Of course not. Now, about your story."

"Just a general brief. Not today. Let's have another look at you. The real story's mine. A real book this time. A novel. So I can get into everyone's heads. Thanks for bringing her."

"I'll go check with Cherry Blossom. Genevieve got married. To her pilot."

"I'm glad."

"Quite a wedding. Your wife will fill you in."

"Can you mail me a bottle of real Scotch?"

"Do my best. You remember Johnny Delany? He came on our flight as the chaperone. I'll ask him. We'll have a good drink together you and I. I fly back to London day after tomorrow."

"How many of us prisoners are you interviewing?"

"As many as possible."

"More than half died by report. Disease from lack of proper food. Tropical disease. She still looks wonderful, Will. Same as the day we first met."

"Tell her that, Bruno. She's a bit nervous. Two and a half years is a long time. Glad you made it, old friend."

When William turned round from the doorway, Bruno's eyes were closed, his head lying back on the pillow. He looked dead. William turned back in alarm.

"Bruno!"

"Just taking a nap. I'm so tired. They only feed us a little at a time or else it goes straight out. Time. Don't you worry. When I come over to England we'll have a drink together in the Duck and Drake. I often imagined that pub in Changi. Kept me alive. Amazing what the mind can do. It's going to be one hell of a book, William. Max Pearl will like it."

"She'll be back soon."

"I hope so."

"Harry Brigandshaw sends his regards. He was at Genevieve's wedding."

"Do I look as bad as Harry in that tropical diseases hospital when he got back from the Congo?"

"About the same."

"He came through that as right as rain."

"That's my boy. Good food, lots of sleep and your wife by your side. You'll come through just fine, Bruno."

Not knowing where to look for fruit, Gillian walked out of the hospital into the street. There were people everywhere going about their business. Her whole body was in a state of panic. With no money, Bruno was her last resort. If he died she would find herself destitute, no longer able to bend men to her will. She was thirty years old. In the plane the men had looked at her but not the same way they had when she married Bruno. They were interested, looking to see if her reaction was the same. When she failed to return their look they went back to reading their books. When she looked again they had forgotten her. Just another married woman like the rest.

The moment Bruno was well enough to make love to her she was going to get herself pregnant. As insurance for her future. The thought of finding herself a spinster shorthand typist wearing glasses appalled her. She had been a fool. The likes of Gregory L'Amour and Nathan Squires were no good to her. For them she was a fling. Convenient. No strings attached for Gregory as she was married. Nathan had been after an easy life at no cost to himself. She hoped he never found a part in a film for the rest of his life. Forcing herself to concentrate and control the panic, she found a Chinaman in a big hat by the side of the road selling bananas. She bought a whole hand, giving him an American dollar. The bananas were quite heavy. With her mind clear, her only choice was nursing Bruno back to health and seducing him. Her life, she told herself, had never been easy. About to begin the most important part of her life to secure her future, she brought the bananas back to the ward on the second floor of the hospital. Bruno was lying back in the bed, his eyes closed. He looked dead. The panic returned with a vengeance. Bruno opened his eyes and smiled. The same smile of wanting she had always seen in his eyes. He wanted her. Wanted her body just the same. Feeling back in control she put the small hand of bananas, still on their stalk, down next to his bed, bent over and kissed him on the forehead.

"Can't you do better than that?"

"Later, Bruno. Oh yes, later. When you are well again."

"William thinks we can move in with Joe and Cherry Blossom."

"That will be nice. When you can travel why don't we take the boat back to England? A sea voyage will do you good. We can sail round the Cape. Make the voyage longer than going through the Suez Canal."

"Do they go that way?"

"We can find out."

"Don't you want to go back to America?"

"Arthur Bumley will want you in London now he's making you famous. The prodigal son, according to William. We're English, Bruno."

"My father's Latvian."

"Never mind. We'll find a little house in Surrey. The trains run well up to Waterloo. A cottage with trellised roses. It will be nicer for the children than living in London."

"You want children!"

"Of course. We're still young enough. Three of them, Bruno."

"What about your friends in America? The rich and famous you like so much."

"I much prefer England. You can write your novel about the war in the weekends. Max Pearl won't mind you living in England."

"Sounds wonderful. Give me a banana."

"You need someone to look after you."

"It's so wonderful to see you, Gillian. You have no idea. All through the years as a prisoner your face in my mind helped keep me going. He's a good friend, William. We can all be friends in England."

When Bruno closed his eyes again, Gillian was back in control. The panic had subsided. The thought of a suburban house in Wimbledon no longer seemed so bad. She would get used to having children, she told herself. It just might be fun. Anything was better than being some man's secretary. The further she kept away from America the better. Quoting again the old saying she had used when having her affairs, 'what the eye does not see the heart will not grieve about'. She began to plan the days and years ahead to make sure their boat sailed together.

When William came back from seeing his cousin she was dutifully sitting on a chair next to her husband.

"When they discharge him, both of you come to Joe's house. Joe likes the idea of recuperating together. They got to know each other in Changi. Joe will be leaving the army. Going into import-export with Cherry Blossom's father. Joe's not coming back to England. Are you all right, Gillian?"

"I'm just fine. So's Bruno. We're going back to England when he's well."

William smiled at her. Gillian rather thought he knew what was going through her mind. Journalists, in her experience, had the bad habit of reading people's minds.

Two days after William flew out of Singapore on the first leg of his journey back to England, Joe and Bruno were discharged from hospital. The army doctor told Joe he would be asked to leave the Royal Engineers on medical grounds, giving them a small army pension for the rest of their lives. One of Joe's kidneys was no longer doing its job properly. Cherry Blossom had never before heard of a pension for life that included her should something happen to Joe. Joe thought the army no longer needed so many regular soldiers. That the medical discharge was the easiest way of getting him out of the army now the war was over. All his kidney needed was a good clean out from the contents of a case of good Scotch whisky.

The same army captain had told Bruno to take a boat trip home. He wrote the recommendation on the discharge from a medical procedure recommending Mrs Kannberg as the nurse to look after him on the trip. When Bruno phoned Arthur Bumley from the Major's office at the hospital, they were given a free trip home, compliments of a generous employer. There was going to be a piece in the *Mirror* about the paper's generosity for one of their own putting his life on the line for the readers of the *Daily Mirror*. Bruno had smiled at the irony of the generous employer deducting his current salary from the overpayment of his wife's pension. In Bruno's experience no one was truly honest when it came to money.

With the squeeze on the *Mirror*, Bruno asked for a double cabin for themselves, not quite having the cheek to ask Mr Bumley for a first-class passage. When they reached England he had his own ideas about the pension overpayment. If they did not stop their nonsense he would turn good public relations into bad. Having the readers howling for the editor's blood. There was always a rogue freelance journalist with an axe to grind with the *Mirror* if William Smythe would not do the job in fear of damaging his own reputation with the paper.

Joe's house was very nice, he told Cherry Blossom, the small box room for the two of them paradise after prison. On their first night alone he and Gillian made love quietly so as not to disturb the rest of Joe's family. His strength was returning with a vengeance. Gillian found a berth on a liner the next day. The liner was leaving Singapore several days later with Joe and Cherry Blossom seeing them off at the docks. When the ship broke away from the pier, hooting, a band playing, streamers breaking, as the first British families left Singapore in three years, Joe took Cherry Blossom by the hand, a small dainty hand that matched her small size. Bruno had told Joe all about Gillian's liking for men, long before he met her. Some men were luckier than others, he told himself.

"Didn't you want to go home with them, Joe?" she asked him, the fear in her eyes outmatching the smile on her oriental face.

"This is my home, Cherry Blossom. Singapore is my home. With the help of your father and some of the civilians I met in prison we are going to be rich."

"Oh, goodie. Really rich, Joe?"

"Really rich, Cherry Blossom. So rich we won't know what to do with the money."

"I never thought we'd ever be rich. Did you hear that, children? Daddy says we are going to be rich."

---

*I*n the following spring, when Patrick Smythe was four months old and Gillian Kannberg six months pregnant, Harry Brigandshaw and Klaus von Lieberman agreed to meet at Romanshorn, on the neutral territory of Switzerland near the shores of Lake Constance. The two families were to holiday together by the lake, Harry having arranged to rent a yacht on which they would live.

The entire family, except Frank who was still somewhere in Rhodesia where he was moving around with his old schoolfriend Brian Tobin, took the ferry across from Dover to Calais where they boarded the train for Switzerland, with three changes of train ahead of them. Beth had finished her two-year course at secretarial college in London and was living at home, getting more bored by the day. Dorian had left boarding school at the end of the last term and was waiting to go up to Oxford. Kim was still one year from leaving school, enjoying the Easter holidays.

Harry, no longer with a job at the Air Ministry, was working with Katherine, his old secretary, in a small office in Holborn trying to find enough work to keep them both busy. The real work in Brigandshaw Oosthuizen was being done by Tinus in New York; he and Genevieve had a small flat together, keeping a low profile while they enjoyed their lives as a couple. Despite trying, Genevieve was still not pregnant.

Klaus had mentioned Gabby and Bergit would be there, but nothing of Erwin or Melina. For the first night the Brigandshaw and von

Lieberman families were booked into the Romanshorn Hotel where Mr Tannenbaum was still the owner. The earlier conversation on the phone between Harry and Klaus had been tense. Face to face, Harry hoped the ice would melt, rekindling their old friendship. As he said to Tina when he put down the phone, "It's worth a try. If this doesn't work, I have done my best."

When the families met in the hotel lobby everything was formal and polite. They could have been strangers.

"Janet Wakefield sends her regards," said Harry. "Your namesake Bergit Wakefield is eight years old. They are still in the same house in Chelsea."

"How nice for them," said Bergit von Lieberman.

"We have a problem with the yacht tomorrow. They say the weather's going to be lousy for a couple of days. I hope you know how to sail a boat, Klaus. Growing up in Rhodesia in the middle of the bush there wasn't any water to sail a yacht. Well, you would remember that from your stay with us at Elephant Walk at the end of your honeymoon."

Harry had thought of asking about their son Erwin. At the mention of Elephant Walk where Bergit had conceived Erwin, she turned away, a look of sorrow on her face. Neither of the senior von Liebermans had asked the whereabouts of Anthony or Frank. The ice, Harry told himself, was still thick. Then they all moved into the lounge of the hotel with its small bar next to a grand piano. A few locals were at the bar, the tourists still not coming after the war. If Harry had not had American money to spend, his fifty pound British travel allowance would have kept him holidaying in England. At the piano with its lid up, a young girl sat playing Gershwin. American music seemed somehow out of place in Switzerland with the Alps outside the window white-capped with snow. Harry had seen Gabby look at the piano with interest.

"Do you play the piano, Gabby? Last time we met was in that lovely restaurant on the pier. We shall all have lunch there again."

"Yes I do, Mr Brigandshaw," she said, looking at the girl sitting on the piano stool.

"Your English is very good. Of course, you were at school in Geneva with Melina. How is Melina? What kind of music do you play?"

"She's married."

"I'm so glad."

"How old is Melina?" asked Beth, looking around the lounge hoping to find some nice young men to relieve her boredom. Her mother also looked bored at all the formality and stiffness.

"She's twenty-three. Two years older than me."

"Then we're the same age. I was twenty-one in January."

Taking their seats at the casual table on which was a big silver bowl of flowers, Tina Brigandshaw ordered them tea from Mrs Tannenbaum, the wife of the owner and sister of the man who owned the jetty restaurant.

"You do drink tea in Germany?" said Tina to Bergit, not knowing what else to say; afterwards she said to Harry that at that point she could have cut the atmosphere with a knife.

"When we can get it," said Bergit.

"The rationing was terrible. Is yours getting any better?"

"No," said Klaus, ending the conversation.

While they all waited for the tea, the silence became physical. The girl at the piano stopped playing and went back to the bar. The bar apparently was open through the afternoon. To Harry, the girl looked more like a local than the resident piano player. Gabby's eyes had roamed back to the piano, standing with its lid up all alone. Harry recognised her look of longing.

"Won't you play us something, Gabby?" asked Harry.

"You won't mind classical music?"

"Of course not."

"A Bach fugue seems appropriate."

For a brief moment Harry thought he glimpsed a brief smile on the girl's face. Then she went to the piano and began to play. The tea had arrived and Tina was pouring into the cups. The few people at the bar stopped talking. Someone from the kitchen appeared at the side door into the lounge, keeping it half open. Mr and Mrs Tannenbaum appeared from reception, a waitress having brought their tea. Dorian had his eyes glued on the German girl playing the piano. Kim had stopped fidgeting. When the first piece was over, Gabby started to play something else. The music was lighter in mood. Even to Harry's untrained ear the music was beautiful. When Gabby finished playing everyone in the room clapped, the people at the bar getting off their bar stools to stand up. Gabby was smiling. Gave them all a brief bow and walked back to the long, low table where the two families were sitting opposite each other looking at the full cups of tea. No one at the table said a word.

"She missed the Berlin Conservatory," said Klaus after Gabby sat down and picked up her teacup. "It was destroyed by Allied bombs so there's nothing we can do about it now. What a bloody waste." For once it seemed Klaus von Lieberman had forgotten his manners.

"I have a friend in New York," said Harry, thinking quickly. "At the Juilliard School of Music. Gabby, could I put in a good word?"

"Oh, that would be wonderful. But how could Father pay for me to go to America?"

"It would be my pleasure. I have an office in New York run by my nephew. You may remember Tinus when we saw you here last time. He's married to Genevieve, the actress. No, I suppose you would not have seen her films."

"Was he the older or younger of the boys at the restaurant?"

"The elder. The younger was my son, Anthony. He was your age."

"Where is Anthony? I liked him."

"He was killed. His aircraft was shot down over Berlin." As Harry mentioned Anthony, his voice choked. "Maybe this visit was not so sensible. There are too many deep wounds that all of us need to heal."

Harry had stood up and turned his face away.

"Oh God, I'm so sorry, Harry, Tina," said Klaus.

"Dare I ask after Erwin?" said Harry turning around after waiting to gain control of his emotions.

"He's alive in body. So I'm told. Russian Front. They didn't have any fuel left to get out when the Russian Army overran their airfield."

"Where is he?"

"In a Russian prison camp."

"Haven't they released the prisoners by now?"

"Cheap labour. The Russians ignore any question of repatriation. For us, the war still hasn't stopped, Harry. They'll never get out of East Germany any more than they'll get out of Poland. You want to go for a walk, Harry? Let the ladies and the youngsters enjoy their tea. Gabby, go and play them all some more music. Everyone seems to be waiting."

"Could I go to America, Papa?"

"Somehow I'll pay you back, Harry."

"You already have with friendship."

Outside it had stopped raining. A cold wind was blowing down from the mountains. They had both put on their overcoats. To anyone watching, it was two old men going for an afternoon stroll.

"Where do you want to walk, Klaus?"

"To the pier. We can have a drink together in the jetty restaurant. Our wives haven't seen each other for a long time. Give them a chance to talk. Did you see the way Dorian was looking at Gabby? She was so looking forward to seeing Anthony again. They caught each other's eye when you came to Romanshorn in 1938. To try and help me. That was all my Uncle Werner playing his games. Running with the hare and hunting with the hounds, I think you English say. Through history, we von Liebermans have survived with our estate by bending with the political wind. After the war you and I fought each other, the estate was bankrupt. I borrowed a lot of money from a Jewish bank in New York. Uncle Werner traded the mortgage on the family estate for the lives of one hundred and sixteen German Jews. Later it turned out Uncle Werner was part of the plot to kill the Führer. Hedging his bets as usual when he realised who was going to win the war. Now he's part of the German committee to reconstruct Germany. General Marshall has a plan to use American money to put Europe back on its feet. Stop us going at each other's throats again. It seems the Americans learnt a lesson from the harsh penalties imposed on Germany by the Treaty of Versailles at the end of our war. Uncle Werner's got some new pet idea of a common market for French and German steel and coal. One minute I thought he was a staunch member of the Nazi Party. Now he claims he was a mole. You never know with survivors like General Werner von Lieberman. He'll likely end up in a post-war German cabinet. If they don't make him chancellor. I don't understand politics. Do you, Harry?"

"I keep as far away as possible. They're all the same. We cherish the winners and lambaste the losers."

"Erwin really believed in a world order under German discipline. Now we will never know. The Russians are trying to manufacture their own atomic bomb. To be able to compete with the Americans."

"It never stops."

"Hopefully Europe has had enough for a while."

"I truly hope so."

"I'm so sorry about Anthony. In a better world they may have married each other. Binding our families together forever. Will you really put a word in for Gabby in New York? She has so much talent that should not be wasted. When you mentioned the Juilliard School of Music her face lit up. I'll pay you the money back somehow. We can only try and do the best for our children."

"He'll come back from Russia."

"I hope his spirit isn't broken. By the Nazis and the Russians."

"What happened to your cousin Henning? Wasn't he a hardened Nazi?"

"Ran off to South America before the Russians collared him. Took one of the girls from Nazi intelligence. Melina, thankfully, saw the light. Married one of our pilots who was invalided out of the Air Force. She's happy. Very happy. Henning's either in Argentina or Paraguay. A lot of the Nazis fled Germany in the chaos... Don't you think we'd better look at this yacht before we enjoy a drink?"

"Do you know how to work the damn thing?"

"I've been sailing on this lake since I was a boy, Harry. I'll teach you how to sail... It's good to see you again, Harry. Really good."

HORNS OF DILEMMA (BOOK SEVEN)

CONTINUE YOUR JOURNEY WITH THE BRIGANDSHAWS

With rumours swirling of his parentage, Frank Brigandshaw wants answers: Who put horns on his father's head?

Returning to England, Frank is heading down two paths. One to make them, the ménage à trois a trifle uncomfortable and admit the truth. The other, to make money and lots of it. And so like father like son, it seems Frank will succeed until he meets Connie Whitaker.

Meantime, Frank's siblings are making their own way in a city that is recovering from the fallout of war. Amongst the jazz set and artists living in Chelsea, Beth falls in love with a man who doesn't love her; Dorian finds himself with a worrying dilemma and Kim sets off on his travels to India.

However, when they are all summoned to Hastings Court, everything the young Brigandshaws have come to love is about to unravel, threatened with collapse and truths are revealed.

With the flame of empire about to go out, along with crippling taxes, the enduring Brigandshaws strive to make their way in a new Britain in this next instalment of Peter Rimmer's historical fiction series, the seventh in the epic saga of the Brigandshaws, *Horns of Dilemma*.

DEAR READER

~

Reviews are the most powerful tools in our kitty when it comes to getting attention for Peter's books. This is where you can come in, as by providing an honest review you will help bring them to the attention of other readers.

If you enjoyed reading *Treason If You Lose*, and have five minutes to spare, we would really appreciate a review (it can be as short as you like). Your help in spreading the word and keeping Peter's work alive is gratefully received.

Please post your review on the retailer site where you purchased this book.

Thank you so much.
Heather Stretch (Peter's daughter)

PRINCIPAL CHARACTERS

~

The Brigandshaws
Harry — Central character of *Treason If You Lose*
Tina — Harry's wife, formerly Tina Pringle
Anthony, Beth, Frank, Dorian and Kim — Harry and Tina's children
Sir Henry Manderville — Harry's maternal grandfather who lived on Elephant Walk
Emily — Harry's mother who lives on Elephant Walk

The Oosthuizens
Madge — Harry's younger sister and wife of Barend
Tinus — Madge and Barend's eldest son
Paula and Doris — Tinus's younger sisters

The St Clairs
Merlin — Eighteenth Baron of Purbeck, Lord St Clair
Robert — Second son of Lord and Lady St Clair
Barnaby — Youngest son of Lord and Lady St Clair and one-time lover of Tina Pringle
Freya — Robert's American wife
Richard and Chuck (Charles) — Robert and Freya's children

Lady St Clair — Mother to Merlin, Robert and Barnaby
Genevieve — Hollywood actress and Merlin's illegitimate daughter

The von Liebermans
Klaus — A WWI German pilot shot down by Harry Brigandshaw in 1917
Bergit — Klaus's wife
Erwin — Klaus and Bergit's eldest son
Gabby and Melina — Klaus and Bergit's daughters
General Werner — Klaus's uncle who is high up in the Nazi Party
Henning — General Werner's son

The Wakefields
Horatio — Journalist at the *Daily Mail*
Janet Bray — Horatio's wife
Harry and Bergit — Horatio and Janet's children named after Harry
Brigandshaw and Bergit von Lieberman

The Rosenzweigs
Sir Jacob Rosenzweig — A Jewish bank owner
Hannah — Sir Jabob's estranged wife
Aaron — Sir Jacob and Hannah's son
Rebecca — Sir Jacob and Hannah's daughter married to Ralph Madgwick
Vida Wagner — Jacob Rosenzweig's German live-in lover

The American Mandervilles
Sir George (Cousin George) — Harry's cousin who inherited the
Manderville title
Thelma — Sir George's wife
George, Henry, Bart and Mary-Anne — Cousin George and Thelma's
children

Other Principal Characters
André Cloete — South African schoolfriend of Tinus and RAF pilot
Arthur Bumley — Editor of the *Daily Mirror*
Betty Townsend — William Smythe's secretary
Bruno Kannberg — Latvian-born journalist of the *Mirror*
Carmel Casimir — Gerry Hollingsworth's wife
Count Janusz Kowalski — Polish lawyer and RAF pilot friend of Tinus
Edward — Barnaby St Clair's manservant

Gerry Hollingsworth — Hollywood film producer, formerly Louis Casimir

Gillian Kannberg — Bruno Kannberg's wife

Glen Hamilton — Editor of the *Denver Telegraph* and friend of Harry Brigandshaw and Robert St Clair

Gregory L'Amour — An American actor and long-standing admirer of Genevieve

Ingrid — Polish girl Janusz is in love with

John Woodall — Flying instructor at Redhill Aerodrome

Justin Hemmings — Trevor's younger brother

Mavis Crookshank — Wife of Phillip

Max Pearl — Robert St Clair's American publisher

Mr Glass — Editor of the *Daily Mail*

Mrs Craddock — The cook at Hastings Court

Paul Crookshank — Eldest son of Phillip and Mavis

Phillip Crookshank — Chief designer and flight engineer for Shorts Flying Boats

Rodney Hirst-Brown — Photographic spy for the Nazis in England

Trevor Hemmings — An Australian RAF pilot and friend of Tinus

Vic 'Ding-a-ling' Bell — Harry's WW2 adjutant

William Smythe — Journalist and friend of Horatio Wakefield

ACKNOWLEDGMENTS

~

With grateful thanks to our *VIP First Readers* for reading *Treason If You Lose* prior to its official launch date. They have been fabulous in picking up errors and typos helping us to ensure that your own reading experience of *Treason If You Lose* has been the best possible. Their time and commitment is particularly appreciated.

Alan McConnochie (South Africa)
Hilary Jenkins (South Africa)
Derek Tippell (Portugal)
Marcellé Archer (South Africa)

Thank you.
Kamba Publishing